PRAISE FOR JENNIFER BROZEK:

"Taut, tense, and terrifying, NEVER LET ME SLEEP grabs you and refuses to let you go until the final page."

–Cat Rambo, author of BEASTS OF TABAT

"NEVER LET ME SLEEP is a disturbing glimpse into an unfolding apocalypse. This is genuine nightmare territory."

–Jonathan Maberry, *New York Times* bestselling author of ROT & RUIN and FALL OF NIGHT

"Action, adventure, humanity, horror, mystery and mayhem mark the pages of the Melissa Allen series. Jennifer Brozek's deft and exciting writing style keeps you wanting more yet also wanting to get to the finish as soon as possible!"

–Jake Bible, author of the Bram Stoker Award nominated novel INTENTIONAL HAUNTING

"It's a cliché to say 'I couldn't put the book down,' but greeting the dawn at about the time I read the final words suggests to me that I really couldn't. The situation is downright creepy, the horror rooted in tension rather than gore, and the protagonist is more than a little fascinating in her own right. Definitely hoping there's a sequel on the way."

–Ari Marmell, author of the MICK OBERON and WIDDERSHINS series

NEVER LET ME

THE COMPLETE MELISSA ALLEN TRILOGY

JENNIFER BROZEK

A PERMUTED PLATINUM BOOK

ISBN (trade paperback): 978-1-61868-626-8

NEVER LET ME
Never Let Me Sleep, Never Let Me Leave, Never Let Me Die
"Never Let Me Feel"

Cover art by Ryan Truso

This book is a work of fiction. People, places, events, and situations are the product of the author's imagination. Any resemblance to actual persons, living or dead, or historical events, is purely coincidental.

Permuted Press, LLC
275 Madison Avenue, 6th Floor
New York, NY 10016
http://permutedpress.com

Never Let Me Sleep was dedicated to Cait Teague, my ideal reader. She was the one in the back of my mind I was writing for. She, and other young women like her, still are. In the end, it's all about the family we choose and those who accept us no matter what we suffer from.

NEVER LET ME SLEEP

BOOK ONE

BEFORE DAY ONE

Joe Davey yawned a huge yawn, then quickly corrected the lane his semi-truck was in. He'd never had this kind of problem at the end of a run before. Just inside the South Dakota border, he only had a couple hours to go to reach his destination. Another yawn split his face and he knew he should've stopped at the Quality Inn a ways back.

Instead of pushing on to the end of the line, he pulled over onto the side of the road in one of the many pullouts for just this sort of emergency. A quick nap would help and he'd still make it on time. He leaned his head back, not bothering to clamber into his semi's small sleeper apartment to lie down, or even to unbuckle his seatbelt. Joe closed his eyes, fell asleep, and died.

*

Gina Clark giggled as she snuck out her back door and crossed over into the neighbor's yard. They had a new playset complete with a slide on one side, a series of large tubes on the other, and swings in the middle. It was exactly the one she wanted. At night, she could pretend it was hers. Scampering into the tubes, Gina sat in the middle of them and pretended she was flying a magical airship, one with huge sails. She was the pirate princess, and after about five minutes of battling other pirates, Gina yawned and declared herself the victor. She curled up against the side of the tube. Her whispered commands to the captured enemy became mumbles, then fell into silence as she fell asleep, and died.

*

Michael Branson stared at the flickering security monitors that flipped through images of the empty building he guarded at night. He knew that Jim should be back from his rounds soon. Then he'd beg a nap. He must have slept poorly. It had been a long time since he'd been this tired on the job. Soon his eyes stopped seeing the monitors in front of them. Then they slipped closed and his head nodded until his chin rested on his chest as he fell asleep, and died.

*

Diane Ramirez and Steve Watts held on to each other as only two teenagers in love could. They kissed and nuzzled in the backseat of Steve's car, sated, satisfied, and tired. Clothing was pushed and pulled back into place as they grinned and kissed some more.

"Hold me," Diane murmured, settling against Steve.

"Always," he whispered in her ear.

She laid her head on his shoulder and he let his head loll back against the seat. The two of them held each other as they both drifted off to sleep, and died.

DAY ONE:

THE DAY SOUTH DAKOTA DIED

CHAPTER ONE

I live by the clock but I survive by the pills. It's eight a.m. and time for my morning dose. Sharon must have had a late night because she usually gets my medicine out for me and watches me take it. Such is the life of house arrest, or 'home detention' if you want to be correct about it. But, I know my pills and I know what they do. I also know what happens if I miss them, even once, especially today. A girl has to do what a girl has to do.

Two hundred milligrams of lamotrigine and good-bye bipolar swings.

Thirty milligrams of Abilify so I see reality as it really is and hopefully the black butterflies and living room sinkholes stay in my imagination and not my field of view.

Twenty-five milligrams of hydroxyzine to keep Captain Paranoia in his cage.

And that's just my morning set. The nighttime set also includes three milligrams of Prazosin to keep the nightmares at bay. It's a mix that finally works. Finally. Everything has ramped up and we're set. Yeah, there are side effects, but nothing like the psychotic swings mixed with the sedation I got on Seroquel. For such a popular anti-psychotic, it really messed me up good.

Excuse me, I need to completely lose my mind, destroy every mailbox on the block, and scream that every hat is hiding an alien.

"Sharon!" I yelled, hoping she'd hear me upstairs. "I took my pills. No need to rush down." No need for her to wonder if she forgot and think I was all messed up—again. That wouldn't do on Doctor Day. Doc Lee is a nice enough guy. A little bit of a prude for my potty mouth but sometimes swearing is all I can do to not kill myself or someone else.

Of course, being in court mandated counseling has taught me a couple of things, including the fact people really *do* care if I have a potty mouth. The way to get around that, according to Doctor Lee, is to get really creative with my swearing. Everyone cares if you drop the f-bomb but no one cares if you shout "Screw!" at the top of your lungs or mutter "mother of pearl!" when you stub your toe. It has almost become a game to see exactly how creative I can get. It also keeps me from getting in trouble. More trouble than I'm already in. When I'm alone or completely forget myself, my mouth returns to its rebellious ways.

I headed into the living room for my mandatory two hours of charging, and my ankle monitor emitted the kind of squeal that would make nuns murder kittens.

"Balls," I muttered, running to the charger and plugging it in.

Somewhere a bit was flipped, alerting security computers that I was either outside of monitor range or I let the stupid ankle monitor run dry. The truth was neither. The damn thing still had a quarter charge. Plugging it in wouldn't stop the forthcoming phone call, but it would prove that I was at home.

I wondered what state or country the call would come from. I was shocked the first time the call came from someone with an accent so thick I couldn't figure out what she wanted for about five minutes. After that, I asked Bill what was going on. Officially, as my probation counselor, he couldn't tell me. Off the record, however, and to help get me to trust him, Bill told me that the great state of South Dakota farmed out its court mandated monitoring to a 'third party vendor' who was already set up and could do the job cheaper than the state government could. Welcome to the global economy. To date, I have had monitoring calls from California, Washington, India, and Ireland.

The worst, though, are the robocalls. The phone rings but instead of a human on the line, it's a computer and I can't hang up on it. I have to answer all of its questions in order and wait for the computer to hang up. Otherwise, Bill gets a call and a black mark goes against me. Too many black marks and it's off to juvie or, worse, the hospital for the rest of my sentence—and four years is a long time to be in a state hospital. I'd come out crazier than when I went in. Everyone knows mental hospitals aren't about curing patients. They're all about containing patients. Nothing more.

Anyway, all my answers are recorded and compared in some sort of voice analysis program so I can't even curse at the thing. I really hate robocalls. I don't care if I'm a fourteen year old 'hardened criminal' under house arrest. I'm still a person and I deserve to have a live person checking up on me. I am not a number.

I settled into my comfy chair and waited for the phone to ring. I didn't want to be in the middle of one of my favorite shows when my watchdog called. It's ironic. My family doctor tells me I need more exercise, the court says I can't leave my house because of "my condition," and the electronic home monitor requires me to sit still for two hours every morning while it charges. That's when I watch TV. Thank God for DVRs. I record my favorite shows and watch them in the morning.

The one thing I miss is playing baseball. I was good at it. It was my main source of exercise and I was one of the team's best hitters. I can always hear about how the local teams did from Matt or Sharon but when it comes to baseball, my heart aches. Now the best I can do is put my treadmill up to some insane number and pretend like I'm running home. It's really not the same. Losing baseball is my one real regret to losing my freedom. I've accepted everything else but I still hurt when I hear about baseball games. It is one of the reasons I never watched live TV anymore.

After five minutes of twiddling my thumbs, I decided that I got the infernal machine plugged in before the false signal of my delinquency hit the queue. Ten minutes later the phone rang. Just long enough for me to relax and really get into my favorite show—*Fringe*. I didn't like the phone to begin with. This particular aspect of house arrest guaranteed I never owned a phone again. Not that I was allowed one now, but that was neither here nor there.

I answered the phone. "Hello?" Not every call to the house was my watchdog. Sometimes we got telemarketers. Joy.

"May I speak to Melissa please?"

"Speaking."

"This is Kelly Monitoring. Please answer the following questions. What is—"

A live person. Awesome. An American male from the sounds of it. Probably California. "Okay. Cool. Where are you calling from?"

There was a startled silence on the phone before he responded. "I'm not allowed to engage in conversation. Please answer the following set of questions. What is your full name?"

Ah, either a newbie or someone with a stick up their ass. I bet on newbie. I waited for the rest of the questions. After a moment Mister Kelly Monitoring asked, "Hello?"

"Hello," I said. "Just waiting for the set of questions. Or would you rather them one at a time?"

"One at a time, please. What is your full name?"

"Melissa Jean Allen. And it will get easier. Though, I suspect some people will curse at you." I could almost hear him reading the next question and checking the expected answer.

"Please give me the name of your supervisors."

"Host family," I corrected. "Sharon and Matthew Moore."

"Uh, right. Host family. What is your case number?"

"66-129-484-7."

"Correct. Thank you. Finally, what is the name of your court mandated psychiatrist?"

I was starting to feel like I was on a strange sort of game show. I was used to bored and incomprehensible. Popping a newbie's cherry was a little unreal. "Usually, you can just say 'psychiatrist.' Doctor Martin Lee. Doc Martin if you're feeling snarky."

He snickered softly before wrapping up with the final question. "The monitoring equipment indicated that your electronic home monitor was out of range. However, it is now showing that it's within acceptable parameters. Please account for this discrepancy."

"My EM is starting to lose its tiny little electronic mind. The battery registered one quarter full when the out-of-battery signal went off. I'll be talking to my parole counselor about it on Thursday. So, where you calling from?"

My watchdog paused again and I could almost see his smile. "California. You have a nice day, Miss Allen."

"You, too." I waited until he hung up before I put the phone back in its cradle. I wondered what he looked like. Probably tan with a mop of unruly blond hair. Not anything like my beloved Deroga Darrington.

My TV viewing routine spoiled, I turned off the screen and grabbed my e-reader. Deroga Darrington was the protagonist of my favorite series of the pulp noir novels called *The Dare Files*. Deroga was the attractive private investigator who always gets the bad guy or girl. Whether or not he gets the girl along the way depends on the story. He's got Pretty Penny as his 'Girl Friday.' At first, I wasn't sure I would like Miss Penny but she turned out to be a kickass fighter who saved Deroga from time to time despite her stupid name. I mean, really, who names their kid "Pretty"?

In the current book I was rereading, Deroga had been hired to find out who murdered a rich man's butler and why. It was a fun take on 'the butler did it' mysteries. Only, in *The Case of the Dead Butler* it was the maid—a redheaded she-devil if there ever was one. I loved me some Deroga Darrington.

An hour and a half later, I clawed my way up out of the clutches of *The Dare Files* to discover that my ankle monitor was once more fully charged and I could go about the rest of my day without it squawking at me. First up, pumpkin whoopie pies.

"Sharon!" I yelled as I headed into the kitchen. "I'm making whoopie pies!" I wondered why she wasn't downstairs yet, then shrugged. She was the grown up. I wasn't.

While I don't have to bring gifts and offerings to my psychiatrist, I like to when I'm feeling good. It is part of my particular brand of 'non-verbal communication' as Doc Lee likes to say. Winter had broken and, while it was still cold, we were well into the slushy, mushy beginnings of Spring. I like Spring and Fall. Transitional seasons make me feel alive. Between that and getting my chemical mix right, it was the best I had felt in a long time and I wanted him to know it. So, homemade whoopie pies were on the menu.

One good thing has come out of house arrest: I discovered that not only can I cook, I like to bake, too. I'm good at both. With limited internet access, a ban on video games, and no smartphone at my disposal, I had little to do that didn't involve the TV, the treadmill, or my books. Sharon assigned me the task of cooking for the family. I agreed as long as I wasn't the only one cleaning up afterward.

With all the ingredients for the cookie part of the whoopie pies on the counter, I went looking for the canned pumpkin to no avail. That was fine; we had extra in the garage where we store the bulk of our extra canned goods. I opened the door to the garage and was surprised to see Matt's car there. Suddenly, Sharon's very late morning made a lot more sense. Matt was still home and she had not been around looking for cold medicine. Which meant they were home together being all snuggly and stuff.

I shied away from thinking more about what else they had to be doing up there. Thinking about your sister having sex with her husband is almost as icky as thinking about your parents doing it. Ugh. No thanks. I found the cans of pumpkin pie and pulled my thoughts back to the topic at hand.

I also made sure to turn on my music when I got back to the kitchen, just in case they decided to get loud.

By the time the cookies were coming out of the oven to cool, the cream cheese filling was made and I got my thirty minutes of dancing around the kitchen exercise in. I really don't like the treadmill unless I have an audio book to listen to. *The Dare Files* aren't on audio, so I listen to the *October Daye* or *Greywalker* series. I'm still debating on the *Dresden Files*. I don't want Deroga to think I'm cheating on him. He has a mean right hook when he's jealous.

I looked at the clock and realized it was noon. Neither Sharon nor Matt had made a peep. I felt my stomach drop and my heart speed up. This wasn't normal. My appointment was at one. Sharon *knew* it was at one. If we were going to walk to the Onida Clinic, we needed to get going in the next thirty minutes or I was going to be late. And if there was one thing Doctor Lee was a stickler on, it was on not being late to any of his appointments. That meant his patients couldn't be late either, barring a death in the family or an alien invasion.

The clinic was a whole half mile from the house. An easy walk in almost any weather. Head up Ginseng Avenue and hang a left on Main Street. Stop when you meet Cedar Avenue and look right. There was a white building that had once been a small white house. It served as one of the two places to get medical attention in Onida. Three if you were one of the two hundred and fifty or so Onida kids in school or one of its thirty-five teachers or administrators. The other was Vilas Healthcare over next to the courthouse building.

Doctor Lee doesn't practice fulltime out of the Onida Clinic. He's a doctor from Saint Mary's Hospital in Pierre. I don't know why he is not over at Vilas Healthcare but it is more convenient and closer for me this way. Doc Lee boots the nurse practitioner out of her office for the day every other week or so. I'm sure Nurse Payne loves that. Yes, that is Darcy's real last name and she is probably one of the sweetest people around.

In any case, I'm not a special kind of special. Doc sees other patients as well. I'm just the only one under house arrest. I have to get special permission to leave the house and see him for our bimonthly appointments. You would think that this would be something that was easy to do since it is court mandated and it happens every other week. You would be wrong. Because of the home detention, Sharon has to call Bill and tell him about the appointment three days in advance every single time.

It is a pain in the ass for Sharon and for Bill but demanded by the system. Lord help you if you try to buck the system.

Be that as it may, I had an appointment to keep and I couldn't be late. "Sharon! I have my doctor's appointment today. Make a noise to let me know you're alive!" I yelled up the stairs at her. I didn't want to go up there. Not yet. I try really hard not to be too much of a burden on them even though they both keep telling me I'm not.

Sharon is my sister and I love her. She is the best big sister a girl could have. Matt is like the big brother I never had, only without all the fights that go along with siblings. Despite being twelve years older than me, she never acted like she didn't want me around. Not even when my brain decided to show the world how broken it was. I've been on some kind of medication since I was ten and even then, Sharon and Matt loved me.

It is a good thing, too. The whole "godparents" thing kicked in after our parents were murdered by a drunk asshole on my thirteenth birthday when he plowed into us on Highway 83. I was thrown from the car and broke my arm. My parents were killed on impact, or so they say. The drunk asshole—one Jonathan Hammer recently fired from the NewGrowth Grain Corporation for being drunk on the job—was charged with manslaughter. I still think he should have been charged with murder.

You might say I really don't like cars. Unlike every kid my age and older, I had no desire to get my license. I already know how to drive if the car's an automatic. But cars meant nothing but loss and grief for me. Cars took my family away from me and took me to appointments I didn't want to keep. They killed my dog one year and my parents the next year. I could probably go my whole life without driving and be happy.

As one might expect, things went downhill for me after my parents' deaths. Between the grief—I still cry when I dream of them—and my broken brain, I'm surprised I didn't end up in court sooner. Probably because my sister is a saint and my brother-in-law is a high mucky-muck at NewGrowth. That convinced the local law enforcement to go easy on me.

Onida is a company town. It lives and dies by the harvest seasons and what NewGrowth can get for the crops. Everything else in town supports the farming industry and its people. If NewGrowth pulled out, there wouldn't be an Onida, South Dakota. It would be simply another dying town near the Lewis and Clark Trail and they would put the State Treasurer's office someplace else.

I thought about writing her a note and doing a quick march through the muck to the clinic. I'm allowed. It would only take ten minutes to get from my house to there. Hell, all of Onida was within walking distance if you were willing to walk a whole mile. Two if you meandered through town the long way. Three if you decided you needed to walk from any part of town out to airport. There really isn't much call for driving unless it's winter or you needed to work the fields or haul something big. Or, of course, you were in a hurry.

I decided to put the whoopie pies together and package them up. If she wasn't downstairs by the time I was ready, I would go up, knock on their door, and tell them I was leaving. They could stay in bed like newlyweds for all I cared. I just didn't like the fact that they did it on Doctor Day.

The entire time I spread the frosting, stacked the pies and covered them in cling wrap, I listened for movement upstairs. That was what I had been missing the whole morning. Even sleeping, people roll over in bed and you can hear it downstairs. If they were doing more than sleeping, I should have been able to hear that—talking, giggling, or even the rhythmic thumping of the bed—this house didn't have soundproof walls at all.

I knew by the time I was done doing everything I could do, I was afraid. Afraid of the too silent house and afraid of interrupting whatever the hell was going on up there. But I needed to. It was Doctor Day and some social rules needed to be broken in order to follow the legally required ones.

I paused at the bottom of the stairs. "Sharon? Matt?" I called. Then I listened.

Nothing.

I crept up the stairs, too aware of how loud my footsteps sounded in the silent house. "Sharon? Are you okay? Sharon?" My hand trembled as I lifted it to knock on their bedroom door. My first knock was so light, I could barely hear it. I chided myself for my fear. Deroga would be ashamed of me if he saw me acting the frightened lamb. My next set of knocks was louder, forceful. "Sharon! It's Doctor Day. We've got to get moving if we're walking like you wanted! Matt! Get up you lazybones! I left you a couple of homemade pumpkin whoopie pies downstairs." I rattled the doorknob for emphasis.

The door wasn't locked and my rattling unlatched it. It swung open revealing two lumps still in bed.

CHAPTER TWO

Sun streamed in through the gauzy white curtains revealing a bedroom with nothing amiss except for the two sleeping forms still in bed at noon. Filled with matching wood furniture that included a dresser, a gentleman's chest, two nightstands, and a sleigh bed, the room was cluttered with the detritus of lives interrupted by bedtime. Yesterday's clothes were still on the floor. Empty wine glasses and books sat on the nightstands. The ancient analog clock tick-tocked over the dresser. Everything was normal.

Only it wasn't.

Sharon and Matt weren't moving.

I looked at them for a moment longer and then backpedaled out of the room in the sudden realization that they weren't *breathing* either. I crashed against the hall wall opposite their bedroom doorway and sank into a crouch, still looking at them.

I shook my head. That couldn't be right. They were sleeping and I was panicking over nothing.

No, I argued with myself. *You know a dead body when you see it. You've seen dead bodies before. Real ones. Not hallucinations.*

I saw my parents pulled from the wreckage of the car. I watched my dad, his eyes open, lay like a broken mannequin on the asphalt with his head twisted at an unnatural angle. I saw him breathe his last breath. My mom, her eyes closed, could have been sleeping if it wasn't for all the blood. I knew as sure as I knew my own name; Sharon and Matt were dead.

How do you know if you don't go look at the bodies and check for a pulse? Maybe they took sleeping pills.

Or maybe they committed joint suicide by sleeping pills.

Was there a suicide note? You don't know. You didn't see. You didn't look.

The other me was right. I didn't really know. (Only I did and I didn't want to believe it.) And I didn't see a note because I didn't look for it.

I pushed myself up from the floor and tottered on shaky knees. Once I had my balance, and my courage, I walked back into my sister's bedroom. When Deroga entered a crime scene, he always took the time to stop, look, and analyze the scene before he looked at the bodies. I took a deep breath. I didn't smell death. I smelled the lingering scent of sleep.

People don't believe they have a sleep smell, but they do. It is very specific. Go into a sleeping person's room and take a whiff. You'll smell it and recognize it. That's what I was smelling here.

Looking around the room, I didn't see a paper or note stuck out of place to be found. Not on the bed, the nightstands, or the dresser. I also didn't see pill bottles on either of the nightstands. There were wine glasses but that was a ritual for them; one glass of red wine before bed while reading. Matt liked sci-fi military books and Sharon liked noir and urban fantasy books like me.

Then I saw Matt's shirt and belt hung out for today. Not suicide. He was planning to go to work today. I looked at the bed. Really looked at it. All I could see was two bodies curled up in comfortable sleeping poses. Both of them were curled towards me. Their faces were slack against their pillows, looking like they were sleeping hard. But there was no movement, no sounds of breathing, no random dreaming twitches.

I was freaked out by seeing Matt lying in bed. The only time I saw him sleeping was in his comfy chair in front of the TV. I was used to seeing Sharon in bed though. She liked to sleep more than I did. She didn't have the same kind of nightmares, or any at all, for that matter. I would come into the bedroom hours after Matt had gone to work and use her own long blonde hair to tease her awake. I didn't want to do that this time. I didn't want to touch her and confirm what my already horrified mind was telling me.

"Sharon! Matt!" I let my voice rise hard and sharp. My fear gave my voice volume. They didn't move. I took another step towards the bed and, not thinking about what I was doing, grabbed Sharon's shoulder to shake her awake.

Her shoulder was hard. Her body was stiff and cool through the fabric of her nightshirt. When I shook her, her entire body moved like a large wooden plank. She was dead as dead could be. Rigor mortis had set in. That meant she had been dead for at least six hours but less than forty-eight.

Dead.

My sister was dead. So was Matt. I didn't need to touch him to know that. I left the room and closed the door behind me. I did this with slow, deliberate movements. Walking downstairs, I had to fight my brain's desire to run in twelve different directions at once. I stopped moving, locked in a Gordian knot of thoughts that chased each other around and around my head. I wanted to shake them awake and tell them this little joke of theirs wasn't funny. Not at all. I wanted to eat one of the pumpkin whoopie pies I made. I wanted to just run, run away.

I needed to call Doctor Lee.

I needed to call 911.

I needed my mom.

It was this last thought that broke me out of my paralysis at the bottom of the stairs. My mom was dead and had been for the last fifteen months. I needed to call Doctor Lee. My brain froze again as I tried to remember the number to the clinic. This was a number I had called twice a month for a year. I closed my eyes, took a breath, relaxed, and let the muscle memory of my fingers remember the phone number for me.

The phone rang four times before it went to voicemail. At least I *had* the right number. I wanted to tell Doc Lee myself instead of a recording but I needed to call 911 next. At the beep, I said, "This is for Doctor Lee. It's Melissa Allen. I'm not going to make my appointment today. I can't. My sister is…" I paused, unable to say it, "dead." The word came out in a choked sob. "S-so is Matt. I don't know what happened. It's not my fault. It looks like they went to sleep and didn't wake up. I… I'm at home. I need help."

I stopped talking then because I was crying too hard. I put the phone in the cradle and tried to control my sobs. With my face in my hands, I cried for about a minute before I was able to pull myself together. I wiped my hands on my jeans, swiped at my tears, and grabbed the phone again. It took me three tries to punch those three simple numbers.

As soon as the phone picked up, I started talking, "My name is Melissa Allen. I live at 585 Ginseng Avenue in Onida. My sister and her husband are dead. I don't know what happened. It looks like they died in their sleep. Please, I need help." I paused, realizing that I had not heard the customary 911 greeting. I listened, and though the phone was connected, I didn't hear anyone breathing. "Hello?"

No one answered.

"Hello? Anyone? Please, I need help. Please."

The silence continued.

I hung up the phone and looked at it for a while. Then I sat down and gave some considerable thought to whether or not I was having another one of my psychotic breaks. When you're a schizophrenic, this is a serious thing to consider. First, I inventoried my physical senses. I took a deep whiff of the air. Pumpkin whoopie pies. The scented candle. My perfumed oil. Okay. No scents of rot, decay, or the ocean. I touched my face, pinched the back of my hands, wiggled my toes, and then punched my thigh. Everything was in working order and nothing was in pain or numb. I listened. I could hear my breathing, the hum of the heater, and the small, tinny whine of the refrigerator. No sounds of things being dragged. No wet footfalls. No barely heard incomprehensible whispers. Finally, I looked around. Nothing was out of place: the walls weren't peeling; the clock remained at 12:36 and readable when I looked at it, looked away, and looked at it again; and there were no sinkholes in the floor.

I wasn't having a psychotic break. I took my pills and all my senses were in place. Maybe I was dreaming. I looked to my left and asked out loud, "Am I dreaming?" I listened and looked around me. It was one of those lucid dreaming techniques Bill taught me to help me get out of nightmares that were so real I couldn't tell if I was awake or not. Nothing changed around me. I looked to my right and asked again, "Am I dreaming?"

No. Not dreaming. Everything was as real as real could be.

But everything was *wrong*. This was real and no one was answering the phone. Not the clinic. Not 911. I reached for the phone again and called the next person I could think of: my parole counselor. Bill needed to know about this anyway. He was one of the good guys. It had taken a little bit for me to believe that but in the end I did. Plus, he would help.

My hand paused over the phone. I would be going back to juvie. My stomach dropped out of my body and I thought I would throw up. With Sharon and Matt dead, it wouldn't matter if my recovery and incarceration was best done in the privacy of a home. I had no other family to turn to. I needed to be medicated. I needed to be supervised. Otherwise, bad things happened.

I grabbed the phone and dialed Bill's number by rote. I was crying again and couldn't see anything in front of me. This wasn't the choking sobs of grief. This was the terrified tears of knowing what hell waited for me. I thought about running away but I couldn't. Not without my medicine. Life wouldn't be worth it without the drugs that fixed my broken brain. When Bill's voicemail picked up, I wanted to scream. Instead, I left him the same message I left on all the other voicemails—family dead, need help.

I needed to do something but I didn't know what. I stood up and walked to the front door. I opened it without thinking about what I was doing until the cold breeze of the lingering winter made me realize I was still in a t-shirt and slippers. If I was going to go for help, I needed to put on real clothes.

Closing the front door, I thought about it. Where would I go for help? All of Onida knew about me, my condition, and the house arrest. After the mailbox incident, it was hard to not know about me. I was the main gossip in this stupid little town for months. Most of them would assume I murdered my sister and her husband.

I guessed that didn't matter. I jammed my feet into my socks and my Wellingtons and had to hunt for my coat—it was one of those warm Anorak coats. It didn't matter that I was on the right brain cocktail, everything was taking me twice as long to do and thinking was hard. Really hard. I wanted everything to go back to normal but I knew it wouldn't, couldn't. That scared me more than anything else.

Opening the front door this time took an unexpected effort of will. I was suddenly afraid of going outside. I was allowed. It was approved of. I really was headed to the clinic. It was the only place I could think of to go. Either Nurse Payne or Doctor Lee would help me. They had to. That was their job. Plus, I really believed they liked me. I was more than merely a patient.

Every step I took told me that this was wrong, dangerous. I didn't know why. I looked around for the source of the danger but I didn't see anything. There was no one on the street but that wasn't unusual; it was the middle of a weekday on a suburban street. People were working or at school. However, my mind wouldn't leave it alone. To the point that it was a relief to see Bella the pit bull puttering around her yard and to see a couple of crows take off at my approach, scolding me as they went.

It was the cawing of the crows that clued me in to what was bothering me. It was damn near silent on the street. Even though people didn't use cars that often in Onida, they did have them. I should be able to hear them in the background noise. But I didn't. This made putting one foot in front of the other that much harder.

I looked ahead, saw the Main Street crossroads and stopped. I didn't want to go any farther. I was afraid that there would be no one on Main Street and that would mean even worse things. Things I wasn't prepared to understand if I was right. Something Deroga always told his clients in *The Dare Files* was to trust your instincts. It was usually right. I took two stuttering steps forward, turned, and then fled back to my house at a dead run.

Slamming the front door behind me while I gasped for breath was the safest I had felt since this whole thing—whatever this thing was—began.

I kicked off my Wellingtons and shoved my feet into my sneakers. I wasn't planning on going out again but I felt safer in comfortable shoes. Rule number two was to wear comfortable shoes in a crisis. You never knew what you would be running to or from.

Back in the living room, I threw my coat on the couch. I wanted it close by and I wouldn't be going back upstairs anytime soon. I stared at the phone and thought for a while. No one was answering their phones. Not yet. Maybe they would now. Three calls led me straight back to two voicemails and that open, silent, empty line at emergency services. It was this last that unnerved me the most.

I looked at the phone base and considered it. When the landline was installed because of my monitoring device, Matt got the best damn phone he could. It had all sorts of bells and whistles. I pulled up the caller history. As part of my house arrest, all of my calls were to be monitored. In this case, it meant the phone records could be looked at or Matt could use the phone history to figure out if I had been using the phone. I scrolled down to the seventh slot. The 1-800 number for Kelly Monitoring was there.

I pressed the dial button and waited. When the phone was answered, I was so startled that I slammed the phone down as fast as I could. It was the automatic queuing system. I tried again. This time when the automatic queue picked up, I punched the appropriate buttons until I got the monitoring department. I hung up again when a woman answered the phone. I smiled. Not everyone was dead. A person had answered the phone. A real, live person. That meant that everyone else was probably busy and there was a glitch at emergency services.

I laughed in relief. There was an explanation for everything. My laughter turned into a yelp of surprise when the phone in my hand rang. Looking at the display, I saw that it was Kelly Monitoring. I was probably in trouble. I would explain and throw myself on the mercy of the person calling back. I prayed they would understand.

"Hello?"

"Melissa?"

It was the California guy from this morning. "Yes. Hello."

"Oh, man," he said, sounding surprised. "I didn't believe it when I saw your number in the queue."

"My number?"

"Your phone number. Kinda hard to forget. You were my first call this morning."

"I'm sorry I called you guys. I've been having the worst day ever and I needed to hear someone's voice." I didn't want to admit that I was looking for his voice or that I was afraid everyone in the world was dead. "Please don't report—"

"Listen," his voice took on a conspiratorial tone, "I could get fired for calling you but I need to know where you are."

"I'm at home."

"In Onida, South Dakota?"

"Yes."

"You need to turn on the TV and watch the news. Like now."

"Wait, what do you mean? Is something wrong?"

He hesitated, took a breath and let it out. "Nobody knows."

I sucked in a breath, mirroring his fear. "What... what's the TV saying?"

"I can't. You need to see it for yourself."

"No. I need you to tell me." I winced at sharpness in my voice. Then the phone went dead in my hand. I listened to the dial tone for a second before I put the phone down and turned to the blank TV screen. Whatever was happening, I didn't want to know about it. Except I did. Maybe it would explain what happened to my sister and Matt.

I sat down and once more considered whether or not I was having a psychotic break. Everything pointed to it: Sharon and Matt, the silence outside, my paranoia, the mysterious call from Kelly Monitoring, the fact that no one, not even emergency services, was picking up. All of it was too much to be real. No outside source could validate the reality I was suffering. Not even the phone call. That could have been in my head. However, if I was having a psychotic break, this was the most lucid I had ever felt while going over the edge.

I stood up again. I would turn on the TV but only after I had counted my pills to make sure I had actually taken them and not dreamed that up. That would explain all of this.

The kitchen smelled like heaven. My baking had not been a dream and I was hungry. Pills first, whoopie pies second. I pulled down all of my bottles of pills. Thirty-one pills for the Abilify, lamotrigine and hydroxyzine. Sixteen for the Prazosin. A little more than a two week supply. We were good. I did take my pills.

I grabbed the plastic container of whoopie pies and a glass of milk. At least I could ease my hunger somewhat while I faced whatever awaited me on Channel 5 News. With a whoopie pie in one hand and the remote in the other, I turned on the TV.

I didn't have to change the channel. The horror was right there on breaking news.

CHAPTER THREE

"Thank you, Jim," said Susan Baker, the blonde TV anchor who usually did the evening news.

I looked at the clock. 12:51pm. Obviously something was wrong. They didn't pull out the evening anchors unless it was big news and, usually, bad. I always liked Susan Baker. She was a blonde like me and had the kind of face that was attractive, more handsome than pretty, and leant itself to serious professionalism. Right now, she looked very serious.

"If you are just tuning in," Susan Baker said, *"the breaking story is the mysterious lack of communication from the state of South Dakota. Starting around two in the morning, everyone who was awake spoke of being tired and needing to sleep. This wouldn't be unusual except for the timing of the matter, and that it came from numerous sources normally awake at that time of night – graveyard shift workers, security personnel, nursing staff, and teenagers."*

The TV shifted from Susan's concerned face to images of Facebook and Twitter messages as Susan read them to the viewers.

"The messages included things like 'I can't keep my eyes open any longer. I don't know what's going on.' and 'Need more coffee! I almost nodded off there.' and 'I've been working the nightshift for years and I've never had a nap attack like this before.'"

Susan's face reappeared. *"More disturbing is the fact that travelers and long haul truckers make it into South Dakota, but not out again. After one reported incident of a truck driver that felt so tired after entering South Dakota that he pulled to the side of the road and called his wife in an effort to wake up then fell asleep while he was talking to her, the Department of Homeland Security quarantined the entire state of South Dakota. We are going live to Peter Tennyson who is at the border of South Dakota and Nebraska. Peter? Are you there?"*

The TV went to split screen mode with Susan Baker on the left and Peter Tennyson on the right. Peter was young and handsome with short dark hair and smoldering eyes. He reminded me of what Deroga would look like if played by a movie star… or TV reporter in this case. He stood on the road about fifty feet in front of a barricade made of plastic sawhorses and orange Road Closed signs.

"I'm here, Susan."

"It's a serious situation there, Peter."

"Yes, it is. I'm standing in front of the barrier on Highway 83 outside the border of South Dakota. At this time, there is no word from anyone inside the borders. The town closest to me, Olsonville, remains incommunicado while the towns south of me, Crookston, Valentine, and Sparks, are all business as usual. The only difference between those towns and Olsonville is distance and a state border. Even the Rosebud Casino and Quality Inn, a popular spot for truckers about half a mile north of this location, is quiet." The camera looked over Peter's shoulder and down the empty stretch of highway. To the left of the barricade, a number of white vans were parked and people in suits and military uniforms were in a quiet buzz of activity hidden mostly by the vans.

"The Department of Homeland Security in conjunction with FEMA, the Department of Transportation, and the CDC, has quarantined the state of South Dakota. This was declared after they lost contact with a CDC scout mission. The CDC scout mission remained in contact with the investigation leader for a total of sixty-three minutes. Afterwards, they lost contact."

"How long ago was that, Peter?"

He consulted his notebook. *"A little over four hours ago."* Peter looked at his notebook again. *"The investigative lead for this baffling and frightening mystery is Department of Homeland Security Agent Tomas Harrison. His team set up a remote viewing vehicle and we are waiting to hear back on what they see using the cutting edge technology in this most baffling and dangerous situation. In the meantime, I have word that Agent Harrison set up a special tip hotline number specific to this case."*

Susan tilted her head into her listening pose and nodded. *"That's correct. Thank you, Peter. The number, 1-800-555-2554, has now been added to the scrolling ticker at the bottom of the screen. If you have any information about what is going on in South Dakota, please call."*

The split screen slid back to one image, focused on Susan's somber face. She paused in her listening pose again. *"This just in. The first pictures retrieved by the investigative team show bodies lying on the ground. It is unconfirmed, officially, but it looks like whatever is happening in South Dakota is lethal."*

"But I'm alive," I whispered to Susan. "I'm alive." I muted the TV. While I sat there, stunned, the TV shifted back to Peter, who looked more scared than serious. It pained me to see my Deroga lookalike seem so frightened. While he was speaking, the people around the white vans were packing things up with an admirable efficiency and Peter was moving towards the news van. I guess everyone decided that they were too close to the action.

I had the presence of mind to jot down Agent Harrison's hotline number. I wondered what they would do when I called it from inside the great quarantined state of South Dakota. I was about to bite into my forgotten snack when the phone rang.

For the second time today, the ringing phone scared the crap out of me. I dropped my whoopie pie with a yelp and looked at the phone. Kelly Monitoring blinked in the phone display. Apparently, California guy decided to call back.

I picked up the phone, "Hello?"

"Hello. This is Kelly Monitoring Services. In compliance with court mandate..."

A damned random robocall. This was the reason only I could answer the landline phone. If Sharon or Matt answered it, the recorded voice wouldn't match the analytics on file and that was a black mark against me. Too many of them and it was off to juvie I go. I glanced at the clock as the mechanical voice prattled on. It was just after one p.m.

Suddenly I was furious. Beyond furious. All I could see was red and black. A missed call was also a black mark. "I'm supposed to be at my doctor's appointment, you fucking piece of machinery!" I raged. "It was approved! You're not supposed to call me while I'm out!" I threw the phone across the room, shattering the TV screen. Even more furious at no longer getting the news, I grabbed the base of the phone, yanked it out of the wall and threw it at the TV, too. Then I screamed and I screamed again. It was a wordless scream of fear and grief.

Then I felt... not good... but better. If you have never given yourself permission to scream a primal scream, do so. It releases all kinds of tension. It also gave me my sanity back. I looked at the destruction and wondered what people would think when they discovered it. Then I saw that I had not only pulled the phone out of the wall, I had yanked the jack along with it. There was no repairing this one.

I went over to the shattered TV and looked at the phone. The phone itself was busted open, its batteries lost in the shards of glass. The phone base was broken six ways from Sunday. It must have hit the cabinet. I shook my head, muttering fake curse words under my breath. No more phone calls for me. Neither coming in nor going out. Sure, both Mark and Sharon had iPhones, but they were upstairs and damned if I was going to go up there to look for them.

I had an iPhone, too. Loved that thing to pieces. It was the last gift my parents gave me. I only had it for about three months before the whole house arrest thing happened and communication had to be restricted. The first time I got caught breaking the rules, Sharon took the phone from me. I was furious but in the end I got over it. I'm not sure where the phone is now.

I sat back down next to my snack. I picked up the whoopie pie from the floor and brushed carpet lint from it. While I ate it, I picked up the note with the hotline number on it. I contemplated the number, eating the pie and washing it down with milk. I ate three more pies and finished off the milk before I decided what I needed to do next.

What can I say? I'm a nervous eater. I'm not fat, so to speak, but I'm not skinny. I'll never look like a model. I'm soft and my hourglass figure is a little heavier at the bottom than the top, though I still look good enough in a skirt. Sharon would scold me for worrying so much about my figure. Sometimes I think she lives in the 1950s. Lives… lived. I swallowed the bite of cookie with some effort.

Then again, who did I have to look good for? I was under house arrest until I was eighteen. I was enrolled in an online high school—which was a blessing in disguise, as I'm getting a tailored education and no crap from bullies. And who the hell is going to want to date me anyway? I was that crazy orphaned girl.

Oh, wait. I forgot, South Dakota is dead. Everyone who knew anything about me was dead.

Maybe, that skeptical part of me who has seen too much already said. *But you haven't seen it for yourself.*

Sure I have. Sharon and Matt are upstairs dead.

Yes. But you could have done it.

There it was. The very real fear I had that I murdered my family. The only way I could be sure that I didn't do it, that I wasn't a murderer, was to go out and find other dead people. As crazy as that sounded, it was the only sane thing to do.

I got up, grabbed my coat, shook it free of TV screen shards and put it on. I debated about my Wellingtons, then decided I could run better in my sneakers. Who or what I thought I might be running from, I didn't know, but better safe than sorry.

This time when I left the house, I didn't hesitate. I needed to be sure that what the TV said was true. Moreover, I needed to know that I wasn't the one who did the killing. I couldn't have killed the state, much less a whole town.

I walked down Ginseng and turned left on Main Street. I paused there to look down the street. Main Street is also South Seventh Street and up until you get to Cedar Avenue and Nile Lumber, it is nothing but houses. Sure, there are some home businesses. Maggie sells Mary Kay and Tupperware out of her house and the Nolans are big into Amway.

There is the Lutheran church at the corner of Elm and Main. Onida, for as small as it is, has five churches: Lutheran on Elm and Main, Catholic on Sixth, Methodist on Ash, Presbyterian on Dogwood and Main. The last is the local Mennonite church run out of someone's house. It moves around and no one really likes talking about them. We do have a former Mormon family, the Smiths—not related to Joseph Smith—and they have a passel of kids but don't wear the Mormon underwear as it were, as far as the local rumor mill is concerned.

Main Street was empty for as far as I could see. This gave the news report credence but made my tummy feel ill. From Ginseng to Fir was empty. I could hear the birds and the dogs and saw Mrs. Sand's cat, but no people—dead or otherwise. From Fir to Elm was empty, too. I looked down Elm Street towards the high school. I hated to admit it but I missed that building. Especially its library.

I stopped in front of the Lutheran church. I wasn't really the churchgoing kind and that made me stand out. I have never been comfortable going to services but I like churches themselves. They feel good… holy… safe. Still, I hesitated before I opened the church door. That was when I saw him; another dead person.

When you enter the church, there is a small antechamber with side passages to the church administration offices. From the antechamber, there is the nave where the pews are. At the head of the nave is a stage and a podium for Pastor Schultz. At the back of the stage was the chancel where the words *"Built on the Rock the Church Doth Stand"* were painted and adorned with doves. The dove motif continued up the back of the wall and onto the ceiling. In the front right pew, I saw the top of a man's head.

"Hello?" I called, hoping he was alive.

The man didn't move or say anything.

I took a breath and walked to the front of the nave to see what I came to see. It was Pastor Schultz. He was slumped down in the pew with his chin on his chest, looking like he was napping. If it were not for the grayish color of his skin and his utter lack of movement, I could believe he was only napping. Next to him was a legal-sized pad of paper filled with notes. A pen lay on top of it. In his lap, his bible lay open. My guess was he had been preparing for the Wednesday night sermon.

"Rest in peace," I whispered to him and left the church. It answered my question—there was no way I killed the pastor. It wasn't enough though. Like the need to wiggle a sore tooth, I needed to see more.

I continued down Main Street, not stopping at the Presbyterian church. I didn't want to see another preacher man dead in a house of God. I paused at the lawyer's office, another house turned into a business, and saw a light on in the window. I guess Bob Pears was working late last night. I walked up to the brick building and tried the door. It was locked. Not too surprising if he was working late. He lived and worked here after converting the entire front half of the home into a receptionist area and his office. Lucy Wallace used to do part-time secretary work for him.

I walked around the building until I could see into the window with a light on. Standing on my tiptoes, I looked in and there was Bob, still dressed in his not-so-starched white shirt and tie. His computer was on but in screensaver mode, and it looked like he had been poring over documents. He had his head resting on his folded arms on the desk. His red pen was next to him. It looked like he had gotten so tired working that it was too much effort to get up and walk the twenty paces to his bedroom. He had laid his head down to sleep and died.

I turned away from him and got out of the muck next to the house. I felt weird looking into people's homes and businesses, like I was a thief or a predator or something. That's not who I was. I was just a girl looking for explanations. And a girl who was relieved to know she wasn't at fault.

The next place I looked was Nile Lumber. Despite the fact that Onida is a small town, maybe eleven hundred people, I didn't know everyone in it. Even though it felt like everyone knew everyone. I'm not the kind of gal to go traipsing through lumberyards for fun, so I didn't know who worked at or owned the place.

I stood by the beat up blue Ford truck that was always parked in front of the yard and looked in. The lumberyard was flanked on two sides by buildings painted in peeling white paint. One of the side buildings was an office with a door. The other side building looked like an open barn with stacks of wood. The building flanking the back of the yard was a long, low building with an open door facing me. I guessed it was for storing wood.

While I was looking at it, something passed in front of the doorway inside the building. A man-sized something. Possibly in a hat. The movement startled and thrilled me.

"Hey!" I shouted. "I'm here. I'm alive!"

I didn't think about what I was doing. All I wanted to do was to see another living person. Dogs, cats, and birds were all well and good but the idea that someone else was alive in the quarantine zone with me was better than ice cream. I ran around the blue truck and into the lumberyard. Dodging around piles of wood and over forgotten tools, I ran straight back to the long building.

I paused at the door of the building. It was dark inside.

"Hello? Hello? My name is Melissa. Hello?" My hand found a light switch and flooded the place with light. It was a storage building for wood. The earthy scent of pine and oak and spruce wafted around me from the stacks of wooden planks. No one answered me but I heard movement.

Hurrying down the aisle between the stacks of boards, I followed the sound. It was a jingling sound, followed by a low cough. As I came out of the aisle and into the workshop area, the golden lab retriever let out a couple of gruff barks and I realized that I had heard the dog moving around. The low cough had been his warning bark.

I watched the dog and it watched me. Babies and animals have always loved me. This Labrador was no exception. Its tail was wagging but it didn't want to leave the desk it was standing by.

"Hey boy. What's going on?"

The dog trotted over to me and bathed my hand in dog slobber. I wiped my hand on my jeans as he trotted back to the desk. I walked closer and saw that there was a man lying on the floor. He must have fallen out of the rolling chair that was now settled against the wall. I sighed, wondering how I could have thought I saw a person walk by the door.

There was a back door to the building on the opposite wall from the desk. It was open. Maybe a breeze had blown a paper by the door and I had seen what I wanted to see. Or I allowed myself to be distracted because I didn't want to do what I knew I needed to do next.

CHAPTER FOUR

I stood on the walk in front of the small ranch style house, now office, adorned with fresh white paint and blue trim. To the right of the walkway was the wooden white and blue "Onida Clinic" sign with its hours and affiliation with Rural Health Care Incorporated. I was as familiar with this office as I was with my own house. I had been in every room and seen every person that worked there.

The Clinic had two doctors, one nurse, the radiology guy, and the receptionist; a lot of people for the small office. The doctors and nurse had their own offices in addition to the two exam rooms and the small room where they took x-rays. May, the receptionist, had her desk right in the reception area. Jeff, the part-time radiology guy, part-time physician's assistant, had his desk in the x-ray room. Most of the time, while one doctor was at the school, the other was here working with Darcy and Jeff. Sometimes Jeff would be at the school, especially during sports physical season.

I saw the light on in the building and knew someone was in there. Either one of the doctors or Darcy or all of the above. They either had worked late, pulled an all-nighter, or came in early. Darcy once confessed to me that some nights when she couldn't sleep, she would come to the office to do paperwork. "If I can't sleep, I might as well do something useful with my time," she would say.

Would.

I knew she was dead, if Susan Baker was telling the truth, but I had to see it for myself. Besides my sister, Darcy was the only other person I considered family. She was there when I was born and saw me through every broken bone, strep throat, and set of stitches. She was also there for me when my parents died. She listened so well, not judging me. When my sister fought to get me out of juvie and in home detention, Darcy was right there as a character witness.

She was my friend and I was already grieving her death with every step down that sidewalk. I walked up to the glass door and opened it. It was unlocked as expected. Whenever anyone worked early or late at the clinic, the door was always open, despite the posted hours on the sign. You never knew when illness would hit or someone would drop in with doughnuts to say hello.

I walked through the entryway, past the receptionist area, and down the hall to Darcy's office. The light I had seen from the walkway was hers and she was there at her desk, waiting for me, her head rested on outstretched arm. In her hand she had her cell phone. It was an iPhone like mine. We used to joke about being technology twins.

I ignored that for now and sat down across from her. Looking around her office, I smiled at the memories. Darcy with the softball league. Darcy with her husband. A family picture. Pictures of her pets; her dog, Beau, and her cat, Esme.

"Oh, Darcy," I murmured. "I'm in an awful mess."

She sat up and nodded, her dead gray skin showing hints of blue and purple in the sunlight. "Don't I know it."

I wasn't surprised when she spoke to me. I wasn't looking directly at her. I recognized the hallucination for what it was: stress breaking my already fragile mind a little bit more and my brain compensating for it the best it could. Still, I didn't fight it or try to banish it. As hallucinations went, this one wasn't so bad.

"What do I do?"

"Well, let's think about this for a moment..." I knew Darcy had her impish smile on. For an older lady with short brown, graying hair, she had the most childlike smile I had ever seen on anyone, including children. When she smiled wide, she looked like a Muppet or some other Henson creature. "You've proven that you aren't the cause of all this."

"I have?"

"Silly girl. This isn't all about you. The world moves on whether or not you're having a good day. Of course you didn't do this."

"What did? What killed everyone? Why South Dakota?"

I saw Darcy's shrug out of the corner of my eye. "I don't know. The government? The military? Aliens? Mother Earth? Something made people sleepy and then they died in their sleep. Honestly, not a bad way to go if you got to go."

"Darcy! How can you say that?" I was smiling now, scandalized.

"Honey, I'm not saying it. You are. I'm dead, remember?" The gentleness of her voice tore at my heart.

I nodded, tears welling up in my eyes. "I know. What do I do now?"

"I think you need to call that hotline. You've seen that I'm dead. That all of this really is real. Why don't you take my phone? I don't mind. Twins share."

I nodded again. "Okay. I can do that." I turned and looked at her. She smiled her most loving smile at me and then laid her head back down on her arm. My hallucination melded with reality as I wiped at my tears. When I could see again, I looked around the office to make sure the hallucinations were all gone. They seemed to be and that was good enough for right now.

I reached forward to take the phone from Darcy's outstretched hand. It resisted me. I tugged harder and Darcy's body shifted forward on the desk. This surprised me. I wondered if rigor mortis could hold a phone so hard. Then I wondered if she was keeping me from taking the phone. I stood up to look at her hand closer, and immediately saw what was keeping the phone in place: the phone was plugged into its charger and part of her body was laying on the cord.

I grimaced and reached around her to unplug the charger. As I did, I could smell the baby powder she wore mixing with the first hints of decay. The four pumpkin whoopie pies and large glass of milk in my stomach did a slow turn and I jerked back from Darcy's body, bringing the phone and its charger with me. My hasty movement messed up Darcy's hair and I paused long enough to stroke it out of her face, being careful to keep my fingers off of her dead flesh. Then I turned and ran from the building.

This time as I headed home, I didn't linger anywhere looking for the bodies I knew were there, all around me. Most of them were in the silent homes in bed. Most of them had gone to sleep last night and not woken up. The thing that bothered me was the fact that I *did* wake up. What made me different? Usually, I hated being a special kind of special but this was something else.

Right before I turned down Ginseng Avenue, I paused and looked around. I had the feeling that I was being watched. Which was stupid. Everyone was supposed to be dead, weren't they? Unless someone else in Onida was the same kind of special I was. Then again, I was a paranoid schizophrenic on an amazing cocktail of drugs who hallucinated in times of stress. So I had a right to doubt my feelings. On the other hand, as Deroga said frequently, "Always trust your gut."

I looked around some more, not bothering to call out, then I headed home. If someone else was alive in town, they needed to be open about it. Me? I was done looking for people. I needed to call a hotline.

As soon as I got in, I threw my coat on the couch and myself into my chair. I scowled at the broken TV and thought about going next door to watch the news at the Blakes'. The idea gave me the shivers. Instead, I plugged in my ankle monitor, not bothering to take off my shoes, and added the phone charger to the power strip on the table. Even though it was fully charged, I was afraid of it suddenly running out of power. I realized the thought was crazy but sometimes you have to mitigate the crazy by obeying it.

I turned the phone on and was thankful Darcy didn't keep the screen locked. However, it looked like she had been in the middle of texting her husband when she fell asleep. He was a doctor over at Saint Mary's in Pierre and had the nightshift. They had been talking about how tired they had suddenly become and agreed they should nap while the world was quiet before the chaos of emergencies started up again. They had just said they loved each other and goodbye.

My throat tightened with suppressed tears as I mourned their love and their loss. At least they got to say goodbye to each other even if they didn't know it was for the last time. I wiped at my eyes, impatient at my emotions leaking all over the place.

Get a grip. You gotta talk to Homeland Security.

I smiled a bittersweet smile at myself. How often did a girl get to do that? Deroga would think I was quite the dame now.

I looked at the note and then dialed the hotline number. A woman with a New York accent answered in a bored voice, "Department of Homeland Security hotline. How may I help you?"

"Agent Harrison, please."

"I'm sorry, Agent Harrison isn't in the call center, ma'am. This is a hotline number only."

"I'm in South Dakota and alive."

Her bored tone didn't change, "I'm sorry, ma'am. Agent Harrison is not available. How may I help you?"

"Um, My name is Melissa Allen. I live in Onida, South Dakota and I'm still alive. Can you get that to message to him?"

"I can get it to the investigative team, ma'am. What number would you like a call back at should the investigative team need more information?"

I was surprised and getting annoyed with her utter lack of care. "Don't you have it on your screen?"

"No, ma'am."

I realized I didn't know what Darcy's private phone number was. It'd been so long since I called it and I'd stopped trying to remember it months ago. Technically, I wasn't even supposed to know it in the first place. "Um, hold on." I touched the iPhone screen and accidentally hung up on the infuriating woman. "Dammit!"

I looked through the phone to get the number. Once I had it, I thought about it and decided that I would give them time to get the message up the chain to Agent Harrison so when I called back, I would get a better reception. I understand answering a hotline can be tedious but that's no reason to treat people like crap. I also bet they had the number in their computer system.

I spent some time looking through Darcy's phone; her pictures, texts and games. It had been almost a year since I'd played with one. Not that much had changed except for the games. I laughed through *Angry Birds* and enjoyed the soothing patterns of *Flow*. I looked through the books she had on her Kindle app and was surprised to see that Darcy was a zombie book junkie. Everything from Max Brooks to Jonathan Maberry to Mira Grant, not to mention the perennial favorite, George Romero.

I hate zombies. I don't like gore. I don't like mindless things that chase and I don't like swarms. Not good with bug books or movies either. Sharon or Matt always had to rescue me from bugs—a spider or a moth or even a crane fly. More than four legs and I can't deal with it. So it was a surprise to learn that about Darcy. I guess I didn't know her as well as I thought. It made me sad that I wouldn't get a chance to learn more.

I put her phone down and snuggled down in the chair. Despite it not even being dinnertime, I was exhausted. I closed my eyes, fell asleep, and dreamed.

I walked through the empty streets of town, looking for something. I couldn't remember what but I knew it was important. Everywhere I looked, things were familiar to me but I couldn't remember the names of the businesses or the owners of the houses I passed, until I was well beyond them.

Up ahead, I saw the Labrador retriever from the lumberyard waiting for me in the middle of the street. When I got closer, he stood up and trotted down the street away from me. I hurried to catch up. He turned right on Fir Avenue and disappeared from sight.

"Dog! Hey dog!" I yelled, following at a jog. When I got to Fir, I saw him waiting about halfway down the block. As soon as he saw me, he trotted away again.

I realized he was leading me somewhere. This time he turned left on South Eighth Street and I knew where he was going: the high school. That brought a pang to my chest. I had not been to the school in long enough that the idea of it made me nervous. I missed it, though, with its purple and gold colors, the Chargers, the library, and the ill-conceived but ever fun radio station KBSB; OBKB!

When the dog turned right and onto the school sidewalk, I wasn't surprised. But the fact that the school doors were wide open did make me wary. The dog paused at the double doors and woofed a gruff bark at me before disappearing inside. I followed him in, no longer able to see him but I could hear the click of his nails on glass. Wait, glass? I looked down and the floor I walked on wasn't tile but a thick glass through which I could see moving shapes.

When I looked up, all of the school walls had turned to glass as well and I wasn't alone. Every classroom was filled with kids I knew and they were all dead. Some were slumped over their desks, others were lolled back in their seats, and a couple had collapsed to the floor. The worst part about it was that all of them had their eyes open and they were watching me. It was horrible, that feeling of being watched by so many eyes.

I ran towards the one place of safety I knew: the library. As soon as I burst through the library doors, the walls became solid again. I breathed a sigh of relief, looked around, and remembered that I was looking for a book. An important book. I couldn't remember what book but I knew I would know it when I saw it. I headed to the stacks, walking through aisle after aisle of books.

Most of the books' spines were blank, with a few random black marks. The ones that weren't had the author name of "Harrison" on them. The random marks grew and wiggled, becoming worms that ate the books I looked at. I closed my eyes and opened them again. The books were fine and had writing on them but I couldn't read the words. I wondered if I could hallucinate in a dream. Then I wondered if I was dreaming.

I looked to my left and asked, "Am I dreaming?"

The verbal cue made me realize that I was *dreaming. I nodded to myself. Dreams helped me understand things.*

"What am I looking for?" I asked out loud.

Nothing happened at first. Then I heard the rumblings of things falling. I looked back and the stacks, now three stories high, were vomiting their books down into the narrow aisle. That massive pile of books tumbled toward me in an avalanche of hardback books with razor sharp pages.

I turned and ran. The aisles through the stacks were a literal maze of twisting passageways and dead ends. I couldn't afford to use the slower, surer way of the left-hand or right-hand rule to get out of the maze. I was stuck with split second decisions and sprinting for my life while being chased by the human-eating book monster.

I turned one corner and saw an endless, narrow hallway before me. I was out of the stacks but I had nowhere else to go. From the sounds of the crashing behind me, the book monster was still coming. I sprinted down the tiled hallway, trying to remember where I was. The hallway, for all its strangeness, was familiar.

But I didn't have time for that. I had to run. Looking over my shoulder, the living avalanche of books was chewing up the hallway, adding long, ragged pieces of wood and broken tile to its form as it snowballed towards me.

And it was gaining.

Afraid and running faster, I fled down the endless hallway, looking for a door, an exit, a hallway. None appeared. I knew I was dreaming but my fear of the thing behind me (and getting closer) kept me from gaining control of the dream.

"Time to wake up," I panted. "Time to wake up!"

I could hear the monster closer still and smell the dusty debris from its mayhem.

"Wake up!" I yelled. "Time to wake up!"

I wasn't waking up. I had died in my dreams before and it sucked. Left me shaky for hours after I woke. I didn't want to die munched into pieces by the book monster but if I was going to die, I was going to face it. I put on a burst of speed and then stopped and turned, facing it head on. I put my hands out and imagined a force field in front of me. Sometimes I could save myself at the last minute and that was what I was praying for here.

Only the monster didn't stop and I was going to die. I stood there, frozen in horror as the mountain of debris and books towered over me. Right when it was about to come crashing down, a hand yanked me out of its path and I found myself held by a man in a trench coat.

The world stopped as snapshot pictures took over.

Snapshot: A man holding me by the arms in a darkened hallway. His head tilted down, face hidden by a tan fedora.

Snapshot: A man in a tan trench coat and matching fedora hat in profile in the doorway of the lumberyard building. His head tilted down. There was something wrong with the shape of his body.

Snapshot: The man holding me lifted his head to reveal a flesh colored mask of a generic, dark haired man smiling a wide, cheerful smile under a plastic mustache.

Reality started up again and something moved under the mask. Something I didn't want to see. I twisted, trying to jerk myself out of his grip, screaming, "Wake up! Wake up! Wake Up!"

I woke in darkness, certain I wasn't alone.

CHAPTER FIVE

I looked around the room, seeking the Fedora Man. Nothing but darkness and silence. Then Darcy's phone vibrated on the table and the sound drilled a hole in my head. I grabbed it and saw that an alarm was set for ten. I turned it off and then disabled the alarm. I put the phone down, three facts penetrating my aching head.

I was hungry.

It was ten in the evening.

I missed my eight p.m. dose.

It was this last fact that jolted me into action. Two hours late wasn't as bad as it could be for missing my pills. Four hours late on the lamotrigine made me want to kill myself. Literally. Ramping up and ramping down that drug is a killer. Two hours only gifted me with the splitting headache I now had. I had a rescue medicine for that but I needed to get my pills *now.*

I jumped up from my comfy chair, took two hasty steps, and fell flat on my face with my left leg still tethered to the ankle monitor charger. Having once walked off still plugged in before and ripped the cord out of the wall, Matt had set up the charging station so that it was attached to the end table first and then the wall. The plug on the ankle monitor was stiff and had the added leverage of being attached to the front of my ankle when I started walking.

Muttering curses, I untangled myself from the power cord and hauled myself to my feet. I needed my pills and my rescue medicine. Then I needed food. Something solid and dinner like. I gulped down my pills with milk and contemplated the freezer. With Matt's sometimes late schedule,

Sharon kept frozen dinners on tap. I grabbed one, opened it, and tossed it in the microwave. When the microwave door closed, I swore I heard a noise outside.

It could've been a coyote or a dog. Or it could've been the Fedora Man. I listened hard but didn't hear anything. My paranoia running as high as my headache, I went to the front door and grabbed the aluminum bat we had there as part of the home protection plan, not that there was a lot of home protecting to do around Onida. Everyone knew about the one sex offender in town and the most excitement we had all winter was when a seventy-seven year old man punched a state trooper. He wasn't even from Onida. He was from Pierre.

Be that as it may, we were one of the few houses in town that locked their doors. It was more for my comfort than anything else and we usually left it unlocked when we all left the house. How was that for bass-ackwards? Now, when I unbolted the door, the click of the lock sounded very loud in my ears.

I crept down the steps and listened. Faintly, I thought I could hear an unfamiliar low buzzing coming from the west. I headed down Ginseng Avenue away from Main Street and toward South Fourth Street. I found myself following Deroga's advice about moving slowly and keeping to the shadows when approaching the unknown. At the crossroads of Ginseng and South Fourth, I stopped and listened.

I heard a dog barking up South Fourth by the grain silos. It was the territorial bark of a dog protecting its turf from something that frightened it. I wondered what could frighten a dog out there. Coyotes had nothing on the local dogs, and raccoons were scarce. The moon wasn't high up and the stars gave scant light to see by but I could see a little more than the outlines of the silos. At the base of them, I thought I could see something moving. It glowed with a faint light; possibly reflected moonlight.

As the dog's barking got more and more frantic, I swore I saw several blobs of faint light moving and heard the buzzing sound of cicadas. The dog's fierce defense of itself and its territory abruptly cut off with a high pitched yelping of pain. It was the kind of yelping that a dog does when you step on its foot… but it kept going. Something was hurting the dog bad. I thought it would never stop. Then it was mercifully silent. I found myself crouched down with my hand over my mouth when I saw three of the hazy blobs converge on a single point. I prayed that the dog was dead, that it wasn't still in pain.

Whether or not this was a particularly bad hallucination caused by the late dose or stress or what, I was ready to be home. I shivered in the night air and wondered why I had thought to come out in the cold at all. I had done exactly what I yelled at movies for—gone out at night without a coat to investigate a strange noise. This was how people got murdered in every horror movie out there. Somehow, I had turned into a bad cliché.

I ran in a bent over hunch until I got back to the safety of the trees and their shadows. Then I sprinted back to the house, closed and locked the door. I decided that me and Mister Bat—his name was written on the bat in purple marker—were going to be fast friends from now on.

The more I thought about it, the more I wondered if the blobs of light were the Fedora Men. Check that, the Fedoras. Because whatever they were, they were *not* men. While I wasn't certain that I actually saw the lights or the Fedoras because of my broken brain, my gut told me that I couldn't discount it.

Most days I accepted the way I was born. Today I cursed it. With everyone I knew dead, I was having a hard enough time dealing with reality to have hallucinations possibly intruding and making it all worse. On the other hand, until something else told me otherwise, I had to treat the Fedoras as a possible threat and maybe the cause of the mass death of South Dakota.

I needed more information and I had just the way to get it. I hurried up the stairs, careful not to jar Sharon's door as I went past and to my bedroom. My bedroom window overlooked one of the eaves of the roof. It wasn't hard to get out there and clamber up to the top of the house. I used to do it all the time in the fall when I wanted to watch the colorful leaves fall and float on the wind. Fall made the town of Onida beautiful and I always watched with love. On a good day, I could see all the way to the courthouse clock tower.

Not used to crawling on the roof at night, I took my time and left the bat behind. If I got jumped on the roof, Mister Bat wasn't going to save me. Once I was out there, I could hear the cicadas' buzzing sound again. This time, it was mostly north of me, towards the clinic. I got myself to the highest part of the roof and stood tall and still.

With the moon higher in the sky and with a higher vantage point, I could see most of Onida, and what I saw scared the crap out of me. I could see at least seven moving blobs of light and they looked like moonlight reflecting off of tan coats. I saw no real details other than man-sized blobs and them moving in a searching pattern. For the moment, they were moving away from me. But Onida wasn't that big. It wouldn't take long for them to come to the south part of town.

I crouched down and crab walked my way back to my bedroom window. I sat down on my bed and hugged my pillow to me. Hallucinations or not, the Fedoras scared me and I really needed someone to come rescue me.

Need? Want, not need. You're being a wimp. What about Wicked Girls Saving Themselves?

"I'm scared," I whispered.

Courage is what you do when your knees shake. What you need *to do is rescue yourself.*

"How?"

Good question. Driving is out – you panic behind the wheel. The Blakes have that pretty little moped you've been lusting after though.

I nodded. "Yes. The moped." It's about one hundred and sixty miles down Highway 83 to get to Nebraska. Julie told me it could go two hundred and twenty on a full tank of gas. At about forty miles an hour, that was four hours. Five with pit stops.

There you go. Fuck this waiting for rescue. You're going to rescue yourself.

"Yes," I said, standing up. First, however, I needed to survive the night. And that meant heading downstairs.

I grabbed Mister Bat and carried him downstairs with me to the end of the hallway where the basement door was. The basement had always been one of my refuges and once I was put under house arrest, it became my solitary safe haven by silent agreement. I turned on the light and closed the door behind me.

The familiar wooden squeaks of the stairs soothed me as I descended into my domain. Fully furnished, the basement was both playroom and survival shelter. There were no windows to the outside and the basement exit to the yard was up a short set of stairs and barred from the inside. The main room had wood paneling, a horrifically orange shag rug that I loved for no explainable reason, and the kind of set up couch potatoes dream of.

Three-fourths of the room was filled with a couch, a loveseat and reclining chair arranged around an old thirty-six inch TV. The TV wasn't connected to the cable, so it didn't have DVR. I had to watch all the new shows upstairs. It was only connected to the DVD player, the oldest X-Box console in existence (no internet on it), and the surround sound system. I wasn't a big TV fan when this room was set up and I didn't have a mandatory two hours of house monitor charging to do. Once I did, I got hooked on old shows and older videogames. Matt bought that lovely flat screen I accidentally destroyed earlier and this room became the room I could be a teenager in. Movies, video games, reading, and sulking or moping if I wanted to without one of the godparents checking in on me.

It was nice. Better than nice. It was considerate. I learned to take my bad moods down here and only go upstairs when I was civil.

The second room was the emergency room. Paneled like the main room, three walls had built-in shelving for canned goods, emergency rations, water, and the like. I once spent a week down here sleeping on the sofa and eating emergency rations and only going upstairs to use the bathroom. Just to see if I could. Sharon and Matt thought I was a little crazy for doing so but it did tell us where there were weaknesses in our survival plan.

Now, I grabbed one of the ration bar packs and tore it open. Lemon flavored, my favorite. Yes, I'd left a frozen dinner in the microwave but I couldn't handle the thought of going back upstairs to get it. I gobbled down two of the four hundred calorie cookies and washed them down with a bottle of water. While I was contemplating the third, the phone in my pocket vibrated. I took it out and looked at the screen. It read MOM and had the face of an elderly woman who looked a lot like Darcy.

The idea of Darcy's mom calling her over and over, trying to find out if she was okay filled me with horror. I could imagine what kind of anguish she was going through. With the quarantine in place and no one really knowing what was going on, it was a solid bet that people from all over were calling friends and family in South Dakota, hoping against hope that their kith and kin made it through despite the odds.

I couldn't do that to Darcy's mom even if I didn't know her. Between the second and third ring, I answered the phone. "Hello?"

An elderly woman's voice quavered with excitement. "Darcy! I knew you were alive. I knew it!"

"I'm sorry. I'm not Darcy." I winced at the confused pause on the other end of the line.

"Who are you? Where's my daughter?"

"My name is Melissa. Darcy is…is dead. I'm sorry."

"You're lying! Put my daughter on the phone this instant, young lady."

The angry command in the woman's voice made me wince again. "I'm sorry. I can't. I wanted you to know. I'm sorry." I thumbed the End Call button and put the phone down, shaking a little. I felt sorry for Darcy's mother but there was nothing I could do.

The phone vibrated in my hand and Darcy's mom showed up on the screen. I thumbed the ignore button and sat back. Thirty seconds later it buzzed again, showing Darcy had voicemail. I knew I didn't want to tap that app. I could just imagine the angry words and accusations. I didn't blame her. If it was my mom or sister or daughter, I would be confused and furious. It would take a bit before I realized I had done me a favor and given me confirmation of death.

Two ignored phone calls later and I was done being understanding and I turned the phone off.

DAY TWO:

THERE BE MONSTERS

CHAPTER SIX

I dozed fitfully on the sofa from midnight until about six a.m. I dreamed but nothing so horrible as the book monster, even though I understood that I was really waiting for Agent Harrison to get back to me. What I could remember was an awful lot of walking down unfamiliar hallways and feeling lost. Usually my brain isn't so literal with my fears.

I rubbed my face and thought about a shower before turning Darcy's phone back on. Sixty seconds later I had four more voicemails and five text messages. I ignored all of them, knowing they were not for me.

I nixed the idea of the shower because I had one the day before and because rule number one said that girls in their skivvies died first in horror movies. Without a doubt, I was in the real-life equivalent of a horror movie. Thus, showers were forbidden until I could get myself to safety.

I needed to pack a three day kit. I had time. I knew it would be another hour before the sun rose and I wanted the clean light of day on me before I took off down Highway 83 on the Blakes' moped.

I thought about that as I pulled out the grab-and-go bag we already had packed and looked in it. I was becoming quite the thief. Darcy's phone and soon, the Blakes' moped. After I went looking through their house for the keys. That brought me up short. I didn't like idea of sneaking through their house and going through their things. Especially since I knew—*knew*—they would be there, dead, in the house.

Desperate times called for desperate measures but that didn't mean I had to like it.

The grab-and-go backpack was good on emergency supplies but light on clothes. Since there was a better than even chance that I would never return to this house, I needed to pack extra clothes to wear. Though, most likely, I would immediately be remanded to federal or clinical care as soon as I got out of South Dakota. I was surprised at how much that thought relieved me.

Wimp, my inner critic chided.

I smiled at myself. At least I was a wimp saving myself. I may be getting myself out of a bad situation but that didn't mean that the courts would pretend the stuff from a year ago didn't happen. I was willing to deal with that. By my choice.

You just don't want to take care of yourself.

I wouldn't mind if I didn't have to worry about a bunch of brain drugs. Those things are expensive and life without them wasn't worth it. Speaking of drugs, while it was too early for them, I needed to go get my supply and keep it with me at all times. If worst came to absolute worst, I could flee on foot and hide out in one of the remote farms or at the municipal airport. I felt like an addict and, in a way, I was. I was addicted to some semblance of sanity.

I opened the door from the basement to the house and listened. Nothing. Only the running heater. I was happy the power substation hadn't decided to crap out. It was mostly automatic and needed some maintenance but the years of South Dakota winters taught us how to build sturdy lines of power. I figured it would run for about another week before something failed somewhere and the whole local system shut down. That was what I hoped. Dad taught me never to put my absolute trust in technology.

When I got to the kitchen, I couldn't help myself, I counted my pills again. Thirty for the twice daily doses and sixteen of the Prazosin. I had forgotten to take it but was happy that I didn't remember any really bad nightmares. I packed the pills into a baggie and stuffed them into my coat pocket. Then I scheduled two daily alarms on Darcy's phone; one for eight in the morning and one for eight in the evening.

As I stood there, feeling very wide awake for the first time in ages, I realized it was the lack of Prazosin talking. It was a wonder drug when it came to getting rid of nightmares but it also left me groggy in the mornings. It was like it would take a couple of hours for my brain to really wake up after I was up and about for the day. I guess that's why I did all my TV viewing in the morning. In any case, I figured I would keep off the

Prazosin for as long as I could. It's not good to be brain dead in the middle of an apocalypse.

While I was mucking with the phone, I looked to see who the text messages were from. All of them were from Darcy's mom. The phone calls, though, came from two different numbers: Darcy's mom and an area code I didn't recognize. My bet was that Darcy's mom had gotten creative and was calling from a different number.

I headed upstairs to my room. I paused a moment in the hall when I smelled something out of place. Then I realized that it was coming from my sister's room. The bodies were starting to rot and the smell was the beginning smell of decay. I couldn't imagine how bad the whole town would smell after a month. The great state of "Under God, the People Rule" would become the great state of "Under God, the Bodies Stink."

My morbid sense of humor made me choke back an unexpected chuckle and I hurried to my room to choose two sets of clothes. That is all that would fit in my backpack along with the rest of the emergency gear. While I was stuffing the last of my shirts into the bag, Darcy's phone rang. It was the second number that had called last night.

I really didn't have time to deal with her grief. I was dealing with my own and bigger problems. I answered the phone but I wasn't polite about it. "Look, I'm sorry Darcy's dead. I loved her, too. Please stop calling."

As I thumbed the End Call button, I heard a male voice ask, "Miss Allen?"

I froze, staring at the phone. Only adults in an official capacity called me Miss Allen. While I was debating about calling the number back—it could be an official someone Darcy's mom contacted but I didn't remember telling her my last name—the phone rang again.

This time, when I answered it, I decided if it was an official someone from Darcy's mom and not Homeland Security like I hoped, I would go look for Shannon or Matt's phone. "Hello?"

"Hello, is this Melissa Allen?" The man's voice was deep and warm.

"Speaking."

"May I ask where you're located?"

This guy was polite but momma didn't raise a fool. "Only if you tell me who you are and where you're calling from."

"My name is Agent David Hood. I'm a Homeland Security Agent calling from Valentine, Nebraska."

I sat down on my bed. "I'm at home in Onida, South Dakota. How did you find me?"

"We've been calling your home number since yesterday after we received your call on our hotline. After that, we monitored outgoing phone calls from the cell towers in South Dakota in hopes that someone would make an outgoing call or an incoming call would connect. Last night you answered a call on Mrs. Darcy Payne's phone but the phone was turned off by the time we tried to call you. We've been monitoring your signal ever since. You turned it on again a few minutes ago."

I felt a thrill of fear and pleasure at this explanation. It was both daunting and cool that the government could actually do something like that. Maybe some of those conspiracy theorists were right about some things. "Oh, yeah. I, uh, had an accident with my home phone and had to find another one. Then Darcy's mom called and I didn't want her to wonder or not about Darcy. Then she wouldn't stop calling, so I turned it off. When are you guys going to come get me?" I felt like I was on the edge of laughing and crying. It was the beginnings of hysteria. I took a couple of deep breaths to steady myself.

David said, "I can't answer that but I have someone here who can."

"Wait!"

"Yes?"

"Do you have an iPhone? I want to see who I'm talking to. I want to do FaceTime."

It was his turn to pause. "Hold on."

I could hear the muffled voices talking in the background. There were sounds of confusion and then David said, "If it works, we can use it to see what she sees." There was quiet and another man's voice said, "Do it." David came back to the phone. "Okay, Melissa. We're going to use my phone. I'll FaceTime you. Are you good with that?"

"Yes."

"I need your FaceTime contact information. I'll text you mine. Text me yours back."

"Sounds like a plan

"Okay. I need to hang up now. I'll see you soon."

"I'll be here."

While I waited for his text message to come in, I searched Darcy's phone for her information. She used her normal email account like I suspected. As soon as his text message came in, I added his information to the cell phone and texted my information back.

In the two minutes it took for David to get back to me, I grabbed the backpack and my bat and headed downstairs. I sat on the ottoman in front of my comfy chair and plugged my ankle monitor in. I didn't want it squawking for juice while I was on the phone. I was sure they already knew about me. They had to have found my court records by now and everything that went along with them. I didn't want them thinking I was sloppy or out of control.

As soon as the phone binged, I clicked the FaceTime app. A young, concerned looking Asian man smiled at me. "Hello, Melissa."

"Hello."

He was not what I had been expecting from the American sound of his voice. He was handsome in the same clean cut way Sulu was handsome in both the old and new *Star Trek* movies.

He was wearing a white button up shirt with the top button undone and a loosened dark blue tie. "I have Agent Harrison here. He'd like to talk to you."

"Okay."

The phone was handed over. I saw flashes of two other people in the room as it moved, a black woman in some sort of military uniform and a white haired man in beige clothing. When the phone stopped moving, the pale face on the screen looked lined and tired. He had to be at least fifty years old, though there was a glint of excitement in his blue eyes. He looked like the kind of grandfather who took his grandkids hunting to teach them about life and death and then made them help butcher the deer to teach them about where food comes from. Both a generous and hard man. I hoped he was going to be more on the generous side with me.

"Hello, Melissa. I'm Agent Tomas Harrison."

"Hello, Tomas," I said and saw how his mouth quirked in a wry half-smile. *Calling me by my given name gives me permission to use yours. Especially if we're going to pretend to be friends.*

"I need to ask you a few questions. Do you mind?"

"No. Not if you answer mine."

He nodded a little. "I will answer them the best I can."

"Okay, shoot."

"First, have you gone to sleep in the last forty-eight hours?"

"Yes. Three times. The first time I woke up and my..." *My family was dead.* I couldn't say the words. I paused as unexpected tears rushed forth. "Sorry." I wiped at my face, collecting my shattered thoughts.

"Take all the time you need."

I took two breaths and then pushed on, choosing to ignore the tears. I made sure they didn't splash on the phone. "The first time I woke up was yesterday morning about seven. I discovered my family dead at noon. The second time I napped from about five until ten in the evening. Then I dozed from midnight until six this morning." My voice shook less the more I talked.

"Have you seen anyone else alive?"

"No." I paused, shook my head. "No. I thought I did, down at the lumberyard but I guess my mind was playing tricks on me." Since I wasn't certain what the blobs of light were, I wasn't comfortable telling him about them. Especially since they might really have been hallucinations.

"Okay. Have you seen other dead people?"

"Yes. Several. I went down to the clinic. That's where I found Darcy and got her phone." I rushed on and asked, "Do you know what's happening? When are you going to come get me?"

"I'll answer the second question before the first. We're not going to come get you. As—"

"Why not?" I interrupted. I wanted to yell and scream at him. I didn't want to be here anymore.

"Please, Melissa. There are a lot of scared people..."

"I'm scared too!"

"I realize that. But please listen. We're in a state of emergency, Melissa, and as far as we can tell, you are the only person left alive in the South Dakota quarantine zone. We've tested it. Within an hour of anyone crossing into the zone, they become incredibly tired and want to go to sleep. If we don't get them out of the zone within minutes of falling asleep, they die. We need you."

Part of me wondered about how they had tested this and who they tested it with. I also wondered how many people had died to figure out as much as they already knew.

"What's the zone? What do you need me for?"

"The entire state of South Dakota isn't dead. Just most of it. Everything south of Tyndall and Hawarden survived. Everything north up to the border between the Dakotas died. It is a rectangular zone and as far as we can tell, there is a signal coming from Onida, Blunt, or Pierre that is causing the zone to exist." He rubbed his forehead. "Blunt is nothing but a suburb of Pierre. Pierre is too busy for something like this to have been set up without notice. That leaves Onida."

"But why do I have to stay here?"

"For some reason, you're not affected by the zone. You're still alive. You may be the only way we have of finding and stopping the signal."

I sat back and stared at him, not wanting to believe him. "But..." I hated the weakness in my voice. Every argument I came up with—send someone else, use satellites, maybe it wouldn't last—was dumb or had a good reason why they couldn't, or shouldn't, do it. In the end, I let the word hang in the air as testament to my reluctance to do whatever it was they wanted me to do.

"Please, Melissa, we're counting on you." His voice was soft and he didn't seem like a man who said 'please' very often.

I nodded even though I didn't want to. "Okay. What do I need to do?" I tried to put on my brave face.

"That's my girl." He smiled. "I'm going to hand you over to Doctor Modell."

Part of me wanted to punch Tomas for the compliment and part of me wanted to hug him. I was a mess of emotions and I had a lot of reasons to be messed up. In the meantime, either I was going to be a hero or I was going to die trying.

Doctor Modell turned out to be the white-haired man in a beige polo shirt. He had wide brown eyes behind expensive glasses and a pale face that made me think it didn't see the sun very often.

"Hello Melissa."

"Heya, Doc. What kind of doc?"

His smile was also tired. "Excuse me?"

"What kind of doctor are you? The doctoring kind or the Ph.D. kind?" Deroga often took control of conversations and learned a lot about the person he was talking to by asking a question that had nothing to do with the topic at hand. In the end, the question was important and usually helped Deroga solve the case.

"Both, actually. I'm a Neurologist and I have a Ph. D. in electromagnetic frequencies. I study the brain as well as the effect of broad spectrum frequencies on the brain."

"Oh, cool. So, you're the brains of the investigation?"

He laughed and shook his head. "No. I'm one of the brains you might say. And you, young lady, need to be our eyes, ears, and hands."

"Okay. What do I need to do?"

"Do you have a radio station in town?"

"Not a real one. Only the high school station, KBSB."

"Good. Do you know if you have a radio tower?"

I shook my head. "I don't know. We might. I mean, I guess we have to broadcast somehow."

He looked to the side when a woman's voice said something. I didn't understand it but he nodded and then looked at the phone again.

"Who was that? What'd she say?"

"That was Lieutenant Kimberly Stoneson. She's a communication specialist. She said if you could get to the school radio station, she would help you identify what we were looking for. First, she needed a little time to find some pictures to send you on your phone. We could be ready to roll within an hour or two. Give you some time to get yourself breakfast."

"Um. Okay."

"I'm giving you back to Agent Hood now."

The phone screen showed a dizzying array of people and equipment as it was handed back to David.

"Heya, David. What happened to Tomas?"

David gave me a half-smile. "Agent Harrison had to leave. He's briefing the president on this."

"The president? As in *the* – "

"Commander in Chief and all that. Agent Harrison wasn't kidding about the state of emergency and people being scared. Whoever or whatever is doing this, some people think it is merely the beginning."

"It's a person or a terrorist group then?"

He shrugged. "That's the best we can think. So, I'm your main point of contact. I will be manning this phone 24/7. If you need anything, call. If you find anything, call. If you want to talk, call. I'm here for you. That's my job now."

"So, you're at my beck and call, huh?" I liked the sound of that.

"Only digitally. In any case, I'm going to go and listen in on the plans so that when we talk next, I can brief you. You get some breakfast and we'll talk soon. Okay?"

"Okay. You get some breakfast, too."

"I will. Bye." He waved at me and hung up the phone.

I looked at the phone in my hand and wondered how the hell I was going to save South Dakota. I couldn't even save myself. I had to try. Food… then into dangers untold.

CHAPTER SEVEN

While I made myself breakfast and took my pills at eight, I thought about what I had agreed to do. From the outside, it was absolutely logical because Homeland Security didn't know what I knew. I was the only person alive they could count on. If it was some sort of signal being generated, me turning it off would make me a hero. Especially if I recovered whatever was making the signal.

On the other hand, there were *things* out there, and I didn't believe they were friendly. Especially since they are the ones who probably caused the whole thing to begin with. Even if Agent Harrison knew about the blobs or the Fedoras—if they were not one and the same—I don't think it would change his mind. I'm still the only person alive that can be their eyes, ears, and hands. Also, I wasn't confident enough in my own senses to admit to seeing the strangeness that I saw.

Then I realized that I could prove it to myself once and for all. I would find the dog at the grain silos. If the Fedoras were real, then the dog would be dead of some violent means. Or there would be evidence of it and its death. If the dog was alive, I hallucinated it all and I could stop being so paranoid. If it was dead, I would show it to David and then we would figure out what to do next.

With the cell phone in my pocket and my bat in my hand, I walked down Ginseng Avenue in the cold morning light. Nothing moved except the birds. Even the dogs were quiet. There was something about the quiet solitude that made me think. It felt weird to have strangers depending on me. It felt weird for anyone having to depend on me at all.

In the olden days, I would have been an adult and married by now. But because of my parents' death and the problems with my brain, not only was I not someone to depend on, I was someone you were not *allowed* to depend on. Until now. I think I liked it. It was good for people to need me as much as I needed them.

I stopped at the corner of South Fourth and Ginseng, realizing that I had left the house for the first time since the house arrest thing began without permission and without thinking about what would happen to me if I did. Things sure changed fast when there was a localized apocalypse. I also realized that it was possible for me to escape into the wilds of South Dakota's quarantine zone and never worry about living anyone else's rules ever again. I could walk away and they would never know what happened to me.

I would also have to give up things like companionship and modern conveniences like electricity since I was certain the power wouldn't stay on indefinitely. And give up being a hero, being interviewed, and possibly going on *The Daily Show* which, until now had only been a pipedream, but suddenly was a distinct possibility. Of course, and most importantly, I would have to give up being sane. No medicine, no sanity.

I shrugged and kept going. The whole time I daydreamed and walked to the grain silos, I was also on high alert. If the Fedoras were around, I wanted to know it before they jumped me. I found myself looking into shadows. Then I realized the only places I thought I had seen something was in the dark or at night. Maybe the Fedoras were nocturnal or were allergic to the sun. It was something to think about.

The first part of South Fourth is wide open on both sides. The right side is a field towards the farmland. The left side is a marshy mess between the road and the houses. At the curve in the road, the skyline shrinks to a huge silo on the left and smaller silos on the right. As the first couple of silos surrounded me, I looked to where I thought I saw the blobs of light converge.

It was a dilapidated shack completely stripped of its white paint sitting next to four squat grain silos; the three closest to the shack were rusty white, the fourth was red rust color painted. Behind them stood three taller, slimmer, rusty white silos. As I got closer, I saw that the grain silos were surrounded by a concrete lip. It was too short to call it a wall.

It was between the shack and this concrete lip that I found the dead dog. He was lying at the bottom of the stairs onto the porch, facing out towards me. It was like he had tried to hold his ground while protecting his sides with manmade barriers. It hadn't worked. Oh, boy, it hadn't worked.

I swallowed my terror and stepped closer. Something had stabbed the dog, a German Shepherd, in the throat and in the guts. There was a hole all the way through his neck with puddles of blood on both sides of his head. And there was a ragged hole in his belly. Thankfully, there was no continuing hole coming out his back. My stomach did a slow roll, tumbling the bacon and eggs in an uneasy spin. I quickly backed away from the poor dog.

This was it. This was my proof. Not only was I not crazy but my paranoia was justified. I pulled out Darcy's cell phone and called David.

His face appeared on the screen but he wasn't in the same place he was before. He was in a place with dark green walls surrounding him. "Melissa? Are you okay?"

"Yeah. Yeah. I'm okay. Where are you?"

He looked chagrinned. "I'm in the bathroom."

"Oh, God! I'm so sorry. I—"

"No. No," he interrupted. "It's cool. I wouldn't have answered if it wasn't. I'm not… busy. I needed to get away from people. I needed some privacy and this was the only place I could get it."

"Oh. I totally understand. Um. I need to talk to you."

"What's up?"

"I wasn't completely honest with you guys before."

He straightened up. "What do you mean?"

"Mostly, I didn't tell you guys everything. I didn't think you'd believe me. I mean… you've read my file, haven't you?"

"Yes, of course. But there's nothing in there about you lying."

"But there's something in there about me needing psychotropic drugs to make it through the day, and that I'm a bi-polar schizophrenic." I looked away from the phone and at the poor, murdered dog. "That sometimes I hallucinate."

He nodded, his face somber. "I did read that. But I also read that you've responded well to medication and as long as there wasn't another incident, you would be released from house arrest on your eighteenth birthday provided you remained on the medicine. What's this all about? What did you see?"

He certainly did know everything about me. At least my files on record were positive. "Remember when I said I thought I saw someone in the lumberyard?"

"Yes."

"I'm really sure I saw someone in the lumberyard building. They walked by the door. They looked like they were wearing a tan trench coat and a tan fedora. And I think it had a mask on."

"Why do you say 'it'?"

I could see that even though he was in the bathroom, sitting in stall, he was writing notes. I hoped it wasn't on his leg. I took a breath. "I don't think it's human. That why I call them 'Fedoras.'"

He looked up from his note taking. "Not human? What do you think they are?"

"I don't know. Monsters? Last night, I thought I heard something. So I investigated. I could see blobs of light. Like moonlight on the tan coats. And I heard a dog barking. And then he yelped like something was hurting him... and then he stopped." I looked at his face with that carefully neutral expression. "See, this is why I didn't want to tell you guys. I knew you wouldn't believe me."

"I'm not saying that. I'm thinking about what you said. Maybe we got it wrong. It's not a radio wave. Maybe it's airborne within a limited range and what you saw were people hiding air filters and oxygen tanks under coats, hats, and masks."

It sounded so reasonable and I wanted to believe him. "Yeah. Maybe. But... but I came out to the grain silos to find the dog. I needed to make sure I didn't hallucinate the whole thing. David, I didn't. I found the dog. I want you to see him."

David nodded, "Okay. Show me."

I walked back to the dog and turned the phone to him.

"Damn," David said. "Get closer. I need to get some screen captures."

I hunkered down in front of the German Shepherd and breathed through my mouth. "Something punctured straight through his neck and into his tummy."

"Man. Get in close to the stomach and then I want to get a couple of shots of the back of its neck."

I did as he asked, making sure not to step in the puddles of jellied blood more out of the gross factor than hiding my tracks factor. I moved in closer and in different angles before stepping around him to let David get captures of the hole coming out of the dog's neck. "Do you have enough?" I asked when I thought I was about to throw up.

"Yes. I'm done."

I hurried away from it and walked down South Fourth towards home. I kept the phone up so I could both see David and where I was walking. "David, I don't think I can stay here. I need to leave. It's not safe."

He grimaced. "You have to stay." He glanced away from the phone and then nodded to himself. "They wouldn't tell you this until they thought they absolutely had to."

"Tell me what?"

"The quarantine. It goes both ways. No one in. No one out."

"But I'm alive. Who do they think might come out of here?"

"I don't know. Terrorists? Once I tell Agent Harrison about what you told me, they are really going to be under orders to shoot to kill. No questions. No quarter."

"What if the Fedoras come after me?"

"Do you know how to use a gun?"

"Yes, but no. My grandfather taught me before he died. That was years ago though. I haven't touched a shotgun since I was six and we aren't allowed to have them in the house. Not even a hunting rifle, and not even locked in the gun safe. Matt was upset at that."

"Matthew Moore?"

"Yes, he's my brother in law. Sharon and Matt are my supervising family." I paused. "Were."

"Okay. No guns."

"I do have this." I showed him Mister Bat and he smiled.

"Smart girl. People underestimate the power of blunt objects. Is that the bat you used on the mail boxes?"

"Uh, yeah. Kinda sorta."

"I'm surprised they let you keep it."

"I didn't ask for permission to keep it and it wasn't taken away from me."

"Gotta love the court system."

"Listen, what's stopping me from getting on my neighbor's moped and rocketing the hell out of here?"

"The fact that they *will* shoot you at the border. I'm not joking around with this, Melissa. Please believe me. They will. Especially after I talk to Agent Harrison about this. I believe you and I know how to talk to him so it doesn't sound so…" He stopped, groping for a word that wasn't the one he was going to say.

"Crazy? Insane?" I was angry and scared. I had monsters in town and military blockades to keep me in the quarantine zone with the monsters.

"Unlikely," he finally said. "Look, I don't like it any more than you do."

"No? Then you come in here and face them."

"I would if it weren't a death sentence." He said this with a straight face and serious expression. There was a moment of silence. Then he added, "I swear. If I could come in and get you, I'd do it myself. I can't." David looked away from the screen and down at his notes.

I stopped and sighed. "Sorry. It's not your fault."

"When I talk to Agent Harrison about these new findings, I'll make a case to extract you from the situation. You're right, it's dangerous and you aren't trained. I'll see if we can't find another way. In the meantime, wait for Lieutenant Stoneson to call. Maybe you two will find the thing that needs finding and we can come get you tonight."

I smiled a fake smile and nodded. "Okay. I'll talk to you later." I thumbed the End button before either of us called us on the lie in our words. It was a waiting game. I couldn't leave and he couldn't help me. We were both stuck in our own ways.

However, that didn't mean I couldn't do something about it.

CHAPTER EIGHT

Instead of going straight home, I headed towards the Blakes' house. Even if I couldn't leave immediately, I could prepare to leave at a moment's notice. That meant getting the moped ready to roll. First things first: find the moped key.

The Blakes live across the way from me in a white ranch style home hidden by a bunch of trees. With spring on the way, the trees were all budding with new growth, partly hiding the house from the road. I turned down their dirt driveway and checked their front door. It wasn't locked. I think I would be surprised if it was.

I opened the door and steeled myself for what I knew I would find. Coming from the outdoors into the closed space, the smell of decay was strong. The front door opened into the living room.

I didn't expect to see the twins, Tanya and Tyler, dead on the couch. They were twelve years old and, unlike most siblings, the best of friends. They were fraternal twins with one being a girl and the other a boy. Sandy blond hair like me with eyes so dark you would swear they were wearing contacts. They had gone to sleep playing a video game. Now it was game over for everyone.

The moped belonged to Tristan, the oldest sibling, and one of the local football heroes. Bets were that he would get out of this crappy little town on a football scholarship. Not anymore. He was good. Cute, too. Never gave me "the look," the one that asks if I'm dangerous or crazy. For a moment, I felt guilty for taking his moped but then decided he would approve based on the circumstances.

I went to the kitchen, looking to see if they had a standard place to put keys like my family. They didn't, but there was a set of keys on the kitchen bar. I took it and headed into the garage with them.

I put my bat on the ground next to the moped. It was a thing of beauty. Electric blue in the front, black on the footrest going up to the seat, and silver on the sides. It was a 50cc Italian Touring Moped. Tristan had saved for months to buy the thing but didn't have enough and, in the end, his parents gave it to him on his sixteenth birthday. I straddled it and nodded. This would do nicely. I went through all the keys on the key ring and none of them fit. Probably Mister Blake's keys.

That meant Tristan probably had the moped key with him. Not something I looked forward to. I left the keys on the beat to crap station wagon and went back into the house. I peeked into closed doors until I found Tristan's room. He was on his bed with headphones on. I guess he fell asleep listening to music.

Images of *Nightmare on Elm Street* suddenly came to mind and I couldn't stop the hysterical bark of laughter that bubbled up. Although the laughter surprised me, I was glad I wasn't crying again. Yes, I had a lot to cry about but I didn't want to cry in front of him.

I turned away and saw Tristan's letter jacket on the chair in front of a rickety desk. Morbid curiosity made me look at what he was studying while I let my hands search the jacket pockets.

Social Studies. Boring. Give me a good math problem any day. Deroga was all about the math, too.

My hands found two pens, one gum wrapper, and a movie theater ticket from Pierre, but no keys. I shrugged out of my coat and put Tristan's jacket on. It was way too big for me but I didn't care. For a moment, I imagined what it would be like if Tristan was my boyfriend. Then I was horrified at what I was doing. Tristan was dead in the room with me and I was trying on his jacket like a lovelorn cheerleader. Suddenly, I understood Deroga's quip that looking at the dead made one long for the living.

I shrugged the jacket off of me, let it fall to the ground, grabbed my coat, and put it back on. Tristan's jacket fell off the chair and open onto the ground. I saw the inner pocket and stared at it. It wouldn't be that easy, would it? I reached down, felt inside the pocket, and triumphantly came up with a set of two keys. One looked like a locker key and the other must be the moped key.

I left Tristan's room with conflicted feelings. I wanted to skip back out to the garage because I'd found the key. I wanted to say a prayer for

Tristan's soul. I wanted this all to be over with. However, normal wasn't something I could have. Though I never really had what everyone else calls normal, I wanted *my* normal back.

Out in the garage, the key slid into the moped ignition and it started up without complaint. The moped's engine purred quietly and I thought about how good it would feel to have her on the road. I didn't know how to drive a car although I have known how to drive mopeds since I was eleven years old. This baby was a beauty.

Then I realized that I had the moped on in the closed garage.

"Smart, Melissa. Real smart."

I reached to turn the moped off, noting that it did have a full tank of gas and while it probably wouldn't kill me, it might be nice if I were dead. Certainly easier.

I sat there astride the moped and thought about suicide. If I died, no one would miss me. I'd be one more statistic. I rolled that thought around in my head, looking to see if it would gain traction.

Do I really want to die?

No. With all that was going on, it was a surprise to realize how alive I felt, and how much I wanted to continue living. Also, I know that David would miss me. If not miss me, he would at least notice I was dead.

I smiled to myself. The thought of David noticing and missing me was far more attractive than anything else right now. It was the only thought that really got me interested. That told me what I wanted—needed—to know. Someone in this world still cared that I existed.

I put the moped key in my pocket next to the cell phone and picked up Mister Bat. Even if suicide seemed like the easier option, it wasn't the more attractive option. It was scary but I had people depending on me. Maybe even the whole world. It felt good to be needed. No matter how much the situation sucked.

I left the house the same way I came in. Walking down the driveway, I saw the Fedora right before I cleared the last tree. I froze and stared, wondering if it was going to turn around and see me. I think I stopped breathing for a couple of seconds and had to pee really bad.

The Fedora had its back to me and it was pressed up against the side of my house looking in the kitchen window. Everything about it made my skin want to crawl right off my body and hide in a deep, well-secured hole. When it stopped looking in that window, it slouched back down into its normal posture that was both standing tall and hunched over with its hat pushed low over its face.

It took an act of will for me not to run screaming when it turned and looked towards the back of the house. It tilted its head back and forth like a dog hearing the word "walkies?" over and over. While it was doing that, I got a better look at its face.

It was wearing a mask. It wrapped halfway around its head. The hat covered a lot of its head but it didn't hide the black hardness that served as skin. The face of the mask did look like a generic smiling man with one exception: the eyeholes were round, twice as big as normal eyes, and black. I didn't see anything that looked like eyes. The hat seemed to protect it from the light of the sun.

It walked back behind my house, and the trees on both sides of the street gave me cover. Both too scared and too curious to move, I tried to figure out what it actually was. It didn't walk like a man. I gave serious consideration to the idea of it being an honest-to-God demon before I wondered where its friends were. I saw at least seven of them last night. I needed to know where the rest were.

Actually, I needed to get off the street and call David again.

I walked as quietly as I could down the driveway and back into the Blakes' home. I locked the door behind me because I wanted warning if one of those things was coming in. The only room I found without a window someone could see through or a dead body was the bathroom.

I closed the toilet lid and sat on it. Mister Bat got carefully put on the floor. No accidental noises to alert the monsters I was here. I pulled the cell phone and its charger out of my coat pockets, thankful I had thought to stuff it in my jacket too. The monsters had found me. I knew I couldn't go back home now. Patting my pockets, I took inventory of what I had on and with me. The phone, its charger, the moped key, my pills, a granola bar, a pair of gloves, and Mister Bat. I was down to my bare essentials. I would have to scavenge for anything else I needed.

I plugged the phone charger into the wall, hooked up the phone, and called David back.

His face appeared on the screen. He was back in the office I first saw him in.

"I haven't had time to talk to Agent Harrison yet." He paused. "You okay, Melissa?"

"Yeah, but it's my turn to be hiding in the bathroom."

"What do you mean?"

"They found my house. While I was out at the silos and talking to you. I stopped by the Blakes' house to check on something—they live across the street from me—and when I came out, I saw a Fedora looking in my kitchen window."

"Did he see you?"

"I don't think so. I hid next to a tree. I was too scared to move. I did get a better look at the mask it wears."

He nodded, encouraging me. "What did it look like?"

"Pretty much like I said but its eyeholes were a lot bigger and they were all black. And the mask only went halfway around. The rest of its head was smooth and black."

"Shiny or not?"

"Not."

"So, an all over rubber hood with a black glass face mask, covered by a human mask to fool the eye at first glance, with overlarge eyeholes to see." David jotted down notes as he spoke.

"You sound so damn reasonable," I said, irritated and scared. I fought to control the anger. It made me want to lash out at everyone, especially David. "You weren't here. You didn't see it. It's not human. It didn't walk like a human."

"What did it walk like?"

"I don't know. Not human. Like it had too many joints in its legs." I gave a frustrated sigh. "Never mind. I need to get out of here."

"No, we already talked about that. Do you have everything you need from the house on you?"

"Yes. Pills, phone, charger, and Mister Bat."

"Okay. Keep all of that with you and head to the school. Lieutenant Stoneson is almost ready."

"What part of 'there are at least seven of them' and 'they found my house' did you not understand? They're *hunting* me now."

David looked pained. "I know. I heard you. The only way we're going to be able to get there and help you is if you help us first. You're smart and brave and you can do this. I promise you, you can. Pretend they're cops and if they catch you, you'll go to jail."

"In Hell," I muttered.

He smiled. It was a weak, uncomfortable smile. "Think 'in Mexico.' It's almost as bad. Whatever, whoever, they are, put them in a context you can work with. Don't let your fear consume you."

"Fear is the mind-killer?"

David nodded. "Exactly. You. Can. Do. This." He enunciated each word carefully. "I believe in you."

"You're right. And I'm scared. But I'll get to the school and call you back. I know a few shortcuts."

"Good deal. By then, I should have had my meeting with Agent Harrison. The fact that there are intruders there, and you've seen them, is a good thing, believe it or not. It gives us more of a face to our enemy, even if it's in a rubber mask. If you can, get a picture of one and send it to me."

"Okay. I don't plan to do a photo shoot with them though."

"Not asking for that. Only one picture. The school is your priority. Now, be careful."

"I will." I hung up the phone and sat there for a minute gathering my wits and my courage. I had to decide if I was running to the school first or trying to get a Fedora on camera.

CHAPTER NINE

The high school is the priority. Get to the radio station first. I can do that.

There's not a kid around here that didn't know a few back ways through town if they didn't want to be seen by the cops or cranky neighbors. Of course, that meant going through people's yards and such. Not that that meant anything anymore except to watch out for noisy dogs and monsters searching for me.

I knew I could get to the path behind the houses here and use it to get to Fir Avenue. Then, I could take a weaving pattern through backyards between Fir and Elm Avenue and come out at the head of Elm through the Pattersons' backyard. After that, cross South Eighth Street and I would be golden.

First, I needed to make sure I wasn't seen by the Fedora searching around my house. I also needed to make sure I could survive in hiding. That meant supplies. Not willing to go back into Tristan's room for a backpack, I raided Tanya's room and was thankful she had a darker sensibility. I'm not Goth by any means but neither am I sparkly pink princess, so the Batdz Maru backpack was ideal.

I dumped her bag out on the bed then scavenged a couple of bottles of water and snack food from the kitchen. I thought twice before I tucked one of Mrs. Blake's good butcher knives into the backpack. It was expensive, probably a gift for something special, and had its own sheath. I also grabbed a flashlight after making sure it worked. I wasn't going to die because I didn't check my equipment first. That was one of Deroga's rules: "Always prepare for adventure."

After that, it was a matter of sneaking out of the house and half mile or so through back ways to the high school. When I was leaving through the back door, I heard the sound of breaking glass come from the direction of my house. That shocked me. The Fedoras were not relying on stealth anymore. They had decided I was a threat and needed to be dealt with, or they had decided that I wasn't a threat and needed to be captured. Either way, it was bad news for me and the sooner I found what Homeland Security wanted me to find, the better.

I stayed close to the trees and away from the sides of houses. Once the Fedoras didn't find me at home—and I still wondered how they figured out which home was mine—they would start a house to house search. I was certain of it.

On a straight shot, the high school was one block north and four blocks east of where I was. I ducked behind a tree near a playset, one that I had not realized the Kittos had put up, and as soon as I hit Fir Avenue, I saw my second Fedora. It was coming out of the Clarks' place. Its hands, if you could call them that, were covered in blood. The Clarks had a dog, Sylvester. Now I knew what had happened to the German Shepherd over by the silos. I couldn't stop staring at its hands.

Imagine your hand, except meld your fingers together into one slab of flesh and sharpen your nails. It looked like a serrated spearhead with a hook to catch prey to serve as your thumb. And make it all black. That was what served as their hands. All I could see in my mind's eye was the Fedora stabbing the dog in the throat and lifting it up to gut it. I was sure that's what happened to Sylvester.

It was this staring that saved me from running into the second Fedora as it came out of the house in front of me. I shrank back into the shadows of the trees I was hiding behind, thankful for the shelter of their new leaves. The Fedoras *were* out in force and searching *every* house. This was both good and bad. Good because they had not actually found me. Bad because I was nearly surrounded. I would have to go back before I could go forward.

I wanted to run but this presented the perfect opportunity for me to get a picture of the Fedoras for David. It was proof for him, for me, and for Agent Harrison. I pulled the phone out of my pocket and took three pictures. When I texted them to David, both of the Fedoras turned towards me and buzzed their droning language. One of them headed for my hiding place with its spearhead hand held high to block the light.

I backpedalled as quickly as I could, dropping the cell phone in the process. I realized if I stopped to retrieve it, the Fedora would find me. Instead I turned and scrambled to the playset and crawled into the blue tube. It was all I could do to keep myself from screaming when my hand landed on Gina Clark's body. I scrambled over her and into the side bubble and prayed that they had not heard or seen me. I wasn't sure what tipped them off but luck was my only hope now.

If I didn't move, I could see both Gina's body and the cell phone where it fell to the ground. I kept my hand over my mouth to keep from throwing up. Gina was the Clarks' seven year old girl. I don't know why she was outside and in the playset tube but she died there and was lying in a puddle of dirty water. In my haste, my knee had come down on Gina's face and had torn the flesh across her cheek. Jelly-like muscle and bone peeked out in ragged smile and I realized it was her cheek muscle staining my knee.

That was when I saw the bottom half of the Fedora walk between my hiding place and the phone. I stopped breathing. It walked around the trees where I'd been standing and I could see its legs moving under the trench coat like it had extra knees based on how the trench coat flexed. The more it circled the phone, the more I didn't want to see what its legs actually looked like. Its feet were hidden in the grass.

It bent down and picked up the phone. For slabs of flesh and a hook for a thumb, it was surprisingly dexterous. I couldn't see what it was doing with the phone but I prayed that David had already texted me back or wouldn't text me right now. After a minute that lasted ten thousand years, it dropped the phone and moved away, back in the direction it came from. I heard the droning buzz that I guessed served as their speech and then all was quiet.

I waited and listened, wondering if it was a ruse. After a count of one hundred Mississippis, I reached out a hand to Gina's coat and tried to pull her out of my way but her limp body was too heavy. There are some terms you wish you didn't understand from experience; 'dead weight' was one of those terms and I now couldn't unlearn it.

When she wouldn't be moved, I knew I had to crawl over her again. This time, without the fear of adrenaline and the terror of the Fedoras, it would be much harder. My choice was to stomp on her head and go out the back or stomp on her body to go out the way I came in. Neither choice was attractive. I chose the path of least resistance and went out the back. I didn't stop or look when I heard the distinctive sound of something—*bone, it's her face*—cracking.

Outside the playset tube, I looked around before I stood up. No one was there. I thanked my lucky stars, retrieved the phone and, stuffing it into a pocket, ran. No more pussyfooting around. If those pictures I sent weren't enough for Tomas, then nothing would be. They also didn't change the fact that I was the only person they knew of that had survived the zone.

I cut across Fir Avenue behind the Clarks' house because I knew the Fedoras had already been there. I continued to zigzag through backyards until I reached Elm Avenue. I listened for about five minutes before I ran across Elm and ducked into the tree line. From there, I did my best impersonation of the movie spy running from shadow to shadow to any other cover I could find—"negative spaces" Deroga called them—a car, an air conditioning unit, a storage shed.

The phone started vibrating before I reached the end of Elm Street. I ignored it. I couldn't report that I had made it to the radio station and I didn't want to answer the phone out in the open. I looked across South Eighth Street and, unlike in my dream, the doors to the high school were not standing open. Also, unlike most of the houses in Onida, the school would be locked. I had not thought of that.

I sprinted across the street and ran up the sidewalk. I yanked on both sets of doors and they wouldn't budge. I didn't want to break in through the front of the building, it felt too exposed. I ran around the left to a side entrance and it was locked as well. The glass in the door was wired to prevent someone breaking in. That was added after the school was set on fire a few years back.

Before I could continue my search, I heard the sound of glass breaking. It came from down the street. I wondered how long it would be before the Fedoras broke into the school.

I remembered something Deroga did to break into a warehouse. No finessing around with lock picks. He'd jammed the slim end of a crowbar against the lock and pushed while jimmying the handle. I pulled out Mrs. Blake's butcher knife and pretended I was Deroga. It took surprisingly little to succeed and pop the lock open. I was sorry what I did to the knife, but it did what I needed it to do.

I walked down the tiled hallway with lockers on both sides of me and remembered my nightmare. I wasn't scared though. I saw my reflection in the trophy case at the end of the hall. In the dim light, I looked bad ass. Dirty clothes, a bat in one hand, a bent butcher knife in the other, and a determined walk. I stopped and looked at myself. I realized something: I no longer wanted to be rescued, no longer felt like I needed to be rescued.

Yes, I was scared, but I wanted to rescue myself and to do what needed doing.

It was a marvelous sensation.

The radio station was set up on the third floor in the northwest corner room. It had two distinct areas: the wall of 8-track cassettes for the ancient radio station set up next to the radio station manager desk. The more tech-savvy kids who served as DJs had rigged up an iPod station and a CD player to broadcast real music but the school system was allergic to getting rid of any obsolete equipment.

There was a low bookcase cutting the large room in half. This marked the radio station mixer and mic set up for the DJ. Curtains covered the walls in a poor man's version of sound baffles while the floor was carpeted to reduce all of the background sound in the room. It was cheap but effective for the high school radio station.

I looked at the papers on the desk and discovered that the radio station manager's desk was now also one of the administrators' desks and included a mic for the PA system. I wondered when that happened and then realized it had to have happened in the last year. It was amazing how quickly things seemed to change.

Enough nostalgia. I had work to do.

CHAPTER TEN

I put the butcher knife and Mister Bat on the desk beneath the mic, which I made sure was off before I pulled out the cell phone. There was one missed call and three text messages waiting for me. The missed call was from David. The text messages were an acknowledgement of receiving the pictures, a text message asking me if I was okay, and a message to call when I got to the radio station.

I called David. Before I could say hello he asked, "Are you okay? Where are you?"

"Yeah. I'm okay. I'm at the radio station. I almost got caught by the two Fedoras I sent you pictures of but I escaped. They are tearing up the town looking for something. Me, I think. What did Tomas think of the pictures?"

"Certainly gave him something to think about and proof that what you were saying was valid."

"That's good." I paused, then asked, "Did you see their hands?"

David rubbed his cheek, then the back of his neck. "Yeah. I did."

"Still think they're terrorists?"

He looked around, leaned close and, with his voice lowered, said, "Officially, yes. Unofficially, no. I don't know what they are. But please don't say 'monster' when Agent Harrison talks to you again. He's a skeptic by profession and needs to stay that way."

I frowned. "If you say so."

David sat up again. "Lieutenant Stoneson is ready. You?"

"I'm ready."

The screen flashed the now familiar brief glimpses of the command center before a black woman with green eyes and short, curly, dark brown hair appeared on the screen. "Hello, Melissa. Call me Kim. It'll be easier than stumbling over my rank and last name."

"Okay, Kim. What do you need me to do?" I liked her attitude. I suspected as a woman in the military, she figured out how to work best with people. I don't go for name, rank, and serial number. I think she understood that from listening in on the conversations I had with David and Tomas. Guess that was why she was a communications specialist.

"You will be looking for a square transmitter or emitter. It will look like a square box with something round and mirrored inside. That is our best speculation."

"I'm going to point the phone outward so you see what I see as I look."

"Good idea."

I slowly panned the phone over the mixer board and mic set up while looking for anything that seemed to be square. "I'm not seeing anything." I raised my voice to be heard.

"Pan up. Look up where the radio antenna might be."

I did as she asked and we both saw the box at the same time. "There," I said. I couldn't keep the excitement out of my voice.

"What's that?" she asked.

I could hear the excitement in her voice, too. In the corner of the room, a thick cable snaked up the wall and to a window. There was something that looked like a makeshift cat door in the window, allowing the cable to travel outside the window while still protecting the room from the elements. I couldn't remember seeing the cable or the black box before. Then again I never did spend much time in this room.

"I don't know what it is. Hold on. I'm going to have to—" I turned to get a chair to stand on with the phone still in my outstretched hand and found myself face to face with a Fedora.

I heard but didn't register whatever it was Kim yelled. I guess she saw a glimpse of what I was looking at now: the smiling mask of a man with a painted on mustache and overlarge glossy black eyes. And they *were* eyes, not a glass mask under the mask of the man. They moved back and forth. They were alive.

The Fedora's right hand shot out and knocked my hand with the phone away from it. Its left hand shot out in a stabbing motion towards my face. I let myself fall back against the desk and to the floor, my bat and the butcher knife falling with me as the backpack dragged them to the floor.

I was lucky I wasn't brained or stabbed. Instead, the bat landed in my lap and the knife hit the floor next to me.

I scrambled back under the desk, pausing first to grab the knife and stab the thing through the foot; a large, black, stubby, hard thing, and into the floor—*oh, God, that's not a shoe, that's its foot*!—before pulling my bat with me. I popped up on the other side of the desk like an evil jack-in-the-box with my bat at the ready. I swung it as hard as I could at the Fedora's head but it was out of reach.

It shoved the desk at me, hitting me in the thighs. Grunting in pain, I held onto the bat with one hand and grabbed the first thing I could throw with the other. I hit it with two speakers, a book, and a mug as I came out from around the desk, flailing at it with the bat. I hit it in the head but without any real power behind it. The Fedora slashed at me with both of its spearhead hands. One missed, the other sliced open my jeans and the thigh muscle beneath it.

I yelled in pain and, using both hands, I swung at the thing's arm. It connected with a crunch. While the Fedora staggered back, it didn't make a sound and that was more frightening than if it had yelled in pain. It stabbed at me with its good arm and I sacrificed my bicep to get in close and slammed it over the head with the bat. The sound of bone or carapace or plastic or whatever was under the hat and mask cracking was enough to make me taste the copper of impending vomit.

I didn't stop as it wheeled back. I hit it again and again, ignoring the pain in my arm and leg. Each successive blow sounding wetter than the last. Finally, the thing fell down and didn't move. When I stopped hitting it, I realized I had been screaming at it. I don't know what but my throat hurt.

I heard a noise behind me. I whirled around with the bat held, looking for the danger. It took me a couple of seconds to realize it was the sound of David and Kim calling my name. I looked around on the floor. Up against the chair leg the phone lay. I picked it up, my hand shaking with adrenaline and fear.

"What was that thing?" Kim asked.

"Is it dead?" David asked.

"It's a Fedora. David will fill you in. Yeah, I think it's dead." I wasn't feeling any pain yet but I knew from experience, I would. "I've got to pull that cable down to look at the box. I need to do it now before the pain sets in."

"You hurt?" David asked.

I moved the phone so it could see the gash in my upper arm and the slice in my thigh. "Yeah. I'm not feeling it right now though. Those spearhead hands are as sharp as knives. Look, I need to put the phone down to get that cable down. Hold on."

Neither of them voiced a dissenting opinion. I put the phone in my pocket and dragged the chair to the corner of the room. I climbed on it to get to the top of the cable sticking out of the top of the window. I pulled on the upper part of the cable. It came loose willingly enough but the rubber in the window around the cable wasn't going anywhere.

I had to trade my bat for the knife still stuck in the Fedora's foot. I tried hard not to think about the black goo on the knife blade as I used it to cut the rubber around the cable. Once the cable and the box was extracted from the window, I got off the chair, moved to the desk, and put the knife next to the bat. I looked at the end of the cable with the black box on it and immediately knew it wasn't what we were looking for.

I pulled out the phone. "You there?"

"Yes, we're here." David answered.

"Is that the transmitter?" Kim asked. I showed it to her and she shook her head.

"It looks like a security camera. I'm going to have to get to the roof of the school to see if it is up there." I tossed the useless thing to the floor.

"Will that be hard?" I knew she was thinking about my injuries.

"Nah. I used to do it all the time. Though, I may have to find bolt cutters."

"Be careful."

I nodded at her. "Look, I'm going to need to focus on this. Plus... I'm beginning to think they can track cell phone signals. They noticed me after I texted those pictures. And then they found me here after being on the phone with you for so long. I want to limit phone calls, okay?"

David took the phone back from Kim. "That's a smart idea. Text if you don't find what we're looking for. Call if you do. You take down that emitter and I'll be there within the hour."

I smiled my fake smile at him. The pain was starting to get through to me. "Promises, promises."

"I do promise, Melissa. I won't let you down."

His face was so serious that all I could think to say was, "Call me Mel. All my friends do."

He smiled. "Okay, Mel. Do you know how to treat those wounds?"

"Yeah. I do. I learned in juvie. I gotta go."

"Okay. I'll be here."

I thumbed the End button and muttered, "I'll be here, too."

First things first, I had to see if there were still bolt cutters in the janitor's closet. Several sets were stashed around the school after some enterprising teenager had chained all the doors shut from the inside, locking the kids in school and the parents out. That had been an exciting hour.

Luck was with me. I popped the lock on the first janitor's closet on the second floor. It had a pair. I hefted with my good arm and decided it was a good substitute for the butcher knife I mangled. After a quick debate, I decided to head to the roof before fixing my wounds. It was better to know immediately if the transmitter-emitter thing was there or not.

I took the stairs slowly, wincing in pain at every step. I was going to have to do something about the gash in my leg. It was deeper than I thought. I needed to make a trip to the nurse's station instead of raiding one of the first aid kits.

At the very top of the stairs, the roof access door was chained like I remembered it being. At least some things didn't change. The bolt cutters made short work of the barrier and I limped out onto the roof. I put the bolt cutters down next to the door but kept my bat. If I was jumped on the roof, I had bigger problems than I thought.

I headed over to the northwest corner of the building where the satellite dish and the antennas were. At first blush, the square antenna transmitter thing wasn't there. But, being as thorough as I could be, I looked through each thing—one satellite dish and three large whip like antennas. None of them were what we were looking for.

Just to be safe, I took several pictures of the whole setup and texted them to David, asking if any of it was what we were looking for. While I waited for an answer, I kept watch on the parts of town I could see. I didn't see movement, not in my immediate area. I could only hope that the Fedora I killed wouldn't be missed for a long time.

The texted answer came back with a "No. Keep looking."

Sure. Keep looking. After I patch myself up.

Despite the pain in my leg, I wanted to go back to the radio station room first. I needed to make sure I had killed the thing. Heroes who didn't make sure with a double tap were surprised later by the same damn monster. If I was in a real life horror movie, I was going to make damn sure it was dead. I stopped by the janitor's closet and traded out the bolt cutters for long-handled hedge clippers. The eight inch blades made me feel better and the tool had a nice heft to it.

The monster's body was still there and now leaking something foul smelling from its head. I looked at it a long moment before I walked over and used the hedge clippers to decapitate it. It took me four nauseating, crunchy cuts but in the end, I was certain the next time this particular Fedora would terrorize me would be in my nightmares. Only then did I feel safe enough to spend some time cleaning and binding my wounds.

CHAPTER ELEVEN

The nurse's station was a small brick building to the left of the high school. I made sure I was alone before I broke the door's window so I could unlock it from the inside. There were all of five rooms in the building: the waiting area, the office that the nurses and doctors used, an exam room, a lavatory, and the holding room.

I knew the office was where they kept the drugs. If there were any painkillers on site, I needed them. After a quick look through of the entire building to make sure it was clear, I went to the office and studied the locked cabinet with the frosted glass. Before I smashed it, I thought to check the two desks. The first desk didn't have the key but it did have a locked file cabinet. I pried it open with the hedge clippers to discover private medical files and a half-filled bottle of whiskey.

"Oh, Nurse Garcia, I knew you drank, only I didn't realize you drank on the job. Of course, if I had to deal with kids at their worst, I'd drink, too."

I put the bottle on the second desk and started going through its drawers. I knew if I had to, that whiskey could be my painkiller, but I really didn't want it to be. Alcohol and brain meds didn't mix well. The middle drawer of the second desk was locked. I pried it open and found a set of keys.

It took me until the third key to unlock the cabinet and, much to my surprise and pleasure, there was a bottle of Tylenol 3 with codeine front and center. That was all I needed. It was a drug I was familiar with, knew how it interacted with my body and my other drugs, and, most importantly, it worked.

With my bottle of painkillers, I moved to the exam room for bandages and other stuff I needed. I mourned the ragged hole in the sleeve of my coat and hissed in pain when I peeled it off my arm and then half shrugged out of my sweater. The sensation of my sweater sleeve dragged over the slash was enough that I stopped, popped two painkillers, and prayed for them to work quickly.

I wanted more but knew I shouldn't have more. I checked the time to see when I could take another, and realized it had been over twenty-four hours since I discovered Sharon and Matt dead. Grief reared its ugly head again and I stomped on it as hard as I could. The tears still welled up and I had to take a couple of breaths to regain my composure. Had it really been only one day? It felt like a thousand years.

The gash in my arm hurt but wasn't that bad. I used three butterfly bandages to pull it closed, covered it with a trauma pad, then wrapped my arm in rolled gauze. It would probably leave a scar. I prayed that the Fedoras hadn't poisoned me. The wound didn't look infected when I looked at it. No weird black or red lines radiating out from it. Just a clean cut with a very sharp weapon.

My leg was another matter. I thanked God that the codeine was working by the time I shimmied out of one leg of my jeans. I looked at the six inch gash and wondered if I had the gumption to do stitches on myself. I wasn't kidding when I told David that I learned first aid in juvie.

For the first month of my incarceration I was housed in juvie, or what served as juvie in Blunt. Honestly, it was more of a halfway house without the halfway part. There were six of us in the house with three adults guarding us. There were two of us to a room and all we had were the bare necessities. To keep us busy, we did chores and had classes. First aid was one. I learned everything from CPR to treating shock to giving someone stitches. I was good at it.

That didn't mean I could give myself stitches without something to numb the flesh. But I didn't want to put any more drugs in my system. In the end, I treated my leg wound like I treated my arm, just with a lot more butterfly bandages, a trauma patch, and two rolls of gauze. I added an ace bandage to protect the whole thing and hoped it would hold.

After that, I moved to the holding room where the beds were. I hurt. I was tired and I needed to rest. I also needed to feel somewhat safe. I blocked the door with the back of a chair, and made sure the frosted window was locked before I sat on the bed. I thought about sewing up the hole in my jacket but dismissed the idea for the siren song of the bed.

I wasn't usually so tired but between my injury, the painkiller, and the running around I had been doing, I deserved a nap. After making sure my backpack and weapons were within arm's reach, I plugged in the phone, lay down on the bed, used my coat as my blanket and fell asleep.

I dreamed so many dreams but only the last one stuck around long enough for me to remember it.

David and I were walking through a hospital, a big one. It was like a maze. I led the way with him walking beside me. We stopped at an intersection and I realized I didn't know where I was or where I was going.

I looked at him, "They all look the same."

"They're all different. You just have to see the differences."

I looked again at the hallway, turned, studying them. They all looked exactly the same. There were eight hallways now.

"How do I choose?"

Darcy answered me. "You choose by finding what you need."

I looked at her and she smiled at me.

"You're alive," I said.

She shook her head and said something to me. I couldn't hear her.

"What was that?" I asked.

Darcy kept talking but I couldn't hear her. Every step I took to get closer made her that much farther away. By the time I was running, Darcy looked like she was shouting at me and I couldn't hear a thing. She kept getting farther and farther away until she was lost in the blackness. I screamed her name over and over and still she disappeared.

I woke with a start. I was sitting up with Mister Bat in my hands with no recollection of grabbing him. I listened for sounds of danger on the edge of panic. I didn't know what woke me but I was on high alert.

Nothing dangerous revealed itself. Nothing moved. No shadow passed by the frosted glass in the door.

After about two minutes of barely breathing, I relaxed, putting Mister Bat on the bed beside me. The scant light coming in from the high window indicated hours had passed while I was napping. I picked up the cell phone. I'd slept seven hours. I never sleep that much during the day. Then again, I'm usually not hurt or running from monsters. I couldn't help but wonder if whatever had happened to the rest of South Dakota was starting to work on me now. The thought scared me. No matter how much stuff sucked right now, I wanted to live.

I reached down to unplug the phone's power cord from the wall and realized that the phone wasn't charging. The phone was charged but its icon showed that it wasn't plugged in when it clearly was. I unplugged the cord from the wall, wrapped up the cord, and stuffed it in my coat pocket.

I listened and sensed what I could. My arm and leg thudded out a concert of dull aches from my wounds. For the moment, that didn't matter. What mattered was the complete lack of sound in the room. No fans going. No distant hum of computers, no background rumble of the heater running.

The power was off.

This could be a problem. While I wouldn't freeze, despite the chilly night weather, I wouldn't be able to see and…

I looked at the cell phone. No text messages. No missed calls. Barely any cell phone reception. With barely one bar, I was essentially cut off. I swallowed my immediate desire to panic. Panicking wouldn't help. What would though?

Getting the power back on.

How do I do that?

Check the power substation.

That opened up a completely new bundle of grief and conflicted emotions. I bit my lip to hold back the sudden loss I felt. Until his death, my father had managed the power substation and made sure Onida had power through rain, sleet, snow, and the dead of night.

Like the mailman, only more appreciated, I heard his voice say and smiled despite the wounded hole in my heart.

Dad used to take me to the substation whenever he had maintenance runs and I was at home. I could remember some of the things he did to reset the power. That was what I needed to do now if I intended to have heat through the night and a way to contact David. Not to mention the fact that I would be easier to sneak up on at night or find if I had light and nothing else around me did.

I put on my coat and stood up, my wounds screaming their pain at me. I took two more painkillers and noted that I wouldn't be able to take any more until after midnight. I walked around the small room for a couple of minutes, letting the painkillers take hold as well as getting the kinks out of my stiff muscles. I had the feeling I would be running very soon.

To get to the substation from the school, I would have to go north on South Eighth, take a left on Ash Avenue, and then a right on the tiny one block street that served as the main street between North Main and South Main. I tried to remember what else was over that way but all I could think of was the courthouse and state treasury building.

One of the landmarks of Onida and the secondary reason for the existence of the town was the one hundred year old courthouse building that served as the official treasury for South Dakota. It was a beautiful brick building with a clock tower and a copper dome. It stood at the T of Ash Avenue and South Eighth Street.

It was also wide open territory. If I remembered correctly, most of Ash Avenue was exposed with very few places to hide. With the sun setting in an hour, this wasn't as bad as it could be unless the Fedoras could see better at night than the day. My best bet was to go straight up South Eighth and go around the back side of the courthouse.

I decided it didn't matter. I needed to get to the substation and fix things if I could. I fashioned a bat holster on the backpack so I could carry the hedge clippers in my good hand and have Mister Bat available if I needed him.

The journey to the courthouse and around back was quiet, if nerve-racking. If I thought the town was quiet before the loss of power, it really was a ghost town now. Everything I did felt amplified; my steps were stomps, my breaths were gasps, I felt like you could hear the sound of my beating heart outside my chest. None of it was true, though as the shadows grew longer, I could understand why settlers feared the night.

I came around the back side of the courthouse and down the dirt road, stopping at the last set of trees between me and the substation. I studied the area. It was about fifty yards down and across Main Street to get to where I needed to be. To the right of the substation were the water tower and its maintenance building. The water tower always gave me the chills. The one time I tried to climb it to prove I wasn't afraid of heights, I did exactly the opposite. I was fine for about the first three stories. Then after that, I couldn't move.

To the left of the substation were the circuit switcher, transformer, the regulators, the reclosers, and the power lines. All of which were surrounded by a locked chain link fence. The red brick building in the middle with two doors and four small windows was the control center of the whole deal.

I studied the shadows around the control center, the hairs on the back of my neck prickling. I never knew what it meant to 'have your hackles up' before now. My lip curled back in a snarl of anger when I saw a Fedora appear around the right side of the building. This one was smaller than the other ones I had seen. Its trench coat barely brushed the ground and its mask met at the back of its head.

While it struggled with the door, I imagined running at it with my bat raised and a war cry on my lips. I knew that wasn't the right way. Stealth was my ally.

Apparently, the Fedora had no such worries. It slammed its spearhead hand down on the doorknob, breaking it off. A little more pushing, and the door swung open. Despite the loud sounds, it didn't look around and no other Fedora appeared to help. I took this as a good sign that when I fought the thing, its allies wouldn't come running.

Distantly, I marveled at myself. I was willing to take charge, take control, and take the fight to the enemy. The girl I was the day before wouldn't have done any of that. If Deroga was with me, he would be proud. Maybe even given me one of his rare compliments.

I moved as soon as it entered the building. I ran down the dirt road and across Main Street, ignoring Mister Bat bouncing against my good leg. Once I got to the dirt plot in front of the building, I slowed to a deliberate walk with the hedge clippers held out open in front of me, ignoring the pain in my arm and leg.

I paused at the doorway to the substation building. The Fedora had its back to me while it looked at the wrong set of controls. I moved in to stab it in the back of the neck but when I entered the room, my bat hit the partially open door, making a dull ringing sound that alerted the Fedora to my presence.

It whipped around impossibly fast and I thrust forward with the hedge clippers. Instead of catching the monster in the back of the neck, it caught the monster in the neck under the chin of the mask. I closed the hedge clippers, chopping open its neck and then slammed the clippers forward, stabbing it deeper in the throat and pushing it off balance.

The Fedora flailed out at me, catching my wrist with a glancing blow that did little more than sting. I opened and closed the hedge clippers again, still pushing its sharp blades harder into the monster's neck. I felt it hit bone and carapace. One of the Fedora's legs kicked out at me, catching me hard in the stomach. I let go of the clippers and collapsed to the ground, gasping for air. I rolled away from the Fedora when it landed on the ground next to me, the hedge clippers falling to the side. The Fedora tried to hit me a couple of times before it stopped moving.

I sucked air into my lungs. When I pulled myself to my feet, I could feel wetness on my arm. My bicep was bleeding again, as was my wrist. Only a little bit, but enough to feel the sting of the cold air. Looking down at the Fedora, I saw that it wasn't dead. One hand and one leg twitched feebly.

I kept my eyes on it and bent for the clippers. I knew what I had to do. The leg that twitched was bare to me and I could see that it had two knee-like joints. Its skin was black and hard looking, and there were fine hairs about an inch long sticking out randomly up and down the leg. The more I studied it, the more it looked like a giant bug leg.

Sickened, I turned my attention back to the creature's neck. It was still bleeding. I thought that meant it was still alive. I couldn't have that. I brought the hedge clippers to bear and used them to sever its head from its body.

"Two down. Who knows how many to go?" I muttered, then turned to the control panel at the far wall. I looked over the dials, alert status, and screens. The substation was running on emergency power after automatically shutting down due to thirty-six hours of neglect and a sudden lack of power usage. It registered this as a faulty reading and sent messages out for confirmation. With none forthcoming, it had shut itself down.

I closed my eyes and tried to remember what Dad would do to fix this particular problem. I could see his hands moving from one control to the next and end with a flipped switch. He used to sing-song the instructions while I watched. I think it started out as a way to keep me entertained but it became a tradition for us both to sing it as his hands moved over the control console.

"Power isn't right, screens blinking bright. The dial to the left, buttons to the right. On, on, off, and a switch to make it right."

I opened my eyes and repeated what I remembered and prayed as I flipped the last switch. There was a distinct clunk of something turning over and the whine of generators spinning up behind the control center. Onida had power again.

"Thank you, Daddy," I said, patting the console in front of me. I resettled the backpack on my shoulders, and adjusted my grip on the retrieved hedge clippers after wiping as much gore off if it as I could without actually touching the blades. Then I checked the bars on my phone. Two bars were better than none. No calls. No messages.

I left the substation building, making sure to close the door as much as it would close with the broken doorknob. The longer the control consoles were not assaulted by the elements, the longer I would have power.

It didn't occur to me then to wonder why the Fedora was trying to get the power back on as well.

CHAPTER TWELVE

I stood outside the power substation for a while, figuring out what to do next. It wasn't quite dark by the time I decided I needed to go somewhere that had maps available. I walked down Main Street towards Ash, keeping a wary eye out for movement. With the power restored—something I hoped the other Fedoras would credit to the dead Fedora within the substation—the streetlights glowed orange in the fading daylight. At the end of Main, right in front of me, was the blue and white building of Dan's Food Center. That looked like a good enough place to start.

I didn't bother to go around to the front of the building. I was sure it was locked. The Food Center closed its doors at nine sharp. However, Dan, the owner, was known to work late into the night, leaving the back door unlocked until he was ready to go for the evening. I entered through the back door next to the loading docks, wondering where I would find Dan's body.

I didn't have to wonder for long.

Stretched out on a doubled sized foam pad that lay on top of two crates, Dan and Cindy, one of the cashiers, were cuddled up together under a ragged but clean comforter. That was unexpected. Either they had just started this affair, or they were both really good at keeping secrets. I mean, I always thought he was gay, and she was half his age. Man, what a scandal that would have been. No wonder he spent so many nights working late.

I kept my face turned away from them out of a weird need to give them privacy until they were out of my line of sight. I headed to the front of the grocery store to see if there were maps like I thought there were. As it turned out, I misremembered a rack of postcards as a map rack.

Not to be thwarted, I returned to the back of the shop and into Dan's office. No map? Fine, I would Google the area to see what I could see. Maybe something about the town, its surroundings, or its history would give me an idea of where to look for the transmitter.

While I figured out what Dan's password was, I took my pills for the evening and snacked on a granola bar. It took me about five minutes to realize I couldn't guess his password and to look for it written down. I found it on a post-it note under his keyboard. Sometimes people are so predictable.

You know how internet time goes so much faster than normal time? You think you spent maybe an hour looking things up and it turns out that three hours have gone by and you are now late for whatever it was you were going to do two hours ago? That was how my time on Dan's computer was.

After three hours, I was no closer to figuring out where the signal was coming from than when I started. However, I had eliminated the following: radio towers, because there were only two that I could find anywhere near us and the closest one was on the west side of Pierre, though I was giving very serious thought to hopping the moped and heading over there despite the fact that we had an infestation of Fedoras here; short wave radio stations, because Agar and Pierre had stations but neither was strong enough to take over the state; military bases, because the only military base we had in South Dakota was Ellsworth and that was all the way west, over by Rapid City; TV stations, because the three in the area were all over in Pierre.

With all of the technological wonders in Pierre and not in Onida, I wondered what Onida had that Pierre didn't that would include the ability to send signals. I knew the answer had to be staring me in the face but I was too close to it to see it. It really was a problem of "not being able to see the forest because of the trees" as Mom used to say.

I decided tomorrow I would break into the courthouse and search the records for something I could have missed. I didn't know what it was but I hoped I would know it when I saw it. Now it was time to find a new place to hide. I didn't want to bed down for the night so close to where I killed that other Fedora.

It was very dark when I snuck out of the Food Center. Clouds hung low overhead, promising rain. I felt the first couple of drops as I headed south, crossed Birch Avenue and started weaving my way west toward 5th Street. I stopped when I heard a huge clanking noise back from where I came from. It sounded like a metal door had been torn from its hinges and thrown onto the paved street.

At least, that was what my paranoid mind told me it was. They had found their dead minion and were pissed. I mean, admittedly, if I were invading a small town that was supposed to be dead and one of my number ended up dead—two actually—I would be pissed, too.

Huddling under a tree, I listened as hard as I could. I swore I could hear something buzzing coming closer to me. Then it was above me for an instant before continuing on south. All my mind would conjure was the image of a five or six foot flying ant and I thought I would wet myself right then and there. That the Fedoras could fly never occurred to me, but it would explain the strange way their shoulders bulged.

When I was sure that I didn't hear any more buzzing and no one was around, I ran half bent over to the house in front of me. It was a mobile home that belonged to Pat Johnson, a local farmhand. The door was unlocked and I ducked inside without looking behind me. Once the door was closed and locked, I looked around to see what I had to work with.

There was a small kitchen with the bare essentials, a living room that also served as the dining room, a bathroom, a bedroom that was now a storage room for all sorts of crap, and Pat's room. Pat was nowhere around and that was a small blessing that I would take. The only thing that smelled of decay was me—my jeans where I scrambled over Gina's body.

Looking through Pat's closet, I saw that he and I wore about the same sized jeans. I grabbed a pair, hesitated, and then look through his dresser drawers. It wasn't what I wanted to do but I couldn't shower so I needed clean clothing. I forced myself to get over the weirdness of wearing a dead man's clothes and changed into fresh socks, underwear, and jeans. While the guy's underwear and jeans fit a little oddly, the scent of soap made me smile. It would do until I could raid a woman's closet or I could get back to my place.

I also dug out one of his t-shirts to wear after peeling off my torn and bloody sweater. I knew it was too cold outside to only wear the t-shirt. I was searching through his tops in the closet, looking for something warm to wear, when I hit pay dirt: a double barreled shotgun and a sweatshirt for me.

Hunting was big in the area. You name it, we have it here: duck, geese, pheasant, grouse, and turkey if you are into hunting wild birds. If you want bigger game, there are antelope and deer. If you want to fish, Lake Oahe has walleyes, perch, catfish, and pike. So it's no surprise that people have rifles and shotguns.

This was the first time I had held a shotgun since Grandpa died. Mom wouldn't let Dad teach me to hunt until I was sixteen. She didn't like guns and wouldn't allow them in the house. Neither of them realized that day would never come. In hindsight, it was probably a good idea. Otherwise, instead of beating up mailboxes, I might have put a shotgun in my mouth.

It took me a little bit to remember how to open the shotgun. Once I did, I verified that it was loaded with live rounds. I snapped it closed and hoped I wouldn't have to use the thing, but knowing I had it and that I understood the principles behind using a shotgun, I felt better having it. This probably meant I was going to shoot myself in the foot. I would take it if it meant I wouldn't be eaten by the Fedoras.

I left the shotgun on the bed while I changed into the sweatshirt, thinking about the monsters. The more I learned about them, the less I thought they were demon monsters. Somehow, I was beginning to think they were giant, sentient insects. It reminded me of the endless charts in Mr. Shindledecker's class of bee bodies where their heart was in their ass but their aorta ran up their backs to their necks.

The idea that the Fedoras were bugs rather than demons was scarier because while demons could be combated with faith, giant insects had no such weakness. Also, if they were insects, this was a scouting party like ones that came into your house, found food, and suddenly you had an invasion of them. I shuddered at the idea of a swarm of Fedoras without their camouflage.

I couldn't figure out where they had come from. The fact that they were here, appeared to have technology, and were intelligent was terrifying. I wondered if the nuclear plant over by Sioux Falls had had an accident that was hushed up but bred a terrible new enemy, one that had blades for hands and, even though I wasn't completely sure, seemed to be able to fly.

I curled up on Pat's bed and took comfort in the scent of another human being, even if he wasn't here. Pat was a good guy who worked hard, and if rumors were to be believed, had the biggest crush on Lucy Driver, a waitress over at the Bakery Café. Word had it that she fancied him, too. I closed my eyes, really hoping that Pat was over at Lucy's place, curled up in bed with her. I hope they had a bit of happiness before…

I sat up straight. Epiphanies are amazing things. They seem to come from nowhere but if you think about it, you will discover that while you have been working on other problems, the main problem vexing you has been stewing in the back of your mind until *WHAM*, what has eluded you for so long becomes blindingly clear.

What does Onida have that Pierre does not? A municipal airport. Pierre's airport is regional. Onida's airport was shut down in the winter and wasn't scheduled to open again for another two to three weeks, but the manager always started up all the equipment the weeks before opening to make sure everything was in working order. What had a radio tower that wasn't obvious? The Onida airport. Where could creatures who worked mostly at night work in secret to affix something to a radio tower? The Onida airport tower. And, why would the Fedoras want to turn the power back on? Because even though the Onida airport had an emergency generator, it wouldn't last forever.

It was ironic that by fixing the power substation, I helped the monsters out. Well, that could work both ways. If I couldn't get to the emitter on the airport tower, I sure as hell could destroy the power substation. I knew exactly what to do. It was definitely Plan B.

I got up, rummaged in my coat for the cell phone and texted David that I had killed a second Fedora and figured out the transmitter had to be at the Onida airport. His return text of "You are awesome!" made me smile. I wanted to call him but it was safer not to.

Instead, I went back to bed, thinking about an early start. It would be about a two mile walk to get to the airport over completely open ground. I needed to see if I could find a bicycle, something quiet. That would make the trip faster, easier, and safer. Most bikes were stored away for the winter but now that spring was here, some would be out. I fell asleep thinking about which houses nearby would have what I needed.

DAY THREE:

SAVE THE WORLD, SAVE MYSELF

CHAPTER THIRTEEN

Waking up morphed from that delicious comfortable twilight of half sleeping into the very real terror of knowing that I wasn't alone in the room. I don't know if the Fedora had been standing in the doorway for minutes, studying me, or if it just arrived. I don't know how I knew it was there before I opened my eyes. Maybe I smelled it, or maybe the animal deep within my hindbrain was on full alert, but when I opened my eyes to see my fear in the flesh, I grabbed the shotgun that lay next to me and rolled off the bed.

I hit the floor between the bed and wall and scrabbled back into the corner like the trapped rat that I was. It watched me with those glossy black eyes, tilting its masked head back and forth, studying me. I fumbled with the shotgun, put it to my shoulder and pulled the trigger. Nothing happened. I tried to fire it another time and nothing happened. I looked down and saw the safety button.

When I looked up again, leveling the rifle at the Fedora, the creature leapt from the doorway to the space above me in a single leap. Braced against the wall on one side and resting on the bed on the other, it was splayed out above me like a giant spider minus the extra legs.

While the Fedora was doing its Shelob impression, its camouflaging trench coat was spread open wide, revealing the body that I had only guessed at before. It was a black, bulbous, segmented thing like a moth's body, with a green-blue iridescence on the bottom and fuzzy black hairs on the top. Its tail ended in a blunt tip and something that looked like it could be a stinger. It was like looking at a giant ant, moth, and bee rolled into one. The only saving grace I could see was the lack of anything that looked like wings.

Then two previously unseen arms unfolded from its side. These arms were shorter and thinner than the other appendages I had seen. At the end of each middle arm was an actual hand with three clawed fingers and a thumb. They moved with dexterous fluidity that was built for fine motor control. Something about its fingers drumming the air horrified me all the more.

I renewed my attempted to shoot the thing as it stared at me. I remembered that this type of shotgun needed to be cocked just as the monster reared back, raising one of its spearhead hands in a striking maneuver. With the butt of the shotgun braced against my stomach, I yanked back both hammers and pulled the trigger. The shotgun slammed into my stomach as it fired, shooting the Fedora, that nightmare body, at pointblank range.

The monster didn't go flying back like it would have if this was the movies. Instead it wavered there, its striking hand slamming back against the wall for balance while what served as its blood or guts poured from its body onto me. I lifted the angle of the shotgun and fired once more. Again, the butt of the gun slammed into my stomach. I grunted at the barely felt pain, knowing distantly that I was going to pay for these two shots later—if I was still alive.

The second shot struck the Fedora in the head, knocking its hat off and tearing part of its mask and face away before it collapsed forward onto me, bleeding all over my neck and sweatshirt. I had a flash of hooked mandibles before the horror of the bleeding monster made my hindbrain panic. It took over and I was moving before I realized what I was doing.

I rolled under the bed, escaping the nauseating stench. I continued to roll, fleeing until I got to the other side and scrambled out from under the bed. Leaving the shotgun on the floor, I ripped the sweatshirt off me and wiped as much of the gore off my neck and face as I could in the seconds I knew I had before the sound of the shotgun blasts brought the other Fedoras running.

I had the presence of mind to grab my phone and coat off the bed and stuff the phone into a coat pocket as I went. I pulled the coat on but didn't take the time to shrug into the backpack before I was out the back door. I paused long enough to get Mister Bat out of his makeshift holster so I had a weapon in hand if I needed it. Then I ran.

Running west, away from the rising sun, I crossed East Dogwood Avenue, through the first set of giant grain silos, and then across South Fourth Street. I continued to sprint through the grain silos towards Cedar Avenue. I saw the building for the Midwest Cooperatives office first and veered towards it. When I reached it, I saw the Sully Pest and Weed supervisor's office and lab and a plan came to mind. If they were giant bugs, pest and weed killer should do a job on them.

Onida is a farming town. We make our bread and butter off of what the land provides and the company sells. We have to make sure that the bugs don't eat the profits. If they do, people are out of a job and no bread or butter. This means crop dusting with insecticides and such. There are all kinds of regulations on the pesticides and weed killers that can be used on commercially grown food.

Which is why the building I was running towards existed. Someone had to make sure we were all following the rules. There was a supervisor and an inspection team to make sure we were using what we were supposed to be using. I bet they had a lot of the local pest killers on site. Hell, enough weed or pest killer would kill a human—or a Fedora—which is what I needed.

I ran towards the building, looking behind me. I didn't see another Fedora but just because I didn't see it, didn't mean it wasn't there. I bashed in the door window without a second thought and got inside. My wounds were screaming their protest and pain but I kept going. Through the offices and into the lab room.

I took a moment to dry swallow two codeine pills, choking on them a little before stuffing the bottle back in my pocket, and using the rest of the water from my backpack to clean monster guts off me. I couldn't stand to feel them sticking to my skin. I waited and listened for the sounds of pursuit but couldn't hear anything. Then I looked around the laboratory to see if I could put my 'poison the monster' plan into action.

Around me, there were tables of computers, microscopes, and other scientific equipment I couldn't identify. There were a couple of portable Bunsen burners, a fume hood with several open jars of clear liquid in them, cabinets filled with books, other cabinets filled with labeled mason jars, a refrigerator, and a row of potted plants. My idea of vats of weed killer waiting for me to flood the room with their killer liquid died an ignoble death. I would have to find something else to do the trick.

In the meantime, I needed to know why David had called. It had to be damn important, knowing that the monsters could sense cell phone signals and he knew it.

Except he had not called.

Looking at the phone, there had been no calls or text messages since the text message last night. How had the Fedora found me then?

The squeal of my ankle monitor demanding to be recharged gave me my answer. It was a GPS device that gave out a constant signal for my location that the charging base back home was supposed to monitor. Just because the people died didn't mean the machines had stopped working. Far from it. I had been wearing the damn thing for so long, I didn't even notice it anymore.

It squealed again as I heard the sound of something coming through the front offices towards the lab. I had no place to run or hide and I couldn't get the ankle monitor off me in time. I had seconds to plan my defense. Then I saw the fire extinguisher and a fire axe. I had just enough time to pull the extinguisher off the wall, pull the pin, and point it at the door when the Fedora burst in.

Still clothed in a trench coat and the smiling mustached mask but no hat, it radiated aggression and hate with its wide stance and raised weaponed arms. I blasted it with the fire extinguisher, advancing on it as it curled back in on itself and away from the cold blast. When the fire extinguisher ran out, I dropped it and reached for my bat. Turning back, with the bat raised high, the Fedora was right there in front of me.

I had turned into its spearhead hand.

Looking down, I saw its hand had pierced my left side right above my hip and below my ribs. The pain was enormous on a distant level. My fear and need to survive kept me moving.

I slammed it in the head with the bat and then stumbled back from it, holding my side. I lost the bat as I fled around the workbench and, once more, was cornered by the invading monster. Without looking, I reached back and grabbed the first glass jar and flung it at the Fedora. The open jar splattered the Fedora with the clear liquid and it reacted like it was acid. Encouraged I grabbed the next two and saw that one of the jars had the symbol for flammable on it. I didn't recognize the second symbol and I didn't care. I threw both jars of liquid at the Fedora, the fumes stinging my eyes.

It stumbled back away from me and around the worktable. I advanced and grabbed one of the portable Bunsen burners. It was exactly like the

Bunsen burner Mr. Shindledecker used in science class. I turned it on, lit it with the sparker, and threw it at the monster. The thing burst into flames and I shielded my face with my hands, moving to the side. When I could see again, it was still trying to kill me, as it flailed at where I had been standing.

I inched around the workbench, trying to keep away from the fire and the Fedora's wildly striking arms until I was next to where the fire extinguisher had been on the wall. My ankle monitor, determined to get me killed for not giving it power, squealed again in a longer burst of teeth-itching noise. I grabbed the fire axe and used it to fend off the Fedora when it ran at me. I dodged one strike of the spearhead hand and brought the axe down on its arm, severing the hand at the wrist. The Fedora reared back from me, flames dancing, spouting black blood from its arm.

With its arms wildly striking about, I struggled around the worktable again to where my bat lay. I picked it up and wound up for the pitch. The Fedora flailed and careened around the room. Its silent struggles with the flames would have been comical if I wasn't so scared or in so much pain.

My ankle monitor gave another demanding squeal for power and this time, it didn't turn off. It kept on shrieking its want for power (or my death) as the Fedora turned towards the sound and rushed me. I gave it my best swing and knocked its jaw into next week. For a moment it stood there. Then, the Fedora fell over backwards, still burning.

I limped out of the room, holding my side. I stopped long enough to jam a chair under the door. While my ankle monitor continued blaring at me in that ear piercing squeal, I debated about beating the monitor on my leg until it stopped making noise, but I figured I would hurt myself more in the process.

Instead, I sat at the nearest desk and ransacked it for a pair of scissors. In a combination of brute force, cursing, and praying, I managed to cut through the hard plastic band of the monitor and only scrape myself once. I thought about beating the ever-loving crap out of the monitor then decided to leave it here next to the room with the burning monster as a warning to the rest. By my count, I had managed to kill four of the seven I had seen. That should be warning enough to stay the hell away from me.

I stuffed the phone back into my coat pocket and dragged myself to my feet. I needed to find a new place to hide that was defensible. Now that I understood the Fedoras were susceptible to fire I needed a place that could supply that. I also needed a place that was nearby and had access to medical equipment. I was bleeding from my side and from my leg again. If my arm was bleeding, I couldn't tell, and that was a blessing.

I stood in front of the building for a moment, looking around. I hefted Mister Bat, the only thing I managed to keep with me through all of this. I didn't see another Fedora but, again, that didn't mean anything. Straight ahead, two blocks away, was the propane store. That would do.

There was no running this time. There was only limping, groaning, and gasping as I took the path of least resistance, the roads, and made my way up First Street and back to Ash Avenue. Stewart and Daughter's Propane was there on the corner, a squat one-story red painted building with a gray tiled roof. It was also the most beautiful thing I had seen all week.

Moments before I broke the front door's glass, I noticed two cars in front of the shop and tried the door handle. It was unlocked. As soon as I opened the door, I knew that more than one person had died in here. I just hoped it wasn't like in the Food Center.

It wasn't. It was worse.

Jody Stewart, the shop manager, must have fallen asleep at the counter and slid off her high chair. When she landed on the floor, she landed on the curved end of a crowbar. I don't know why they had a crowbar in the shop but it was now embedded in Jody's throat. The puddle of blood had attracted flies and maggots squirmed all over Jody's face.

I backed out of the shop and did my best not to throw up by gulping in fresh smelling air.

My phone vibrated in my pocket and I wasn't afraid of picking it up now that my ankle monitor was gone. It was the Department of Homeland Security calling but not on FaceTime. I thumbed the answer button.

Before I could say hello, Tomas said, "This is Agent Harrison. I need a status update."

"Hello, Tomas. I'm fine," I said, limping my way to the bench on the side of the building.

"This is not a game, Melissa. What's your status?"

"I'm bleeding profusely and killed two more of them this morning."

"And the transmitter?"

I looked at phone for a moment in disbelief. No congratulations on being alive or killing the damn things. No concern about the fact that I was hurt. "Thanks for caring. Jesus. Like I told David last night, the only place the transmitter could be is the municipal airport. Didn't David tell you?"

It was a moment before he answered, "Agent Hood is not available right now. You said you're bleeding. Were you joking? And you killed two more?"

"No. I'm not. I figured out too late that they were tracking me by my ankle monitor. Fortunately for me, they're just as allergic to shotguns and fire as we are."

"Can you continue your mission?"

There was a tightness in his voice I didn't like. "If my mission is to get to the airport and find the transmitter, yeah. I think so. I need to find some stuff to patch up my side but I should be there today. If I don't call you back by tomorrow morning, nuke Onida from orbit. It's the only way to be sure."

"I'll await your call. Melissa?"

"Yeah?"

"Good luck."

Agent Harrison really was an odd duck. "Thanks," I said and meant it.

He hung up the phone before I did and I wondered where the hell David was. Maybe he was getting some much needed sleep. I didn't know. I looked at the cell phone and saw that it was nearly eight in the morning. Time for my pills. At least one thing in the day could be sane.

I patted my coat pocket with my daily pills in it and it was empty.

CHAPTER FOURTEEN

The disbelief came before the panic did. I put the phone on the bench next to me. Then I emptied out all of my pockets, not just my coat pockets. I still had the cell phone, its charger, the bottle of codeine pills, a granola bar, and a forgotten receipt. The key to the moped and the bag of my pills were gone. I had no idea where to look.

I didn't realize I was cursing until the cell phone vibrated with David's number on the screen. It wasn't FaceTime, it was a normal call. I ignored it, checking and rechecking my pockets until the fourth ring.

"David?" I said, trying to control my panic.

"Where are you?" he asked.

"I was about to ask you that." My voice was surprisingly calm for the complete and utter panic going on in the background of my brain.

"I'm a mile outside of Onida, coming up Highway 83."

I blinked at the phone. "What?"

"I promised you I would help. I always keep my promises. Where are you?"

"I'm hurt and I can't find my pills."

"That's not what I asked, Mel." His voice was patient. "Where are you?"

"I'm at Stewart and Daughter's Propane. Make a right on Ash Avenue. The sign might say Onida Road or 185th Street. I can't remember. Take the first right after the Chevy sign and then look for the little red building on the left. It'll be past hangar looking things and the squat silos." While talking to David was making me feel a little better. I still wanted to throw up and I was feeling dizzy. I wondered if it was from the blood loss, the adrenaline shakes, the panic, or the lack of drugs.

"Don't hang up, Melissa."

"I wasn't planning on it. I figured out how they were tracking me."

"It's not the phone?"

"No. I mean, I don't think so. I think it was my ankle monitor." I could hear the sound of his car. "I can hear you."

"Come out in front of the building."

"If I can hear you, so can they."

"The Fedoras?"

"Yeah. They're pissed. I killed two more this morning. One stabbed me, though."

"Come out front where I can see you." His voice had that patient tone of someone not understanding something important.

I stuffed the pain pills and the phone charger back in my pocket and picket up my bat. "I'm coming. I'm hurt though, and I need to find my pills."

"Can you move?"

"Yeah." I took a couple of painful steps to the corner of the building.

His car, a cherry red Ford Mustang, roared into sight. "I see you," he said, making a beeline for where I stood.

I leaned against the wall, waiting for him but also looking for the three Fedoras I knew were still around. They had to have heard him with a muscle car like that. He turned off the car, jumped out of it, and looked at me. "Christ, Melissa, what happened?"

David was taller than I expected, about five foot ten. He was wearing a light blue button up shirt over a white t-shirt and a brown leather jacket over jeans. He had a bowie knife strapped to his leg. His face was pale against his black hair and black eyes. He had a generous smile despite the circles under his eyes. I wondered how he managed to fight off the sleeping effects of the quarantine zone.

I looked down at my torn and bloody coat, saw that my wound on my thigh was bleeding again and tried to smile. "Just showing the Fedoras a real good time. What the hell…heck…are you *doing* here? Does Tomas know?"

"I'm helping you and no, he doesn't. Did he call?"

I nodded. "If you want to help me, help me find my pills. How are you staying awake?"

"A massive amount of drugs and if I need them, I've got a couple of epi-pens." He showed me a handful of yellow and black pens. "Adrenaline will keep me awake." He came closer to me, gestured to my side and asked, "Can I see?"

I nodded and looked away as he lifted my coat away from me. My breath steamed in the cold morning air.

He whistled. "How are you still standing? We've got to stitch you up before we do anything else. I brought medical supplies."

"No. We've got to get away from here first. Your car could be heard all over Onida."

"Then let's move." He went back to the car and grabbed a first aid shoulder bag. "Can you walk?"

I was surprised that he took me at my word without a quibble. Most adults questioned everything I said. I nodded. "Slowly."

"Need help?"

I was pleased he asked instead of assumed. It was nice that he made the choice mine. "Where we going?"

"Up to you. You know this town."

"How about the NewGrowth Grain Company next door?" I paused and then said, "If we have to get there fast, I'll be faster with help."

"All right." He dropped the shoulder bag to one hand and transferred it to the other. His right arm free, he tucked it around my waist. "Think of it as a three legged race."

I understood what he wanted and wrapped my arm around his waist. With my bad leg and wounded side between us, we made good time to the NewGrowth building. It was small and white. David let me go long enough to pull out the bowie knife and used it to pop the lock. "Misspent youth," he said when I looked at him.

Once inside he had me lay down on a work counter on my side so he could stitch up the side that was hurt. He was pulling out medical supplies including gauze, thread, needles and such, and I saw he handled them like he knew exactly what he was doing. I stopped trying to watch him once he walked around behind me.

"How did you learn to patch people up?"

"Trauma medic in the Army. Lots of practice." He rubbed something on my skin.

It was cold and stung. I hissed in pain.

"Sorry. Cleaning the wound. This is going to hurt but it's a numbing agent so I can put your stitches in without you twitching in pain. It's a clean through and through. You're lucky it didn't hit anything vital."

I bit my lip as he injected me with the numbing agent. When I could speak again, I asked, "So, Army to Homeland Security?" Whatever he was using worked fast. All I could feel was the pulling of flesh and thread through flesh. I wondered how bad this one would scar.

"Yeah. Did my four years, got out, got interested in the State Department. Got hired. And here I am."

"How old are you?"

"Older than I look."

I could hear a "don't ask" when I got one. However, I needed the distraction. "So… forty?"

He gave me a frowny look. "Twenty-nine, thankyouverymuch."

"So, old but not that old." I smiled a brave smile at him.

He returned the smile with a hmph. "Thanks."

I listened to him work, his movements steady and sure. "How long have you been in the Quarantine zone?"

He looked at his watch. "One hour and forty-seven minutes."

"How do you feel?"

"Pretty good but that's the drugs talking. The zone is still up."

"Any idea why Tomas didn't tell me you were missing when he called?"

"What did he say?"

I could hear the change in the tone of his voice and it scared me, though his gentle fingers didn't stop their work. "He wanted my status and he wasn't nice about it. I told him about the airport. Told him that if I hadn't called him by tomorrow morning, he needed to nuke the place from orbit."

"Did he agree?"

"Yes, but I don't think he's—"

David interrupted me. "Yes, he is. He *is* planning to nuke the place. Just not from orbit. You bought us an extra twelve hours."

I felt him cover the stitches with gauze and tape it down. My heart beat double time. "Would he really?"

"You can sit up now. And yes, he would. We need to get to the airport now."

I shook my head and shifted myself into a sitting position with slow, careful movements. The stitches felt good but I didn't want to chance tearing them. "No. We need to find my pills now."

He came around and looked at me. I could see he was trying to understand and also looking to see signs of addiction. "Mel…"

"No, David, listen. I'm already thirty minutes late for my dose. Within ninety minutes, I'm going to have a splitting headache and will have trouble with anything that needs fine motor control. Within four hours, it will be a migraine. I'll be dizzy, uncoordinated, nauseated, and that is the *least* of the possible symptoms. Not to mention hallucinations. Within eight hours, I will wish I was dead. Very seriously dead. Within twelve, I will hate you, too. Within twenty-four, if I have not already found a way to kill myself, I will be actively trying to kill me *and* you."

His brow furrowed as he studied my face. "For real?" he asked, his voice soft.

"For real," I said and then paused. "Actually, not trying to kill you. Just me. But if I have a really bad hallucination, I might try to hurt you. The hallucinations are real to me and stress makes them worse."

David nodded. "Okay. Where do we look?"

I thought about it, thought about the first fight this morning and decided. "Backtrack to where I had my pills last."

He helped me down from the counter. "You lead. I'm here to protect you."

I picked up Mister Bat and said, "I've done pretty well so far. I've gotten four of the bastards."

"I guess that leaves the rest for me." Outside the door, he asked, "Take the car?"

"No. Too noisy. They knew I was here by the dead carcasses lying around. They know you're here because of your car. But just because they know we're around doesn't mean we should flaunt it."

"You can walk?"

"Yeah, but for the airport, we'll need to find bicycles."

He gave me a look that reserved judgment but said, "All right."

Back the way I had come except using the roads this time, we backtracked down South Fourth Street to Cedar Avenue and then up 5th Street until we reached Pat's house. The two of us walked around the backyard, looking for the missing bag of pills until I finally said, "If it's here, it's inside. Probably in the bedroom with the Fedora." I didn't want to go back in there but I had no choice. I went up the three stairs to the door and opened it.

Standing there without its camouflage coat, hat, and mask was a Fedora monster and I was face to face with it.

It was about six feet tall with four sets of inward curving mandibles that were as black as the rest of its head. Its eyes were oblong and three times larger than a human eye. It had no nose I could see and was hairless on its head. Its body was the same segmented iridescent blue-green I had seen on the other one with a fuzzy, black, blunted stinger. Its upper arms were jointed like human arms with discernible shoulders, elbows, and wrists that ended just above the serrated spearhead hands. It had its middle set of limbs curled close to its body and its legs had two sets of knee joints.

It was by reflexes alone that the monster didn't stab me with its intended blow. The spearhead hand skittered off the aluminum bat and shot past my face. I stumbled backwards and fell down the short flight of stairs. As I hit the ground hard, I heard David yelling. Then the sound of gunfire. I counted four shots and saw the monster still coming for me. I shouted, "The head! Shoot the head."

David shot the thing four more times with deliberate and measured shots. Both of its eyes exploded, and the spot between the eyes and mouth caved in. Still it wavered and then it tumbled forward onto me. I had just enough time to roll partway out from under it before it hit the ground.

David rushed to my side. "You okay?"

I grunted as I pulled myself up. "I think so."

"I thought you said you killed it." He put out a steadying hand. "Good God, they are ugly."

"I did kill it. It's still inside. This is another one and makes five. And believe it or not, it's less creepy with them out of their human camouflage than in it."

David kept his gun out and looked down at the dead Fedora monster. "I'll believe that when I see it."

"By my count, we only have two more to go." I stepped around it and into the house, keeping my eyes on the floor, looking for the missing bag of pills. No dice. I would have to go back to the bedroom.

I went down the hallway to the back bedroom with Mister Bat at the ready. Even though I was sure I had killed the Fedora monster that attacked me I had not taken that final step of cutting off its head. I could hear David following me.

"You sure it's dead?" he asked.

"Mostly. I didn't stop to get a pulse after I shot twice." I stopped where I was. "Maybe you should… you know…"

"Go first?" He smiled as he passed me.

"Yeah." I stepped back while David cleared each of the small rooms until he got to the bedroom.

He lowered his gun and nodded to me. "It is definitely still dead."

I walked up next to him and saw the monster laid out on the bed. It was a mess. Its chest was ripped open and one of its eyes was a gory hole. I noted that there was no real blood on its body or on its face.

"It wasn't like this. I guess the other one was its mate or something. It cleaned it up." Next to one of its small arms was the baggie with my pills. I could have passed out with relief. I stepped up to the bed and reached for it, accidentally touching the Fedora.

The Fedora's closest little hand grabbed my hand as it closed around the baggie. I shrieked and jerked back in surprise. David fired at it and its second eye disappeared in an explosion of fluid. A second bullet followed the first as I lifted my bat, prepared to go toe-to-toe with the monster again. But it stopped moving.

I got up and ran down the hallway to the living room, hysterical laughter bursting forth. I couldn't stop myself. It really was like a horror movie where the monster came back for more. Only this was real life, and for some reason, I found this hysterical. David came down the hallway. "You okay?"

I nodded, still laughing.

"No wonder it was so aggressive. It was protecting the injured one." He looked up and down the hallway, and then out the open backdoor.

"And we... and we..." I continued to laugh. "Monster. Movie." I felt the hysteria starting to win. I punched myself in the leg, striking my wounded thigh. The pain was immense, blossoming out in waves of red and black. It hurt worse than when I got the wound in the first place. For a moment, tears welling in my eyes and grayness descended, I thought I was going to pass out. I took a shaky breath and held onto consciousness with all that I had and promised never to do that again.

"Feel better?" David's face was a conflict of emotions. I could see he wanted to smile but he was still both on high alert and concerned.

"Yeah." I went into the kitchen and opened the refrigerator. I turned back to David when the Imperial March suddenly erupted from his coat pocket.

CHAPTER FIFTEEN

David gave me a grin that was half dorky and half embarrassed. "It's the boss."

"Tomas?"

"Agent Harrison, yes." He answered the phone. "Agent Hood here."

I could hear both sides of the conversation from where I was. I grabbed a pop from the fridge, downed my pills like the addict I was, and listened.

"I hope you have a good explanation for what you're doing now, Agent Hood."

David rubbed his cheek. "Yes, sir. We have limited time and a great need to get this situation solved as soon as possible." He walked over to the nearest chair and sat down.

"So, you broke into the quarantine zone."

"Yes, sir."

"If I understand your reasons, you willingly risked your life to assist Miss Allen in achieving her mission objective?"

"Yes, sir."

"You understand that if you don't succeed in your mission, you will *not* be allowed out of the quarantine zone."

"Yes, sir."

"Even if you do succeed with your mission objective, there will still be consequences."

"Yes, sir."

That blew my mind. I yelled at the phone, "Way to encourage proactive thinking! If you don't succeed, you're screwed. If you do succeed, you're still screwed!"

David winced and waved a hand at his throat in a silencing gesture.

"She can hear this?"

I answered before David did, "Yes, Tomas. I can. Hello to you, too."

"Hello, Melissa." David shrugged and put the phone on speaker as Agent Harrison continued to speak. "You were the next call. I have sent your request for more time up the chain of command. Due to the change in circumstances, it has been denied. If I don't hear from you or Agent Hood by twelve hundred hours that you have found and destroyed the transmitter array, we're going to commence Operation Zeus."

Before I could respond or ask any questions, David said, "We understand, sir." To me he mouthed, *I will explain.*

Agent Harrison sighed. "A lot is riding on your shoulders." He paused, "David, Melissa, good luck. I really hope to hear from you before noon."

"Thank you, sir," David said. "We won't fail. It's been an honor working with you, Agent Harrison."

"It's been an honor working with you, too, Agent Hood."

That served as good-bye on both sides and David thumbed the End Call button.

"Operation Zeus?" I asked.

"I wasn't kidding about him bombing us. Though, not with a nuke. A MIM-14 Nike-Hercules should be enough to wipe Onida off the map."

I sat down at the table across from him suddenly understanding that if we didn't stop the monsters, the United States Government was going to stop all of Onida with us in it. "What changed in circumstance? What made you make a suicide run to help me?"

"Hey, it's not suicide. I've come prepared and I believe we can do this."

"Suicide to your career."

"Agent Harrison is by the book and I will be reprimanded but it won't be that much more than a black mark on my record. I'm sure he has plenty from his younger days."

"The change in circumstances. You're avoiding the topic."

David sat back and wouldn't look at me. "Honestly, it's unbelievable."

"Oh, I don't know. I've spent the last couple of days running from giant, sentient, insect-like things I've been calling Fedoras because they used human clothing as camouflage. I just might believe it."

He glanced at me, looked away and said, "We discovered the source of the signal that is causing the quarantine zone. It's being sent from a geosynchronous orbit above the upper atmosphere. It's being received and retransmitted from some place in or near Onida."

I looked at him for a long time. "Geosynchronous orbit. Outer space."

"Yeah."

He leaned forward on the table, looking suddenly tired. "From higher up than the space station but we can't find it. No one knows why."

I nodded. "All right. Aliens. There, I said it. Aliens. And this is the advance scout group that, what? Is looking to see if we're susceptible to their sleep-death weapon?" David yawned wide and closed his eyes. "Hey now! None of that!" My voice was sharp with fear.

David's eyes flew open and he stood with an abrupt jerky motion. "Damn. We are susceptible. Some of us are. You're different though. You existing might have saved the world."

"We haven't saved the world yet, agent man." I looked at my phone. "We still have three hours. It won't take more than thirty minutes to get to the airport." I picked up my bat. "C'mon." Then I said, "Wait there."

I went back down the hallway to the bedroom and found the shotgun on the floor where I left it. My stomach ached just thinking about it. I wiped the gore from the barrel on the bed and searched the closet until I came up with a box of shells. I stuffed these in my coat pocket after reloading the shotgun. When I returned to the living room, the bat in one hand and the shotgun over my shoulder, David was standing by the open door.

"Good idea," he said, nodding at the shotgun. "You say there are two more Fedoras out there?" David asked as we headed out the door and westward towards the airport.

"Yeah. That I know of. I saw seven glowing bodies the first night. But, honestly, I've been hiding. So I really don't know."

"And we can't take a car because if they are at the airport they'll hear us coming, and if they aren't they'll know we're headed that way. A car would be faster though."

"Look, if you think we'd do better with that Mustang, I'm all for it but I've been surviving on stealth."

"I think every minute counts."

I thought about it as we walked back towards Ash Avenue. "All right. Only if you can stay awake. Then again, it's all of two minutes down Ash and a left on 3rd street. We'll have to take the streets anyway. The fields are muddy marshes. You could get stuck in one of those mud holes. It's not quicksand but almost as bad."

"We need a plan," David said.

"I've been following the 'Get 'em, Ray!' plan." He gave me a look. "What? Sharon and Matt made me watch movies from their formative years. Besides, I really don't have a plan. Do you?"

"I'm just the muscle. You're the brain. This is your territory, you know the lay of the land. What are we going to encounter at the airport? What's the layout?"

"Um, it's got two runways, both lit. There's a hangar bay for the Cessna airplanes and ultralights and a helicopter. Most of the main building is one floor but there is a two-story part to it where the manager spends his time, especially when crop dusting is going on. On top of that is all the radar tower and antenna equipment and its own cell tower. It's got its own emergency power supply but if we stop and mangle the power substation, that won't last for long. We could cut the power before we get there. In case, you know, something happens. It's not really on the way but it's close enough once we get to Ash."

"That's a good idea." That made me beam inside. The warmth disappeared when David frowned and asked, "So, if we cut the power, we'll still have cell signal? Got to have a way to call Agent Harrison back."

"Yes. I still had cell signal when the power went out. The airport cell tower must be on the emergency power line, too."

David considered this. "All right. How do we get to the antenna array? Do we have to go inside or is there a way to get to it from the outside."

"I don't remember. It's been a while since I've been there. I mean, I know a lot of kids go out there and climb up. I think there's ways to get up from the outside and the inside."

"Okay, we can look around and figure out if there is an easy way or only a hard way."

When we arrived at Ash Avenue, we turned right towards Main Street. "Um, I killed one of them in the substation."

He stopped and looked at me. "Really?"

"Yeah. When the power went out, I went to the substation to get it back on. I found one of them there, trying to get the power on. It didn't occur to me that they might need it for their signal thing and I hadn't thought of the airport then. I just wanted to make sure I was warm."

"Makes sense. You sure it's dead?"

"Yeah. I chopped its head off. I did that with the first two. The third one I shot and then had to run from the all the noise I made but the fourth one caught up with me at the Pest and Weed Supervisor's office."

"What did you do to that one?"

"Set it on fire, cut off a hand, and hit it in the head with my bat." I lifted my bat up. I noticed a couple of new scratches and a dent in it. Poor thing.

"Then I locked it in the lab. It could still be alive but if it is, it ain't happy." I pointed out the water tower. "The substation's over there."

We saw the substation door in the middle of Main Street as soon as we made the turn.

"Damn," I muttered. "They did tear the door off after they found the little one."

"Between the one in the house cleaned up and protected, and this show of real anger, not only are they displaying they are self-aware but are also emotional beings. This makes them a lot more dangerous than we first thought."

"People fight harder for other people than just themselves."

"Instead of an invasion force looking for resources like a hive mind, they might be looking for a new place to colonize."

I stopped at the foot of the substation driveway. "Whoa, invasion force? You didn't say anything about an invasion force."

He shrugged. "There's a signal coming from a geosynchronous orbit that we can't find the source of. It's hidden. If one ship is hidden, why can't an entire armada be out there?"

"Because they'd be down here invading?"

"Not if this is their idea of safely exterminating a lesser species."

"I'm *not* a lesser species, thank you very much."

"No, but they may believe we are. So they picked a less populated area delineated by random lines to test out their euthanasia field. It means they've picked up our communications, studied our regions, and tested it out on a large area suited to their needs. They assumed we wouldn't recognize them in their human clothing camouflage. If I were going to colonize an already populated planet, the sleep-death weapon is a humane way to do it. Especially if I didn't want to fight the indigenous population for the land."

"In what universe?" I was horrified by the fact that I could see our own government doing the exact same thing. Most natives don't fare well against colonizing forces.

"This one. Right here, right now. Only, we aren't the superior species this time."

I turned away, not wanting to contemplate this. "C'mon. We're wasting time." I walked up to the doorway of the substation and wasn't surprised that the Fedora's body was gone. The blood was still there. "No one is going to believe this."

David stood behind me. "What? That they look after their dead?"

"No. That they were here at all. The government will make something else up to explain the deaths. If we survive, I'm going to be put in a very dark hole where people will experiment on me to find out why I survived when the rest didn't." I went to the console, put the shotgun down, and started the shutdown procedures Dad once taught me. He told me I had to learn because, maybe, someday, he wouldn't be here to turn out the lights when they needed to be turned off.

"I won't let that happen. I promise. And I keep my promises. You see that. I'm here now, aren't I?"

I snorted. "You're going to be in the cell next to me."

"I doubt that. Besides, I think it has something to do with the way your brain works. I looked up what you take and thought about doing the same before I headed out here. In the end, it was too much work to get that many controlled drugs. Adrenaline is the better choice."

I looked at him, horrified by the thought. "Are you crazy? Did you look at the side effects? Ramping up a new psychotropic is hell. Some of the side effects can kill you. I mean, lamotrigine has a possible side effect of a death rash."

"You're joking."

I shook my head. "I'm not."

"Damn."

"Yeah."

He came over to stand by me while the system shut itself down. "All I'm saying is if we get out of this, and I'm sure we will, you'll be a hero. This is too big to cover up."

"We'll be heroes. You're here risking your life, too."

"Not for much longer. C'mon." David headed out of the substation and down to the end of the driveway.

I followed, pausing at the doorway to silently say goodbye to my father and to thank him for showing me what to do. I saw I had forgotten the shotgun. Then a buzzing sound caught my attention. It was the same sound I heard the night before but I wasn't certain if it was a hallucination or not. I looked at David. He was looking around with his gun out. If he could hear it, it was real.

"Stay there!" he ordered.

I stayed in the doorway, looking around for what I thought it was. Then, from around the water tower, a flying Fedora dove at David.

CHAPTER SIXTEEN

David got two shots off before the thing was on him, grabbing him, and lifting him off the ground, knocking the gun from of his hand. This Fedora was solid black, no hints of iridescent blues, greens, or purples. Its wings were like the wings of a giant termite; long, thin, and insectile. They were wings that didn't look like they could fly but they were and were strong enough to carry the Fedora and a human.

It appeared larger than the other Fedoras and, worse yet, its stinger looked sharper and it was trying to sting David with it.

I couldn't help but wonder if this was a female Fedora or not. It was larger and not colored. I vaguely remembered something about female animals having a duller, drabber coat so they had an easier time hiding. The fact that she could fly meant she might be able to breed and I had killed a bunch of her mates. It might mean she was a queen of this hive or colonizing force or whatever the hell it was.

David struggled in her grip, twisting his body back and forth to avoid the stinger while punching her for all he was worth. I could see blood on his face and hands and realized he wasn't punching her with his fist but with the bowie knife he wore on his belt. While he was getting pummeled, he was giving as good as he got.

I couldn't let him fight her alone. I ran out to the street and picked up his gun. The safety was off and I pointed the gun at them but I had never fired a pistol before and it was different than the shotgun. I followed them with the gun, not sure I could hit her. I might hit David and make things worse.

He was tiring and it looked like the queen was tiring too. She flew higher and higher, four stories up, the buzzing of her wings taking on a jerky quality. Sudden she dropped him and he caught one of her legs before he could fall to the ground, losing his knife as he did so. The queen, losing altitude, tried to stab him in the face with her stinger.

I followed them with the gun and then fired five bullets from the gun before it was empty. I had no idea how many bullets hit her but I know at least one hit her wing and she spiraled in a controlled fall with David holding on for dear life. I dropped the gun and ran back to where my bat lay. I thought twice about it and retrieved the shotgun.

When I turned around, David was lying on the ground and the queen was crawling away from him, leaving a trail of black blood behind her.

"Oh, no you don't, you bitch." I cocked both of the hammers and went after her. "You don't get to live." I put the shotgun to my shoulder like I'd been taught, aimed it at her head, and pulled the trigger twice. My shoulder hurt like crazy from the shotgun's recoil but that Fedora wasn't going anywhere without a head.

"Six down, one to go," I told David then turned around to see him twitching on the ground. I ran to his side, dropping the shotgun at his feet. His head was lolling back and forth and he was gasping for air. It looked like he was going into an anaphylactic shock. There was a puncture wound near his clavicle and I realized that he had been stung.

Patting his pockets, I found several of the epi-pens he brought with him to help keep him awake. I read the instructions and then jabbed the business end of it against his upper thigh and pushed the button. There was a jolt as the needle deployed, I held it steady and counted to ten. When I pulled back, David's breathing had evened out.

"David? You okay? David?" I shook his uninjured shoulder. I stuffed the rest of the epi-pens in my coat pocket next to the shotgun shells.

His eyes rolled in his head and then focused on me. For a couple of seconds he blinked without recognition and then nodded. "Yeah. Okay. Yeah."

I helped him sit up. "You were having a reaction. It stung you."

He tried to look at his shoulder and winced. "Yeah. I think it did."

"Trust me. You've got a hole the size of my little finger. Now you have to get up." I stood and offered my hand, terrified he would refuse it.

"Do I have to?" He rested his head in his hands.

"If you don't want to die, you do."

He looked up at me, suddenly remembering the sleep-death field.

I gestured again with my hand and put on my best Arnold impersonation and said, "Come with me if you want to live."

David laughed weakly and accepted the help up. We were both a little unsteady on our feet; him from the sting, the fall, and the adrenaline; me from all my injuries reminding me they were there. I pulled out my phone and looked at the time. "Two and a half hours before this place goes boom. Let's go."

While David stopped to pick up his dropped pistol and his fallen bowie knife, I retrieved the shotgun and reloaded it. I had four shells left. Four shots. I had to make them count. Every movement hurt but I knew it was finish this or die. David looked a lot worse for wear when I turned back to him. He must have seen the concern on my face because he visibly straightened and smiled. "Lead on."

"It's up this way. Maybe we should drive."

David thought for a moment. "I don't think I should try driving like this. I'm woozy."

"Do you want me to drive?" I frowned at him. His face was starting to swell. It made his skin shiny.

"Do you know how? Are you old enough?"

I pretended a nonchalance I didn't feel. "If we find a car with an automatic transmission I can. Most kids around here know how to drive by the time they're ten. So yeah, I'm old enough. Even if it isn't legal." I looked closer at his face. He was white now. "Are you sure you're okay?"

He shook his head. "No. All I want to do is sleep. I don't think I should sit at all. I think we need to walk."

"All right. We're about two miles away."

On any normal day, the two mile walk would have been a breeze. As it was, my side and my thigh were throbbing within half a mile and all I really wanted to do was lie down and nap. Again, I wondered if my recent weird sleeping habits were because of what had been going on and getting hurt or if it was because of the sleep-death field. Maybe a little of column A and a little of column B. When I realized that I was staring at my feet instead of straight ahead I pulled myself together and shook my head. I would have tapped my cheeks but my hands were full of Mister Bat and Mister Shotgun. It was scary how comforted I felt carrying these weapons.

I noticed David had fallen more than a step behind me. When I looked back, his face was an unhealthy shade of gray and he had dark circles under his eyes.

"How you doing?" I asked.

"I've been better," he admitted.

"Is it the sting?"

"No. I think it's the quarantine zone. It's getting to me."

That scared me. "Even with the adrenaline? Do you need another?"

He shook his head. "Not yet. I'm still moving…" He dug a small white packet out of his pocket.

I blinked at him,. "Cocaine?"

It was his turn to be surprised, "No. Smelling salts. Cocaine? Really?"

"You said you had drugs. You didn't say you had those."

He broke open the package and inhaled deeply. It was like he had slapped himself. His eyes opened wide and he jerked his face away from his hands.

"Damn." He blinked his eyes clear of the tears. "I'm awake. I'm awake." He started walking again with renewed energy in his step.

We walked along in silence for a couple more minutes before he asked, "So, wanna tell me about the whole mailbox incident?"

"What's there to tell? It's all in the file." I glanced sideways at him, wondering why he asked.

"What you did is in the file but why did you do it? What happened? I'm asking because if I have something to concentrate on, I won't remember how tired I am or how much I hurt."

I was silent for a few steps before I said, "You know that my parents were killed on my thirteenth birthday." He nodded. "From the moment that happened, I ceased to be me. I became that girl whose parents were killed by a drunk driver, that girl who was orphaned, that girl who survived. I became a thing, an object, something to be pitied, a statistic."

I tucked the bat under my arm and wiped at my face, surprised that I wasn't crying. I guess I was all cried out for the moment. "What no one cared about was the fact that the guy who hit our car stopped and pulled my parents from the wreckage before he got back in his car and drove away. I saw him do it. I was thrown from the car and lying in some tall grass. He never even noticed me. He would've gotten away with it. The kicker? My dad was still alive and bleeding to death. He had a broken neck. The driver could have helped my dad. All he did after pulling them out was look down at them, say 'Well, damn,' and readjust his hat before he got back in his car and left."

"Harsh."

I nodded. "For the next three months, someone had to come over and say how sorry they were. They weren't. All they really wanted to do was get a look at me and see how Sharon and Matt were dealing with suddenly being my guardians. We were the talk of the town and I hated it. I was already on meds and this made it all worse. After a while I stopped being polite, stopped smiling, and stopped playing the small town polite chitchat game. I started telling people to fuck off."

"Makes sense." His voice was neutral. It was the kind of thing people said when they had nothing to say but wanted you to know they were listening.

"So that day, someone had come by to see if they could get new gossip for the mill and I wouldn't see them. I pretended not to be home. By that time, I couldn't stand to be around anyone who wasn't family. I don't even know who it was. They left a sympathy card in the mailbox. I can still remember what it said. *'There is a reason and a plan for every pain that comes our way. What does not kill us makes us stronger.'* Handwritten was, *'Be happy. Now God has two new angels to keep Him company.'"*

David grimaced. "First, that sympathy card writer needed to be fired. Second, that person was an asshole."

"Yeah. I lost it. I ripped it up, stomped on it, and then got my bat to beat the ever-loving crap out of the mailbox so I never received another piece of mail like that again. I didn't stop at my mailbox. I kept going down the street."

"And the hat thing?"

"The next day, my doctor upped a couple of my meds. Seroquel. That doc didn't believe me when I told him it wasn't working. It didn't go well. I already didn't like people. I tweaked. I started thinking people wore hats to hide the alien inside. Somewhere along the way, I decided the guy who left my parents to die wasn't human. One thing led to another... I was arrested for destroying Federal property and then juvie which, with my meds, was a bad idea. Which eventually ended the court case with house arrest and bi-monthly meetings with my doctor and probation counselor."

He glanced at me. "You seem to be doing well now."

"Yeah, I guess. I suspect I'm going to have a complete breakdown after we save the world."

"I hope not."

"I hope not, too. I do have problems though. I hallucinate under stress. There is a small part of me that is praying to God you aren't one." I didn't realize I was going to admit that fear until it was out of my mouth.

He put his hand on my shoulder. "I'm real and here. Just like I promised."

I didn't tell him that when I hallucinate, sometimes it is so real I believe I feel things. Like now. I smiled and covered his hand for a moment. "I know."

His hand was too hot. I knew he had a fever. The epi-pen must not have stopped the poison. We really were running on borrowed time. We knew it, and we were both ignoring it. I looked up and saw the airport within sight.

"What about you? I told you my deepest, darkest secret. What's yours?"

David looked off towards the horizon and I wasn't certain he was going to tell me until he began to talk.

"I told you I was in the Army. I spent most of that time over in Afghanistan. It was hard going. Kandahar. We got shelled a lot. In the movies, there's a nice whistling sound when any form of incoming indirect fire comes down. Rockets, however, travel faster than the speed of sound. If you aren't looking in the right direction, the first time you know you're under rocket attack is when the first rocket in the volley impacts and explodes." He shrugged at me and smiled a sick smile.

"When it comes to explosions, the sound is ambiguous. It's the fact that the shockwave from the blast is slapping you in the face and your body that eliminates all doubt about it being an explosion. You can't tell exactly what kind of explosion it is or how large it is. Essentially, how an explosion feels is mostly a factor of how large it is and how far away you are. So, a small explosion close by can feel about the same as a big bomb farther away."

He rubbed his cheek, a habit of his, it seemed, when he was uncomfortable. "We were out on a mission—I can't really tell you about it—it was highly classified, highly dangerous, and very important. Someone messed something up somewhere and we got caught between a rock and a hard place and someone started shelling us. It was loud and close. I think we were all practically deaf before we got out of there."

His voice had taken on an emotionless quality that seemed weird next to his normal way of talking. "An extraction team was called and when they got there, we got hit hard. One of my guys, Sergeant Crusett, was killed. Because of the fire we were taking, we couldn't even get his tags from him. We left a man behind because we had no choice. *I* left a man behind. It was my decision, my command."

I could see the pain of the memory on his face as we made the turn down the road towards the airport in front of us.

"Only he wasn't dead. He was unconscious and hurt but alive... and I was the one to leave him behind. Three days later, we got word that he was a prisoner of war. Three months later, he really was dead—beheaded on camera."

David looked at me, his eyes bleak. I didn't think he was looking at me. He was looking at the man he'd left behind and I suddenly understood why he was here, risking his life to try and save mine. I had no idea what to say to him until the words popped out of my mouth.

"You're here now."

He looked at the airport, checked his gun and his knife, and nodded. "I'm here now."

We both looked at the airport and knew that it wouldn't be as easy as turning off a switch. We just didn't know how hard it would be in the end.

CHAPTER SEVENTEEN

There were three buildings at the airport: a hangar bay for the Cessna planes and ultralights, a maintenance building next to the fuel pumps, and the main building where the planes were loaded for crop dusting, paperwork was filed, plane inspections were held, and the rest of the day-to-day management of the airport was conducted. We could ignore the maintenance building and the hanger bay to concentrate on the main building.

We walked in, inspecting it from the outside. I told David what I remembered from the inside.

"The building looks like one big building, but really it's half that size with hangar bays. Those bays are closed and locked up when the airport's down for the winter. During the rest of the year, it's mostly open to the general parking area." I pointed out the huge metal roll up doors in front of a parked Cessna.

As we came around the south side nearest the runways, the delineation between the hangar bays and the indoor workspace was clear by where the windows started, revealing a wall with a row of chairs facing outward. Once we turned west we both stopped at the same time. Halfway down the west side of the building, the second story of the building started. Between us and it was a solid wall that looked like it had holes punched into the side of it.

"Is it normally like that?" David asked.

"No, not that I remember."

"Does it look like there was once a ladder there bolted to the wall and is now gone?"

I nodded.

"Do you see the ladder anywhere?"

I looked around. "No. I don't."

"Looks like there's only the hard way to get to where we need to go."

We both looked up at the second story level and saw a metal ladder bolted to the wall on the corner farthest away from the edge. It looked like what I imagined the missing one should look like. "Maybe. I think there's supposed to be another one on the other side." While I thought it might be true, I didn't hold hope that that ladder would be there.

We looked up to the top of the second story to the radio tower at the top. I didn't see anything unusual from this distance but I was also not that familiar with the antenna set up. I did see the blinking red light on the very top of the tower. It was faint in the morning light, indicating that the backup power was still on. I didn't remember how much backup power the airport had or how long it would last.

I checked my cell phone. I still had two bars.

The east side looked the same as the west. David pulled his bowie knife from his belt and headed towards the side door with a deliberate stride. I looked around for the missing ladder and didn't see it. However, I did see Barry Tyler's dark red Chevy truck parked in its usual spot.

"Wait," I called, hurrying up to him. David gave me a questioning look. I held up a finger for quiet and then reached for the doorknob. It was unlocked. David grinned and motioned me back as he sheathed his knife and drew his gun. I stepped back and let him go first.

From this side of the building, we entered into a wide open room with twelve foot high ceilings that looked like it could be used for storage, classes, and as a makeshift rec room or lounge. There were a couple of old vending machines in one corner near a Ping-Pong table and a disreputable looking couch. At the far end was a door to the hangar bays. Across the way was the wall that had the lookout chairs and a set of stairs headed up to where the radio tower switchboard was.

In the middle of the room from ceiling to floor, wrapped around one of the support pillars, was a structure my mind wanted to deny. It was round and wide, sixteen feet across, with thin walls made from what looked like a mixture of shredded wood and metal. There was one man-sized entrance into it and something pulsed red from within on the left side. The smell of bile and wood pulp made me gag. It was undeniably alien and terrible.

We stared at it, unable to move until a cold breeze urged us onward.

Finally I whispered, "We are *not* going in there no matter what. I've seen what happens to the curious in horror movies."

"We're not in a horror movie," he whispered back.

I looked at him. "The heck we're not."

He saw the look on my face, and nodded. "We'll burn it on the way out."

I closed the door with a quiet thump and followed him around the right side of the thing—*the giant hive*, my mind screamed at me—keeping our backs to the wall. In my worst nightmares, I'd never dreamed something so awful. Now, it was stuck in my brain forever. I really was going to need to take Prazosin for the rest of my life.

Once we were a quarter of the way around it, we saw the second horror waiting for us. Sticking out of the backside of the thing, the hive, and stacked like cordwood, were people. Lying with half of their bodies stuck into the wall of the hive, they were covered in a glistening, clear sheath of *something*, maybe crystal, that looked like it would be hard to the touch. Not that I was going to do something so stupid.

"The hell?" David muttered when he saw it.

"Are they alive?"

"I don't think so."

"What... why?" I couldn't figure out what the bodies were doing there, stuck in the wall. They didn't add to the structure. My mind tried to make sense of it.

David's answer was flat with disgust. "Food."

That was when the emotional part of me took a powder and hid behind my analytical mind. I stared at them. There were seven bodies stacked on top of each other with a layer of the crystal between them. From what I could see of their clothes, all of them were men, farmers and pilots. I pointed to the bottom one with the bat. "That's Barry, the airport manager."

"How can you tell?"

"It's the boots. Chinos. People used to laugh at him because he mail ordered them from Zappos. Teased him for being too good to wear real boots." He gave me a look of disbelief. It was a stupid thing to notice and I shrugged. "Small town. Entertainment's hard to come by."

That was when the Fedora came out of the bathroom door next to the vending machines and I discovered the error of carrying two weapons that both need two hands to work effectively.

In the movies, there is always a moment of hesitation on both sides when the hero meets the monster unexpectedly. It heightened tension and anticipation. There was no such thing here. The Fedora leapt from the bathroom doorway, across the room, and straight at me. I don't know if it even noticed David. It wanted me with a vengeance and I knew why: it was the one I set on fire in the lab.

I don't know how it got out but I saw parts of melted mask on its face under a bandage and one of its spearhead hands was missing. I wondered how it managed to escape from the lab.

I raised the bat and the shotgun to ward it off as it jumped on me. I ended up dropping the bat and jamming the long part of the shotgun barrel in its mouth, crushing some of its mandibles, as it pinned me against the wall. I screamed when its pair of middle hands shot forward, clawing at my torso, leaving long tears in my coat and bloody furrows in my stomach.

I kicked out at it, flailing, and I shoved against the shotgun trying to escape but it was too strong. Hurt or not, that thing wanted my blood and it was going to get it. I was aware of David dodging its one good spearhead hand as it kept him at bay. It leaned in closer and even though the shotgun was jammed in its mouth, it spat a stream of noxious fluid at me. I jerked away, causing most of it to splatter against the wall. The dregs that did hit my coat steamed, burning through the fabric.

There were two loud shots and part of the Fedora's head disappeared.

For an eternity, the thing still pressed against the shotgun and then it slumped towards me. I shoved it away, dropping the shotgun. I ripped what was left of my coat off as the first bits of its acidic spittle burned the skin on my shoulder. I was bleeding and burning. David took the time to shoot the downed Fedora in the head a third time to be sure.

If I thought I was a mess before, I was wrong. Now my pilfered t-shirt was ripped open at the stomach and being burned away by monster vomit at the shoulder. I hesitated at taking the t-shirt off but pain won over modesty. I pulled the t-shirt off, leaving me only in my sports bra, and wiped at my shoulder with it. "It burns," I said.

"The bathroom," David said.

He led the way with his pistol at the ready. He cleared the bathroom before he let me come in. By the time I got to the sink, my shoulder felt like it was on fire. I looked in the dirty mirror above the sink and saw that my shoulder was red with small blisters. "It looks like a chemical burn."

David was already rummaging in the first aid kit on the wall. It was the only thing in the bathroom that looked new. The rest of the bathroom was muddy and had an odd smell to it. I didn't want to think too much about that smell and what it might be.

"It was probably digestive acids," David said as he returned with burn gel. His face had an odd, distant look to it. One I recognized. It was a look of retreating into the logical mind. His look probably mirrored mine. He spread the gel on my shoulder. Its relief was immediate and I relaxed as much as I could.

"I don't want to cover this for too long but we'll have to until we've completed our mission objective."

I nodded. "We're almost there."

He bent to look at the scratches on my stomach. When he did so, I saw black lines snaking away from the sting site on his shoulder. My stomach dropped in fear and I wondered how much pain he was in.

"It doesn't look too bad. I saw some liquid bandage. It should do the trick." He went back to the first aid kit and came back with a small can of New-Skin and sprayed it on my stomach. "At least we got them all."

"No. There's still one more."

He looked at me. "That's seven. The four you got and the three we killed."

I shook my head. "I'm pretty sure that was the one I locked in the lab."

"Dammit," he muttered.

"Yeah." I stood there, trying not to look as weird as I felt, standing there in just a pair of jeans and my sports bra, bandaged about my middle and on one arm. I crossed my arms over my chest, trying to make it seem natural. "We should get going. I'd rather not race the clock on the whole bombing of Onida thing."

He nodded and then looked at me. Really looked at me, coming back from that distant logical place in which he had taken refuge. I wondered what he was seeing. A scared girl with a lot of wounds? A woman without a shirt on? What? He coughed and holstered his pistol long enough to shrug out of his leather jacket. "You're going to need this if we're going back outside."

I took his jacket with a half smile. "Thanks." I slid it on, wincing a little as the leather dragged itself across old and new wounds. I zipped it up anyway and immediately felt better. It was warm, felt like armor, and smelled like him and his cologne. Stetson. A favorite around here. I put my hands in the pockets and felt three more of the epi-pens and his cell phone.

David quirked me a smile and I liked seeing him here and not in that distant place. "C'mon. If we're going to save the world, we'd better get moving."

He led the way out to the stairs to the second floor and I was happy to let him do it. I stopped to get Mister Bat. He was going to be with me until the end, one way or another. The shotgun, half covered in the acid, looked like it had fired its last shot. I stopped behind David as he looked up the stairs.

"You know this is a horror movie, right?" I asked.

David nodded. "I know. I mean, metaphorically speaking."

"Yeah. That. What I really mean is that the last one is going to be up there somewhere."

He looked relieved. "I know."

"How many bullets do you have left?"

"Thirteen."

I was happy he knew off the top of his head. "I hope it's enough."

"It will be." He smiled. "The heroes always win in the end."

I had a sinking feeling about it all and prayed that it wouldn't be a sole survivor kind of thing. He had the same kind of reckless air I have when I'm about to do something stupid to myself. I suddenly wondered if he suffered from depression or PTSD and hoped he wouldn't make a kamikaze run on the last Fedora that had to be around. I think I would rather have Onida blown up than have that.

"Ready?" he asked.

No, I thought. I nodded anyway and we both turned towards the stairs.

CHAPTER EIGHTEEN

It was a single flight of stairs, twelve steps, and we were on the second floor. There were two rooms. This first was half walled with glass and faced the runway. There were two long tables and two chairs. One table had a computer, monitor, radar screen, microphone, and a couple of other pieces of equipment I couldn't readily identify. On the other table, stacked in neat piles, were trench coats, fedoras, and the mustached masks.

David looked at them for a long time before he asked, "Is this…?"

"Yeah," I nodded.

He picked up one of the masks and shook his head. "I think you're right. I think it would be worse to see them in the disguise." He dropped it back to the table with a grimace and wiped his hand. "That isn't plastic, either."

"What is it?" Despite the look on his face, or because of it, I was curious.

"Don't know. Might be skin or a biological polymer."

I wrinkled my nose, "Ew."

"Yeah. Ew."

I turned towards the second room. It was a storage room with a door to the outside of the first story roof. The metal door had a push bar handle. I considered it. With no monster on the second floor, it had to be outside.

David came up behind me. "I'll clear the exit. If it's out there, I'll deal with it. You get to the antenna array and destroy the emitter. Good?"

I nodded. "I'll destroy everything up there if I have to."

He turned to the door, cracked it open and led with his gun. It was clear from the one side. He opened the door all the way and said, "I will deal with this. You complete the mission." From the grim set of his mouth, I knew he was looking at the last Fedora.

My mouth suddenly dry, I nodded. "I'm on it."

He flung the door open and was already shooting and running at it by the time I got my first look. It was a Fedora in full human disguise, standing on the other side of the roof, near the edge. It was dodging as many bullets as it was taking. In David's need to distract it, he wasn't aiming.

I turned from that, knowing he had his job and I had mine. I ran to the metal ladder at the corner of the second story. I climbed three rungs before I looked up and saw another Fedora on the roof of the tower. This one wasn't camouflaged. It launched itself at David's unprotected back, and I screamed his name.

He didn't have time to dodge and the second Fedora plowed into him. David hit the roof face first and, losing his grip on his gun. I couldn't let him fight both Fedoras alone. I knew he would lose and then I would die and all this would be for nothing.

I jumped down from the ladder and ran at the Fedora on top of David. It heard me coming and backhanded me with one of its spearhead hands. Only David's leather jacket kept me from getting hurt. I hit the roof, still gripping my bat. When I got up, I saw David wrestling with the second Fedora and the first one dragging itself towards David's unprotected head.

I rolled to my feet and charged the first one with my bat held high. It looked up right when I hit it as hard as I could. Mister Bat meet Mister Head. There was a satisfying crunch of bug carapace and the Fedora skittered backwards away from me towards the edge of the building. I followed it and hit it again, this time in the chest as it tried to stand. It stumbled again, closer to the edge.

I raised my bat again and hit it across the face. It stumbled back again, one foot only partly on the roof. It started to fall backwards, and one of the hands caught my bat either to pull itself back to the roof, or to pull me into the fall with it. I wasn't strong enough to hold the creature and I wasn't willing to go off the roof with it. I let my beloved bat go and watched them fall.

When the Fedora hit the front part of the Cessna parked below, it impaled itself on the Cessna's propeller, my bat tumbling from its grip. Cursing, I looked back at David and the other Fedora. David was bleeding from stab wounds in his arm and chest.

His gun was too far away for him to reach. He had resorted to his bowie knife once more and had cut off one of the spearhead hands. I ran to the pistol, picked it up and fired at the Fedora. It was the last bullet in the clip. I did the only thing I could do: I threw the gun at the Fedora where it bounced harmlessly off its back.

I had no weapons and no way to fight the thing pinning David down.

"Get the emitter!" he yelled at me.

Then I remembered the epi-pens. I had no idea if they would work but I had nothing left to try. I pulled out two of them, uncapped them, and ran for the Fedora's back. When I leapt on it, I heard David cry out, crushed by the weight of the Fedora and of me. I pressed both epi-pens in the back of its neck and fired them. If I was lucky and if it was built anything like the bugs it looked like, both adrenaline shots would reach its aorta and give the Fedora a heart attack.

I held the epi-pens to its neck until it threw me off of it. It whirled around towards me as I hit the ground. David grabbed one of its feet and it turned and stabbed him in the stomach. I screamed my rage even as it advanced.

Suddenly, it stopped, tilted its head, and opened its mandibles wide. It made the clicking noise I had heard off and on over the last three days. Then its body seized up, it limbs curling on themselves. It fell over and twitched with spastic jerks of its neck and legs, then after a moment, it was still.

David rolled to his side, groaning in pain. I ran to him and knelt. "David, are you okay?"

"The mission?" He asked.

I looked up at the radio tower and antenna array. "It can wait. I've got to help you. We've got time."

"No!" He gripped my arm in a tight grip. "Finish the mission. Save yourself. Save us." His eyes were filled with pain and need. He nodded at me.

I nodded back. "Okay. I'll destroy it. You stay here. You… you don't die."

He smiled bloodstained teeth at me. "I won't. Promise. I'm just going to rest my eyes." He let go of my arm and closed his eyes.

"No. Don't sleep!" I shook his good shoulder and he didn't move. "You can't sleep. It'll kill you!" I shook him harder and he didn't move. Panic set in and I knew if I didn't get that emitter destroyed, he would be dead within minutes.

I ran to the metal ladder and climbed up it. Once I was on the roof, I wasn't sure how to destroy the emitter when I found it. The tower was about fifteen feet tall in a pyramid shape with a lattice of steel beams to keep it stable. The rest of the myriad of equipment at the base of the tower were normal human things; a shortwave radio antenna, power cords, and a TV cable. However, I could see on the top of the tower was a square thing with what looked like a mirrored ball in the middle. It stuck out against the other panel looking emitters. That had to be it.

I looked around for something to destroy the tower with and found nothing. I wouldn't, couldn't let that stop me. I would rip it out with my bare hands if I had to. As I reached for one of the cables running up the tower to yank it out, I recognized it for what it was. Stepping back and looking up, I realized that the tower I was about to destroy was the one and only cell phone tower in the area. The airport radio tower was coupled together with the cell phone tower. Two birds, one stone.

No cell phone tower meant no cell phone signal. No cell phone signal meant no way for me to call Agent Harrison and get him to call off the bombing of Onida. David wasn't kidding when he said it was going to be 'the hard way.' And that hard way was to climb the cell tower and deal with the emitter array from up there.

My stomach dropped to the floor at the thought but I wasn't going to let my fear of heights stop me from saving David. While the tower wasn't meant to be climbed without special gear, it was possible. The canted beams connecting the sides of the metal pyramid created a makeshift ladder.

It was cold to the touch and while it was hard to balance on the tilted beams, I took one step at a time, climbing towards the goal of destroying the thing that murdered my friends, my family, and my future. I refused to look down, despite my paranoid brain's insistence that if there were eight monsters, there were probably nine, and one was either chomping down on David's face or clambering up after me.

Despite my cold hands, I was sweating by the time I got close enough to see the thing. Every muscle in my body hurt and there was a good bet that half of my wounds had reopened. Instead of thinking about that, I concentrated on my goal, my mission objective.

Now that I could see it clearly, it was about three feet across with four outer panels. Each panel was a six inch by twelve inch rectangle that bowed outward a little. It looked like it was made of wire mesh. The mirrored globe turned out to be a faceted ball of hexagonal mirrors. It was like looking up at a mirrored bug's eye. I saw how it was attached—more of that glistening crystal stuff.

I grabbed the first panel and pulled on it. It didn't budge at first and then, under my weight the arm holding it bent but wouldn't break. That had to be enough. I did that to all four panels, rocking the top of the tower back and forth. I tried not to hurt the cell tower panels but one fell when I knocked into it. I ignored that and prayed that it would still allow calls out.

The mirrored ball wouldn't come loose. In frustration I hit it, and one of the mirrors cracked. Tucking my hand into the leather of David's jacket sleeve, I pounded the mirrors, cracking and shattering them until there was nothing but bent wire stems. I grabbed what was left of the center column with both hands and pulled until the crystal cracked and the thing came loose. I nearly took a header off the top of the tower as it did, and only the power cable glued into in kept me from falling. I felt a couple of the stitches in my side tear through my flesh. Clinging to the steel support, I used the edge of the pole it was mounted on to sever the cable. Then I let it fall to the rooftop where it bounced, losing more pieces.

Exhausted and in pain, all I wanted to do was sleep. However, David was hurt. I needed to let him know that the mission was accomplished and I needed to stop the bomb. Climbing down the cell tower took a lot more out of me than I wanted to admit. At the bottom, I picked up the central piece and tossed it down to the first story rooftop before making my way down the ladder.

Every part of my brain screamed conflicting thoughts at me: *He's dead, you're too late. Call Agent Harrison. He's not dead, you saved him.*

I limped over to David holding my side. Kneeling beside him, I shook his shoulder.

"David, I did it. Mission accomplished. I did it." He didn't move or even groan. I shook his shoulder harder and felt for a pulse. I was trembling too much to tell if there was one or not. The black lines from his shoulder wound had grown and I wondered if it was the poison.

Leaning over to try to feel his breath, I felt the stitches in my side give a warning jolt of pain. I put my hand to my side and pressed in, trying to stop the pain. I felt the hardness of the last epi-pen. I still had it.

"Please, please, please," I prayed as I pressed it to his outer thigh and depressed the plunger. He didn't react. Not when the needle stabbed him in the leg. Not when the adrenaline hit his system. I went from praying to begging. "No, no, no!" I muttered over and over. In a fit of panic, I searched his pockets for more smelling salts.

I could have cried when I found four used packets and one unused one. He must have used the other four while he was driving. If not, he had been using them in secret to keep me from worrying about him. It made me want to shake him all the more. I cracked the last one under his nose and begged, "Wake up. Please, wake up!"

For a second he didn't move. Then his head twitched back away from my hand. Alive. He was alive. I grabbed his hand and said, "You can't die, you promised me. You promised you wouldn't die." I squeezed his hand hard and thought I felt a twitch in return. "You can't leave me behind. You can't leave a man behind." I knew it was dirty pool but I didn't care at the moment what was fair and what wasn't.

When the Imperial March erupted out of my pocket, I thought I was hallucinating. Then I realized I had David's phone and it was Agent Harrison. I answered the call and Tomas was there before I could say anything.

"David? Are you alright? What's your status?"

"He's hurt really bad. He's alive but I don't know for how long. You've got to send help."

"Did you succeed?" Agent Harrison asked after hesitating a moment. "Did you take down the transmitter?"

"Yes!" I wanted to rail at him for caring about that and not immediately sending help. "It's down. I killed it."

"I need proof."

I looked at the phone and realized that it was past eleven and he was determining whether or not to set the missile launch in motion. I also realized that he didn't believe me, and I had only minutes to change his mind.

"Okay. Can your phone get text messages with pictures?"

"Yes."

As much as I didn't want to leave David's side, I had no choice. "Stay on the line. I'm going to get a picture of the thing I broke and send it to you. Stay on the line."

"I'll be here."

I went over to where the broken emitter array was with its bent tines and panels. I took two pictures of it, and sent them while I told him about how I climbed the tower and broke the thing off. My panic subsided as I forced my brain to work in a logical manner. I needed to be as calm as he sounded. I needed him to believe me.

"All the mirror shards are up on the second story roof. Do you want me to go get a picture of it?"

There was no answer either way. I realized Tomas hadn't barked orders or questions at me the whole time I was talking and taking photos. I looked down at the phone and knew before I saw it that I had no signal. The emergency power to the airport had finally given out. I had no idea how much of that they heard and no way of contacting them. As far as I knew there were no other towers in the area. And even if there were, without power to them, they were just as useless as the tower right next to me.

At that moment, I had a choice. I could run downstairs, jump into Barry's truck, and try to make it to the nearest town ten miles away, hoping the truck wasn't a stick shift and that Agar still had power so I could call Tomas back... and leave David behind. Or, I could put my faith in the universe and pray that Tomas had all he needed to make his decision.

I dropped the phone and walked over to David. I was done trying to save myself and the rest of the world. I did what I could. If a missile was coming, I wasn't going to leave a man behind. I sat next to David, ignoring the waves of pain and protest coming from most of my body. I took his hand in mine and let go of the death grip I had on my sanity.

"There were eight," I muttered, rocking back and forth. I stared at nothing, painting a pretty picture in my mind's eye, one that I was willing to die happy with. I imagined David and I limping down the stairs, stopping just long enough to set the Fedora hive on fire, and then taking Barry's dark red Chevy truck out of town. David smiled at me as he drove us down Highway 83 and away from the city of the dead. He congratulated me on a job well done and told me he was proud of me. I knew there would be a hero's welcome waiting for us at the Nebraska border.

"There were eight," I repeated and smiled.

CHAPTER NINETEEN

We listened to the radio as we headed towards Valentine, Nebraska. An old-fashioned soap opera radio play was on. I leaned against David's shoulder, smelling his antiseptic cologne.

"This is Melissa Allen," Doctor Lee said. "She won't give you any trouble. The restraints are to keep her from unconsciously scratching at her bandages."

"Is she awake?" Nurse Payne asked.

"Yes, but she is non-responsive. She has been like this for nine days. This medication is the same medication she was on when she was brought in. Her file indicates that she is bipolar and schizophrenic."

"There were eight," I murmured to David as he stroked my hair.

"We don't know what that means," Doctor Lee continued. "It's the only thing she's said this entire time."

"What about her guard?"

"That's a matter for the courts." His voice was prim and disapproving as he moved around the room.

"Unofficially, why does she have a guard? If I'm to be one of her nurses, it is a good idea for me to know what she's capable of. Or what someone else believes she is capable of."

Doctor Lee lowered his voice to a confidential tone. "Rumor has it that she murdered her family. Smothered them in their sleep."

"Good gracious, this girl? And how'd she get these injuries? Running from the police? It looks like someone took a machete to her."

I didn't like the way they were talking about the patient.

"There were eight," I said to David but he didn't change the station.

"More likely, she took a serrated steak knife to herself. Look at where the wounds are: the meaty part of the thigh, the side of the bicep and a slash above her hip. It looks like she put in stitches to close the side wound. Good thing, she might have bled out otherwise." Doctor Lee's voice was unsympathetic. "Though, we still aren't certain what kind of chemical she used to burn her shoulder."

"I just can't see how a girl could do this to herself." Nurse Payne clucked her tongue. "Poor thing."

"Don't underestimate the insane. This 'poor thing' has a record."

"Then why isn't she in Ward Five?"

"Orders from on high."

"What do we do if she becomes responsive? Call the police?"

"No." Doctor Lee's voice was firm. "This goes higher than that. The Department of Homeland Security. There is a number in her file."

"Goodness. What did this girl do that warrants the DHS?"

"I don't know but I do know there is one Homeland Security agent who really wants to talk to her when… if… she recovers." Doctor Lee's tone of voice morphed from the confidential tone of prurient gossip back to cool professionalism. "Miss Allen is your most interesting patient in that regard. She eats when fed and takes pills when they are introduced, though liquids are easier through the IV. In all other aspects, you treat her like a coma patient for hygiene and the like."

"Yes, Doctor Lee." Nurse Payne's voice still had a curious, speculative quality.

"Now, as a part-time nurse…" Doctor Lee's voice faded as the two of them walked away.

I leaned forward and turned off the radio. Looking at David I asked, "There is one?"

He turned from the road to gaze at me and nodded. "Yes. There is one. Maybe you should check it out."

Coming back to myself was like seeing hours upon hours of the most boring movie in the world punctuated with exciting bits. The sound for the movie was like a half remembered dream. It was better understood in freeze frame pictures:

Snapshot: A helicopter flying in towards the airport.

Snapshot: Men in green uniforms and guns swarming the airport roof.

Snapshot: Gurneys brought out and being laid down on one.

Snapshot: A clear mask put over my face.

Snapshot: The white room with the white curtain.

Snapshot: People coming and going. Some in white. Some in green.

Snapshot: A white haired man standing by my bed, talking.

Snapshot: The head nurse and the new nurse – not Doctor Lee and Nurse Payne – walking around my bed and talking.

I looked around the room and for the first time in over a week I was seeing what was really there. I was in a private hospital room with a side glass wall and a privacy curtain. There was a TV on the wall in front of me. I was dressed in a blue and white polka dotted hospital gown and both of my wrists were restrained in soft brown leather straps.

I had a sense of déjà vu at the scene. The one previous time I had checked out like this was when I was twelve and my dog was hit by a car. It died in the street while I held it. I never did find out who killed him but I woke up, came back to myself, three days later in Saint Mary's in Pierre. This room looked exactly like that one. It made me wonder if there was a required standard for hospital rooms.

I looked down to see if my fingers could reach any of the buttons that controlled the bed or called for the nurse. I didn't like being restrained, no matter how much it was for my own good. This time, the call button was right there. Last time… I didn't like to think much about last time.

I hit the call button. I remembered what the nurses had said and wondered if I had made the whole thing up. I hurt a lot but the idea that I murdered Sharon and Matt hurt so much more. I decided that if it was true, I would find a way to kill myself. Anyone who could murder their own family didn't deserve to live.

I waited for a couple minutes for the nurse to come in and then almost gave her a heart attack.

"Did you twitch against the call button again?" the head nurse asked when he came in.

"No. I'm awake now," I answered. He froze a couple steps from me. He was a short, slender guy with blond hair and glasses. "I pushed the button so you could sit me up and inform… whoever needed to be informed… that I'm awake."

He stepped to my side, did as I requested and asked, "How are you feeling?"

"I hurt but I'm okay. I'd like to have the restraints removed but I'll understand if you say no." I saw the chagrined look on his face when he realized that I had heard what he said to the other nurse.

He nodded. "I think it will be fine. I do have to ask you not to leave the room, and if you need to go to the bathroom, call for assistance." As his hands worked to free me, he added, "I need to inform people that you're awake and aware of yourself again."

I smiled wryly, looking past him, at the guard in the doorway on the phone. "I think that's already being done."

The guard by the door was moved into my room with me. He spent his time reading or sitting quietly. I had no wish to make small talk. Nor was I ready to ask about David, not that I was sure he would know anything about him. Plus, I still wasn't sure I hadn't created David as an imaginary partner in crime. Fortunately, I only had to wait a couple of hours for Agent Tomas Harrison to show up.

I knew Tomas as soon as he arrived. He was shorter than expected but still imposing. His lined face looked tired and his eyes were much bluer than they appeared on the phone. He walked into my room and dismissed the guard with a nod. He closed the door and I wondered if he had changed his clothes from a stiff button up shirt to the polo shirt to make me feel more comfortable. I decided he hadn't. He didn't seem like the kind of man who made allowances for anyone.

After a moment of sizing each other up, I asked, "Is he dead? Was he ever there at all?" It was better to rip the Band-Aid off all at once than to deal with a thousand tiny pains.

"If you are speaking of Agent Hood, no and yes." Tomas walked over to my bedside.

The relief I felt was overwhelming. Tears sprang to my eyes. I hadn't realized just how much I was holding back. The fear that I was so insane that I made up the Fedoras and murdered my sister and her husband was gone. With those two words—no and yes—I was able to trust myself again. Even better, David was still alive. He'd made it.

Tomas put a warm hand on my forearm. "He is alive and well enough. He was in surgery for a few hours due to some of the wounds he sustained but he is alive. I'm told the adrenaline shot you gave him kept his heart beating."

"Did we kill them all? The Fedoras?" It was important that I knew this. If not, I would be having nightmares about them for the rest of my life—which I probably would be anyway, but who's counting?

He nodded. "As far as we can tell, yes. We found eight carcasses. One in the school. One near the water tower and one on it. One outside a house and one inside that house." I saw him watching me count off each one he mentioned. "One in the airport. One on top of a Cessna. One on top of the airport roof."

"There were eight," I said with a sigh. "And the signal? The one that created the sleep-death field?"

"Gone. We never did pinpoint its source but we believe that this was only a scout force. We'll be studying the stars and scanning for that signal from now on."

His face changed to a more neutral expression and I knew that there was bad news to come. He took his hand off my arm and I understood that he was no longer being empathetic. He was back to being coolly professional.

"You and Agent Hood did a good job and I commend you. You might have saved the world from an invasion."

"But…?"

"But the world can never know."

"Is that why the hospital thinks I murdered my family?"

"Yes."

"What about what happened to South Dakota? What are you going to tell the world about why all those people died?"

Tomas looked away from me for a moment before he said, "We're not going to tell them anything. It will remain an ongoing investigation. A mystery and a quarantine zone for years to come. By the time we open up South Dakota again, we *will* have a plausible explanation."

"You really think that's going to work?"

"I think the thousands of conspiracy theorists out there will do our job for us for a while." He half-smiled. "Besides, what would you believe? A rushed explanation with holes or one of the many theories that are already floating around out there—like this was a terrorist attack or an experiment gone wrong? Or a field of electronic transmissions from an extraterrestrial source that made the victims fall asleep and then turned their brains off?"

He had a point. No one would believe the truth. The more I thought about it, the more I realized they shouldn't know the truth. "If they did believe the truth, there would be a worldwide panic with no way to soothe people. No enemy we could point at and say, 'There's your danger.' Unless, of course, you showed them the Fedora bodies."

"So, for now, we all keep our mouths shut. Also, the official designation is *Mega Aphis*."

"Good to know." I closed my eyes and wondered when he was going to get to the part about tossing me into a very dark hole for the rest of my life. "And me?"

"You still have three and half years left on your house arrest sentence and no sponsoring family." He hesitated and I could see him choosing his words carefully. "By order of the highest authority, in thanks for your service to your country, you will be remanded to a special care facility run by the State Department."

I tried to figure out what that meant and failed. "I'm going to be put in a government hospital where I will be considered an insane murderer?" I guessed.

He frowned. "No. You will remain under house arrest and fostered by the State Department until you are eighteen. We're not going to punish you for saving the world. But you have special needs and your experiences can never go public. At the age of eighteen, your case will be revisited."

I thought about this for a long moment and he allowed the time for me to think. I appreciated that. I did have special needs—Abilify, lamotrigine, hydroxyzine, and Prazosin—not to mention I was only fourteen. No state in the world was going to allow me to emancipate. I was stuck between a rock and a hard place.

"Okay," I said, feeling a little like I was giving in, even when it was the best option I had.

He smiled at me. It was a genuine smile by the crinkle of his eyes. "You really did an amazing thing, Melissa. We're going to take care of you."

"Can I see David?"

"No," Tomas said. "He's not on site. He's in recovery and being debriefed."

My heart sank. "Is he in trouble?"

"There's trouble and then there's *trouble*."

I think he meant to be comforting. It didn't work. Not in the least. I really wanted to see David with my own eyes to make sure he was okay.

"In the meantime, we need to get you out of here and get you to where you're going."

Getting me out of the hospital in Valentine, Nebraska was much ado about nothing. A matronly woman with gray hair in a bun who introduced herself as Mrs. Drury brought me new clothing. She stayed in the room to help me dress. She moved through the process of dealing with my IV, bandages, and clothing with the calm efficiency of a nurse. In truth, she made me so nervous that I didn't try to make small talk like I usually do with new people. There was no asking questions to keep her off balance.

She escorted me to the admissions desk and signed me out. By escort, I mean, led me around by my unhurt arm. The nurses watched me like they would a cute but vicious animal—with a wary curiosity. I was bundled into a black SUV, and I wondered if Tomas had lied and I was going to some sort of government prison.

The trip was quiet and tense for me. We drove straight to Miller Field Airport. Without a call to anyone, the SUV drove up to the terminal, stopped, and let us off. Mrs. Drury pulled a satchel from the back. She hit the side of the SUV twice and stepped back.

As soon as the SUV drove away from the terminal, Mrs. Drury looked at me and smiled, her stiff posture relaxing. "There now. Plenty for them to gossip about for a while."

I was surprised. "Pardon?"

She pulled her hair down out of its bun and laughed at the look on my face. "My name is Heather Shaker and I'll be your guardian for the next three and a half years. Call me Heather. But not Mother, despite the fact that I do appear to be a professional mom from a certain point of view." She offered me her hand.

I shook it out of habit and asked, "What?" My mind couldn't wrap itself around the change in her demeanor.

"There were appearances to be kept up. No one will question where you've gone because everyone who's treated you already believes they know. You were taken into custody and to jail by the government. There will be gossip, of course, but no one will really care or look into the matter." She turned towards the waiting private plane. "They're happy and we're happy."

"Where are we going?" I still wasn't sure if I should be happy or not. I hurried to catch up with her.

"I actually don't know. You're my new assignment. A special kind of special."

"What did you do before… this?" I didn't even know what 'this' was but I was beginning to like her.

"I ran safe houses abroad until some government idiot blew my cover. I've been dangling in the wind for the last couple of months. You might say I'm also a special kind of special. It's kind of nice to know what I'll be doing for a while." She tilted her head. "We can be special together."

I stopped at the ladder to the plane, "If you don't know where we're going, who does?"

"The pilot and our new liaison."

"Who is that? Tomas? I mean Agent Harrison?" Now that I was back in the real world, I knew I needed to mind my manners a bit more.

"No, that would be me," a male voice said from the top of the ladder.

I knew that voice. I turned and saw David standing there with a cane. He looked like he had been through the wringer but the black circles of fatigue were gone. I hurried up to him and gave him a careful hug. He hugged me back. I looked at him, searching his face. "Are you okay? Are you in trouble? I'm so glad you're... real-ly alive." I almost said real. I think he understood that.

Heather made us get in the plane and sit down before we talked more.

"I'm all right. You saved my life. Thank you. I'm still recovering. And, not really in trouble, though, I've been taken off of field duty pending an investigation and my injuries and such." He waved a hand. "Until then, it has been determined that I'm the best one suited to be your liaison to the department."

"Really?"

"Yep."

"Where we going? Also, are you sure this isn't just another way of..." I glanced at Heather, not wanting to offend but not knowing how to say it any other way, "...putting you in a cell next to me?"

"I'm sure," he said with a smile. "If it is, we'll deal with it together."

I sat back and nodded. "All right."

Come what may, I had someone I could depend on and he knew he could depend on me.

NEVER LET ME LEAVE

BOOK TWO

In the state of North Dakota, there stood an improbable building in the shape of a pyramid with its top cut off. Once used as a radar system for a brief time, it was now a supposedly defunct complex. The reality was something more. It was a government building filled with secrets—both personal and federal. For those in the know, this building was now referred to as "the PAR Lab."

The PAR Laboratory had two above ground floors filled with offices and communication equipment. It also had five below ground floors filled with much more esoteric projects, experiments, and test subjects. A small group of scientists and guards manned the complex twenty-four hours a day, seven days a week. Level E, the lowest of the underground levels, housed the most dangerous test subjects and experiments. There, the secrets bred like rats.

The underground levels were a marvel of secret technology. Impenetrable walls with the ability to become airtight at the push of a button. Ambient lighting that gave the rooms and hallways a soft glow. All of it was on an automatic timer that matched the earth's rotation and motion of the rising and setting sun.

The human and the alien stood on either side of the glass barrier. The clear wall looked weak, but both knew from experience that it was stronger than diamond—stronger than either of them could break. They spoke in the only way the alien could speak: mind-to-mind.

"Soon."

"Yes. Soon. We cannot make it go any faster. When all of the children are here and are a distraction, that's the best time for your escape."

"You've been wrong before."

"Yes. I know. I'm sorry. Is there...?"

"Shhhh."

The alien began to pace in front of the barrier. The other followed in an unconscious mimic. They were silent for a time, walking the clear wall between them. The human's feet made soft sounds against the uncarpeted floor. The alien made no sound at all.

"Time is of the essence."

"Yes."

"The testing begins next week."

"Yes."

"Escape is possible. I promise."

"Escape is inevitable. I can share myself with many if need be."

"Then what?"

They stopped and stared at each other, not moving and only one of them breathing. The lights in the hallway dimmed, indicating the time change and the coming shift change. The human glanced around and stepped to the glass, breath fogging it. The alien moved forward until they were face-to-face.

"Then what?

"Then we find suitable shells and we come."

"How many?"

"Many."

"And you'll fix this world? You promised you'd fix everything."

"The pact will be upheld."

The human stepped back and smiled. "The pact will be upheld." The words were murmured aloud with pleasure. Then, with another look up and down the hallway, the human hurried away. The alien watched and waited.

THE PYRAMID OF NORTH DAKOTA

CHAPTER ONE

It's not every day that you get your ass handed to you by a forty year old woman… unless, of course, you're me and you're in the middle of your daily training exercise. I'm Melissa Allen, savior of the world and convicted delinquent. My reward for saving the planet was to *not* be sent to juvie. Instead, I've been remanded into the custody of one Heather Shaker, DHS agent and the woman currently giving me a new set of bruises.

Believe it or not, I haven't been this happy in years.

Heather came at me with a series of punches to cover the leg sweep she was going for. I managed to block and dodge both like clockwork, but I fell for a gut punch feint, leaving my face unprotected. Her fist lightly clipped my jaw. I took it and tried to press the attack. Part of training is knowing how to take a punch—even if it was only at sparring strength. She blocked my punches with ease.

"C'mon, Mel. You'd be down by now. Focus." She moved forward, her feet barely touching the padded floor of the finished basement that was now our own private workout room.

I danced back out of her range—and by "dance," I mean backpedaled as fast as I could. It wasn't graceful and I didn't run into any of the other exercise equipment stationed around the edges of the room. Dodging didn't require grace, thank goodness.

I didn't have the breath for a snappy comeback, despite wanting to give her one. Not that I could think of anything at the moment. Heather pulled back as well and made me come to her. Not a smart move. Never said I was smart. Just determined. I rushed her, throwing her a solid kick to thigh and following with a couple punches that she blocked by reflex. I longed for the day that my reflexes were as trained as hers.

I needed more power to get through Heather's defenses. We both knew it. Continuing my advance, I threw my entire weight behind a punch, trying to bring her down. She beat it aside and stepped in, placing her hip next to mine. Before I could pull back, she had my wrist in hand and used my momentum to toss me over her hip and hard onto the thankfully padded ground.

I lay on my back, panting for breath, gazing at the white ceiling of the workout room. My eyes, as always, were drawn to the north corner. By the time I'd traced the crack from the corner to the end, Heather was standing over me and I was well on my way to getting control of my breath.

"What did you do wrong?"

"The same thing I do wrong every morning now, Pinky: I got into a sparring match with you." I wiped at my dripping face with a grimy sleeve and grimaced. Laundry was a never-ending battle of stinky, sweaty workout clothes.

Heather shook her head and suppressed a smile. "Be serious." She offered me a hand.

I groaned as she helped me up. "Too fast. Too much. Didn't control it enough."

"Right. I controlled the fight from beginning to end. I made you come to me. I made it so you over extended yourself. What should you have done instead?"

Before I could answer, my phone binged its 8:00 A.M. alarm. "Saved by the bell." I stretched my back and heard it pop before I went to the phone, silencing it. There, at the table, as Heather watched from across the room, I took my pills: Two hundred milligrams of lamotrigine for bipolar swings. Thirty milligrams of Abilify so I see reality and not something that isn't there. Twenty-five milligrams of hydroxyzine to keep Captain Paranoia at bay.

It was a chemical mix that finally worked and would probably keep on working for another half-year or more—if I was lucky. I used to say that I lived by the clock but I survived by the pills. These days, I still live by a clock but I do more than survive. The pills are there to help me enjoy life and to keep me on an even keel. Though, taking them is a constant reminder of everything I've lost: My parents, my family, my dog, my favorite nurse. I even missed Doctor Lee, the man who'd discovered the right pharmaceutical mix for me; and Bill, my parole officer. All of it, and them, were gone. It was nice when I didn't think of these things twice a day.

"Okay. Rest time is over. Let's go another round." Heather stretched her neck side-to-side then moved to the center of the room.

I wiped my face with a hand towel and shook my head. "You know I'm better at shooting than hand-to-hand."

"That's why we spar daily and only shoot twice a week."

"Along with accelerated school work."

"Better to get you your G.E.D. next year as soon as you turn sixteen." Heather smiled and beckoned. "C'mon. One more round."

I was the kid Heather never had because she was too busy running safe houses in Europe for the DHS, or some other three-lettered government agency, until some idiot blew her cover on national TV. She had high hopes for me. In truth, she was the best guardian a girl like me could have. But, sometimes, her grand plans scared me.

"Really? C'mon... I'm not in the mood. Can't we be done?" Sometimes, the whine worked. Sometimes, it didn't.

Her face darkened like storm clouds on the horizon. "Moods are for movies and candlelit dinners. Defend yourself." Then she was running at me.

I knew she meant business by the thin press of her lips and I needed to fight. I threw my towel at her. It gave me a scant second to get ready and get away from the table so she couldn't pin me to it. She threw a couple of hard punches that would've knocked me for a loop if I hadn't gotten out of the way.

Moving in quickly, I feinted to the left and came in hard from the right with several punches, followed by a quick knee. Heather blocked most of the blows and returned at least one for each I delivered. She surprised me with a high kick that glanced the side of my head and made me blink, seeing double.

When she didn't press her advantage, I rushed in and grabbed her shirt in both hands. Twisting my hips as I was taught and driving down with my fists, I rolled Heather over my thigh and sent her crashing to the padded floor.

Heather lay there for a moment before giving a soft groan that was half laugh. "I'm going to feel that in the morning."

Still surprised that the move worked, I offered her my hand. She took it in both of hers and put all her weight against me. As I braced my leg to pull her up, she snapped her foot out and tapped the back of my locked knee. It buckled as she pulled and I landed on the ground next to her, face first.

"That was good improvisation with the towel and good on hip throw," Heather said. "But the fight's not over until both parties agree."

"Sometimes, I hate you." I lay there for a moment longer before shifting up to my elbows. "Would you have actually hurt me if I… I don't know… not fought back?"

"I'd have given you a black eye to remember me by. Fights are a surprise. Fights don't care if you're tired, hurt, or just not in the mood." She rolled to her feet in a smooth motion of long practice.

She didn't look at me as she spoke. Something was off. I could tell that much. I considered her for a long minute. "You know, you don't usually fall for the hip throw. I'd like to say I'm getting better but…" I let the unspoken question hang in the air. My stomach turned over in drunken loops when she looked away.

"Maybe I was distracted." She popped her neck and glanced down at me then turned away.

"Oh, hell. What's going on?" Heather had been pushing me hard the last couple of days. I thought she was irritated at something I'd done. Guess I was wrong.

Heather walked over to the table, grabbed her water bottle, and drank. She wiped the sweat from her forehead, her eyes still on the floor.

"Heather?" I curled up, hugging my knees to my chest. This wasn't like her. In the four months we'd been together, Heather had been my surrogate mom, parole officer, teacher, combat trainer, and friend. She'd been open and honest with me the whole time. I didn't always like what she had to say, but she was on the level. This new reluctance to speak scared the crap out of me.

"David's coming over." Heather turned, her eyes looking above me. "He's going to tell you about a… thing… you're going to participate in."

I stood, all my aches and pains forgotten. "Thing? What kind of thing?"

"I can't tell you. I'm not allowed." She took a deep breath and let it out. "I don't have all the details. Or practically any details."

My mind raced with ideas of this "thing" I would be participating in. I got up and walked to her. We were almost eye to eye when she finally looked at me. "You've got some details."

"Yes." She glanced again.

"Tell me?'

She shook her head. "I can't."

"You're killing me." I turned to the table, leaned on it, and spoke in an exaggerated wounded tone of voice. "First, you basically say that I didn't get that hip throw because I'm good but because of a *thing*. Now, you know something about this *thing* but won't tell me." I glanced at her out of the corner of my eye to see if my lame attempt at humor had any effect.

Heather gave me a half-smile and shrugged. "All I really know is that you'll be gone for a week."

She had my attention. "Gone? Where? With whom? Will you be there?"

"Gone. Yes. Where? I don't know, yet. With who? I don't know. Will I be there? No." Heather shook her head. "We both have to wait until David gets here and lets us know what's going on."

CHAPTER TWO

I sat in the living room, watching for David out the front window. I hadn't seen that much of him since he got me and Heather settled in our place in Grand Forks, North Dakota. He was always off seeing to his other duties. The one time I asked about it, he just said, "You're not the only one who's saved the world." He wouldn't say anything more after that.

The idea of it made me jealous and still does. I suppose after a DHS agent comes running into a quarantine zone to try and help you, you get attached. Especially when your family is dead. It's not like I'm in love with him or anything. He's old. Like more than twice my age. Had to be over thirty with his time in the army and then Homeland Security.

I jumped out of my seat as soon as his fedmobile—a generic silver, four door sedan—pulled up. I was out the door and running down the path before he was out of the car. I stopped at the edge of the walkway and watched him, not believing what I was seeing. I laughed, shaking my head. He was in a black suit, black tie, and white shirt. He gave me a look as he left his sunglasses in the car and closed the door.

"You're taking this *men in black* thing a bit seriously," I said as he approached.

He gave me a wry smile and then a hug. "Had a meeting. Needed to look like I knew what I was talking about to the suits."

Older or not, I had to appreciate how cute he was. A couple inches taller than me, David was an attractive Asian man with the clean cut features of Mr. Sulu from Star Trek. "With Tom? How is he?"

"If you mean Agent Tomas Harrison, yes. He was one of them. And he is as he always is."

"Grumpy." David gave me a wink of agreement. We walked to the front door together. "So, meeting with him and other high mucky-mucks?"

"As you say." David nodded. "Hello Heather."

"Hello." She gave me a look. "Couldn't even wait for him to get in to pounce on him, eh? We're going to have to add lessons in patience to our curriculum."

"Ha!" I said. "Lost cause." I skipped inside and led the way to the living room. "Besides, I didn't pounce on the *thing*. I'm going to wait until he tells me about the *thing*." Heather and David glanced at each other in a way I did not like. "I mean… that's why he's here, right?"

David shrugged and took a seat across from me on the couch. "Well, yes. There is something I'm here to talk to you about." He glanced at Heather again. She shook her head.

I noticed she leaned against the doorjamb to the room, making herself available as needed but not really part of the conversation. Her face was in a neutral, hiding-her-feelings pose. I turned back to David and saw that he had the same neutral expression as well.

"So, I'm going somewhere?" I prompted.

"Yes. What else do you know?"

I shrugged. "That's it. I'm going somewhere and Heather won't be there." I was surprised at how much that last bit scared me. I felt my happy mood drain away bit by bit. My gut told me I wasn't going to like whatever this *thing* was.

David nodded, face still neutral. "Okay. Both are true, but it's not going to be all that bad. Promise."

"Right. So… details?"

"I told you that you weren't the only one who's saved the world, right?"

"Yeah."

"Well, there's enough of you, and enough highly classified things going on, that my superiors want to see if there's a correlation between you guys. You'll be going to the PAR Lab for a week for medical and physical evaluations."

I slumped in my chair, thinking, as I stomped on my rising panic. Panic wouldn't help now. Information would. "More of 'you guys.' Adults or teenagers?"

"Teenagers."

My relief was mixed with annoyance. I wasn't all that special after all. How many different ways could the world be saved? "Just a week? Seven days?"

David hesitated. "Yes. I believe so. That's what was scheduled."

I jumped on that. "But you don't know for sure?"

He shook his head but raised his hand to placate me. "I'm hedging because they may find something that might need more study. Most likely not."

My heart crashed to the floor. "This is it. They've decided that they're locking me up."

"No." Heather took a step into the room. "They won't."

"No." David's word echoed Heather's. "No. I promise you that. You are coming home."

I looked at Heather. She came over and put a hand on my shoulder. It was a comforting warmth, but it didn't do a thing to shift the lump of fear in the pit of my stomach. "Can you make it so, if there needs to be more studies, I get to come home in-between? I mean, I'm going to need my pills and… stuff."

David looked between me and Heather as he nodded. "I'll see to it. For all of you. This isn't a prison. This is a research lab. All of you should have time to go home after the first round of tests."

I couldn't see her face but I think Heather was just as unhappy as I was. "Where are you going to be while all this is going on?"

"Nearby. You'll be staying at the PAR Lab itself. I'll be offsite but still within the campus proper. But, I'll be there during the day. I'm going to have daily meetings and progress reports. Remember, I'm a glorified go between. Agent Harrison is working on something for all of this. I think you'll like it when everything gets approved."

I tilted my head at him and said nothing. Everyone had grand plans for me but no one was asking me what *I* wanted. Part of me appreciated it. Part of me was irritated. Either way, I knew I couldn't do anything about it. Technically, I was still serving out my house arrest sentence and not just living a normal life—no matter how much I enjoyed living with Heather. The absence of an electronic monitor was nothing more than a privilege. In truth, the government could do what they wanted with me until I was eighteen, when my sentence was done and I became 'of age' as they say.

"I like what Agent Harrison is working on for you guys if that counts for anything." David cocked his head, mimicking my posture. When I didn't say anything, he asked. "Are you going to be alright?"

I shrugged, still feeling deflated and scared. "I suppose I will be. I don't really have a choice. Do I?" I didn't wait for an answer I knew I wouldn't like. "When does this week start anyway?"

"Today. Well, tomorrow officially. But I need to take you in for processing today."

"What?" Heather's hand squeezed my shoulder hard and kept me in my seat as I started to jump up. "What do you mean?"

He gestured to me with open palms. "I mean, I got the call yesterday that everything was in place. All of the doctors and equipment had arrived and that they were just waiting for you to arrive."

"Holy crap," I breathed. I wanted to run in ninety different directions at once.

Heather hunkered down next to me. "Think of it as a working vacation. You won't have to spar with me or do school work. Take your books and relax while you're there. And," she glanced at David for confirmation, "there will be other kids who have gone through something like what you've gone through. Maybe you'll make some friends."

"Oh, yeah. Broken kids like me who happened to save the world. I'm sure we're going to be the best of buds. We can have sleepovers after we get tested like rats." I stood, pushing her hand off my shoulder. I ignored her hurt look. I needed to be alone to process this betrayal. "I'm going to go pack for a week's vacation in a lab."

Neither of them tried to stop me as I stalked out of the living room. I stopped partway down the hall and listened. Adults speak the truth when they think the kids aren't listening. I learned that lesson a long time ago. David and Heather were both quiet. Then Heather said, "Promise me on your honor that Melissa is coming home. Don't you dare lie to me."

"I promise. All it is, is a series of tests. They want to test all of them at once to see what they can find." David paused. "I swore to her that she wasn't going to be locked away and I meant it. I still mean it."

"You realize if something like that does happen, I'm coming after her." Heather's voice was soft and made me shiver, but also made me feel a tiny bit better.

"I'll be right there with you." David sounded just as determined as Heather had.

Mollified that at least Heather and David were still on my side, looking out for me, I headed upstairs to my room to do the packing I needed to do.

What does one wear to a laboratory for testing? I decided comfort was key and my usual uniform of jeans, t-shirts, and sweatshirts should do.

I paused and thought about it. I would be meeting other kids. I decided at least one nice shirt as well. I doubted the doctors in the lab would be interested in what I was wearing as they poked and prodded me.

I scowled. I wasn't overly fond of doctors and the last two I did like were dead. The new one I had—my DHS assigned psychiatrist—wasn't too bad. At least she listened when I told her my current drugs were working.

Brushing the black cobwebs from my suitcase, I put it on the bed and started to pack. A week's worth of jeans, shirts, and exercise clothing takes up a lot of space. But not too much space that I couldn't bring Mister Bat with me. There was no way I was leaving what amounted to my best friend behind. Next to the bedroom doorway my trusty friend stood. Twenty-two inches of hard hitting aluminum with "Mister Bat" written on him in purple marker. He wasn't the original Mister Bat but he would do.

I was dismayed to see black cobwebs wreathing him. Had it been so long since I'd practiced with him? Looking around my bedroom, I realized that there were black cobwebs in the corners of the room and a black cobweb crawling up one side of my mirror. I brushed Mister Bat free of the dust and cobwebs before I put him in the suitcase. A little grimy or not, I wasn't going anywhere without him.

As my hand came away dirty, I wrinkled my nose and rubbed my hand against my jeans, leaving a black smear there. I knew I needed to give the room a quick cobweb clean up before I left. I didn't want Heather thinking I was a disaster of a kid when she looked at my room—no matter how true that was.

Hurrying to the bathroom, I stopped at the sight of me covered in dust and dirt. Even my hair had straggles of black cobwebs in them. This was going from bad to worse in a hurry. There was no way I was going to let David or the doctors see me like this. I quickly washed my hands, then my face. My skin shone pink and squeaky clean against my grubby clothing. I would have to change before I went back downstairs.

I turned and came face-to-face with Heather. I jumped with a yelp of surprise. Heather twitched back, her hands coming up in a defensive pose.

I rubbed the side of my face, trying to push my bedraggled hair behind my ear in an attempt to look neater than I was. "You scared me."

"I'm sorry." Heather relaxed her stance and half-smiled. "I just came up to see if you needed any help."

I looked at her. She could see me. She wasn't reacting to the dirt and grime. Something wasn't right here. I shook my head. "No. I'm good. But… I want to take two weeks' worth of my pills with me. Is that alright?"

She nodded. "Yes. I'll put it together for you." Heather turned away then turned back. "You sure you don't need help? You look a little out of sorts."

I glanced in the mirror and was not surprised to see the dirt, grime, and cobwebs all gone. I did look a little shaken. I put on a brave smile and shook my head. "Nah. I'm good. Almost ready. Thanks for getting my pills for me."

"It's going to be okay, kiddo. I promise. So, shake a leg. You need to leave soon."

I waited until she was gone to look at myself in the mirror again. Still clean. I looked down at my jeans. Also clean. I returned to my room. Once more, I wasn't surprised to see the black cobwebs were gone. Sitting on my bed with a sigh, I rubbed my face and thought about what it meant.

Great. Hallucinations. Just what I needed. Black cobwebs were new. I wondered if they were the new black butterfly. I also wondered what they meant. There was so much they could stand for: Feeling unused, unloved, obsolete. Foggy in mind. Feeling dirty and worthless. Or, maybe they were just what my mind conjured on the spot with no rhyme or reason. I was broken in the brain after all. It could be any or all of those things.

Not surprised. Months without stress and then a sudden shock, my mind commented.

The question is... are the hallucinations because of the stress or do they just have crappy timing?

No, my other voice said. *The real question is: have you had hallucinations in the last four months and just not noticed they were hallucinations?*

I had no answer for that. I really didn't know. But now, I had no choice but to continue to get ready and go get tested at a federal lab. I really hoped my hallucinations didn't follow me there. And, if they did, I'd catch on to them being not real before it was too late.

CHAPTER THREE

We spent most of the ninety minute trip in silence. David tried to make conversation but I couldn't keep up my end of it. I was too worried about what the week was going to bring, how I was going to hide my hallucinations, how I was going to convince everyone not to lock me in a cell. In my mind's eye, I was already locked in an oubliette and forgotten.

I'd write about the hallucinations in my journal once I had time. It was something my new doctor, Doctor Ferguson, asked me to do. She had listened to me when I told her everything was working as expected and hadn't immediately tried to experiment on me with new drugs and treatments. I figured I owed her honesty at our twice monthly meetings. I mean, she knew the truth of me and what I'd been through after all. Besides, the short, black woman with iron in her hair and her spine seemed like the kind of woman who could tell when you were lying. I had the feeling that it wouldn't go well for anyone if she did catch me in a lie.

"Almost there," David said, breaking me out of my spiraling thoughts of dread.

I looked up and all thoughts of hallucinations and honesty fled my mind. Before me in the distance, but coming closer, was a fenced complex with nine standard buildings between one and six stories tall in a cluster. They stood to the side of a huge building that had my attention. It looked like a pyramid with its top chopped off. Wide, open fields spread out from the complex until they hit several dozen three-pronged windmills.

"I don't believe it." I shook my head. "It's a pyramid. Why didn't you tell me?"

"What? So you could go look up 'pyramids of North Dakota' on Google Maps or *Atlas Obscura*?" He gave me a half shrug as he turned off the main road, through the unguarded fence opening, and into the small group of very ordinary looking government buildings. "Where's the sense in that? It would've made you worry all the more."

"You're damn right it would've." I only had eyes for the pyramid structure with a large disc on each of its faces. "You should've told me. I'm going to be living in there for the next week?"

He parked the car in front of building nearest to the pyramid—which wasn't all that near in the grand scheme of things at about a football field away. "No, you aren't going to live there for the next week. You're going to live *under* it for the next week." Then he got out of the car.

I scrambled out after him. "Under? What do you mean under?"

David pulled my suitcase from the trunk, popped up the handle, and handed it to me. "Just what I said. Think of the PAR Lab like an iceberg. You're only looking at the top ten percent. What you can see is normal offices and communication equipment. All of the secured offices, labs, quarters, and such are underground." He headed towards the building.

For a brief moment, I thought about refusing to go inside. But, that would just embarrass him and me. I hurried to catch up to him but didn't get there in time to ask my last question—why wasn't there a guard at the entrance to the complex? Instead, I shut my mouth and followed him inside the building.

It was about as generic federal décor as you could get: off white floors, pale green walls, old pictures of architectural drawings of the complex, and an American flag in one corner. There was a dark haired woman in a green army uniform at a desk with a counter. To either side of the desk was a closed door. David neither stopped nor spoke to the woman. He gave her a nod then walked through the left hand door. I followed while she watched us, her hands hidden beneath the desk.

We entered a long hallway with no doors with the same pale green walls and off white floor. The flickering florescent lights were an added bonus of creepy.

"This is every murder hallway ever. I'm going to have nightmares about it," I whispered. I couldn't help it. I felt like I needed to keep my voice low. The wheels of my suitcase added an unnerving soundtrack to our muffled, echoing footsteps.

"It's all part of the plan." David's voice was low, too.

"What? To give me nightmares?"

"No. To keep intruders confused and at bay." We came to a T intersection and David turned left without hesitating. We were treated to a duplicate long hallway. "Most people who don't know where they're going automatically choose the right side choice of door and hallway. That way leads to a set of benign offices were the normal administration of the complex happens. It's also staffed with well-trained armed personnel." He paused at the closed door at the end of the hall. "No one comes here who shouldn't be here. If they do, they are escorted off immediately."

"What if they fight?"

He glanced over his shoulder. "Then they are dealt with." Pulling out a white keycard, David showed it to me. "Here's where the real offices begin." He swiped the card against the upper part of the doorjamb that didn't look any different than the rest of the doorjamb. The metal door automatically swung inward.

It was like we stepped into another world. The room was clearly an antechamber into the rest of the offices. The floor was carpeted in an industrial grey-blue office carpet. There was a couch on the wall opposite the desk. The walls were white. Two people waited for us: a visibly armed white man in black fatigues standing behind the desk and a dusky-skinned woman in slacks, button up blouse, and lab coat standing in front of the door opposite us. The woman smiled. The man did not.

The woman stepped forward and held out her hand to me. "Hello. I'm Lakshmi Gowda. You can call me Lakshmi if you like. Or Doctor Gowda if you'd be more comfortable with that."

I gave her an awkward handshake as I glanced side-eye at David. He was smiling. "Uh. Hi. I'm Melissa."

Lakshmi nodded to the guard then to David. "I'll take it from here."

"Wait!" I grabbed David's arm, then paused when he looked down at me. "Can I call you?" It was the only thing I could think to ask. "While I'm here, I mean?"

David glanced at Lakshmi and she nodded. "There's a cell tower close to here. Your phone should work underground."

David patted my hand still gripping his arm. "Sure. No problem. FaceTime?"

I shook my head. "Skype. That way it won't matter if you're at your computer or not. 8:10pm each night after I take my pills?"

Again, he looked at Lakshmi. This time she paused and thought before she said, "I think that'll work. If there's a test happening during that time, I'll let you know that day and you can reschedule."

"Okay. 8:10 each night."

I let go of his arm and gave him a smile. "Cool. Talk to you tonight."

"Will do." David returned my smile and touched my arm briefly before he turned away and walked out the door we'd come in.

I didn't have time to do more than watch the door we'd come through close before the other door opened. I followed Lakshmi down the hallway filled with doors—both open and closed as she spoke. We passed offices, meeting rooms, a break room, and a kitchen. Her long black braid tick-tocked like a pendulum as we walked.

"We have a pretty busy week planned for you and the other kids: physical stress tests, mental stress tests, psychological tests, blood draws, problem solving skill tests. There's so much we need to pack in because we only have a week that all of you are here. You're not afraid of needles, are you?" Lakshmi didn't look at me as she spoke.

I shook my head, then I answered aloud, "No."

"Good. I never liked needles myself."

I noticed that while there were windows, they had a white film over them obscuring everything outside. Though, they glowed with sunshine. At least, I thought it was sunlight.

"Lakshmi? Are we already underground?"

"What do you think?" She paused before yet another door at the end of the hallway to peer at me with interest.

I paused before I spoke, looking back the way we'd come. There was a faint but noticeable uphill feel. "I think we are. I think we've been going down this whole time. And the windows… I think they're just lights."

"Good eye. Yes. We're underground. But not in the secured part where we'll be."

"That guard wasn't secured?"

She gave a laugh. "Ben? He's more window dressing and monitoring. Oh, don't get me wrong. If need be, he knows how to do his job of keeping people out." She swiped her white keycard against a blank part of the wall and the door opened. "This area is administration and our 'public' offices. Through that elevator," she pointed to the middle of the hallway, "is where the real work of the PAR Lab happens."

We walked to the elevator. It looked ordinary enough when it opened. Though, the buttons were labeled: 2, 1, A, B, C, D, and E. Lakshmi swiped her card against a visible black plate. The light at the top turned from red to green and she pressed the "A" button. We went down one level from Level 1 to Level A. When we exited, we were at one end of a long hallway.

It was disorienting after entering in the middle of a hallway. I hesitated just outside the elevator door and got my bearings. To the left were a series of doors, irregularly spaced out, starting with a storage closet door, then open double-doors where I could see a refrigerator. Most of the other doors were single and closed with no windows into the rooms. About midway down the long, uncarpeted hallway, I saw lavatory signs for men and women. The walls were sky blue with small signs of wear and tear.

"This is basically the living quarters of the Lab. Eight bedrooms. Shared shower and washrooms—separated by men and women. A kitchen and the lounge. This is the level you'll be on when you're not being tested. Your bedroom, the kitchen, or the lounge. In general, we'd like you to stay in the lounge during you free time. That's where the others are now."

Lakshmi opened a door near the washrooms. "This one is yours." She waited in the doorway after I entered.

I gave the room a good look. I don't know what I was expecting but this wasn't it. It was a large room with a desk, dresser, wash area, a sitting area with loveseat and a chair with a lamp, and a bed. The walls were still that pleasant shade of blue but it had a thick piled grey carpet that squished underfoot. The closet doors were mirrored. The main lighting was a soft glow from recessed lights around the edges of the room. "This is nice."

"What did you expect?" She seemed amused at my surprise.

I rolled my suitcase into the sitting area and left it there. I could tell that I wasn't done with the tour. "I don't know. Something more hotel-like?"

She laughed, a rich warm sound. "Oh, no. Our visiting scientists wouldn't stand for that. When you need to live here for months on end, they try to make things as homey as possible. But better, because you don't have to do the dishes or your laundry. We've got people for that."

I turned to her. "Am I going to be allowed on the other levels? Or am I restricted here?"

"Well, technically, you aren't restricted to this floor. You have free run of Levels B and C but we prefer that you don't go to Levels D and E unless you've been specifically called there."

"Why is that?" I noticed that I wasn't forbidden from the lower levels and she used the word "prefer" rather than a more definite rule. It was interesting. My immediate thought was that it was a test: to see who broke the courtesy of the request first and how long it took. I mean, that's what I'd do.

Lakshmi shrugged. "Some of the experiments are delicate or sensitive. Some of them are dangerous. But, in truth, some of the scientists are particular about who goes in and out of their labs. They can be territorial. It's just better to be polite."

"Polite." I watched her, trying to see if she was testing me. It really was stupid for an adult to bring a teenager to a new place and say, 'You can go here and here but not there. But if you go there, you won't really get in trouble.'

"Yes, polite. Scientists aren't known for their social skills. We can be a grumpy lot."

Everything she said made sense. But, in my mind, it was a test. And thinking of such… "Do I have any tests I need to do today?"

She nodded. "Yes. Not the actual test, but I will be giving you a baseline medical examination. Get your numbers before the tests so we have something to compare them to. Though, that won't happen until after lunch. So, you have a couple of hours." Lakshmi beckoned me to follow her.

Once more in the hallway, she brought me back to the elevator at the end of the hall and pointed to a sign. It was floorplan showing the rooms and the exits. "There are emergency stairwells that go from Level E to the first floor, if there is a fire and we need to evacuate. Just go straight up to the first floor. There will be emergency lights to guide you out of the building. Don't use the elevator."

Lakshmi turned and pointed at a double set of metal doors to the right of the elevator. "That's the stairwell. If there is a lockdown, the stairwell door between Level A and first floor won't open and you'll need to use the elevator. It won't go up unless you're with someone with a proper access card. So, fire—take the stairwell. Lockdown—take the elevator with me, another scientist, or a guard. The alarms are very different. You'll be able to tell which is which. A lockdown will have red lighting."

Despite her casual tone of voice, I could tell she was uncomfortable. "What's the difference between a fire alarm and a lockdown? What would cause a lockdown?"

She shook her head. "It won't happen. I'm just required to tell you the difference."

This did not fill me with confidence. "But…"

"Now," she overrode me and walked back down the hall. "There's the kitchen. Standard fare. One of the other kids will show you how things work if you don't know or have any questions." Lakshmi gestured left at the kitchen with four round tables in it. "Washrooms and showers." She threw a hand right at the pair of doors with "MEN" and "WOMEN" emblazoned on them. At the end of the hallway there was a large room with another set of double doors. "And, here is the lounge."

I followed her in, still wondering about the difference between a fire alarm and a lockdown alarm, and found myself under the scrutiny of four pairs of eyes. I froze as Lakshmi said, "Everyone, this is Melissa Allen. She'll be here for the week. Help her get oriented."

There was a quiet chorus of agreement from the four teenagers staring at us.

With that, Lakshmi sailed out of the lounge, leaving me to fend for myself with nowhere to hide.

CHAPTER FOUR

I stood where I was, fighting the urge to flee as the four of them stared at me and I stared back. There were three boys and one girl. The first to catch my eye was the pale, red-headed boy nearest me. He had a watchful look and circles under his eyes. He barely looked at me. Instead, his eyes flicked from me to the doorway to the mirror at the far end of the room then back again. When he realized I was looking at him, he gave me an uneasy smile.

"Hello." It was the only thing I could think to say. I stepped to the nearest seat—a battered couch—and perched on the edge of one arm. "I'm Melissa."

"Hi. I'm Ian Brown." A tall, tanned, brown-haired boy walked to me with his hand outstretched. "Don't mind these barbarians."

"Uh…" I shook his hand but he didn't stop talking.

"That one over there," he indicated the red-head, "is Sean MacGregor. He's the one with the funny accent."

"Sod off," Sean said without rancor. I heard a touch of a lilt.

"That lovely lady is Carlita Lopez, our resident brainiac." Ian grinned at her and winked.

Carlita, a Latina girl with long black hair, dimpled. She had an open laptop cradled in her arms. "Call me Carrie."

"Hello Carrie."

Ian pointed to a handsome black teen in the back of the room. "And that surly fellow is Adam Erickson, resident lab rat."

Adam didn't say anything. I stared at him. He was gorgeous with high cheekbones and the darkest skin I'd ever seen on a living person. I wanted to look at him forever. He was like looking at art. Then I realized I was staring and I looked at my hands, my cheeks burning. "Hello."

When I glanced up again, Adam was smiling. My heart gave a stutter and my stomach hit the floor. Maybe this lab thing wasn't going to be so bad after all.

"So," Carrie said, looking at her laptop, "you're the one responsible for what happened in South Dakota, huh?"

I sat up straight, nearly falling off the edge of the couch. "What? No. I stopped what was going on." I paused and chose my words carefully. "Guess you could say I saved the world." It sounded trite, meaningless, and didn't say anything about what I'd been through. Part of me wanted to say so much more. Here was a group I was allowed to talk to about what had happened.

"Saved the world?" Ian laughed. "Been there. Done that. Got the t-shirt." He sauntered back to his original seat.

"Been there. Done that. Got the scars to prove it." Sean pulled his t-shirt up and revealed a livid set of red scars against his pale skin that looked like bite marks from a triangular head. His English accent was clear now. As was the bitter pain of what he'd obviously been through.

I looked between the two of them. "Are you serious? You've both really saved the world, too?"

Ian and Sean nodded. Ian shrugged. "Looks like the world is always in trouble, eh?"

"You fought off eight of the *Mega Aphis*?" Carrie was reading from her laptop. "What was that like? What were they like?"

"Awful. I mean, imagine six foot tall intelligent insects that look a bit like a cross between an ant and a bee. With spearhead hands and can spit acid. And it really hates humans. I still have scars from it, too." I bit my lip. "Are there pictures of them?"

She shook her head. "No, this is about you, not them. Though, there's a lot in here about them. Did everyone really go to sleep and then die?"

"Yes. Except for me." I tried to slow my breathing and not panic. This was more than I had expected. It's one thing to discover you aren't special. It's another for people to… question you like what had happened was an interesting video.

Carrie nodded. "Except for you because of your interesting brain chemistry."

I frowned at her, my stomach flip-flopping again. Did these guys already know how messed up I was? "What are you reading?"

"Your file." She wrinkled her nose. "Wore human masks made of an unknown biological matter? Ew..."

I got up and walked to her. "How'd you get my file?" Peering over her shoulder, I saw official-looking documents open and typed notes. There were no pictures that I could see.

Carrie closed the laptop and spun around to look at me. "That's what I'm doing here. I suppose you could say I'm a reformed evil hacker."

"Not evil," Ian said. "Just... naughty."

Carrie ignored him. "Computers and I get along really well. And I know enough social engineering that I can get the things I need to get into even the most secure locations."

She smiled at me and tapped her laptop. "It's a game now. Sadie, Doctor Giacomi, knows I'm going to do this no matter what rules they give me or firewalls they put in place. So, she keeps changing things up. Sometimes, I think they're just using me to test their security system. But, too many people do dumb things like write down their passwords on a post-it note and put it under their keyboard. But she doesn't know just how much I can do. Right now, my VPN session into their secure servers looks like *EVE Online* traffic."

"That's a lot to do in a short amount of time..." I stopped as she shook her head. "Not a short amount of time?"

"I live here. The lab is my home."

"Wait... what?" Now I was completely confused. "I thought that... this was just a test. For a week. We get to go home after a week." Flushing, I moved away from her and towards the couch under the mirror opposite Adam. I noticed he spent most of his time just watching the rest of us. He gave me a close-lipped, half-smile as I sat.

"Orphan," Carrie waved a dismissive hand at me. "Never knew my parents. Lived in an orphanage. Couldn't get adopted because of my hand. Found I had a knack for computers. Got in trouble and, after 9/11 with people who couldn't tell Arabic from Spanish, getting remanded to the State was a godsend."

An orphan. I knew what that was like. It also explained the lack of a foreign accent in her cheerful voice. I wondered where she'd grown up. Midwest for sure. Our voices could be sisters. I looked at her hand and saw nothing wrong with it. "Your hand?"

Carrie grinned. "Not this one." She pulled her left hand out from under the laptop. "This one."

She waved a hand that was actually half a hand. I could see that her fingers ended at the first knuckle but she had a whole thumb. I tried not to stare but failed. "Oh, wow. Does it hurt?"

Shrugging, Carrie said, "Sometimes. A lot of times, in a general achy way. But that's basically my story. I've been living here for a couple of years now. Already graduated from high school and I'm in my second year of college."

When I didn't say anything, just looked at her offered diminished hand, she continued, "My hand is a simple congenital defect, not caused by any disease or condition. The doctors actually don't know the why of it. The only surgical correction available to me when I was younger was the addition of two more joints, but they would be stiff and inflexible. There is probably more now, but I really don't care.

"The most important thing in dealing with something like this is attitude. It's just your hand. You accept it as part of who you are. You do what you can with what you've got. For instance, typing was a challenge, but I developed my own system. One thing I've noticed is that if I don't pay any attention to it neither will anyone else. I never have a problem showing it to little children who have noticed and are curious. I let them look and touch to their heart's content; I don't make it a big deal, so they don't either."

I couldn't help but smile. "That's really amazing. Thank you for telling me. I don't know if I could be that brave."

Carrie grinned. "I can't be all perfect. I gotta have something that brings me down to mere mortal status, right?"

"Like I said, resident brainiac." Ian cocked his head. "Me? I'm just handsome and talented."

I could tell Ian wanted to talk about himself or he wanted the attention off of Carrie. Either way, I obliged as I saw Carrie give him a quick smile and tuck her hands under her laptop. "So… if I'm not the only one to save the world, how did you do it?" I added Sean to the conversation. "And you? What happened to you?" Out of the corner of my eye, I saw Adam relax and sink into his end of the couch more. I wondered what about the conversation made him tense. Maybe he thought I was going to be mean about Carrie's hand.

Ian shifted forward in his seat. "I'm from Colorado. Colorado Springs. We lived near one of the substations. We, my family, we all started hearing voices coming from the TV, radio, and our computers. At first, we thought the NORAD was doing something funny to communications. Then, we realized it was just our house. We joked about being haunted. Then, one day, they came through."

"They? Through what?"

"The scientists here call them Minkowskians after Doctor Herman Minkowski, the time-space scientist. His grandson, Doctor Kai Minkowski is the resident expert on inter-dimensional creatures. It's kinda of a stupid name if you ask me, but what do I know? I'm just a teenager." Ian shrugged. "In any case, they came through, I'm really not sure how, and invaded our house and…" He paused, shaking his head. "We fought. They killed my family. I accidentally captured one using a stun gun."

I looked around. Everyone had the bored expression of people who had heard this story more than once. "When did this happen?"

"About two months ago, I guess. When the DHS got hold of it and me, I became ward of the state. I'm living with Agent Kress right now. But when I turn eighteen, I'm on my own with my inheritance. I'm gonna be a rich man."

I gazed at him, surprised that he was taking everything so well. The crack about his inheritance was downright ghoulish. Then again, some people dealt better with adversity than others. They also didn't have a brain chemistry that hated them. I turned to Sean. Again, I was struck by how haunted he looked.

"Mine just happened a few weeks ago. Three, I think. Time is the same here in the lab. It happened off Orcas Island in Washington state. I was vacationing with my family. There were these sea creatures called Nehrings. Serpent-like and telepathic with wicked bites. Venomous—in mind, body, and soul. Killed my family and my friends. Only, I didn't succumb to their poison. Nobody knows why the poison didn't kill me.

He gazed at his hands, far away. "I think they were supposed to be some sort of advance force, testing an attack from the sea. The Navy captured a couple but they died soon after. It was like they couldn't live here, in this world."

"The government, Homeland Security, has custody of you? Aren't you from somewhere else?" I glanced at Adam and noticed something odd about his reflection in the mirror.

"It's a bit sticky. I was born here. My mom was American. Dad was English. I spent most of my life in London. But, the report said all hands lost. They don't really know what to do with me."

"I'm sorry." The words were lame and inadequate but that was all I had to give.

"His file is just as conflicted," Carrie said. "What happened to him is a matter of national security but he does have both an American passport and a British passport. They're still wrangling out the legality of it all. Trying to figure out which country has custody without revealing the fact that the world has been under attack from... well... aliens. For at least the last year." Carrie tilted her head. "There have been other attacks. Smaller. But everyone died."

"Then, how do they know about them?"

"Evidence in the aftermath. Biological anomalies. Scraps of video. Journaled accounts of the dead. The evidence goes back a year. That's when it hit the federal radar. But, it could've been going on a lot longer."

I rubbed my cheek. "That's really scary."

Adam spoke for the first time. "That's why we're all being tested. There's something different or important about each of us. Carrie's smarter that most of the scientists here. You three have fought off alien invasions because of immunity to poison, immunity to a euthanasia field, and the ability to fight off the Minkowski's attack. I'm the baseline. I'm genetically perfect."

I blinked at him. "Genetically perfect? That's a new one on me."

"What he means," Ian interrupted, "is that he's genetically created in a lab. Not born of man or woman."

Adam's relaxed posture stiffened and he glared at Ian.

"You are such an ass." Sean pushed himself out of his seat, moving with the slow motions of an injured person. He shook his head at Ian. "Just because he lives here with your girlfriend it doesn't mean you need to constantly bring him down to try and make yourself look better. Christ. You have such a fragile ego. You're one of the reasons why I hate being here." He stalked out of the lounge.

I saw Carrie cover her face with her hand, flushing, and realized the easy camaraderie between the four of them wasn't so easy after all. Sean was still reeling from his attack and loss. Ian was feeling out of sorts and needed to prove himself as...something. Or maybe he really was just a mean boy trying to show off for a girl he didn't get to see that often.

Adam stood and walked to Ian, puffing up a little. "What's your problem with me?"

Ian squared off with him as Carrie stood. "Guys. I really don't feel like being confined to quarters again."

"You do realize we're being watched right now," I said. All of them paused and looked at me. "Haven't you wondered about this mirror?" I put my fingertip against the mirror and saw its reflection butted up against my finger. "I read that you can always tell when a mirror is one way. If you put your fingertip against a regular mirror, you see its reflection, but there's a gap of glass over the silver metal backing. If you put your fingertip against a one way mirror, there's no gap. Just like this. This whole mirror is a window into an observation room." Thank you Deroga Darrington and *The Haunted Mirror*.

Silence hung in the air for a few beats. Then Adam returned to the couch, reached out a finger, and tested his part of the mirror. "Huh. Score one for the new girl." He smiled at me. "I never knew."

I flushed and ducked my head, to hide my pleased smile.

Ian scowled at him. "Look at you, still trying to be a real boy."

Adam turned from the mirror and shook his head in a way that reminded me of a disappointed professor. "You really are an ass. In a week, you'll be gone, and I'll still be here, at home, with my family." He gazed at Ian. "You'll be nothing but text on a screen once more."

Ian balled his hands into fists as Adam strode past him. Carrie reached out and touched Ian's arm and he relaxed. The two of them looked at each other. Suddenly, I was a third wheel in a car full of baggage. Apparently, Ian wasn't as well put together as I first thought. He was acting out and grieving in a much more aggressive way—by attacking the person closest to Carrie.

Possessiveness, I thought. *Afraid to lose someone or something else.* I got up, eager to be gone. "I need to unpack and get ready for my baseline physical." I didn't wait for a response.

"Well, you sure know how to make a first impression," I heard Carrie say as I hurried out of the room and down the hallway.

*

I wasn't lying about needing to unpack or to get ready for my baseline physical. I figured I needed to be in workout clothing. Also, I didn't want to be in the lounge anymore. Knowing I was being observed felt too much like being back in the hospital "for observation."

My room was the same as before. But, I felt the need to test the mirror above the sink and the mirrors in my closet doors—just to be safe. They were real mirrors. If there was a camera or something like it in here, it wasn't visible and it wasn't in any of the places Heather told me about—like in clocks or the fire detector. Feeling better about my privacy, I unpacked and changed into sweats and a t-shirt.

After glancing at the clock, I figured an early-ish lunch would be okay. I didn't exactly know when the physical would be. Better fed than hungry and cranky. A perfect time to check out the kitchen with the expectation that we were going to be responsible for ourselves.

Adam was in the kitchen at one of the tables, staring at his half-drunk bottle of orange juice, when I entered. I paused. Again, I was struck with how handsome he was. "Oh. Hi. Should I go?" Damn my stupid tongue. Sometimes, I can be so lame.

He shook his head. "Nah. It's a free country." The microwave beeped and he got up to retrieve his lunch. A hot pocket. It looked good.

I checked the freezer and there were at least a dozen boxes of hot pockets and other frozen meals. I selected one and popped it in the microwave. I looked everywhere but at him because I didn't want to stare at him. I froze when I glanced at him and saw he was watching me with a smile. I smiled back.

"It's okay," he said. "Ask what you want to ask. It'll be easier that way. Carrie's got the right of it in that regard."

I bowed my head and watched the hot pocket turn in the microwave. "That obvious, huh?" I saw him shrug out of the corner of my eye.

"Anomalies are always interesting."

"What's it like being genetically perfect? I mean... how...?"

"Like? I don't know. I'm never sick. My physicals are well above average." He took a bite of food and paused. "As for how, Doctor Erik Vandermeek broke some laws, put together the exact genetic makeup of what should constitute a perfect human, grew me in an artificial womb, and birthed me at the nine month mark. I honestly don't know any other way to be than me."

I pulled my meal from the microwave and sat down, freeing the hot pocket from its cooking sleeve. "Did you grow up here? In PAR Lab?"

"Yep. I've had a bunch of different caretakers but, Lakshmi, Doctor Gowda, has been my most consistent parent, I guess you could say."

That explained one thing. The way he spoke reminded me of the doctors and scientists I'd visited. I guess when you lived around them all your life, you emulated what you heard. "What happened to Doctor Vandermeek?"

He furrowed his brow for a moment, then smoothed his face into something neutral again. "He left when I was eight. I don't know if he left willingly or not. I think yes. He called me Adam Erikson. He didn't give me his last name. Never let me call him 'Dad' or 'Father.' I think..." Adam shrugged, "it was because he was white and I'm not."

I wanted to deny that but I couldn't. People were still hung up on the color of a person's skin no matter what they say. It happened every day in Oneida. I paused and wondered if part of my immediate attraction to Adam was the fact that I'd never seen a guy with skin as dark as his. I looked at him, his face, his dark eyes, his uneasy smile. I looked at him and admitted, maybe yes. He was handsome. He also felt exotic to me. That was something I needed to stomp on and now. Adam was a person, no matter what Ian insinuated.

"Penny for your thoughts?"

I blinked at him. Then flushed and stammered, "Uh. I was, uh, wondering if you knew what the baseline medical examination was like."

He smiled a broad smile, white teeth flashing against his dark features. The smile turned into a grin as I blushed all the more. "It won't be too much. Maybe blood work, a physical exam, some stress testing maybe. It all depends on the data they are looking to get out of their experiments with you. Lakshmi will be in charge of it. You'll be fine."

I'm sure I would be. I just wondered if I'd be fine within the group of kids here. They all seemed pretty cool on the surface but there were, as Deroga might say, dangerous waters beneath that could drown anyone who didn't take care.

*

Not ten minutes later, Lakshmi came to get me. We took the stairs next to the elevator down to Level B. I was surprised to see that we did not come out on a single hallway but in the corner of two hallways. I considered this as we headed down the lefthand hallway. "Is this Level bigger than the first floor? I mean, Level A? Or, was there part of Level A I didn't see?"

Lakshmi was quiet for a moment then seemed to come to a decision. "Level A is a square of hallways like all of the other underground floors. Each level is built like a Roman domus. Except, the interior courtyard is more of a maintenance shaft where the generators and protected well water pumps go. Not to mention the air filtration system."

"So, why did it look like there was only one hallway?"

"Security through obfuscation. The storage room next to the elevator has two doors. The second one opens on the rest of the U shape of Level A. The permanent residents live on that side of the floor." She glanced at me as we entered a doctor's office—her office by her ease of use and knowing where everything was.

"You mean like Carrie and Adam?"

She nodded. "And me. Also, there's a server room, a security office, and as you guessed yesterday, an observation room. Though, it's rarely used."

"How come Carrie and Adam didn't know about it?"

"Their keycards don't give them access to everything. Actually, they are pretty limited as things go. But, I suspect it's because they didn't really care to look. The interesting stuff is on the levels below." She pointed to a chair. "No more questions for now. Let me do my job."

"Yes, ma'am." I sat as requested and let myself be poked and prodded.

The next three hours was round after round of medical tests and they sucked. Who wants to have blood drawn, a gynecological exam, elbows and knees pounded, lungs tested for capacity and strength, eyes puffed at and dilated, muscle flexibility and strength pushed, my scars noted, and a tooth examination in one day? We moved from Level B to Level C a couple of times. I also had x-rays done and would've had an MRI if the machine hadn't been busted. It was one of my first inklings that not everything worked perfectly at PAR Lab.

The other thing of interest was the fact that, despite the large complex and huge number of rooms—offices, laboratories, a full-sized gym, and meeting rooms—I saw, at least twenty rooms per floor, I didn't see more than a dozen people working. Most of them were there for me, taking measurements and performing tests.

As we headed back to the stairs, I stopped in front of the elevator on Level C and looked around. It was almost identical to the Level above it. I listened and heard almost nothing.

"Are you alright?" Lakshmi stilled and mimicked my movements. "Do you want to take the elevator instead of the stairs?"

"Where are all the people?"

She shook her head. "I don't understand."

I gestured to each hallway. "With this big of a place, shouldn't there be a lot more people? I mean, this place wouldn't be this big without more people. Or... wouldn't you shut down some of the levels to conserve energy and save money?"

"Ah." Lakshmi nodded. "Yes. There are a lot more people who work here but they will not be here while your testing is happening." She pressed the elevator button. "It's best if they don't know you and you don't know them. And I mean "you" as in all of the kids being tested. Of course, they know Adam and Carrie. Some of the scientists here seem to think of them as interns. Which, I suppose, in a way, they are."

"Is that for their protection or ours?"

"Both. There are some sensitive projects that happen here. You won't see them because they've been secured. You don't have the clearance to even know what they are, so don't ask. We're working on a skeleton crew for the next week or so. You kids are our main focus."

"Great. I think."

She smiled at me. "I think so. Studying you guys might unlock new ways to protect us from these incursions."

"Are they getting worse?"

Lakshmi's smile disappeared. "That's something we can talk about later in the week."

CHAPTER FIVE

I was up at seven for breakfast and my pills by eight. I used to think that eight was barely time enough for me to wake up and pretend to be alive. However, the last four months of being up by 6:30 A.M. (thanks to my training schedule), left me bright-eyed and ready for whatever. Adam let me know where we were to meet and when.

By 8:30 A.M., the five of us were in the large gym on Level C, where Lakshmi and three other people waited. All of the teens were in shorts and t-shirts. All of the adults looked like stereotypical doctors in white lab coats. One woman even had a clipboard. I wanted to laugh, but everyone was being too quiet and serious for me to do so.

Lakshmi nodded to us as we instinctively lined up in front of them. "Just to get everyone on the same page, I'd like to introduce you to the three people you'll be spending most of your time with for the next week. This is Doctor Aaron Dudetsky." She gestured to a stern looking older man with graying temples and glasses. "He's the lead on this part of the project."

"You may call me "Doctor" or "Doctor Dudetsky." I am not interested in any pet names you may come up with for me." His voice was a smoker's gruff and he gave Adam and Carrie a glare. Carrie and Adam glanced at each other with a knowing smirk.

Lakshmi pointed to an athletic black woman with a neutral expression on her face. "This is Doctor Sadie Giacomi. She's our staff psychiatrist. You'll be having daily sessions with her on an individual and group level."

"Hello. I have an open question policy. If you have a question, just ask." She stepped forward as she spoke and had a nice smile.

"Do you have any pet names we can call you?" Ian sounded as innocent as could be but I saw the devilish grin on his face. He really liked pressing buttons.

She gave him a long, quiet look that made the grin falter, then fade. "Doctor, Sadie, or Doctor Giacomi will do." Looking up and down the row of us, she asked, "Any serious questions?"

We all shook our heads. That quiet authority and confidence pushed us all back in line. I decided I liked her as Lakshmi pointed to the youngest of the trio waiting for us, an elfin red-head woman holding the clipboard. "This is our assistant, Miss Jolene Lake."

Like the psychiatrist, she stepped forward. "Hello. Call me Jolene. I'm fine with it." She glanced at Doctor Dudetsky. "For the most part, I will be assisting Doctor Dudetsky. As he will be balancing the tests for all five of you, if you have a question, ask me first. I might have the answer for you."

Doctor Dudetsky clapped his hands. It was loud in the quiet room, startling us. "Right. Now that all that nonsense is out of the way, let's get to work. We've got a lot of tests to get through. First up, stress running. I want to see who can run the fastest for the longest period of time. Everyone up on the treadmills."

I suppressed a groan. I hated running. The only time I liked running was sprinting from base to base in a softball game—not that I'd had any of that lately. In the last four months, Heather had been working my butt off with all sorts of exercises and running continued to be my least favorite. I suspected that the workouts were because it was something we could both do. Her other love, crochet, was still black magic to me.

Still, as the five of us started up on the treadmills with oxygen masks strapped to our faces and heart monitors strapped to our wrists, I was glad I'd been doing something to prep for this—albeit, unknowingly. Sean, still recovering from his battle with the Nerhlings, dropped out first.

Doctor Dudetsky looked at the treadmill numbers and nodded to Jolene. "That's Subject 223." When Carrie dropped out, he remarked, "Subject 222. I expected better from you." Jolene marked the numbers down without comment. Though she gave Carrie a sympathetic smile.

Carrie, scowling and gasping for air, gave him the finger as he turned his back.

I dropped out next. I did better than I thought I would at 15 minutes and 6.5 miles an hour. Though, my heart felt like it wanted to pound through my chest.

"Subject 225." He pointed at the treadmill as if Jolene was blind.

"I. Have A. Name." I continued to gasp as I walked around, trying to calm my frantically beating heart.

Doctor Dudetsky ignored me as he stood between Ian and Adam. He crossed his arms. "Well, it's down to you two."

Carrie walked with me, keeping her voice low. "Don't let him get to you. He's always like that. Most of the time, I think he forgets that I'm *not* one of his test subjects."

I shook my head, my breath coming easier now. "Just because he's always been an asshole doesn't excuse his attitude. We're people. People who've done some damn impressive things."

She smiled at me as she glanced at him. "Yeah. I know. Old habits."

"Old dogs, new tricks," I muttered and decided my mission this week was to get the good doctor to call me by the right name. Grumpy old man, meet surly, stubborn teenager.

We both turned and watched Ian and Adam duke it out on the treadmill. Already I could see that Adam was going to win this one. I could tell by the ease of his running form. I smiled, taking the time to admire him from the backside.

"This is the perfect view," Carrie whispered to me with a wicked gleam in her eyes. "Look at those ass... sets." She held out both hands, palms up, and rocked them back and forth in time to the boy's movement.

I couldn't help but giggle and agree. I tried to stifle it but that just made us both giggle harder.

Sean popped his head in-between us. "What are you girls laughing at?"

"Look at those ass... sets," I said, repeating Carrie. "It's like watching a pair of metronomes."

He considered Ian and Adam's increasingly moving and sweating backsides and nodded. "I'd do 'em. Both of them."

Carrie and I gasped in unison.

"What? I can appreciate the male form. I'm an equal opportunity letch. Captain Jack Harkness is my patronus." He gave us a serious nod and a lascivious wink.

"Really?" I asked as Carrie raised her hand up. "Me, too. Good ol' Captain Jack Hardness... I mean, Harkness."

I clapped both of my hands to my mouth, giggling madly as Carrie and Sean high-fived each other. I didn't say anything. Where I grew up, LGBT was barely known, much less accepted, and bisexuals were supposed to be merely confused. I only knew about it all because I'd been through the state's correctional system and saw a lot more than any of my guardians knew. Neither Carrie nor Sean looked confused. Just amused. I turned away and saw Doctor Giacomi watching us. I poked Carrie. "Do you think we're being psychologically evaluated right now?"

Sean and Carrie glanced over at Giacomi. Carrie nodded. "Yeah. Most likely."

"She's not taking any notes."

"Sadie has a great memory and an amazing ability to mimic voices and hand gestures. You should have her do some of her impressions for you sometime. Also, I'm pretty sure this whole thing is being recorded."

Sean and I exchanged a surprised glance. "Oh. Well. Okay. Yeah. I guess that makes sense."

Just then, Ian stumbled, then tumbled off his treadmill with a great crash of noise. Carrie and Lakshmi rushed to his side as he lay there gasping and panting, his oxygen mask askew on his face. Sean and I shifted towards each other, touching shoulders and looking around. I don't know what I was looking for but I was tense and so was Sean. I felt like we were ready to go back-to-back to fight all comers.

Doctor Dudetsky pointed at Adam and hissed, "Keep going. Don't ruin the test." To Jolene he said, "Subject 224."

Right then and there, I decided that Doctor Dudetsky was more than just an asshole. He was the kind of man who sacrificed people to get the numbers he wanted. That made him dangerous. It also meant I was going to call him on his shit if he endangered us.

I got my chance on the very next test.

We all stood around the weight bench watching Doctor Dudetsky and Jolene confer. When he was ready, Doctor Dudetsky turned to us. "This is the weight stress test. Each of you will benchlift to failure. It's a simple test. It shouldn't take that long. Subject 221 will be first." He gestured to Adam. "We'll start with one hundred pounds and go from there."

"Excuse me, who do you want to be the spotter?" I glanced between Jolene and the doctor. Both of them gave me a blank look.

"I didn't say I was going to accept questions." Doctor Dudetsky turned his back on me.

There was no way I was going to let him get away with that. I raised my voice. "Don't care. The question stands. Who will be spotting? Because my guardian taught me that you don't do strength training without a spot. Especially if you're going to the failure point."

He turned back to me as the rest of the room went dead quiet. "Your guardian isn't here. Subject 221, get on the bench."

Adam took a step forward, looking conflicted. I stepped in front of him. "*I'm* here. You *don't* do something like this without a spotter. Someone could really get hurt. Like dead hurt." I could feel my face flushing and my hands tremble. I clenched them into fists to keep them still. I tried to keep my voice level but already it was shaking with fear and anger. "I will spot if needed."

The scowl lines in his face grew and his bushy eyebrows furrowed, looking like two pissed off caterpillars on either side of the deep V wrinkle in his forehead. "Do you want to fail this test, Subject 225?" His voice was low, menacing.

Shaking, I repeated, "I will spot for Adam and the rest if needed."

He raised his chin and declared, "Subject 225 has failed this test." When Jolene didn't immediately make a note on the clipboard, he yelled, "Mark it down!"

That was exactly the impetus I needed. "Do you think that scares me?" I laughed, sounding hysterical to my own ears. "I spent days in a quarantine zone with monsters hunting me. I've been stabbed, threatened with being shot, and burned. My whole family is dead. And you think one little black mark is going to scare me?"

Red clouded my vision and my voice shook. I gestured to Sean. "He's still recovering from being attacked and having his family murdered by monsters. Do you think your black mark scares him?" I gestured to Ian. "Or him? His family was murdered by monsters, too." I looked back at Adam. "Do you think Adam—his name is Adam, not Subject 221—hasn't listened to your threats all his life?" Tears ran down my face as I grabbed Carrie by the left arm. "Do you think your little black mark scares the smartest person in the room when she had this to deal with all her life?" I pulled Carrie's left arm and up, showcasing her deformed hand.

"We're not numbers. We're people, we've done amazing things, and shouldn't be treated like this. I'm not going to let you hurt us for the sake of your test. These tests are important to someone, right? Well, if you don't want me skewing your results all week, you're going to start treating us like people." I sniffled, face hot with anger and fear. "So, make your black marks. Make them til the cows come home. I don't care."

Ian stepped up beside Carrie. "I weight lift on a regular basis. She's right. We need a spotter. I can spot, too." He put an arm around Carrie. "Also, we need a wrap for Carrie's hand. It's the only way you're going to get a true test." Sean and Adam stepped close to the three of us, presenting a united front. I've never been more relieved in my life.

Doctor Dudetsky looked back and forth at our faces, scowling all the more. He focused on my face, glistening with tears. "I will not—"

"Doctor." Doctor Giacomi's calm voice cut off whatever Doctor Dudetsky was about to say. "May I have a word?"

"This isn't over," he grumbled then walked to the side of the gym to confer with the psychiatrist.

I turned away and covered my face with my hands. "Oh, god. What've I done?"

"That was brilliant," Carrie whispered.

I looked down at her hands. "I'm so sorry. I shouldn't've... I didn't think..."

She pushed my chin up to look her in the face and shook her head. "I didn't know how to ask about it. I'm so used to his tirades, I wasn't sure... Weight lifting is going to suck. I don't care about my hand. It's just a hand. It hurts all the time. But, I just don't pay attention to it. Dudette probably didn't remember it. I needed help. So, thank you."

"Dudette?"

Adam leaned in and whispered. "Yeah, what else do you call a man like him with his last name?"

I smiled at Adam and looked around at the group of us. "Thank you for sticking with me. Thank you for not leaving me hanging out to dry. I didn't know it was going to be like this. I didn't know he was going..." I shrugged

Sean shook his head. "No problem"

"Are you okay?" Ian gestured to my face.

I looked up at the wall mirror and blushed all the more. My face was very pale and blotchy. "Yeah. Just... I cry when I'm angry. I can't help it. Oh, god. I look a mess." I swiped at my cheeks and eyes with the backs of my hands, sniffling.

The closing of the gym door alerted us to a decision. Looking up, I saw Lakshmi and Doctor Giacomi walking towards us. I wavered, wondering if I should apologize for my outburst. I was rude, yes. But he was being stupid. Adults aren't always right.

"I will finish the morning tests," Lakshmi said, her voice neutral. "Doctor Dudetsky needs to revamp his testing schedule. He will have me present the test instructions before the tests and, if there are any questions, he and I will review them. I will review this afternoon's tests while you are having lunch. Questions?"

We all shook our heads, not daring to act out after my outburst.

Lakshmi nodded. "Good. We will continue with the strength test. Ian and Melissa will be the spotters. Carlita, let's figure out how to make it a viable and safe test for you."

Adam leaned to me as Carrie consulted with Lakshmi. "Doctor Dudetsky isn't going to forgive or forget this. He holds a grudge. I've seen it. Now that he's figured out he can't cow us into submission, he's going to get a lot more subtle and vicious. Especially since we all sided with you." He smiled, his eyes dancing. "And I'm really glad I got to see that. No one stands up to him."

"I'm sorry," I mumbled. I didn't know what else to say.

"Don't be. He needed it. Just… watch your back, you know?"

The rest of the morning's tests went without incident. Even Ian, who seemed to always be ready to mock or start something, was on his best behavior. He was actually pleasant to be around, working as part of the team, instead of trying to stand outside it. Strength tests gave way to flexibility and balance tests, and the morning ended on reflex tests that involved sprinting from one side of the gym to the other, then to building a four-story house of cards.

While none of it was fun, by the end of the morning, we were all joking with each other in an easy camaraderie born of being stuck in the same situation after the blow up with Doctor Dudetsky. It allowed us to finish early.

CHAPTER SIX

Thank goodness we had a long break for lunch. We all needed showers and to retreat to separate corners and prepare for the next set of tests: all mental and psychological. Unfortunately, it wasn't a long enough break for me.

The tests started off all right: pairing words, word searches, maze running. They were timed tests and Carrie smoked us all. For the most part, I did all right. Not first, not last. Very middle of the pack and very normal. It was nice to feel that way for once.

Ian, who did not do well, scowled and sulked through most of the tests. The easy camaraderie we'd built up for the morning started to bend against his moods. Adam didn't make it any easier as he slapped his pen down on the table when he was done. The first time he did it, he noticed Ian's discomfort. After that, he made a point of being noisy whenever he finished. The third time Adam pulled attention to himself, Sean rolled his eyes and muttered, "Bollocks. You two need to get a room."

It was during the maze tests that the black butterflies came back. I waved a couple away before I realized what was going on and clamped down on my reactions. Instead, I had to let the butterflies flutter about my head, their all-too-real-to-me phantom wings tickling my face and hair. I gritted my teeth and held on. I wasn't willing to have the "I'm having hallucinations" conversation with Doctor Giacomi—no matter how calm she was. We hadn't had our first private session yet. I didn't have a feel for her. I didn't know how she'd react.

I worried about it all throughout the tests. I knew the butterflies were a hallucination, probably brought on by the weirdness and stress of this whole situation. It also didn't stop the butterflies from getting into my face and distracting me. I tried to keep my reactions to a minimum.

I failed.

I reread and reread the brain teaser paragraph, trying to puzzle out the answer when, right above my head, Doctor Giacomi asked, "Melissa, are you alright?"

I squeaked my surprise as I jerked halfway out of my chair. I heard one of the guys chuckle. Looking up at her, I nodded. "I was. Until you scared the daylights out of me." Inside, I ran through every curse word I knew, trying to calm my racing heart.

"I'm sorry." She took a step back from me. "You were waving your hands around. I wanted to check on you."

I knew she knew about the hallucinations. It was right there in my file. I still didn't want to admit to them in front of the others. I turned away and saw a gnat crawling on the edge of my desk. "There's a bug. It's bothering me."

"A bug? There aren't any bugs down here." Giacomi glanced around as if to confirm this. "Are you sur—"

I slammed my hand down on the edge of the desk, making everyone jump, and cutting her off. I lifted my hand, saw the small smear of black and clear wings on my palm. "Looks like there's a bug to me." I lifted my hand, palm up, to her. I prayed that the gnat wasn't another figment of my imagination, too.

"Ah. So there is." She nodded and walked back to the front of the meeting room. "Adam, you're going to have to make sure the garden is secure. At least one of your pets has escaped."

"Yes, ma'am." Adam didn't bother to raise his head from the test. I wondered what she meant by garden as I rubbed my palm clean on my jeans.

"Fifteen minutes," she announced and took her seat.

I sighed softly and glanced up. My stomach hit the floor as I met Doctor Giacomi's gaze. I gave her a weak smile and turned back to the brain teaser questions. She had her eye on me. I wondered if I was being paranoid. Then I remembered it wasn't paranoia if it was true. Needless to say, I didn't do well on the test.

As soon as it was over and Doctor Giacomi said we had the rest of the day to ourselves, we split up like a mandatory support group. Ian all but sprinted from the room with Carrie following. I made a beeline for my room, dashing up the stairs.

Adam ran up behind me. "Melissa, wait."

Surprised and pleased, I did. "What's up?" I watched him with interest. I wasn't used to people my age wanting to talk to me.

"You wanna see the garden?" He rubbed the back of his neck. "I mean, the bug did, you know, bug you. You should see where it came from."

I shrugged. "Sure."

"We could grab dinner and eat it there. It's pretty cool. I do a lot of work there."

Smiling, I nodded. "Okay. I'd like that."

Sandwiches, chips, and sodas in hand, Adam led me to the elevator and pressed the "D" button. "You're going to love this."

"Level D? Am I allowed to go there?" I was nervous and excited. I'd already pissed off Doctor Dudetsky today and caught Doctor Giacomi's discerning eye. I didn't need an official reprimand from Lakshmi for doing something I wasn't supposed to—especially after she'd told me to be polite and avoid Levels D and E.

"Yeah. It'll be fine." Adam made a face at my hesitation. "Really, there won't be a problem. One, it's not like anyone cares. Two, anyone who would care isn't down there. Three, I know both of the guards on rotation. Patton and Forester are good guys. Four," he smiled a shy smile, "you're with me. If there's a problem, I'll take the blame."

"You know, you have to live here after we go. Unlike me, they can actually ground you."

He shrugged. "I know. That's why I'm fine with it. They know me. I know them. It's not like they're going to ground me, you know. Half the scientists here use me as an unofficial intern. Or, more like, an assistant. Seriously, I think they'd be lost without me. It'd be like pissing off the acquisitions admin. They'd be shooting themselves in the foot by telling me to stay in my room."

"What do you do here at the lab?"

We walked out of the elevator and down the hall in front of us. This floor looked like the ones above it except that it had fewer doors, larger windows into the laboratories, and dimmed lighting. It reminded me of going into an office building on the weekend or during the holidays. It was very easy to think of it as "apocalyptic." That brought me a bit too close to what happened in Oneida and I slammed the door on that train of thought.

"Things like this garden. The scientists designed it. We all put it together. I maintain it and do a lot of the measurements. In other projects, I gather data for them. Or, they give me their data to put into the computer. Really, I suppose some people think of it as scut work. Not me. What I do for everyone is valuable. I know I'm making a difference. Especially when one of them looks up from their experiment long enough to tell me so."

I heard the pride and happiness in his voice. It washed away a lot of the doubts I had about how horrible it would be to live underground all the time. Adam seemed pretty well adjusted. That might be because he'd never lived outside the lab. I couldn't tell.

He brought me to a small antechamber room with no windows. There was a door opposite us that looked a lot like a pressure seal door that you have on submarines. After he handed me his dinner to hold, he opened it with a turn of the round handle. As he did, I was struck by a blast of warm, wet air filled with the loamy scents of moist earth and growing things.

Adam held aside the hanging plastic strips, and let me enter before him. As soon as I was through, I saw why the strips were there. There were small birds flitting throughout the room. I was stunned by the size of the room and the variety of plant life. There were small trees, planted flowers, growing vegetables, grass, and small bushes. They were in all stages of growth and life. The room itself was huge. It must have taken up part of Level C. The ceiling was hidden by gauzy nets and a watering system.

"This," I said, "isn't just a garden. It's more like a… a…" I was at a loss for words. And yes, there were small patches of flying bugs.

"Technically, it's an ecosystem. It's not a biosphere because we can come and go as we please. But, this is one of my main projects."

I couldn't fault the pride I heard in his voice. I understood what I was hearing so much more. "It's amazing."

"Thanks. There are benches over here." He took his meal back and led me to two parkside benches on either side of a bird fountain. "I insisted. This is a nice place to come. It's a good place to remind the scientists that there's more to science than experiments."

I looked up at the lighting. It felt like late afternoon even though I knew it was later than that. "It's like being outside. Except the lighting is wrong."

"It's as close as I like to get to being outside." Adam unwrapped his sandwich and dove in. "And the lighting is one of the tests. It never changes. Never gets brighter or darker. But it is full spectrum. They want to see if plants from earth could live in a 24/7 lighted environment. I mean, do plants *need* downtime?"

"Why do they want to know?"

He shrugged. "Above my pay grade."

"You get paid?" I opened my sandwich and picked at it. I should be ravenous but I wasn't. I was too interested in Adam and his strange life.

"Oh, sure. How else am I going to buy stuff from online? It's not like I have parents to bum money off of."

I nodded. "I guess so." I paused. "Why don't you want to go outside?"

He took a large bite of his sandwich and chewed. I looked around the garden, watching the birds and picking out the different kinds of vegetables growing: tomatoes, cucumbers, lettuce, corn, scallions, and carrots. There were a bunch I didn't recognize off the top of my head.

"There's a ceiling in here," Adam said finally. "I can't really see it because of the way the room was built, but it is here. I know where the world ends. When I go outside the lab and see all that space that just goes on and on and on..." He shook his head. "I can't deal with it. I feel like I'm going to fall into the sky. I can't move, but I want to run away. I don't like it. I don't feel... real out there."

"Agoraphobia." I half-smiled at him. "Because you've lived here, inside, all your life. What are you going to do when you grow up? Or when it's time to go to college?"

"Melissa, I'm not getting out of here."

His voice was so matter-of-fact, it hurt my heart. "What do you mean?"

"I'm a test tube baby. I have no real family. They run tests and experiments on me all the time. They... I'm an anomaly. None of Doctor Vandermeek's other creations lived. I think that's why he left, or was sent away; to try to focus on that instead of his one success." Adam looked across the garden. "I think I'm going to live, work, and die here. At least I can make something of my own. That's why I do this and the other projects. I already took my G.E.D. even though I don't officially exist. I can take all the online college courses I want, but without a social security number and all that, I can't do anything officially."

"But, you order things from online?"

"Yeah. There is a credit card in my name but I don't actually pay the bill. I get an email from accounts payable who deducts it from my running account. It's not like I have a real bank account. Or, if I do, I don't have access to it."

The more he talked, the more upset I got. I didn't know what to say or do. "Are you a prisoner here?"

"Where would I go if I left? I read the reports of everything that happens to young black men. Can you imagine what the first cop I met would do when I told him I didn't have ID? I couldn't identify myself in any meaningful way? I'd end up in jail or worse."

Adam shook his head. "At least here, everyone knows me. I'm not judged by the color of my skin or the assumptions of most of society. Here, I'm accepted. Here, I'm known to be intelligent and polite. Here, I'm home. It may not be much to some people. But compared to others… I live like a king. I know this. It is a gilded cage and I have golden handcuffs, but most of the time, I'm really happy. How many other people, much less young black men, can say that?"

I bowed my head. I had no answer. With all that had been going on in the news: the shootings, the riots, the injustice, and the cops killing unarmed black people, Adam had a point. Especially if you were standing in his shoes. Throw in the fear of open spaces on top of that and he had no way of experiencing the good people in the world… except for the people who worked at the PAR Lab. Suddenly, my situation seemed a thousand percent better than it had before, and I was already grateful for Heather and David.

We both looked up as the door to the garden opened. Carrie walked in with Ian behind her. They stopped when they saw us. "I'm sorry," Carrie called. "I didn't know anyone else was here. I wanted to give Ian the tour."

Adam stood. "No worries. I was giving Melissa the tour, too. This place is all yours. I've got one more thing to show her." He looked back at me and beckoned. "C'mon. You'll like this."

I stood in a hurry, balancing my partly eaten meal as I followed him out. I heard Carrie whisper, "Thanks." to Adam as we passed and saw him give her a wink. Once we were outside, the sealed door and the antechamber room, I asked. "Did I miss something?"

He grinned. "Carrie gave me the 'clear out' sign. I think she wanted some private time with her boyfriend. Too bad she's got such bad taste in men."

"She did? I missed it."

"Yeah. We have all kinds of signals for each other. It makes managing the scientists that much easier."

He didn't sound like the same guy who was sad at not having a family, was afraid of falling into the sky, and knew he wasn't leaving the lab. He sounded confident and comfortable once more. I couldn't tell if he was just good at hiding his feelings or what.

"Hey, I do have something to show you. I wasn't lying about that."

I tilted my head at his anticipatory tone. "What is it?"

"It's a surprise."

"Okay. But I want to change my shirt. This one is itchy." In truth, I wanted to dump my dinner somewhere so I could stop carrying it around and not eating it. I'd eat it later.

"Cool. No problems. You're really going to like this." We headed back up to Level A.

Adam waited for me outside my door. In the time it took me to situate my dinner for later and change my shirt, he had made the rest of his dinner—sandwich, chips, and all—disappear. I suspected he was like every teenage boy I'd ever known: a champion speed eater. The crumbs on his shirt told me that I was correct.

"Right. Is it still a surprise?"

He nodded. "Yeah, sorta. C'mon." Again he led me to the elevator. This time, he hit the button marked "E."

"What's on Level E?"

"The holding cells."

I blinked at him a couple of times. "What do you mean?"

"Remember when Ian said he accidentally captured a Minkowski?"

I nodded, getting a very bad feeling about all this.

Adam's excitement was clear. "Where do you think they're keeping it?"

CHAPTER SEVEN

I stared at Adam, trying to wrap my head around what he was telling me. "They keep the captured... *thing*... here? Why didn't they warn us? Don't you think that's something important to know?"

"My bet is that they didn't even think about it. They're studying it. It's already here. It's a sorta known quantity. It's probably why they're testing all of us here at the same time instead of sending me and Carrie with you guys elsewhere." He led me down the hallway with the confident step of a person who knew exactly where they were going and had been there before.

I followed, looking into each empty cell as we passed by. Each was a smooth cube of about twelve feet by twelve feet with rounded corners. I saw no seams where wall met floor or ceiling. I couldn't tell where the cell's illumination came from. I stumbled a little, my feet dragging. I took hold of myself and gave Adam a brave smile as he glanced back with a wordless question. *I'm fine*, I lied to myself.

Adam reached the last cell and waited for me. I could see colored light from within radiating out to flicker red, then green, across his face. Heart pounding, palms sweating, I thought, *I'm not fine. I'm afraid.* I didn't know if I wanted to see the alien. I didn't know if I even wanted to be here anymore. But, with Adam watching and waiting for me, I had no choice.

I stopped a couple feet away from him, at the edge of the cell, and peeked in. I don't know what I was expecting but it wasn't what was in front of me. Behind the glass in the center of the cell was what looked to be a large gaseous blob of light about three and a half, maybe four, feet in diameter. As I watched, the light pattern shifted from reds and greens to blues and yellows. Tiny streaks of lightning flickered over and through it.

"This is a Minkowski?"

Adam nodded. "Yeah. Pretty, huh."

Pretty is not the word I would've chosen. But, I had to admit it was interesting looking in a totally what-the-what kind of way. I didn't say any of that. Instead, I nodded and noticed that one wall had a row of small globes on it.

"It killed Ian's family?" I approached the glass.

He nodded again. "Yeah. Parents, sister, uncle. Maybe you shouldn't get to close, eh? The wall is a super strong polymer that isn't available for commercial use. Still, better safe. You know?"

I stopped and stepped back, closer to Adam. As I did so, the blob became humanoid shape without arms, but had a distinct head, torso, and legs. "What's it doing?"

"What do you mean?"

"Why did it change shape?" The creatures color flickered through the rainbow before shifting back to primarily reds and greens again.

Adam glanced at me. "Why is a soap bubble round?" He said it with the tone of someone quoting a beloved phrase.

I didn't recognize it. "Surface tension?" I shook my head and shrugged.

His shoulders slumped and I knew I'd missed something. "Because it's appropriate for the environment."

I tilted my head in invitation for him to continue because, again, I wasn't getting it.

"Because humans are here and it, he—I kinda think of it as a he—is mimicking his visitors." Adam shrugged. "I think he's trying to be polite."

"Is it sentient?" I couldn't think of the murderous blob of light as a he or a she. It was too alien. Something about it screamed of otherness that did not belong.

Before Adam could answer me, the Minkowski whipped out a tentacle of light filled with tiny lightning bolts and touched one of the globes in the wall. The globe lit up green with a faint crackle of sound.

I yelped, jumped back, and was already starting to run down the hall before Adam's voice, yelling that it was okay, caught up with me. I stuttered to a stop and looked over my shoulder. Part of me, the part that was still in Oneida with the Fedoras—and probably would be there forever—was yelling to keep running, to get away from the monster, to flee. I stopped because Adam looked so conflicted, but not hurt.

He took two steps towards me. "It's okay. It's okay. That's how he talks. Through the lights. I'm sorry. I should've warned you."

"It talks? You talk to it?" I heard my voice rising with my fear and surprise. I couldn't help it. My heart continued to pound and my mouth was dry. "It killed Ian's family and you want to talk to it?"

Adam rubbed his arm. "How else are we supposed to understand it? Maybe it didn't mean to kill Ian's family. Current theory holds that they communicate with each other by melding a little and exchanging, uh, electricity."

I didn't hear the crackle of the tiny lightning bolts but I did see the green glow from the wall. I walked back towards the cell, sticking to the far side of the hallway. When I could see the Minkowski again, I saw that it was next to the wall with the globes. Two light tentacles flashed out and touched two different globes. One pink. One blue.

"Me. Feel." Adam looked at me. "Pink indicates him. Blue indicates a feeling. I think he's apologizing for scaring you."

"How long has it been here?"

"Ever since Ian captured it. Just over two months, give or take."

I kept looking at it. "Four months for South Dakota and the Fedoras… Mega Aphis… murder. Two months later, these things. Three weeks later, the Nehrings off of Orcas Island. Is it me or are the incursions coming faster?"

Adam shook his head. "There've been other attacks going back at least a year. There were others captured. The others died, as far as I know. The Nehrings, even though they came from the ocean, died in their ocean based prisons. It was like, there was something hostile here, that we couldn't tell." He gazed back at the Minkowski. "This is the only one that has lived."

I glanced at it then asked Adam, "Did it know what it was doing when it killed Ian's family?" Out of the corner of my eye, I saw the creature move, to flickers of motion. A red light. Then a green light.

Adam watched me. "He says, no then yes."

"Were you scared?" I addressed my questions to Adam but we both knew I was talking to the Minkowski.

So did it. Green light.

"Yes," Adam translated.

Sentience meant it could lie. Meant possible malevolence. Meant it knew what it was doing. The thoughts and their terrible potential rolled around and around in my head.

"Were you angry?"

Green light. "Yes."

"Were you hurt?"

Red light. Green light. "No. Then yes." Adam paused. "When Ian tased it."

"Do you know why you came here to Earth?"

Green light. "Yes."

"Why?" The whole time I spoke to Adam, I could see the Minkowski out of the corner of my eye. In the side view, it looked like it was expanding. But not really. Like the shadow of it was expanding. It reminded me of an afterimage when someone takes your picture with a very bright flash. But it wasn't expanding in a bubble. It was expanding in almost a star-shaped pattern. I tried to keep myself calm when one of the points passed through the glass and moved slowly towards us.

Pink light. Pink light. Blue light. "We feel." Adam shrugged when I furrowed my brow at him in question. "We think hitting the "me" light more than once means the Minkowski as a group.

"But what does it mean by "we feel"? Why did it come here?"

He shook his head. "I don't know."

All the while, the afterimage shadow moved closer and closer to us. I knew with every fiber of my being that I didn't want it to touch me, touch us. I wanted to flee. I fought my fear then finally gave in to the Deroga's advice, "Sometimes, fear is the only thing that keeps us alive. Go with your gut."

I grabbed Adam's hand and gave him a weak smile. "Let's go. I want to walk." I didn't wait for an answer. I pulled him along with me and saw the afterimage shadow seem to lunge at us. Letting go of his hand, I broke into a run and yelled, "Race you!"

At this point, I didn't care if he was following. I needed to get away from that creature, its light, and its shadow. I didn't know or care if the shadow was just my imagination or not. Part of me knew the monster was dangerous. I sprinted down the hallway. I'm good at sprinting but Adam was better. He caught up with me, flashing a wide grin before pulling ahead.

I laughed. It felt good to run, to get away. I almost didn't stop in time and half crashed into the wall next to the elevator. Laughing, Adam reached out to stop me. I smoothed my hair down, feeling the warmth of his hand on my shoulder. It felt wonderful. It anchored me and pushed back the panic. We looked at each other and started to laugh again.

But panic still bubbled under the surface of that laughter. I could hear it even though Adam couldn't. I needed to get to my room to calm down before the laughter became tears. "You won," I said as I pushed the elevator button.

Adam nodded. "Genetically perfect."

Something about that made us both start laughing again. We giggled all the way up to Level A, fighting to keep some semblance of calm. Just as we had it under control, the wrong mingled glance would set us off again. It was a good thing that no one was in the hallway to see us acting like loons.

We stood outside the elevator for a long minute before Adam asked, "So, where else do you want to go? I can give you the whole tour, level by level if you like."

I shook my head. While I was feeling better, I knew I needed some quiet time away from people and to consider the ramifications of the day, my fight with Doctor Dudetsky, and the Minkowski. "I need to call David, Agent Hood. I promised. Plus I have to write in my journal. Part of my agreement with my doctor."

Not technically a lie. I did promise to call, just not this early. Also, the journal was completely true. Not that I didn't skip a few days here and there.

Adam nodded. "Okay. I'll be in the lounge tonight if you want company after your call and stuff." He stood there a moment longer then turned away just before it got awkward and walked down the hall towards the lounge.

I watched him go, not sure if I should wait until he was gone to go to my room or what. He turned into the washroom and answered my question. I hurried to my room, already pulling out my phone. I texted David: "Need to talk ASAP. Skype in 5?"

My phone vibrated as I closed the door. The answer was simple: "Yes."

I threw myself onto the bed with a great sigh of relief. David would know how to set things right. Maybe I would call Heather afterward. If that was allowed. I frowned. Nothing was said either way. Better to ask forgiveness…

Exactly five minutes later, David called. I think he set a timer or something. I sat up and thumbed the answer icon. As soon as he appeared, I knew he was worried. In truth, I was worried, too.

"Hey," I said, not sure how to start.

"Hello." David must have set up his phone in a stand or was using a laptop with a webcam because I could see him head on. He wasn't looking up or down at me. He tilted his head. "So…?"

"So... I hate it here and I don't want to do this anymore." The words came out before I realized what I was saying. I glanced away and back again.

David's worried look turned into something a lot more parental and relaxed. "But, nothing's wrong?"

"Yes. No..." I paused, then remembered the afterimage shadow. "Yes."

"Which is it; yes or no?"

I buried my face in my hand. "I don't know. I just don't. I... things are wrong and weird."

"All right. Tell me."

I looked up at the return of his worried tone. Already I was feeling silly for insisting on the call hours before the scheduled time. "You have time?"

"Melissa, you say that something is wrong. I trust you. Remember how we met? Tell me and let's work this out."

"You sure?"

"Yes."

I nodded. "Okay." I told David everything except about the hallucinations and the afterimage with the Minkowski. From the schedule to the fight with Doctor Dudetsky to the other tests to the garden and ended with meeting the Minkowski. "And then I got wigged out and convinced Adam to race me to the elevator because I needed to give you a call. And I did."

David was quiet for long enough that I thought he'd disconnected. "David?" I hoped I hadn't confessed almost everything to a dead phone.

"I'm here." He shifted and flashed me a brief smile. "Just thinking about what you said. I warned them that you kids survived because you were unusual. The argument with Doctor Dudetsky might have been a test to see what you'd do when presented with a situation that could be dangerous to you."

"For me?"

"For all of you."

I shook my head. "Nah. Adam says that Doctor Dudetsky is always grumpy and isn't used to being defied. At all. He's kinda an alpha scientist or something."

"Ah. All right. I wonder what your report is going to say."

"That I'm uncooperative and a pain in the ass."

That brief, closed-mouth smile appeared. "It's true. But, I think you had a good reason."

"Did you know the Minkowski was here?" I didn't want to ask but I needed to know.

He nodded. "Yes. And yes, we figured that all of you were going to meet it at one time or another. Officially or not."

"Why didn't you tell me?"

"I tried to talk to you on the drive over but you didn't really want to talk. I decided it was better to let you not stew about it. I mean, would you have been happier knowing it was there?"

"I guess not. But why are we all here?"

David tilted his head. "The tests are real. There's something going on and three of you have some innate defenses… or flaws that serve as a defense against these incursions. Also, in all honesty, we wanted to know how all of you kids reacted to it. You, in particular."

I felt both oddly pleased and confused. "Me? Why?"

He shrugged. "You have a very different way of looking at the world. Your brain works in odd ways. I know Adam likes it and Carrie doesn't care. Ian is curious but cautious, and I can't blame him for that. He's the one who captured it after all."

"What about Sean?

"As far as I know, Sean hasn't ventured past Level C. He goes where he needs to go and no more."

"Well, he's still healing."

David nodded. "Yes. He's still healing."

"Tell me about them? I mean, Carrie's read my file. My real file. Adam's amazing but I can't help but feel like he's getting the short end of the stick. Ian is hurting and acting out. And poor Sean. He's reeling from what just happened to him."

"There's not much more to tell than what they told you in the lounge—I received a transcript of the interaction, good job on the mirror thing. Carrie hacked into some really sensitive places. In truth, she's the one who caught the hint that there were alien incursions and that they were happening more and more frequently. Until she started putting it together, they were just a bunch of separate, unusual situations we had files on. It's her curiosity that made her break into databases she shouldn't have even known about.

"You know about Adam, from what you've told me. He's the one I've had the least interaction with. Ian… is fighting some personal demons, but he's doing all right. And you're right about Sean. He's hurt. Bad. And his status as officially dead is a complication." David leaned forward and put his chin on his hands. "We really do want to do right by you kids. This is a new situation. There will be stumbling blocks."

He paused and leaned back. "But none of this tells me why you're so upset. Why did you want to talk now? You were so pale when we first connected. What happened? Does it have to do with the Minkowski?"

This was the do or die moment. Do I trust him with the truth or not? He did come into the quarantine zone to protect me and help me find what was causing the euthanasia field. I took a breath. "About that…"

"Yeah?"

"I've started hallucinating again. Not big things but it started yesterday and has happened two… maybe three… times."

David pursed his lips and repeated. "'Two maybe three times.' All right. Tell me."

"I saw black cobwebs in my room when I was packing and black butterflies during the afternoon tests."

"Black cobwebs are new but not the butterflies." David kept his face neutral as he spoke. "Definitely write that down in your journal and talk to Doctor Giacomi when you have your first personal session." He looked down at something. "That'll be tomorrow."

"She can't change my meds, can she?"

"No. But her thoughts will be sent to Doctor Ferguson."

I breathed a sigh of relief. "Okay. Good."

"Now, tell me about the maybe third time. Why is it maybe? What was it of?"

I hesitated, feeling my cheeks flush. "I don't know what I saw. I don't know if I'm wrong. I… I really can't tell if it was real or not."

"Melissa, it's okay." David gestured to the screen. "It's me. I understand you. Caveats heard and accepted."

I laughed a little. "Thanks. The Minkowski. I saw… I think I saw it expand. Out of the cell."

His eyes got wide, then they narrowed and he stared at me. "Explain."

I explained it as best I could with the afterimage example and how it spread out from the creature in the shape of a star and how I could only see it out of the corner of my eye.

"Honestly, it was more like feeling the thing than seeing it. I mean, you can't see someone looking at you from behind, but you can sense it. It was a lot like that. And I swear, it did move for us when I pulled Adam away from it."

I dug my hands into my hair. "That's why I think, maybe, probably, it wasn't real. I mean, it was so alien and weird. I think my brain was pulling out all the stops to get me to run away."

David nodded. "All right. I'll talk with a few people and have them send all of their surveillance video for that time period to analysis. They watch the thing in multiple spectrums. We'll see what we can see and I'll let you know our progress tomorrow.

"In the meantime, you need to write about this in your journal—your confusion and your fear. We'll talk about what you write before you see Doctor Ferguson. I'm certain her security clearance is high enough, but I need to make sure." He paused. "Don't talk about this last bit with Doctor Giacomi. Stick to the concrete as much as possible with her. You can talk about being afraid of the Minkowski but not the rest."

I nodded, feeling my shoulders relax. "Deal. I can do that."

"Hey."

"Yeah?"

David smiled, a broad, reassuring smile. "Thank you. I know that must've been hard. Telling me about the hallucinations. I'm proud of you."

"You're welcome." My smile mirrored his.

"I've got your back. Just remember that when you're talking to Doctor Giacomi tomorrow. Even when it's scary. I'm there. Courage is what you do when you're afraid."

"I know it'll be okay in the end. I'll call you tomorrow."

"Bye." David gave me a little wave.

I returned the wave as I thumbed the Skype call closed. I was proud of me, too. At that moment, I knew everything would be okay. Feeling so much better, I called Heather's cellphone. It went to voicemail.

"I'm sorry I can't answer your call. Leave me a message. Also, if this is Melissa, I'm thinking of you. I've been called out of town for a couple of days. Don't worry. I know you're doing great."

It hurt that she wasn't there but I was happy to hear her voice and that she was thinking of me. That was one of the reasons she was the best agent and guardian a girl like me could have. At the beep, I said, "Heya Heather. Just checking in. Don't work too hard. I'm doing fine. Call David if you have questions."

I ended the call and hugged the phone to my chest. "I can handle this. Everything will be just fine."

I hate it when I accidentally lie to someone—especially when I lie to myself.

LOCKDOWN

CHAPTER EIGHT

"–NOT A DRILL. PAR LABORATORY IS NOW IN LOCKDOWN. REPORT TO APPROPRIATE STATIONS. REPEAT. THIS IS NOT A DRILL. PAR LABORATORY IS NOW IN LOCKDOWN. REPORT TO APPROPRIATE STATIONS."

I woke to a world bathed in red light, shouting robots, and an alarm signal so loud it almost made my ears bleed. At the first shrill alarm, I rolled out of bed and hit the floor hard enough for my head to bounce, adding stars of pain to my already confused state. I struggled to my feet, Mister Bat in hand, looking for the danger. While I didn't see anything, I was half certain I was back in Oneida and a Fedora was coming for me.

Two attempted steps later and I was on the floor again with bruised knees. Muzzy headed from the Prazosin, I couldn't get my thoughts in order, even with the shouting robot quiet. I pushed the sheet and blankets away from me and stood with deliberate intention. Brain fogged or not, this was an emergency and I needed to get in gear.

My body moved on automatic as I continued to scan for danger. I pushed my feet into socks, then jeans, keeping Mister Bat nearby. Next came the bra, the t-shirt, and the sweatshirt. I kept my movement fast and as clean as possible. I was wearing what I'd worn the day before because it was handy. But I wasn't going anywhere unprepared. I grabbed my cross-body purse and shoved my phone, its charger, and my pills into it. Everything else was unneeded or already in it or on me. Last came my sneakers. You never knew what you'd be running from or to.

Three shrill notes sounded, making me shriek and jump. I swung Mister Bat in an involuntary arc, expecting an attack. Nothing was there, except the shouting robot.

"THIS IS NOT A DRILL. PAR LABORATORY IS NOW IN LOCKDOWN. REPORT TO APPROPRIATE STATIONS. REPEAT. THIS IS NOT A DRILL. PAR LABORATORY IS NOW IN LOCKDOWN. REPORT TO APPROPRIATE STATIONS."

I peeked out my door and saw an empty hallway bathed in red. In the unfamiliar light, the hallway looked like one of my nightmares. The blue walls were now black and the white floor was red. The recessed lighting was also red.

"Jesus wept," I whispered before I sprinted down the hallway to the lounge. Adam and Sean were already in the room. Both jumped as I burst in, Mister Bat held high. Adam backed away in flight response. Sean raised his weapon, a cricket bat, in fight response, and took a step towards me before he realized who and what I was.

"Melissa, what the hell?" Adam recovered and came towards me.

Sean nodded to me and Mister Bat. I nodded back to him. He was fully dressed and armed. Sean got it. He understood. I came deeper into the lounge and turned, watching the door, waiting to see what would come through next. In my heart of hearts, I was babbling that the Fedoras had finally come for me. They wanted revenge.

"Melissa? Did you see anything?" Adam didn't touch me. Instead, I felt him recede into clinical observation.

"No." I glanced at him. Shorts, t-shirt, bare feet. This was Adam's home. The only home he'd known. Of course he was comfortable here. Of course he'd be unprepared in a crisis. "Is this a test? Are they testing us?" I looked over his shoulder at the mirror. "And why aren't you wearing shoes?"

"I never wear shoes at night." Adam peered at me as if I were some strange insect he didn't quite recognize. "And, I don't know. I don't think it's a test. The only time a lockdown happens is on a scheduled maintenance test. Never on a random one. We all know when it will happen. Events kick off when a lockdown occurs. We go to designated areas until we're evacuated. Security patrols, making a clean sweep. There's a computer component but I don't know the ins and outs of that."

Ian came through the door at a good clip. He was wearing sweatpants, a t-shirt, and socks. "What the hell is going on?" He was breathing hard like he'd been running. "What's happening?"

I noted the lack of shoes and knew that we needed to get that fixed for him and Adam. And soon. I also found myself shoulder-to-shoulder with Sean. Both of us held our weapons at our sides.

"We don't know," Adam answered. "This isn't right."

Carrie hurried into the room, fully dressed, with her laptop in hand. Her hair was disheveled but she also had a jacket on.

"You're late," Ian said, looking relieved.

"Naked girls die first." Carrie hefted her laptop from one arm to the other and opened it. "Besides, I couldn't leave Morpheus behind."

"Deroga Darrington." I smiled at her.

Carrie nodded. "Pretty Penny, actually. But, yeah."

Three shrill notes sounded, warning that the shouting robot was back.

"THIS IS NOT A DRILL. PAR LABORATORY IS NOW IN LOCKDOWN. REPORT TO APPROPRIATE STATIONS. REPEAT. THIS IS NOT A DRILL. PAR LABORATORY IS NOW IN LOCKDOWN. REPORT TO APPROPRIATE STATIONS."

After the end alarm signal rang, Carrie stared at the ceiling in a listening pose. "That's three. Nine minutes since the alarm was set off. That should be it for the noise."

"What about the lights?" I asked. "It's a horror show in here. Who decided on red lights against blue walls? Or didn't anyone test this before spending the money to make it happen?"

"Don't know." She shook her head as she typed furiously on her computer. "Well, shit. Lockdown locked all the servers and booted all the users. Even the admins. I can't do anything about the lights until I get into the server room or we get security to flip the appropriate switches."

I looked back towards the mirror. Adam saw me. He raised his chin in understanding and moved to the mirror. Cupping his hands around his eyes, he pressed his face to the glass. For a long moment, no one said or did anything except watch.

Adam straightened and shook his head. "No. I can't see anyone through there. But I did see a table and a row of chairs facing us."

"Well, that answers that." I looked at the rest of them and saw Ian move for the door. "No! Ian, stop." He did and looked at me, cocking his head to one side in an unspoken question. "We're in a horror movie now. No one goes anywhere alone. At all. No one."

Carrie smiled briefly and Adam laughed. But the other two nodded. When Carrie and Adam saw Ian and Sean nodding, Adam shook his head.

"We're not in a horror movie. We're in one of the most secure labs in the world."

"That's on lockdown and has a monster in its basement." Ian's voice was quiet as he spoke. "With a skeleton crew manning the helm. Yeah. Sounds like a horror movie to me." He looked to me. "I just want to see if anyone's coming."

I wanted to argue with him, but I couldn't think of a reason to say no. "Just peek. And if you come back headless, it's your own damn fault." Oh, yeah. I was stressed. I couldn't stop my swear words and I wasn't really trying.

"Heard and accepted." Ian took a breath, squared his shoulders, walked to the doorway, and looked out. He yelped in surprise and backpedaled fast.

There was a second gasp from outside the room. Then Doctor Dudetsky came barreling through the door. "What is the matter with you, boy?"

"Sorry, sir. I was just looking."

Doctor Dudetsky looked around the room. "Good. You're all here." He eyed me and Sean and our weapons without comment. "I'm going to take you kids out of here. Elevator, now." He turned on his heel and expected us to follow.

Carrie and Adam were already moving out the door with Ian in the lead, close behind Doctor Dudetsky. Sean and I followed, bringing up the rear like guards. In truth, that's exactly what I was doing. I wasn't going to let anything get us from behind.

"Where's Lakshmi?" Carrie was asking when we got to the group crowded around the elevator, waiting for the doors to open up.

Doctor Dudestsky shook his head. "I expected her to be in the lounge. You are her first priority. Though, I thought she might wait for me to arrive before taking you to the surface of the complex."

The elevator doors opened and the old man stepped in. "C'mon. Everyone in. Squeeze if you have to."

We didn't need to squeeze but we were elbow to elbow. Ian put his arm around Carrie to make a little more room. Doctor Dudetsky pressed the "1" button and nothing happened. He scowled and waved his wallet at the sensor. Again, nothing happened. The elevator doors closed and he sighed to himself. Again, he waved his wallet at the sensor and pressed the "1" button.

"Nothing's happening," Sean said.

I couldn't tell if he was pale under the red light reflected against the metal of the elevator walls but I knew from his rapid breathing and darting eyes he was having a problem. "You okay?" I whispered.

He shook his head. "Tight spaces."

Doctor Dudetsky took his featureless white access key from his wallet and held it to the sensor, then he mashed the "1" button and then the "2" button. "I know nothing's happening. It should. I have the highest access rating in the building."

"Maybe the elevator is broken?" Carrie asked in a small voice.

Ian reached out and pushed the button for Level B. Immediately, the elevator jerked into life. "Oh, shit," he muttered and tried to shift Carrie behind him.

We all watched the elevator doors, as we shifted positions, getting Sean and Carrie to the rear of the small room, trying to protect them if something was there. The doors opened on an empty black hallway filled with red light. It would've been funny if it wasn't so scary. The elevator doors started to close but Sean shot his cricket bat out to stop them. Then he was shoving his way through me and Ian to get out of the small room.

"Sean MacGregor, you get back in here right now," Doctor Dudetsky rumbled.

I looked back at the doctor and saw the strain on his face. He looked terribly old in the red light.

"No, sir. I'm sorry. I can't. I'll take the stairs back up. I'll meet you in the lounge."

I put out a hand to stop the elevator doors from closing. "No one goes alone. Horror movie rules."

Doctor Dudetsky glared at me. "The young lady is right. Get back in this elevator at once."

Oh, was that how he wanted to play the game? The old codger could say Sean's name but not mine.

Adam gave me an "I told you so" glance.

"I can't, sir. I'm sorry. I just can't." Sean looked around, trembling.

I stepped out of the elevator. "All right. Claustrophobia sucks. I'll go with you and you won't be alone." I smiled at him before I turned and addressed Doctor Dudetsky. "We'll take the stairs and meet you in the lounge.

"Get back in here, both of you!" This time, the doctor put a hand out to stop the elevator doors from closing. Five seconds later and the elevator alarm started, complaining that it couldn't do its job.

The doctor and I glared at each other, facing off in the ultimate 'who could out stubborn the other' match.

"We should go to the security office," Ian said, interrupting what promised to be quite the argument. "That's where we can turn off these lights and figure out why the elevator isn't going up to the surface."

I nodded to him with a grateful smile. "That's a good idea but I don't know where that is." I looked over my shoulder at Sean who had put his back to me and was scanning down both visible hallways. "Do you?"

He shook his head, "No."

I couldn't see his face but he was standing taller than before. I hoped he was better. I looked back at Doctor Dudetsky who was seething at me. Whatever he was about to say was interrupted by Adam stepping out of the elevator. "I know the way. I'll take them, Doctor. It'll be faster this way. You guys go by elevator. We'll take the stairwell. We can check the door at the top, too."

Doctor Dudetsky's face ran through the gamut of surprise, betrayal, resignation, and the neutral acceptance at Adam's defection. I thought Adam would pay for this act for years to come. This was the second time in two days that he'd defied Doctor Dudetsky to back me up. But, that was a battle yet to come. Now, as the elevator doors shut, Adam was on our side.

"I go first. Sean, you're second. Adam, you keep the monsters off our back. Okay?" I looked each of them in the eye and got a head nod before I turned for the stairwell door. I kept my bat ready as I pushed the door open and was met by almost total darkness. There was no red light in the stairwells but there were faintly glow strips on the outsides of the stairs. That was the only light and the only way to tell where the stairs and landings were.

"Well, shit. Hold on. Keep the door open."

Adam did as I asked. He shook his head, frowning. "This isn't right. There should be emergency lights in here. Power doesn't go off. We're not on the grid. We've got our own generators." He sounded scared for the first time. "Either someone turned them off or we have no power in the lab."

"Either way," I said, "it's bad news on burnt toast." I fumbled for my phone and found the flashlight app. As soon as it lit up the stairs, I saw a woman's hand dangling over the edge of the stairway landing.

CHAPTER NINE

"Holy crap." I ran up the stairs to the landing, afraid that it was Lakshmi. It didn't make me feel any better to discover it was Jolene. She was facedown against the cold concrete, her red hair spread out around her, hiding her face.

"Is she dead?" Sean came up behind me with Adam behind him.

I shook my head. "I don't know." Crouching down, I hesitated to touch her, to roll her over, but I knew I needed to. I grabbed her by one shoulder. It was warm and pliant as I pulled. I took that as a good sign. The last shoulder I'd pulled on like this had turned the whole body over like a log. It was a memory I would never forget.

I handed my phone to Sean. "Keep the light on her."

Pulling her over onto her side, then her back, we all saw Jolene's scorched clothing and burned skin. The damage was mostly centered around her chest. It look like something had electrocuted her. I put a trembling hand to her neck and found a fluttery pulse. I leaned down to her and felt her breath on my cheek. "She's alive. We've got to get her out of here."

Adam moved up. "I'll take her. I'm the strongest and you need both your hands."

I didn't argue. I got out of the way and took my phone back from Sean. Adam easily scooped up the smaller woman and cradled her close to his body. He looked back to me for instructions.

"Me first. Then you. Then Sean. Three across when we get to the hallway." I didn't wait for comments, questions, or contradictions. I was scared out of my mind and if I stopped to think about what we were doing, I would falter. I knew me. I had to go with my gut. I led us up, my phone light and the glowing stripes on either side gave us enough light not to fall on our faces.

Emerging into the red lit hallway was both a relief and awful. With Adam carrying an injured Jolene, my nightmare analogy was becoming far too real. "Which way?"

Adam nodded to the left. "Through that door." He indicated the featureless door that looked like every storage room door I'd ever seen.

I went first, opening the door. There was a small room that was part storage, part antechamber, and part short hallway. There were shelves on both sides of the room filled with office supplies: paper, tape, pens, and other such necessities of a paper based company. The closed door opposite me was just as featureless as the first. I opened and saw a hallway that was a twin to the floors below us.

"Where's the security station?" I led the way pretending a confidence I didn't feel. Talk about faking it until you made it.

"It's just around the corner." Adam shifted his body sideways to get him and Jolene through the semi-closet. Sean followed, closing the door behind us. He stayed behind us as Adam and I walked next to each other.

As we turned the corner, I saw Carrie standing outside a door, looking in. She hugged her laptop to her like a security blanket. The look on her face, wide eyes and mouth in a small O, was pure fear. By tacit agreement, we sped up, hurrying to her and the rest.

"Carrie, what's wrong?" Adam shifted Jolene closer to him to keep her from being jostled.

"He's dead." Her eyes went even wider when she turned and saw Adam carrying Jolene.

"Who's dead? What happened?" I brushed aside them and looked into the room she was staring into. I saw a windowless room filled with computer equipment and monitors. All of the monitors were dark. Ian and Doctor Dudetsky were crouched over one of the black uniformed guards.

"It's Joe Chambers." Carrie's normally chipper voice was barely a whisper.

"What happened?"

Carrie shook her head and backed away from the door and Adam. "Is Jolene…?"

I moved inside the security office, talking as I went so I didn't startle the doctor or Ian. I raised my voice loud enough for everyone to hear me. "We found Jolene in the stairwell. She's alive but burned."

Ian's head shot up at that. "Burned? Burned how?"

He was already moving towards and past me as I answered. "I don't know. Electrical, maybe." He didn't answer and I didn't follow up. My eyes were on the large wet smears on the ground next to the guard—*Joe Chambers,* I reminded myself —as Doctor Dudetsky examined the body. When he turned the guard over, the stab wound to the heart was apparent.

Doctor Dudetsky shook his head and stood with a groan. "Dead. How could this happen?" He leaned to the computer and jiggled the mouse. The monitors remained dark with no signs of movement. I watched and stayed out of the way as Doctor Dudetsky moved with methodical skill to try to get any of the computers and monitors to boot up. "Why isn't it working?"

"Is it plugged in?" I didn't mean to ask but it's the first thing any tech person asks of an unresponsive machine.

He gave me a hard glance but didn't say anything. Instead, he leaned down and looked under the desk. "Huh. No. The power strip is dark." He looked at it, considered, then gazed at me, gesturing to the floor. "Would you get it? I'm getting too old to be creeping around under desks."

I was aware I had an audience. This was a time of crisis. Snarky (or petty) comebacks weren't appropriate. "Sure. You may want to look at Jolene. She's alive but her pulse is weak."

He furrowed his eyebrows at me, confused. "Jolene?"

"We found her unconscious and burned in the stairwell."

Doctor Dudetsky looked up and beyond me. "Where's Doctor Gowda?" We all shook our heads. He grunted then nodded. "Get the computers working if you can."

"Okay doc." I looked over my shoulder. "Carrie? You're the computer whiz." I hunkered down and crawled under the desk. I put my bat next to me and fumbled for the power strip cord. I found it. It was wet and tacky to the touch. Grimacing as I plugged it back in, I heard Carrie say, "That's it."

I lifted my hand to my face. Even though I couldn't see my hand very well, I knew it was covered with blood. My nose did all the verifying I needed. I crawled back out with awkward shifts as I dragged Mister Bat with me. I didn't want to rub blood onto my pants and I wanted to show someone else. Why would the end of power strip cord be covered in blood?

Carrie scowled at the monitor as I made it to my feet. "Everything is either frozen or in a weird state or trying to reboot."

"Can you get the regular lights to come back on?" I held my gore covered hand away from me as if it were a dead fish.

"No. Not until things all reboot or I get into the server room." She looked at me and my hand. "What the what?"

"Blood. There was blood on the end of the power strip cord."

She looked down at the guard's body. "Why would Joe unplug the computers? What would that solve?"

I leaned to her. "Better question: who the hell stabbed him?" I found a couple of paper napkins and cleaned my hand off as best I could. I knew I would be digging blood traces out from under my nails until I could get a shower. This did not fill me with glee.

Carrie shook her head. "I don't know. We can't get out of here until I get the system fixed."

"Can you do it from here?"

She smiled. "Oh yeah. I can make this baby tap dance if I want to. But it's going to take time. Until then, we're still in the horror show."

"At least it's quiet now."

"Guys. Guys. We got to go." Sean stood in the doorway, looking glassy-eyed and terrified. "Now. We got to go now!" Adam ran past him towards the opposite way that we came in with Jolene slung over his shoulder like a bag of potatoes.

My heart sank and I stuck my head out the door. At the far end where we'd come in, the Minkowski hovered. It seemed larger as it waited there. Ian shook his head in terrified denial as he backpedaled until he was even with me and Sean. Then, without a word, he brushed past me into the office, grabbed Carrie by the arm in one hand and Carrie's laptop in the other. He ignored her squawk of protest and pulled her from the office, dragging her towards the path of escape.

Doctor Dudetsky moved between the teens and the monster. "You go. I'll hold it off."

Already backing up, I asked, "How? C'mon!"

"With this. We know it's effective." He held up his hand and brandished a two-pronged stun gun at the Minkowski. "Now go. Dammit, Allen, obey me for once."

Sean and I turned and ran down the hallway. I paused at the corner to look back. Right then, I saw the Minkowski rush towards Doctor Dudetsky and envelop him. Lightning crackled in and around both of them as Doctor Dudetsky stiffened with a cry of pain.

Sean grabbed my arm and pulled me around the corner. Doctor Dudetsky's pain-filled shouts followed us. We sprinted down the hallway, past the observation room on the other side of the lounge, and into a wall.

I looked around for another storage door and didn't see it. "Where's the door? How do we get out? Where'd they go?" We looked around frantically, pressing and hitting anything that looked like it could be a door but nothing moved. There had to be a door near here.

"Oh, god." Sean's voice took on a tone of resignation.

I looked to where he was looking and we both saw the Minkowski's light preceding it in horror show colors under the lockdown red light. It was bright enough to bounce off the end of the hallway. That's when I realized that I hadn't heard Doctor Dudetsky in a while. I didn't like the man but he didn't deserve to die like that.

"Here's the plan," Sean said, taking a couple steps forward. "I'll distract it and you go around it and escape."

I shook my head. I knew there had to be another way. There was. I could see the observation room through the open door. I shook his shoulder and pointed at it. "Here's the plan. You stop being an idiot and you come help me break through that mirror." I grabbed his wrist and pulled him towards the room.

The Minkowski turned the corner and filled the entire hallway with its light. Tentacles of light and electricity stretched out to the sides, skimming over the artificially black walls, briefly making it other colors—including the sky blue shade. It didn't rush towards us. It seemed to be searching, seeking, questing.

I filed that away for later. "C'mon," I mouthed. We hid in the room, closing the door quietly. Both of us moved on instinct. The quieter we were, the less likely we would be caught. At least, I know that's what I was thinking. For the moment, breaking the mirror was out of the question.

I looked around and took stock. There wasn't much here. A long table with chairs in front of it and a large metal cabinet to the far right of the room. It was large enough that one of us could hide in it if it wasn't too full of crap. The other could hide behind it. I shifted my purse, tucked my bat under my arm, and grabbed both handles, turning them slowly to mask the sound of metal scraping against metal.

To our surprise, the whole thing was empty. Sean and I didn't hesitate. We both stepped in and pulled the doors shut behind us as the light of

Minkowski reached the observation room door and shone through under the crack. It wasn't until we were inside the cabinet that we realized something was weird about the cabinet doors

"Why are there handles inside?" Sean whispered.

I shook my head and whispered back. "I don't know. I think this might be—"

I didn't get to finish my sentence. The cabinet wall behind us opened and hands grabbed us, yanking us backwards into blackness.

CHAPTER TEN

I did not scream and neither did Sean. What I did do was make sure I kept Mister Bat because I was going to beat the crap out of whoever had hold of me as soon as I could—friend or foe. I raised my bat to stomach height and twisted hard away from Sean. I didn't want to hit him. I did hit someone. Not hard. Just enough to make them let go.

"Ow! Shit!" A male voice hissed low and in pain.

"Who the hell are you?" I kept Mister Bat up in a defensive posture. I still could not see anyone—or anything for that matter—in the darkness. "Sean?"

"Here." He was now on my right instead of my left. The darkness wasn't completely pitch black. Without the red light, my eyes quickly adjusted to the new dimness.

"No. It's Ian," the other voice grumbled. "Christ, that hurt."

"I'm here, too. Adam." That voice came from the same side as Sean.

"Do any of you have a light?"

"No." It was Adam again. "But we don't need it. Just put your hand on the person next to you and follow me. The passageway is clear and we don't have far to go."

I put my hand on Sean's shoulder and felt Ian put his hand on my back. We moved in the herky-jerky movement of the blind leading the blind in an unfamiliar place. We couldn't have gone more than ten or fifteen feet before the group paused and Adam opened up another door.

This one let the familiar red light in and allowed us to see. We walked into a bedroom almost identical to the room I was staying in. As soon as

I was through, I looked to see what we'd come through. It was a hidden door behind a wall-mounted mirror. I noted that it was a real mirror and not a creepy one-way mirror.

"How'd you find out about this? I thought you didn't know about the observation room." I noted that Jolene was on the bed and Carrie was at the desk with her laptop open.

"I asked Lakshmi to show me. I hadn't known about the observation room." He shrugged. "She did when I asked. She rarely says no to me. But when she does, she has a reason. I guess, since the secret was out, there was no more reason to hide it."

"Are we safe here?" Sean hugged the cricket bat to him. "That thing was right at the observation room. Can it find us?"

"It can open doors. I know that. I saw Sean shut the other door behind us." I went over to Jolene and checked on her. Her breathing was normal but her heartbeat was irregular.

Adam looked from one to the other of us. "I don't know."

"Okay," Carrie said. "Before we start panicking, let's figure out what we *do* know. Like, who's alive, dead, missing, or injured. Let's start with that. Then we'll move on from there."

"Injured: Jolene Lake," I said.

"Dead: Joe Chambers," Ian said.

Sean looked up. "Dead: Doctor Dudetsky."

"We didn't see that." I gazed down at Jolene's charred clothing and pointed at it. "She got hit with the monster's electricity and she lived."

"Doctor Dudetsky: unknown, possibly injured or dead." Carrie paused in her typing. "Anyone see Lakshmi or Patrick Forester?" We all shook our heads. "Okay. They also go in the Unknown category."

"So does Doctor Giacomi." I thought about the calm psychiatrist and wished she was here.

"One dead, four unknown, one injured, and us. As far as I know, that's all the people that were in the underground levels this week." Carrie looked up. "What do we need to do now?"

"Get out of here as soon as possible." Ian moved over to the desk. "And part of that, I think, is getting you into the server room."

Carrie typed as she spoke. "What else?"

"Radios. We need to split up to look for the missing people but we have to be able to talk to each other." Ian looked at me as he spoke. "We're in a horror movie after all. If we have to do the dumb stuff, we need to be smart about it."

"Access cards." Adam shifted from the wall where he stood and held up a black white access card. "The only reason the observation room was open was because Doctor Dudetsky gave me his access key. The door was locked. My keycard and Carrie's only have the basic access to them. They won't open practically anything now."

"Doctor Dudetsky's card will get me into the server room." Carrie tapped the side of her computer as she thought. "There were radios in the security station and I'm pretty sure that Joe had his access keycard on him. That should give us a second access key that actually opens secured areas."

I looked down at Jolene. "Hold on." I patted her pockets, looking for her access keycard. They were all empty." I paused. "Anyone know if the Minkowski can use or carry a physical object?"

Ian shook his head. "No. Not that I saw. They're pretty intangible."

"Okay. Radios, access cards, and getting us into the server room to see if we can get us out of lockdown. That's the top priority." I pulled my phone from my purse. It had about three-fourths of a charge and two bars. "We also have to let the world know what happened here. That the alien has escaped."

"Tell who?" Carrie asked. "We're wards of the state. Adam and I live here. Sean hasn't been assigned an agent. Ian's agent got called away on business as soon as he came here. So, unless you have someone up your sleeve…"

"You read my file. I've got Agent David Hood. He's the one who brought me here. I talked to him last night. He's staying in one of the nearby buildings. If anyone knows what to do now, he would be it."

"So, call him." Sean looked at each of us then gestured to me. "Let's see what they have to say. Maybe they've already got a plan to get us out of here."

The room grew quiet as they all stared at me. "All right." I shifted until I had my back to everyone and called David. I put the phone to my ear and listened to it ring. It rang six times before his voicemail picked up. *Dammit*. Nothing to do but leave a message. "Heya David. I know we just talked but there are some serious problems down here. We're in red light lockdown and… the thing that scared me… it escaped. It's killed at least one person. We need help and we need out of here. Call me as soon as you can."

I hung up and turned around. "He's probably in an emergency meeting. On the good side of things, cell phones are still working."

Everyone slumped, disappointed. I felt bad for raising their hopes, then dashing them. "Don't worry. David will call. And if something happens that he can't, we got a message out. Speaking of which, who else has cell phones?"

Adam and Carrie looked at each other and shook their heads. "We're not allowed to have them down here. Besides, we have our computers and IM."

"Mine was lost at sea." Sean looked away. "I don't have a new one because they don't know what to do with me."

"My agent told me not to bring my cell phone," Ian said. "How come you got to bring yours?"

I shrugged. "I don't know. We weren't told not to and Lakshmi knew I had it. We talked about me calling David to report in on a nightly basis."

Carrie waved a hand. "None of that matters now. What matters is that we tried and that they know we're in trouble. That means we've got to do what we need to in order to survive. So, call made. We need radios. We need in that server room."

"Where is the server room?" I asked.

"Problem number one," Adam said. "It's two doors down from the security station. It was one of the doors with a small window and no windows into the room because it needs to be kept at a consistent temperature."

Sean cleared his throat and shifted the handle of his cricket bat from hand to hand. "How are we going to get in there with the Minkowski running around? Is there another secret passageway?"

"Not that I know of." Adam glanced at Carrie who shrugged. "The only thing we can do is see if it is still there. We know it can open doors."

Ian raised a hand. "I volunteer as tribute."

"What? No." Carrie half-stood, then swat at Ian's shaking head. "Oh. Damn. You're right."

"Yes. I am." Ian smiled at her. He continued to look at her as he said, "For those who don't understand, I know the Minkowskians best. I fought them. I captured it. I should be the one to go."

"Not alone. Horror movie rules." Adam nodded to him. "We go in pairs."

"All right. You both scout. You both come back. You have ten minutes." I looked at my phone. Was it really only three in the morning?

"Fifteen. It's a big place." Ian looked at Adam who nodded his agreement.

Carrie shrugged. "Fifteen but no more. And go out this side. See if you can come up behind it if it's still on this floor, trying to figure out how we all disappeared into thin air."

Ian gave her a mock salute then gestured to Adam. The two boys peeked out the door at the hallway. They were quiet for a moment then Ian slipped out, followed by Adam. Sean closed the door after them.

We stood there, looking at each other for long enough that it got uncomfortable. I didn't know what to say. I turned to check on Jolene and took refuge in the fact that someone needed a skill I had. I checked her breathing and her pulse. It was the same. I resisted the urge to shake her awake.

"Dammit," Carrie muttered, typing on her laptop. "I wish I had wi-fi or something. Can you turn that cell phone into a hot spot?"

"No. It's not something we have on the service. I wish David would call back." I picked my phone up again.

"It doesn't matter what I wish," Sean said from his place by the door. "It won't change anything. At least the two of you have a chance of getting your wish to come true."

With that, my phone vibrated, startling me so bad that I almost dropped it as I stifled a yelp of surprise. I don't know if it was me or my phone that startled the other two but Carrie jumped to her feet, pulling her laptop to her and Sean went from a comfortable lean into batter's up before we realized we were all overreacting. I answered the phone, relieved to see that it was David.

"Hello?"

"What the hell is going on down there?"

Again, I turned my back on the people in the room so I could concentrate on the call. It wasn't David, though. It was Agent Tomas Harrison. David's boss. That made my stomach drop. Where was David? "It's bad, sir."

I don't know if he paused because I called him "sir" instead of "Tomas" or because of the tone of my voice. "How bad, Melissa? Oneida bad?"

I paused, then decided to be as honest as possible. "No, I don't think it's Oneida bad but I think it has the potential."

"Explain."

Good old Tomas. Verbose as ever. "We're in lockdown, red lights and everything. But, Doctor Dudetsky's access card wouldn't make the elevator take us to the first floor. We're locked down here and the... is this a secure line?"

"Secure enough. Speak plainly."

I could see his intense blue eyes and buzz cut in my mind's eye. "The Minkowski escaped. It attacked, Jolene Lake, who is hanging on but needs medical. It attacked Doctor Dudetsky, condition unknown, probably dead. He tried to stop it while we escaped. Accounted for: All five teenagers. Alive and well. Joe Chambers, dead. Unaccounted for: Lakshmi Gowda, Sadie Giacomi, Patrick Forester."

I paused to see if he had any other immediate questions. I could hear a hubbub of activity in the background.

"Tell me what you're not telling me."

I bowed my head and lowered my voice. "It's an inside job. The guard, Joe Chambers, was stabbed. The Minkowski's attack is electrical. Also, whoever killed the guard didn't stop to make sure he was dead. I think they were too busy releasing the alien."

"Why do you say that?" His voice was neutral, probing but unbias.

I wished I could look Tomas in the eye. "I had to crawl under the desk to plug the power strip to all the security computers back in. The end of it was covered in blood, as if a bloody hand pulled it out of the wall. I don't know why the guard would do that."

"Hold on." His voice pulled back and I heard Tomas say, "The security computer was unplugged." There was more incomprehensible babble in the background. Tomas came back on the phone. "Right. That explains things better. The system is acting as if there was a power failure and sealed the bottom levels."

"You mean, there's a double secret lockdown mode?" I didn't intend to sound snarky. I couldn't help it. "How do we get things back to normal?"

"In the event of a power outage, the system will believe that it has been in lockdown for three days—the amount of power reserve—and seal the underground levels. Let me speak to Carlita."

I blinked at the phone. It never occurred to me that Tomas might know the other kids here. But, on second thought, it made a hell of a lot of sense. I walked over to her and handed her the phone. "Tomas wants to talk to you."

I was surprised again when Carrie's face lit up with pure joy. She took the phone from me. "Agent Harrison! Are you getting us out of here?" She listened for a short time, then started typing one-handed as she answered with "Uh-huh." and "Yeah." and "Oh. That *is* good. Okay. Got it." She ended the call with, "Okay. Hope to see you soon."

Carrie handed the phone back to me with a huge smile on her face. She seemed a thousand percent better and much more determined. I put the phone to my ear. "Tomas?"

"I've given Carlita everything I can to help her fix the lockdown. Your job… protect her. She's probably your best bet for unlocking the seal."

"I can do that. I've got Mister Bat and Sean has his cricket bat."

"Never go anywhere without that thing, do you?"

I heard the smile in his voice. "No. With my history, would you?"

"No. Agent Hood is your point of contact. He's currently going through security records sent to him last night. I'm up to speed with that situation, too."

"Should we look for the missing people?"

"Only if you can do so safely."

"What do we do about the Minkowski… and the person who let it out?" I hated to think that someone I'd just met was working with the monster.

"Defend yourself as best you can."

"Yes, sir."

"Melissa, I'm not going to lie. This does have the potential to be as bad as Oneida." He paused like he was going to say more then said, "David will call you soon."

"Okay."

He hung up without a formal good-bye. I looked at Sean and Carrie. They were a study in contrasts. She looked happy, excited even. He looked like he was going to throw up.

"They're working the problem from their end," I told Sean in hopes of boosting his morale.

Sean visibly pulled himself together and straightened his back. "What do we do now?"

"We wait for Adam and Ian to get back." I glanced at Carrie. "Then we get Carrie into the server room. After that, it depends."

CHAPTER ELEVEN

With a minute to spare before I panicked, there was a quick knock on the door signaling Adam and Ian's return. Sean stepped back to let them in but neither he nor I let down our guards. They hustled in but were quiet until the door closed behind them. I saw that they returned with more than they left with.

"This level is clear as far as we can tell. We opened every door." Ian pulled two radios out of his pocket and handed one to Carrie and one to me. "Doctor Dudetsky is dead. We checked. He was all burned up like Jolene."

Adam handed Sean a third radio. "We took his body to the security room. We didn't know what else to do."

To my eye, they both looked shaken and subdued. Heather taught me that most of her job in managing a safe house was to keep morale up. "You did good. And you got us radios. Plus, Agent Harrison called."

Ian perked up at that. "Are we rescued?"

It was Carrie who answered. She closed her laptop and stood. "No. Not yet. The system's been FUBARed and I need to do exactly what we all thought I needed to do: get into the server room and fix all the things as an admin. It won't be easy, but Agent Harrison gave me some pointers."

"Also," I added, "they know we're in trouble and they're working the problem from their end, too." I didn't want to say anything about Tomas' vague warning. I would get more concrete answers out of David when he called back.

"How, exactly, is the system so messed up?" Adam walked over to the still unconscious Jolene and picked her up as easily as before. "I mean, this system's the best that money can buy."

Before Carrie answered, I interrupted. "Me and Ian in front. Adam and Carrie in the second row. Sean follows behind. Talk while we move."

Waiting until everyone was in the hallway and in place, Carrie answered. "The best we can tell is that the system was put into lockdown. Then, Joe unplugged the computer, making it seem like the power went out, which flipped a bit somewhere, telling another security system that the lab had been in lockdown for at least three days. At that point, it sealed the lab. All exits locked and no amount of security clearance can open things without a lot of effort.

"I'm going to guess—and this is just a WAG—when we plugged the system back in, the secondary protection software got confused and said, "Nope. Screw you, hippie." and kept us sealed. My job is to figure out what happened and reset systems enough to let us out."

While Carrie talked, we walked down the hallway, around the first corner, and then the second corner to the hallway where the Minkowski attacked Doctor Dudetsky. One thing I noticed, and I'm sure Ian did, too, the wood around the door handles was scorched. It's possible the alien was using electricity or magnetism to turn the handles. I wondered, if it was mostly gas and electricity, why it didn't just go under the door or through cracks. Maybe it did have mass after all, in an alien biological way.

Adam used Doctor Dudetsky's access card to get us into the server room. It was a large room with rows and rows of racks with thin servers filling them but it wasn't anything like I imagined. First, it was a lot quieter and darker than I thought it would be—and not just because of the red lights. Almost all of the server blades were glossy black with almost no lights at all. In the movies, server rooms are filled with whirling fans and blinking lights from the server racks.

A quick estimate told that each eight foot high column had about fifteen servers and I counted six columns per stack and eight stacks in the middle of the room with a bunch on the sides—at least another eight, though not all of them filled. That meant there were at least eight hundred server blades in this room alone. I couldn't tell how many of them were actually working but, the sheer number of them made my head spin.

Weirdly, this whole room reminded me of the stacks in a library. It was just that big and quiet and orderly. It was also a lot cooler than the rest of the floor. I was glad I had my sweat shirt on.

While I was gawking at more computers than I'd ever seen in my life, Carrie led us to the back wall of the room where a workstation area was set up. It had four monitors, a comfortable looking office chair and sitting area to the side—complete with a couch, a low table, and a mini-fridge. More battered and scruffy office chairs sat around the sitting area or were abandoned by the walls. The discarded remains of microwaveable lunches and candy bars littered the entire area.

Ian grinned and moved to look around the sitting area to see what was there. He came up with two full bottles of red wine. "This is a techie's dream come true. Almost. All the comforts of home. Minus the gaming station."

Sean and Carrie stood side-by-side at the computer station. Sean held Carrie's laptop while she leaned over the keyboard and typed. Sean leaned down and murmured to her. She nodded as she continued to type.

I turned and watched Adam move to the couch and gently lay Jolene on it. He leaned over the couch and pulled a large fuzzy blanket up, and draped it over her still form.

"Gopal had his own gaming laptop. So did Annie. They'd hide in here when they wanted to avoid work because no one else could come in here except people like Dudette." Carrie, already sitting at the workstation, paused. "I mean, Doctor Dudetsky."

We were quiet at the reminder that the doctor was dead. Carrie opened her laptop and consulted her notes. I looked at the guys. Only Sean was prepared for the crisis. "Maybe Sean and I should get some food and the two of you should get warmer clothes on."

"I'll be good here." Carrie turned on monitors.

"No. Sean and I will go. Then Adam and Ian will go. Better to stay in pairs." I put on a fake smile. "So, any requests from the kitchen? No one starves on my watch."

Sean and I peeked out of the server room to make certain the coast was clear. But instead of heading directly to the kitchen, I turned towards the security room. "We need Joe Chambers' access card." Sean didn't comment. He just nodded.

It was very easy for both of us to fall back into siege mode. I know he hadn't had time to recover from what had happened to him and I guess I wasn't as recovered as I thought. Only Ian seemed comfortable. But, from what I knew of him, that was just a façade.

As we entered the security room with two bodies in it, I was glad for the hellish red light. The blood smears on the floor still looked like mud rather than blood and the red wash gave both the guard and the doctor a pretense of life. I tried not to get my hands too bloody as I searched Joe's pockets until I came up with his card. It was in his wallet. Right next to a picture of a woman and a baby. He had had a family. That was something I wish I could forget. I knew I never would.

Turning away, Sean held out a gun holster and a stun gun holster. "Pick your poison."

"You ever shoot a gun?" I asked.

"Once." He gave me a half-shrug and looked away.

"Gun then. Heather's been training me for the last four months on them." I checked the weapon to make sure it was loaded before clipping the holster to the waistband of my jeans. "Any more stun guns? Ian said that he captured the Minkowski with one."

He shook his head. "There should be three more, but all of the slots are empty."

"Well, that's worrisome."

"Maybe. Maybe not. Maybe the other guard has one."

"Wherever he is." I gazed at the monitors. They were all still dark.

"Can we go now?" Sean kept his head turned towards the door.

I realized that he wasn't just watching our backs. He didn't want to look at the bodies anymore. I guess, somewhere along the line, I had come up with the coping mechanism of ignoring the bodies. I didn't know if that was good or bad. "Yeah. Sure."

We both hurried out the office and down the hallway. We turned the corner with caution but the hallway was still clear. The door to the hallway I was most familiar with was closed. But it also had the same sort of scorching that was on the other side. The Minkowski left the same way it had come in.

"Do you really think they'll come for us?" Sean asked while we filled grocery bags with drinks and nonperishable food, half emptying out the kitchen. It was very easy for me to see us living out of the server room for days while the alien stalked the lab hallways.

"Yeah. I do. I know David. I know Heather. David broke into a quarantine zone to come help me. I don't think he's going to let a little thing like a foot-thick steel door stop him."

Sean grabbed my arm just before I opened the server room door. "You told him that one of us helped it. Do you know who? Who killed the security guard?"

I shook my head. "I don't know. I don't think it's one of us kids. We're the ones being tested. It wasn't Doctor Dudetsky. It wasn't the guard. It wasn't Jolene."

"How can you be sure about Jolene?"

"There wasn't any blood on her clothing. Whoever helped the alien and stabbed Joe Chambers probably got blood on them."

Sean thought about it for a moment. "Okay."

"Why? Do you think it's one of us? One of the kids?" I did not like that idea. Not one bit.

"I don't know. I just know I'm scared."

"We all are." I swiped the guard's card against the door's sensor to make sure it worked and was relieved when it opened up. "We come bearing food," I called as we entered.

The server room was quiet except for the hum of machines and the clack of a keyboard. Back at the workstation, Ian and Adam came forward to claim the bags and set them up on the coffee table. They'd rolled a couple extra office chairs up near the computer.

I walked over to Carrie and looked over her shoulder at the computer screen. She had two windows open. One was to a manual and the other was a command line window. I didn't understand what she was typing at the CMD prompt. "How's it going?"

Carrie stopped typing. She didn't look up at me but by the stiffness of her neck, she was irritated. "Here's how it's got to be. If you want things fixed, everyone needs to leave me alone. Got it? Don't talk to me. Don't ask me questions. Don't bother me unless something is on fire. And *don't* stand over my shoulder."

"Okay. Sorry." I backed away and looked at Ian and Adam. Both of them were specifically not looking at me or Carrie. It didn't take a genius to know that both of them had bothered Carrie as well. "Okay guys, you're up. Ian, Adam. Get better clothes on and shoes you can run in."

"Can we look for the missing people?" Ian asked.

Adam, who had started for the door, nodded. "Might as well."

"Yeah. They might be hurt and need help" I nodded. "Here's the guard's keycard. I'll keep this one." I handed it to Ian and pocketed Doctor Dudetsky's access card.

Sean stepped up. "We can go, too. Cover more ground."

I shook my head. "I need to stay here. Keep an eye on Jolene and Carrie." I lowered my voice with the last but she heard me.

"I'll be fine. Go. Just go." Carrie didn't look at us, still typing in a fast, one-handed dance over the keyboard with the thumb of her left hand keeping time on the space bar.

"No. I have my orders from on high. You aren't to be left alone. Besides, David should be calling soon." I paused glancing between the guys. "But Sean could go with you. The three of you should be able to manage anything that came your way. And Sean has a weapon." I looked at Mister Bat. I thought about giving it to Adam but I couldn't make myself do it. "Either of you two know how to use a gun?"

Ian raised his hand. "Yep. I'm a Halo champion." He paused at my glare. "Yes. Been shooting since I was knee-high to a grasshopper, as my dad liked to say."

Shaking my head with a smile, I handed the 9mm over to him and watched as he took it from the holster and checked it. He handled it like a pro. "Okay. I've got a bat. You guys have a stun gun, a cricket bat, and a gun. Look for the rest. Check in on every level at the start and end. Level A is already clear so you can start with Level B."

Ian gave me a mock salute and turned to the other two boys. "Clothes then Level B as our lady commander says. No talking unless you see something that needs words." The three of them trooped to the door. Sean peeked out through the tiny window, then through the cracked door. He gave the all clear and they slipped out one after another.

There was silence except for the electronic humming. At the lack of typing, I looked over my shoulder at Carrie. She was staring at me. "What?"

"How do you do that?"

Confused, I shook my head. "Do what?"

"Make them obey you? Ian and Adam hate each other but they're working together like BBFs because you're telling them to. It's like you've become the adult or something."

"Oh, that." I half-shrugged. "My dad used to call it the 'Voice of Authority.' You talk like you know what you're doing, speak firmly and confidently, and that's it. People think you know what's what and obey. We all kinda want to follow the herd." I patted my purse with my phone in it. "Also, it doesn't hurt that I have a line to the outside."

"Back in the orphanage, you would've ruled or you would've been beat down and hard."

"Was it really that bad?" I took a step towards her and stopped. "No, wait. I'm not supposed to bother you."

"It's okay. I'm compiling. Yeah, it was pretty bad. Like I said, getting caught and ending up here was the best thing that ever happened to me. Gilded cage and all that." She eyed the scrolling computer screen for a moment as she asked, "Tell me about these 'marching orders'?" She crossed her arms, half turning to me, half keeping her attention on the scrolling window.

"Tomas said that I needed to watch out for you. So, that's what I'm doing. Call it enlightened self-interest meets the demands of the higher ups." I looked around the quiet room. "Besides, I'm sure the guys will find the rest. Then someone else will be in charge. We can relax and let them deal with everything."

"You don't actually believe that. Neither do I. And for the record, gimpy hand or not, I'm not helpless." Carrie held up a stun gun like the one Sean had. "I took it while I was in the security office. Never pass up an opportunity to go armed in a dangerous situation."

I grinned at her. "Deroga Darrington."

"You betcha."

Someone pounded on the door to the server room.

We both jumped. I pointed at her. "You don't leave this room for anything. And I mean anything." Turning, I ran for the door at the front of the server room.

CHAPTER TWELVE

I looked out the small window in the door and saw another of the black uniformed guards. FORESTER was emblazoned on his chest. He relaxed when he saw me in the window. "Miss Allen, I need you to let me in. I was attacked and my access card was stolen."

His voice was muffled but I could hear just enough to read his lips and understand what he was saying. I reached for the door handle and paused. "How did you know to find us in the server room?"

"I ran into the boys."

Ah, of course. It made sense that they'd send the guard to the server room to protect us. I opened the door and wondered a moment too late why no one had radioed back to me that they'd found the missing guard. As soon as I opened the door, he grabbed me by the shoulders, pulled me from the server room, and threw me across the hallway. Mister Bat went flying as I stumbled, rebounded against the wall, and hit the floor hard enough to make me see lights. Pain radiated out in enormous waves where my head cracked against tile.

Forester rushed at me as I tried to get to my feet. I fell back and kicked out, connecting with his shin. I scrambled back and he hissed in pain and stumbled. I got to my feet, reeling. Grabbing me again by the upper arms, he slammed me into the wall. I tried to knee him in the groin but he blocked the blows with his thighs. I stomped down on his foot and jabbed at his eye. My thumb sunk into the soft part below his eye ridge. Crying out, he let me go and backed up.

When he pulled his hand away, electricity danced across his face from injured eye to uninjured eye.

"What the hell?" was all I had time to say before he rushed me again. I pivoted and grabbed for him, tossing him over my hip just like Heather showed me time and time again. He went down hard but before I could bask in my victory, the guard was on his feet, electricity coursing across his whole face.

This time, he'd pulled his weapon. It looked like a 9mm semi-automatic. Exactly like the one I gave Ian. I backed away, hands raised, looking for anything I could use for cover. "Wait. Wait. Whoa. You don't have to do this."

"We feel," he said, and pulled the trigger.

I screamed as pain seared my shoulder, as bad as any I'd felt while fighting the Fedoras. Another shot sounded almost in my ear and I jerked away from the noise… and found myself almost face-to-face with Lakshmi. She had a gun pointed at me. It crashed again, this time, as I looked at it, the muzzle flash damn near blinded me. Ears ringing and spots in front of my eyes, I put my back to the wall and my fists up to defend myself, blinking as fast as I could, trying to clear the tears and lights from my eyes.

"It's all right, Melissa. We got him." Doctor Giacomi didn't touch me. She stood near me for a moment, then approached Lakshmi and Forester.

The doctor knelt over the downed guard. She had hold of his wrist and was also checking for his pulse at his neck. Blood pooled out from his body. Lakshmi shook her head. "I'm sorry. He's dead. I had to do it. There was no choice."

As I looked at her, I swear I saw a thin arc of electricity run up Lakshmi's braid. Was it real? Was the lightning in Forester's eyes real? Or was I hallucinating again? My mouth went dry as my stomach did flip-flops. Had I missed my 8 A.M. pills? I dug in my purse for my phone. Its screen was shattered. I thumbed it on anyway.

4:23 A.M. At least, that's what I thought it said. I couldn't be sure. But, it wasn't 8 A.M. I hadn't missed my pills. I breathed a sigh of relief. Okay. Maybe it was a hallucination based on my fear of the Minkowski. Maybe it wasn't. I dug into my purse to make sure my pills were still there. That was the last thing I wanted to deal with—missing pills and their catastrophic lack. They were. I sighed again, comforted. I shook my head to try and clear some of the pain and dazzle. It must have been just the knock to the head.

Lakshmi looked up at Doctor Giacomi. "What are we going to do, Sadie? I just killed a man."

I couldn't see Lakshmi's face but I could see Doctor Giacomi's expression. It was neutral as usual, but there was something else there I didn't understand. A cold hardness.

"We do what we need to do." Doctor Giacomi reached out a hand. She was holding a stun gun. "I'm sorry." She pressed it to Lakshmi's neck and thumbed the trigger.

Lakshmi arched her back and screamed loud and echoing in the hallway. I backed away as I watched Doctor Giacomi mouth the words, "One. Two. Three." Then she stepped away from Lakshmi's spasming body. She looked over her shoulder. "You want to move back."

I backpedaled halfway down the hall and stopped. Doctor Giacomi also backed up a good ways but she kept her body between Lakshmi and me.

Lakshmi was covered in electricity as she knelt, body arched in a display of agony. Multicolored light streamed out of her mouth and coalesced into a mini-Minkowski the size of a dinner plate. It hovered there in front of Lakshmi's face then rose as Lakshmi collapsed backwards.

I covered my mouth to keep myself from screaming in the horror of it.

"Don't move," Giacomi said. "It tracks by ripples of sound waves. It's not really the Minkowski. Just a small bit of it. It's more instinct than anything else when it's not possessing people." The whole time she spoke, her voice was soft and controlled.

"That's right. Come here. I'm the only thing worth going after." The blob of light moved towards her as she raised the stun gun in front of her, poised to strike. "Come get this. I'm going to stun it. Electricity is part of its makeup. But feed it too much, like a tick that gets stuck... I tell you this because if it doesn't work, you need to run because I won't be me. I'll be it and I'll come for you."

The whole time Doctor Giacomi spoke, her voice was soft, calm, and neutral. Almost like she was narrating a scene in a play. It scared the crap out of me. Who was she? How could she face something like that? How could she have killed Lakshmi?

The blob darted for her center of mass and she stabbed into the middle of it with the stun gun already lit. There was a loud crackle of electricity and then the Minkowski light was gone.

"Holy fuck," I breathed. "You're not really a psychiatrist, are you?" I didn't mean to reveal my thoughts but I couldn't help myself.

She turned to me with a bemused look on her face. "What makes you say that?"

I gestured towards Lakshmi. "That. What you were saying. How calm you are."

"In fact, I am a fully licensed psychiatrist." Doctor Giacomi tilted her head. "But I have had other training. Now… we have a problem, you and I."

"We do?" My stomach hit the floor again and I felt my scalp prickle with fear. I saw Mister Bat a few feet beyond her and my heart sank. At least, Carrie was safe. As if in confirmation to that, the red light disappeared and was replaced with the normal soft glow of the hallways. *Thank you, Carrie!* I thought, pleased to know she was getting somewhere with whatever she was doing. Though, all the blue and white after the red still made me blink.

"Yes. We do. It's a matter of trust." Doctor Giacomi gazed at me but did not move. "How do you know you can trust me or that I can trust you now that we know the Minkowski can influence people?"

"I'm not possessed. That guard was trying to kill me." I gazed at her, my brows furrowed. "How did you know Lakshmi was possessed?"

"The possessed show small arcs of lightning over their skin and in their eyes. I saw signs of it when Patrick locked us in my office. And I saw what was left in him jump to her as she knelt over him. She knew he was dead. She was just collecting the alien bit from the body before it," Doctor Giacomi paused, "…died. I guess that's the right word. The small pieces don't seem to be able to survive for long without a host. Incidentally, I don't believe that you are possessed."

Relieved that I didn't hallucinate the lightning and relieved that she didn't think I was possessed, Doctor Giacomi was right. I didn't really trust her. She was with Lakshmi. I glanced at the stun gun in her hand. "I think, based on what I've seen, the only way I can trust you is if I stun you and see what happens. If light come shooting out of your mouth…"

She gave me a half-smile and a nod. Then she put the stun gun on the ground and stepped three paces away. I gazed at her. "You knew I was going to say that," I accused.

"I knew that I couldn't give you the idea. I'm going to turn my back to you. Let's get this over with quickly." Doctor Giacomi did as she said she would do. She also braced herself against the wall.

I hesitated. She could grab me if I got close. I've seen it in the movies. But, there really wasn't anything else I could do to break the standoff. The moment I moved, I realized my shoulder still hurt like hell. I looked down.

The left side of my sweat shirt was soaked with my blood. I really hate the sight of my own blood. But we would deal with that later.

I walked over to the stun gun, picked it up as I kept an eye on her, and tried not to look at either Forester or Lakshmi. I couldn't help but notice the burn marks around Lakshmi's mouth where the alien was forced out of her body. I turned away and straightened.

Before I could raise the stun gun and use it on Doctor Giacomi, she said, "Stun me for a count of three. It will hurt but it won't do lasting damage."

"All right." I didn't say anything else. I took two steps forward and pressed the prongs to her arm. "One. Two. Three."

She shouted through gritted teeth, her muscles locked tight. As soon as I counted "three" I stepped back and her knees buckled. She held onto the wall, twitching, and trying to control her fall. I took this time to retrieve Mister Bat, though it hurt like hell to pick him up. I tucked him under one arm and watched Doctor Giacomi.

She wiped her face with a trembling hand. "That always sucks."

"You've been stunned before?"

Nodding, she got to her feet. "For the record, the other way you knew I wasn't possessed is because I didn't pick up one of those two pistols and finish what Forester started. Why don't you..." She stopped and eyed the blood on my sweatshirt. "Never mind. I'll do it." After collecting the two pistols, she patted down Forester and swore. "Dammit. They're taking all the access keys."

"Not all. We've got two." I glanced at the server room. "We should probably tell Carrie what's going on." Doctor Giacomi nodded. I walked to the server room door and keyed it open. "Carrie, it's me. I've got Doctor Giacomi with me."

"Is this a Pretty Penny situation or is this a usual Deroga situation?"

I stopped. I couldn't tell exactly where Carrie was but I knew what she'd really asked, *Is this where Pretty Penny has to save the day* or *is this Deroga coming in from a fight?* Carlita Lopez was one smart girl. I appreciated that. "It's a usual Deroga situation and he needs whiskey." Which was my way of warning her that I was hurt.

When we got to the back of the server room, Carrie was standing with a stun gun in one hand and her other hand behind her back. I didn't know what she could do with that half-hand of hers and I wasn't willing to find out. I raised my one hand, holding the stun gun. "It's okay. Well, okay enough." I put the stun gun on the coffee table and groaned as I shifted the bat out from under my arm and rolled it under the table. I wasn't going to be able to use that for a while.

Carrie still didn't sit. "Well?"

"The alien can possess people. You can tell by seeing lightning on their skin. You can force it out with a stun gun." I paused. "Patrick Forester is dead. He did this to me. Lakshmi is, too. She died when Doctor Giacomi forced the Minkowski out of her." I was tired. I didn't have the will or the words to sugarcoat anything. "How's your end?"

"Hi Sadie." Carrie smiled at the doctor as she put the stun gun down. When she did so, I saw she had a syringe in her other hand. Well, that was new. She put it in her pocket. "I've reset the low level security. I'm working on convincing this damn lockdown code that we're not in lockdown but something is borked somewhere. I need time."

"Hello Carrie. We have time. Good work with the lights. The red was giving me a headache." Doctor Giacomi pointed at my shoulder after she set the pistols next to the stun gun on the low table. "We should do something about that."

"There's a first aid kit on the wall to the right." Carrie sat back down as Doctor Giacomi retrieved it. "It feels like forever since the guys left, even though it's only been about fifteen minutes."

I frowned. "Why haven't they radioed in? I told them to."

Carrie shrugged. "Boys?"

I watched Doctor Giacomi dry-swallow three ibuprofen. She offered me the bottle. When I nodded, she poured four little orange pills into my hand. I dry-swallowed them as I pulled the radio from my pocket and realized we never even tested to see if the radios worked or not. We didn't even assign a channel to talk on. I just had to hope everyone was on the same channel. I pressed the talk button. "Radio test."

Nothing happened for a moment. Then Ian's voice came back. "Five by five. Over."

"Where are you guys? Over."

"Level C. Over."

"You were supposed to let us know when you got there and when you were done with each level. Over."

"Forgot. Sorry. Half way done. Over and out."

I gazed at the radio, my eyes narrowed. There wasn't much I could say to that. Besides, Doctor Giacomi was waiting with the open first aid kit. I pulled my sweat shirt collar open so she could look at it.

She tilted her head this way and that. "Hell of a scar there. I think it protected you some. What happened?"

"Alien bug spit digestive acids on me." I tried to play it off cool, like it was no big deal. But I watched her out of the corner of my eye to see what she did. No reaction. Part of me was disappointed.

"Ah. The bullet basically shredded the skin on your shoulder. A couple of stitches and antibiotics should to the trick until we get another medical doctor in down here."

"I think I should sit for this."

"I think you should, too."

I grabbed one of the extra office chairs and pulled it away from the workstation. I sat with a sigh. The adrenaline was wearing off and the Prozasin I'd taken was making me muzzy-headed again. I tried not to whimper as Doctor Giacomi cleaned the wound then began to stitch me up. "Do you have a cell phone?"

She shook her head. "Forester stomped both of our phones. He also took our access cards."

"And mine's got a shattered screen now. At least it still works."

"Did you contact anyone? Let them know our situation?"

"Ow!" I winced as she tightened a stitch. "Yeah. Agent Harrison called back. He's the one who gave Carrie the information to help break us out of here. He knows there was an inside guy. Forester, I guess. Makes the most sense. How did you get out of the office anyway?"

"Brute force and anger. I'm afraid that office door will need to be replaced. Or, at least the doorknob will."

I watched her mouth twitch. It wasn't the twitch of someone trying to hold back a smile. It was the twitch of someone getting ready to give someone bad news. "What?"

"You're not going to like this."

I gasped as she tied off the stitches. "I already don't like it, Doctor Giacomi."

"I'm going to recommend a full quarantine for all of us. We don't know who's been compromised and for how long."

My heart sank. "Permanent?"

"Thirty days." She dabbed more antibiotic on my wound, then covered it with a sterile pad. "I know it scares you, but it's the right thing to do. And I'm going to be right there with you. We have to do it. You know that."

I did. But it didn't stop the paranoid me from running around inside my head, screaming *"No! No! No!"* Fortunately, I didn't have to answer her. My phone erupted in my purse, vibrating loud enough for all of us to hear it while the strains of "Secret Agent Man" played. I pulled it out and thumbed the call button. "Hello?"

CHAPTER THIRTEEN

"Tell me you have some good news."

David's voice was tired and clipped but I was really glad to hear it. I glanced upward at the server room's white ceiling. "Carrie got the lights working. So, we don't look like we're in a horror movie… even though we are."

"That bad?"

I nodded and gasped as my phone, pressed to my ear, cut me. I pulled the phone away, wincing. "Yeah. Actually, it's worse." I got up and walked to the farthest corner of the room. "I mean bad." He didn't say anything. So, I ran down the list of the dead, injured, and living. "Is there anyone else in the underground levels?"

"Not that I know of. But, yeah, this is bad."

"I haven't gotten to the worst part yet." I took a breath. "It looks like the Minkowski can actually possess people. It's obvious. There are electrical arcs that run over the body when stressed. If you kill the human, it finds another host or rejoins another piece of it. That's what happened to Lakshmi. But, you can force it out of the person by stunning them with a stun gun for a count of three. Except, that's what killed Lakshmi."

David was quiet for a very long time. "Next time, start with the worst news first, okay?"

"Okay. And my phone screen is smashed. I can't call you but I can receive calls." I paused, then pushed on with what I thought was the worst news. "Doctor Giacomi is going to recommend a thirty day quarantine after we get the lab open. I think… I think that's the right thing. I'm scared out of my mind about that but… you can't let any of us leave. I think the alien is trying to escape."

"New objective: Capture or kill the Minkowski." David's voice was calm and cool.

I pulled the phone away from my head and looked at it. I really wish I could see his face. "Are you serious? How the hell, heck—sorry, are we supposed to do that? It's a blob made of electricity and gas and it can electrocute people. Oh, and did I mention the possession?"

"Let me talk to Sadie, Doctor Giacomi. If you can wake up Jolene, between those two, I think they'll have some of the stuff Doctor Kai Minkowski thinks we need to fight and capture the alien. Also, talk with Ian. He was the one who captured the alien that's running lose."

"All right. Anything else? World peace while we're at it?"

"Melissa…"

I sighed and reigned in the snark. "I know. I know. I'm just…" I didn't want to say 'scared'. I think he knew. "I'll give you to Doctor Giacomi." I hurried back through the server room to the good doctor and held out the phone to her. "Agent Hood would like to speak to you about a plan to capture the monster. Careful, the phone bites."

Doctor Giacomi took the phone and held it near her ear. I went over to the first aid kit to see if I could find smelling salts. Miss Jolene Lake needed to stop being a sleeping beauty and start being a badass, monster-capturing, scientist. I grabbed some of the burn salve as well. I figured she could use it.

I broke open the smelling salts and waved it under Jolene's nose. She barely responded but I kept the salts there until she moaned and her eyes fluttered open. I let her try and get her bearing before I gave her the bad news, and then the worse news. While I did that, I kept half an eye on Doctor Giacomi pacing one of the server aisles as she listened to what David and Doctor Minkowski said.

"What?" Jolene grimaced and winced in pain. She looked down at her burned chest. "Where?" She looked around, blinking in confusion as her eyes darted from me to Carrie to the rest of the server room then back to me.

"You're in the server room. You were attacked. Do you know who you are?" It's always a good thing to get a baseline for someone who has been unconscious for hours.

"Yes. I'm Jolene Lake."

"Do you know what attacked you?"

She nodded. "The Minkowski. It was in the stairwell. I didn't know it could climb stairs." Jolene peeled back the part of her shirt, hissing, and looked at the burned skin above her heart.

I handed her the burn salve, then helped her sit up. "Things have only gotten worse. I wouldn't have woke you but we need you now. You got any idea how you survived that?" I pointed at the burn mark as she gingerly applied the salve.

"Implantable defibrillator. I have a bad heart." She handed me the salve. "It zaps my heart if it stops ticking."

I exchanged it for a sterile pad and held the tape for her. "It tried to shock you to death and your implantable defibrillator gave it the finger. Cool. You're an actual cyborg and it saved your life."

She finished taping herself up. "Yeah. So what's worse?"

I handed her a bottle of water. "Seven living. Four dead. The lower levels are sealed in lockdown mode, the Minkowski is still running free, and we have orders to capture it." I stood suddenly. "Shit. I forgot."

Pulling the radio from my pocket, I thumbed the talk button. "Guys, come on back. We've found the missing people. We've got a new objective. Over." I rubbed my forehead. I felt like such a heel. I had no idea where they were and the whole point of them being out and in danger was to find Forester, Giacomi, and Lakshmi. Thank goodness they hadn't found Forester before he'd found us in the server room.

There was no answer. I counted to twenty Mississippi's before I tried again. "Guys? Respond. Over." I wondered if my radio broke in fight with Forester. I looked up. "Carrie? Can you hear me over your radio?"

Carrie turned from the computer screen and nodded. "You're clear over here."

I hadn't noticed that she had an earbud plugged into one ear, but that explained why I wasn't hearing an echo of myself. I was just about to call for them again when the radio in my and exploded in shouts of fear.

"It's here! It's coming for us!"

I had no idea which one of the guys was shouting. I tried to stay calm as I answered, "Use the stun gun. The stun gun will hurt it. Don't let it touch you. Over." I released the talk button and started counting. I stopped when I got to nine. "Screw it."

I rushed to the coffee table, grabbed the stun gun and one of the pistols, and ran for the door. "You and Jolene come up with a brilliant idea to kill the monster or capture it. I'm going to help them." I didn't wait for permission or for Doctor Giacomi to tell me not to. I was out the door and into the hallway without a pause.

Of course, the bloodied and burned bodies of Forester and Lakshmi were there to greet me. We really needed to move them somewhere more dignified. Now that I could see them in the clear white light of the hallway and I wasn't scared out of my mind, my stomach gave a slow, rolling flip. I turned and ran down the hallway towards the elevator and stairs.

No one was in the hallway with the kitchen and my quarters. Part of me longed to get out of this bloody sweatshirt. That would have to wait. The guys were in trouble. As I burst through the door to the stairwell, I made myself slow down. No, there wasn't an inside man to worry about anymore, but there was a monster on the loose.

The scrape of metal on metal and the soft click of a door below told me I wasn't alone. I waited and looked over the rail. The noise came again. It wasn't a hovering monster. "Hello?"

There was a pause, then Ian asked, "Melissa?"

"Yes." I ran down a set of stairs to get to him.

"What are you doing here?" He was leaned against the rail, one foot off the ground. He was now in sneakers in addition to sweat pants and a t-shirt "What happened to you?"

"Rescuing you guys. And I got shot at by Forester. Where are the rest?"

Ian blinked at me a couple of times, then shook his head. "I don't know. The Minkowski came for us. It was in a room. We got split up. Last I saw, Sean and Adam were sprinting the other way."

"On this level?" I looked up and could almost see the alien coming through the door at us.

"No. Level C."

"Well, come on. I want to get you back to the server room before I go looking for the rest."

"I need help. I hurt my ankle." He limped up the first stair.

I put an arm around his waist and he put a hand on my non-injured shoulder. He was trembling hard. I didn't know if it was from fear, adrenaline, cold, or all of the above. "Why didn't you grab a jacket or a sweat shirt? You're shaking."

"I..." Ian shook his head. "I guess I didn't think about it. But I do have shoes on."

"At least there's that." I helped him up the stairs, one by one. "Where's your radio?"

"I dropped it as I ran. I'm sorry."

"It's okay." I made a mental tick that we were a radio down.

Together, we did a slow three-legged race up the stairs. When we got to the top, I pulled my radio out of my purse. "Carrie, I'm coming in with Ian. No one shoot us. Over." My voice, muffled, echoed through the stairwell.

"Roger. Over and out." Carrie sounded distracted but happy.

I helped him down the hallway and shook my head at his wide-eyed, unspoken question when he saw Lakshmi and Forester. "Don't ask. I'll explain when we get everyone here. Or Doctor Giacomi will. Things are worse than we thought."

I got him into the server room and onto the couch. Carrie typed a couple more command line instructions and turned from the computer. It looked like things were compiling again. She moved to Ian's side and pushed some of the food out of the way to clear a spot on the coffee table. "You should elevate your ankle."

Ian gave her a soft smile and did as he was told. Then he took hold of her hand and kissed her check.

I looked around then did a quick up and down the head of the server stacks. "Carrie, where are Doctor Giacomi and Jolene?"

"Sadie got off the phone with David, said, "I know what to do." Then took Jolene to the storage room." Carrie pointed at the workstation. "She left your phone with me."

Part of me wanted to shout at people for not telling me what they were doing. There was still a monster out there. Then again, they were the adults and they didn't answer to me—no matter how much I wanted to control the situation. "Okay. Did she say anything else?"

Carrie shook her head. Even though she had most of her attention on Ian, I saw that she kept an eye on the scrolling computer screen.

"Right. I'm going to go see if I can find Adam or Sean."

Ian looked up. "They're okay. They've got to be. They're together."

I nodded as I retrieved my phone. It made me feel better. If I couldn't carry Mister Bat and be effective with it, then my phone was the next best thing. "Yeah. Probably. You guys stay here. I've got a radio and so does Carrie. Let Doctor Giacomi and Jolene know I'm getting the boys."

I left without waiting for a response. I needed to get out of the server room. There were way too many corners and shadows and the black cobwebs were back. They pushed and pulled at me. I could feel them wanting to wrap me up. If I stayed in the server room any longer, I'd be cocooned and then smothered. As much as I wanted to, I couldn't logic the grimy, suffocating hallucinations away. Worse yet, part of me yammered that they were really there this time.

But out in the hallway, even as my breath came easier, I couldn't avoid looking at the crumpled and bloody bodies of Lakshmi and Forester. I grimaced as I turned away. With my shoulder, I didn't think I could move the bodies to the security room without re-injuring myself and, honestly, I didn't want to drag them. They deserved better. I needed Sean and Adam.

I radioed again. "Adam, Sean. You need to come back to the server room now. We've got a plan. Please respond. Over." Listening as I hurried towards the stairs, my heart sank. Neither of them responded. Had the Minkowski killed them? I needed to go to Level C where Ian saw them last.

I heard the pounding of someone running as soon as I opened the stairwell door to Level C. I stopped and listened, trying to pinpoint what direction it was coming from and what direction it was going to. The pounding got softer as it got farther away. Whoever was running, was moving clockwise around the level. I debated using the radio again. But, if Adam and Sean couldn't use the radio because they were fleeing for their lives, there was only one thing they could be running from.

I pulled out the stun gun and waited. I didn't want to get close enough to use the stun gun on the Minkowski, but I was ready to if I had to. The pounding feet paused, then started up again. Louder. Coming closer.

Adam burst around the corner of the long hallway in front of me. He sprinted towards me, gasping. "Stairwell. Get in the stairwell." Behind him, colored light flickered around the corner and the Minkowski appeared. It was smaller than it seemed in the cell but it was moving fast.

I pushed open the door to the stairwell and stepped inside. I held it open for Adam, looking for Sean, as the alien gave chase. Sean was nowhere to be seen. Adam slowed as he came through the stairwell door, then yanked it out of my hand and pushed it shut. He bent down and shoved something under the door. Then kicked at it. It was a wooden doorstop wedge.

Eyes wide at the implication, I stepped back from the door. Adam went to grab my arm but stopped at the blood covering the left side of me. "Stairs," he said as he pulled back his hand. "I don't know if this will actually stop it."

We ran up the first flight of stairs to the landing, then watched as light shone out under the door. I wished the door had a small window. Then

I was glad it didn't as lightning arced around the door handle, slowing turning it. When the door didn't swing open, there was a pause and the crash of a bolt of electricity hitting the door again and again.

Adam grinned as he panted. "I knew it. It doesn't have the strength. It's trapped. I had to run around and around, stopping here and there to search for a doorstop. Then run again as it caught up. That thing doesn't get tired."

"Good job." The electrical lashing grew furious, crashing one after the other against the metal door. "C'mon." I headed up the stairs.

"You okay? What happened? Why are you bloody?" Adam followed me.

"Got shot by Forester. The Minkowski can possess people." I paused on the stairs in front of Level B. "Why didn't you answer your radio? I've been calling for a while."

"I don't have one. Sean and Ian do. But we got separated." Adam opened the stairwell door to Level B.

"I know. I found Ian. Where's Sean?"

Adam shook his head. "We were checking different rooms when the Minkowski came out of one. I ran. I don't know where Sean and Ian went. It's been chasing me for a while. I led it down the stairs to get it away from Ian and Sean. Sean wasn't doing too well. I'm hoping he found a place to hide."

I followed him at a slower pace. Something wasn't adding up. Ian said the attack happened on Level C. Adam said the attack happened on Level B. Both thought Sean was with the other. "Maybe he turned off his radio."

"Sean!" Adam yelled, his voice bouncing off the walls. "You stay here. I'm going to do a quick run around this level and see if he hid." He raised his voice again. "Sean, it's safe!"

I stood there as Adam ran down the hall. He stopped at the corner and yelled for Sean again. Then he was gone. I hear him yell at the next corner and twice on in the opposite long hallway. My radio came to life. It was Doctor Giacomi. "Melissa? Jolene and I have a plan. Return to the server room, please. Over."

"Got it. Over." It made sense that Doctor Giacomi had taken over radio duty, giving Carrie the needed space to do the black magic needed to beat a malfunctioning security system back into shape.

Adam rounded the last corner and paused a final time. "Sean! I trapped it on Level C." He slowed to a walk and was barely breathing by the time he got to me. "I guess he made it to another level."

"We need to get to the server room. Doctor Giacomi has a plan." I kept my opinions to myself. It was possible that the attack was startlingly enough that either Adam or Ian didn't realize what floor they were on. It could be an innocent mistake. But, not knowing where Sean was worried me.

"At least the Minkowski is trapped."

"Yeah." I didn't say anymore until we were back on Level A.

I knew that Adam could help me move the bodies in the hallway and that needed to be done. I wasn't sure how to approach it. I reached out and grabbed his arm to stop him before we turned the corner.

He furrowed his brow at me in confusion. "What?"

"Adam, I told you the Minkowski could possess people. It possessed Patrick Forester who did this to me." I gestured at my shoulder. "Lakshmi shot him before he could kill me." I took a breath. "When she went to check on him, she was possessed." That wasn't exactly right but details would complicate the situation. "They're in the hallway. We need to move them."

His eyes went wide. "Lakshmi?" He turned from me and ran.

I heard his cry of disbelief and pain. I closed my eyes as I heard his choked sobs. I hadn't wanted him to see Lakshmi like that. I hadn't forgotten that she was as close to being a mother to him as could be in a place like the PAR Laboratory. When I turned the corner, Adam had Lakshmi cradled in his arms. His face was buried in her hair.

I swallowed hard, my throat tight and tears springing to my eyes. I recognized that grief. I shared it when my dog died, and when my parents died. Then again when my sister and her husband died. I walked slowly down the hallway until I stood next to him. Not knowing what else to do, I put my hand on his shoulder and waited.

He didn't look at me. "How?" The word was ground glass in his mouth.

"She was already possessed. After she shot Forester, she came to him in the guise of checking his pulse. She... the thing inside her... was just collecting the piece of the Minkowski within. Doctor Giacomi used the stun gun on her."

"That killed Lakshmi? Sadie killed Lakshmi?"

I didn't really know what to say. "It came out of her mouth, burning. I... I don't know what killed Lakshmi—the stun gun or the Minkowski." I paused and glanced at the server room door. "Will you help me move these bodies to the security room?"

Adam's answer was to stand, still cradling Lakshmi to his chest. His head bowed, he turned away, carrying his surrogate mother to the security room. I didn't follow. I wanted to give him all the privacy he needed for such raw grief.

I also needed time to get myself back together. Watching Adam ripped a scab off a wound in my heart. I missed everything I'd lost in the last couple of years all over again. I didn't succeed. Work always helps. I patted Forester down for the access cards he had but I didn't find any. He should have at least one—his—but if he took Lakshmi's and Doctor Giacomi's access keys, he should have all three on him.

Tears were still running down my face when Adam reappeared. He didn't say anything to me. He just grabbed Forester under the shoulders and pulled him into the security room.

I wiped at my tears, took a couple of breaths, and turned towards the server room door. My heart nearly came out of my chest. Doctor Giacomi was standing at the small window.

CHAPTER FOURTEEN

Doctor Giacomi—I couldn't bring myself to call her Sadie, even if everyone else did—opened the server room door for us. She made no comment about our puffy eyes and downturned faces as we walked in. Back at the workstation, Carrie had earbuds in with music going. She kept her eyes on the scrolling screen in front of her, occasionally typing something that made the screen scroll more. Ian was on the couch with his injured leg elevated. Jolene wasn't in sight.

I made a show of looking around then asked, "Jolene?"

Ian shifted his leg and answered, keeping his voice low. "She's run down to one of the supply rooms for stuff. I gave her my... Joe's... access key."

"By herself?"

"Yes." Doctor Giacomi answered before Ian could. "What we need is on this level at the end of the hallway in Doctor Minkowski's quarters. He's got a private lab attached to it where he stores an amazing amount of stuff." She gave us a slight smile. "It's why I was by the door, to see if she needed help getting the equipment in. I deemed it safe enough."

I looked at her and she looked away from me to Adam. There was something she wasn't saying. I didn't know what it was and I didn't like it. At all. When adults hide something, badness is on the way.

"Where is Sean?" Doctor Giacomi addressed the question to Adam.

He hadn't looked directly at her since he entered the room. Instead, he'd kept his head down and stood to the side. I couldn't tell if it was because he was trying to hide his grief or because he was trying to hide his fury. Probably a little of column A and a little of column B.

"Adam?" she prompted after about a minute of silence.

When Adam looked up, grief outweighed anger on his face. He shook his head. "I don't know. When the Minkowski came for us, I ran. Sean wasn't with me. I don't know where he is. I'm sorry." He spoke with dull pain and helplessness.

"He might've gone to ground and just hid." I shrugged. "I've thought of doing that a couple of times."

Doctor Giacomi stepped to Adam and put a hand on his shoulder. He turned to her and hid his face against her. She didn't say anything. She didn't have to. Adam was a boy who'd just lost another of his surrogate family. I looked away from the scene, feeling guilty for intruding on its intimacy.

I found myself looking at Ian. His eyes were wide and disbelieving. He shook his head slowly and mouthed the words, "Lying. Sean was with him." Glancing between the grieving Adam and the alarmed Ian I didn't know what to think.

Fortunately, Jolene's return kept me from having to do anything about this—just yet.

Jolene dumped a roll of thick copper wire, a roll of insulated copper wire, two four-foot iron rods, two pairs of long rubber gloves and metal snips on the floor near the server room door. She knelt and started to lay everything out in order. Doctor Giacomi looked down at it and nodded.

"What's this?" I wasn't sure what they were going to make.

"In good time," Doctor Giacomi said. Then she raised her voice. "Ian, Adam, come here, please."

They came from different parts of the server room. Ian from the couch. Adam from the farthest wall. My bet was that Adam just wanted to be alone. The new puffiness in Adam's face said that he'd been crying again. I felt my throat tighten, feeling for him. I spent days crying for my lost loved ones. It never gets easier and it never would.

"Ian, could you explain how you captured the Minkowski, please?"

Ian blinked at Doctor Giacomi and frowned his confusion. "Uh, okay?"

"I'm sorry if this brings up bad memories, but it's relevant to my plan to capture the creature."

"Yes, ma'am." Ian looked at his sneakers, gathering his thoughts. "Um. Okay. This was on my family's farm. We're a bit of distance from

Colorado Springs but near one of the substations. The Minkowskians had come through to our world, somehow, and we'd fought them—badly—for a few hours. They killed everyone but me because I kept moving. Nothing physical would stop them. Not a gun, a shovel, a bat. The thing that had been most useful was a fan, actually. It kept them at bay. Gaseous as well as electrical."

Ian took a breath. "My mom was the last to go. When it zapped her, we were running for the car. She fell and her stun gun fell out of her purse. I saw it when I tried to help her. But," he shook his head, "she was already dead."

He mimed the movement of leaning over his mother's body. "The aliens were right there. There was nothing I could do. I dove for the ground and grabbed the stun gun. I activated it as one of them tried to engulf me. That possession thing, I guess. I didn't know they could do that. But, when it hit the stun gun, it froze in mid-air. Like it was stunned."

Ian held a hand out, holding a pretend stun gun. "I moved away from it and it stayed still. The others, the ones that had come to keep me trapped, ran away." He shook his head. "They zoomed back into my house and were gone by the time Agent Harrison and his team got there."

"How long was the Minkowski stunned?" Doctor Giacomi asked.

"About ten minutes. I hit it a second time when I thought it was moving." Ian gave a half shrug. "The whole attack on my family took about an hour. I didn't know it then, but the government had recorded the anomaly near NORAD and scrambled a team to my house." Ian looked at his feet again. "If they'd been faster, they might've saved more than just me."

The entire time that Ian spoke, Jolene and Doctor Giacomi worked on whatever it was they were making. Jolene wrapped one end of the iron rods in thick copper wire. Doctor Giacomi wrapped the other end of the iron rods in the insulated copper wire. Except, she didn't snip it off. She connected the two iron rods with about ten feet of the insulated wire between them. It made the whole thing look like a strange set of antenna connected by a big piece of black licorice.

"How did they move the Minkowski?" Jolene asked.

It was a good question. How *do* you move a monster made of gas and electricity? I looked between the strange invention and Ian.

"I think it was an electrified glass box." Ian shrugged. "Something about electromagnetic pulses. I don't know. I was hurt. And my family was dead. They took me away before they shoved it in it. I only saw a little bit."

"Thank you for telling us, Ian." Doctor Giacomi got to her feet and dusted her hands off on her pants leg. Jolene followed suit but also held the long rubber gloves. Her attention was on the doctor. "I have a plan. It's based on Doctor Minkowski's theories. It won't be easy. It will be dangerous. But, I believe it will work."

"To capture the Minkowski?" Adam looked alert once more.

"Yes." Doctor Giacomi pointed at the copper wrapped rods. "These are grounding rods. It's a designated electrical path designed to dissipate a static discharge voltage, such as the lightning that the Minkowski uses to attack and that the Minkowski appears to be made of. We have them linked together through an insulated conductor so that the electricity that goes in one end will traverse the wire to the other rod."

She took one pair of the rubber gloves and put it on. Jolene put the other on. Both of them picked up a grounding rod. "Our intention is to ground on both sides with these rods. Any electricity the Minkowski attempts to discharge will flow in a circle back into itself. It won't be able to harm us, and we should be able to move it."

"Move it to where?" I asked. "Back into its cell?"

"Yes, that's the plan." Doctor Giacomi put her part of the trap down. "I haven't quite figured that part out, though. I didn't spend time with the Minkowski." She nodded to me. "Melissa will have to talk to Agent Hood to get the information on how to open the cells, pass codes, and such."

Ian raised his head. "Uh, I sorta know how." We all looked at him. Ian blushed and pushed on. "I asked Joe when I first got here. I mean, it had killed my family and tried to kill me. I needed to know I was safe." He rubbed the back of his neck. "Joe told me that the cells could only be opened from the security office and that they had rotating pass codes in a book. I don't know what book but I'll bet it's in the security office."

Where all the dead bodies were. Great.

I raised my hand. "Why not see if Carrie can open it from here? I mean, she's in the guts of the security system now. I think, maybe, capturing the Minkowski's more important than getting us out of here twenty minutes faster. I mean, hell, I'm pretty sure Tomas… Agent Harrison… has someone burning a hole through the stairwell door right now."

I paused and blinked in a sudden realization. "Ah crap, we never actually checked to see if the stairwell door was locked to access cards."

"I checked," Doctor Giacomi and Ian said at the same time then smiled at each other.

Doctor Giacomi nodded to me. "You're right, though. Let's figure out the feasibility of that idea. Then I'll tell you the rest of the plan." She disappeared into the server stacks to talk to Carrie.

Adam stood back, removed once more. Everything in his stance said, "Leave me alone." Ian sat on the floor and stretched out his injured ankle, grimacing as he did so. Glancing around the room, I saw the black cobwebs beginning to grow again. Just what I needed. I looked for something, anything, to distract me.

Jolene leaned against the wall next to the door. I moved to her and kept my voice low as I put my back to the guys and the cobwebs. "How are you?" I gestured to the patch above her heart.

She eyed me. "Probably as good as you. Sadie told me what happened."

"All of it?"

Jolene gave me a tight-lipped nod. "Yeah. What's it like to stun someone?"

"Pretty awful, actually." I tilted my head. "So, what happened to your keycard?"

She shook her head. "I don't know. I had to use the one Ian gave me."

"That's four missing keycards. And we know the Minkowski can't carry them." I considered this. "Also, Forester stomped the cell phones. I guess he could've hidden them."

"Maybe. I don't know. I really don't. I just want to get out of here."

"You and me both."

While I was talking to her, she seemed younger than what I first thought. Instead of in her upper twenties, I guessed she was maybe twenty-two. That put me at her level. Yeah, I was only fifteen. But Doctor Ferguson told me that kids who go through a traumatic experience, or multiple traumatic experiences in my case, tended to grow up quicker than normal kids. No one could ever say I was normal. Especially not me.

Turning back to wait for Doctor Giacomi, I thought I saw an arc of lightning snake down the server stack that Ian sat next to. I twitched to warn him to get away, then stopped myself. Was the lightning like the cobwebs? How could I tell?

"Ian?" I tried to keep my voice calm and neutral. "Can the Minkowski possess machines?"

He looked alarmed for a moment then slowly shook his head. "I don't think so. I mean, I didn't know they could do the possession thing to begin with. But, if they're electricity and gaseous… where would the gas go?"

I nodded, trying not to watch the electrical arcs moving up and down the server rack closer and closer to him. "Makes sense, I guess."

"Why do you ask?"

I shrugged. "Just curious. You know…?"

Doctor Giacomi returned. "It appears that Carlita can open and close the cells from here. Good idea, Melissa."

"What's the plan?" Adam stepped forward again. He looked eager despite his attempts to stay dispassionate.

"This is the dangerous part. We need to set up a trap. Also, we need to bait that trap." She gestured to Jolene. "Jolene and I need to set up in a room across from the bait. We need to get the Minkowski to go for the bait. When it does, we trap it with the grounding rods. If it works like we believe it will, then we will need to move the creature down to the cell and lock it away again."

"We have it trapped on Level C," Adam said.

Everyone looked at him with varying degrees of surprise and disbelief. Oh, right. We forgot to mention that little fact in Adam's grief and my inability to keep more than two thoughts in my head while fighting against hallucinations. Damn the Prozasin. Great for killing nightmares but awful for letting me be on top of everything I needed to be. "Yes. I'm sorry. Adam wedged a doorstop in the stairwell door. It couldn't get out. Unless it used the elevator and we hadn't seen that happen yet."

Doctor Giacomi nodded, considering this. "Then, we need bait and someone to lead it to the bait. This actually lets us control the situation a little bit more. Jolene and I can set up and…"

Ian raised his hand. "I volunteer as tribute."

"Why you?" Adam asked, his voice sharp.

"Because I can't run." Ian gestured to his ankle. "Because I'm the one who got away when it killed my family. It won't be able to resist me."

I nodded. "Makes sense. Carrie will need a radio. Jolene and Doctor Giacomi will need a radio."

"I will need a radio," Adam said.

"*We* will need a radio," I corrected. "No one goes solo. Carrie will be safe in the server room." I didn't want to say that I needed to keep an eye on him, but with Sean still missing, I did. Especially since Ian was certain Adam was lying.

Doctor Giacomi nodded. "That's correct. Jolene, Ian, and I will set up on Level B. We need at least ten minutes to get ready and to practice the maneuver."

"Okay. Adam and I will go wait in the stairwell."

"I'll radio you when we're ready. You need to lead the Minkowski up from Level C to Level B and down the hall." Doctor Giacomi met each of our eyes to make certain we understood. "You two will run past Ian, then wait at the end of the hallway. When we capture the Minkowski, you two will need to block open the stairwell doors—so spend your ten minutes finding another couple of doorstops. One for Level B and one for Level E. Everyone understand what they need to do?"

"Yes," Jolene said.

Adam nodded.

Ian pulled himself to his feet. "Ready when you are."

"What happens if the grounding rods don't work?" I asked. This was a Hail Mary plan if I'd ever heard one.

"Stun guns," Doctor Giacomi answered. "You, Adam, Ian. You three will be the only ones in a position to stun it. Until it is dead."

Or we are, I thought. She and I looked at each other. I knew that was what she was thinking, too.

As we walked into the hallway, Ian touched my arm. I hung back and looked at him. He leaned close and whispered, "You be careful. Seriously. He's lying about Sean." We both glanced at Adam. "Be careful," Ian repeated.

I nodded, freaked out by Ian's intensity and what he was implying. "I will be. I promise."

CHAPTER FIFTEEN

"Let's go to Level D. I'm sure there's doorstops on B but I don't know where and I do know where they are on D. The garden is just one of my main projects. I remember seeing doorstops in the closets of a couple of the labs." Adam kept his voice low as he spoke.

I didn't blame him. The stairwell, no longer the dark obstacle course filled with boogiemen, still echoed with every sound—steps pounded and voices came to you changed—unless you took care to be quiet. "Sounds like a plan," I said as I descended the stairs with as light of a foot as I could, following him. I watched him carefully for signs of betrayal and danger. I didn't have to wait long.

Lightning arced over his lanky form. First, from left hip to right shoulder; then from right clavicle around his back to under his left bicep. I had no idea if what I was seeing was real. I could be hallucinating the electricity because I was so worried about Ian's warning. Or, Adam was also possessed and I might be in a lot of trouble. I put my hand in my pocket, and held the stun gun for comfort.

We were quiet until we passed the stairwell door to Level C. The metal looked bent and blackened, but the doorstop held. "At least we know where it is," I said.

Adam's voice floated back to me. "I wish we knew where Sean was."

"Are you sure you were on Level B? Ian said you were on Level C."

"He was wrong. The Minkowski chased me down the stairs. Scared the crap out of me. I don't know why it focused on me and not them. I mean, Ian's right in the fact that he was the one who got away. Shouldn't it have focused on him?"

"I don't know." I couldn't tell if he was lying or not. "Ian hurt himself running away from it. I had to help him up the stairs."

"Ian is a weird guy." Adam opened the door to Level D and held it for me. "I mean, he's smart and he's fit but he hurts himself running away. His family was killed by monsters but when the lockdown happened, he didn't look scared. Not like the rest of you."

"I don't understand what you mean." I stopped next to him as he closed the stairwell door with a quiet click.

"I mean, you, Sean, and Ian lost…" He grimaced and faced me, his jaw tight. "Your families were all murdered. You fought monsters. All within the last four months. You, four months ago. Him, eight weeks ago. Sean, three weeks ago. How come only you and Sean showed up in the lounge with weapons, dressed for a siege, with a wild look in your eyes? I mean, you two were ready to kill. It scared me. But when Ian came in, he was loud, yes, but not scared. No weapons. No shoes. No panic."

I considered this. I understood Adam's confusion. "From what he said, it sounded like the Minkowski attack took like, at most, an hour? No more than two. It was over and done with. I was hunted for three days by the Fedoras, the Mega Aphis monsters. Sean… it sounded like he had several days of fighting and was trapped on a boat with nowhere to go. Maybe that's why."

I couldn't tell if Adam was trying to throw suspicion on Ian or off him. But now that I was looking at him in the face, I didn't see any signs of electricity. He was just a guy trying to make sense of something that didn't add up to him.

Adam shook his head. "I don't know. He got shy and wouldn't let us into his quarters when he got his sneakers and a jacket. It's not like he even changed clothes. I just don't get him and how he acts. You guys are more normal to me. I just… Ian is strange."

I half-smiled, thinking that, maybe, it was a jealousy thing. Ian was allowed out and about. Ian was the one teen here that could almost rival Adam's physical abilities. It made sense that they would butt heads. Also, he was dating Carrie.

Glancing at my face, he shook his head again. "No. This isn't about me and him not getting along. He's jealous that me and Carrie are close. He hates that I get to spend time with her and he doesn't. I think he wants to live here."

"How did Carrie and him start dating?" I tried to hide my grin. He was protesting a little too much.

Adam turned away and started walking down the hall. "He was here for a week after the attack. That's how he met us. They've been exchanging emails since then."

"Ooh. It's a new thing." I started to say more but my radio came to life. "Radio check. Over."

"Loud and clear. Over," I said. I wasn't looking at the radio, though. Somewhere, down here on Level D, another radio echoed.

"Five by five as Ian likes to say. Over." Carrie had a smile in her voice.

Adam and I looked at each other then both of us pointed down the hallway towards the garden. The sound was muffled, full of static, but it was definitely there. Adam took off in a jog, calling, "Sean? Where are you? Sean?"

I stopped to listen to the radio. Jolene was talking again. "We're just about ready. Melissa, when you and Adam have the doors blocked open, and are ready to get the Minkowski, let us know. Over."

"Understood. Over and out." I put the radio back in my pocket instead of in my purse. I was more used to pockets on a regular basis. I watched Adam hurry down the hallway, looking into the open offices. He gave each one a quick glance, then continued on.

About ten feet from the antechamber to the garden, Adam slowed, then stopped in front of the open door. He stared inside the room and rubbed the back of his neck. The look on his face was a mixture of horror and denial. Bowing his head, he walked forward, half-entered the room, then went to his knees.

Even from where I stood, I could hear Adam muttering, "No, no, no, no."

Clenching my teeth to keep from screaming, I pulled the stun gun from my pocket and walked with careful, measured steps to the antechamber. If Adam was faking all this time, I knew he could easily overpower me. I didn't have enough training to protect myself from someone like him. I didn't have a pistol anymore, either. Those went to Carrie, Jolene, and Doctor Giacomi.

I stopped behind Adam and I knew what I would see—Sean dead—but I didn't know how he died. Or how bloody it would be. I gazed at Sean. His eyes were open and staring. His shirt and jacket were covered in blood. It looked like he'd been stabbed only once. Maybe twice. But he didn't immediately die. Blood was smeared everywhere as he'd pulled himself away from the door toward the garden. His body was stretched out, as if even in death, he was still trying to get to his cricket bat in the far corner.

"Who would do this?" I asked. "How? Why?"

Adam shook his head. "I don't know." He reached out and checked for Sean's pulse at his wrist. Then shook his head.

At that moment, an arc of electricity ran up Adam's back so reminiscent of Lakshmi, I had no doubt in my mind that Adam was possessed. Most likely, as Ian said, he did this. I hesitated a moment. Was I willing to kill Adam as Doctor Giacomi killed Lakshmi?

Yes.

This wasn't Adam anymore. This was an alien possessed person who'd just collected another piece of the monster. I triggered the stun gun and pressed it to Adam's neck. I didn't look away and counted. Adam arched giving out an undulating cry of pain. Every muscle was tense and shaking. But, in the time it took for me to count to three, nothing happened except for Adam's pain and his clenching, spasming body. No exhalation of light from his mouth. No burning of flesh. No piece of a Minkowski forced into the open.

I pulled the stun gun from Adam and caught him as he fell backwards. I stretched him out until he was laying out on the floor, trembling and twitching. It hit him harder than it hit Doctor Giacomi.

"What the hell?" Adam tried to yell at me but couldn't. "Why?"

I felt horrible, my heart racing and my palms sweating. I'd just stunned Adam because I couldn't tell my hallucination from reality. This was way too close to my break after my parents died. I backed away from him, trying to keep it together. "I'm sorry. I'm sorry. I thought you were possessed. I kept seeing electricity on you. I thought... Ian said..." I shook my head. "It was the only way to be sure."

Adam turned over, shifted to his knees, and took a few breaths, moving his arms, clenching and unclenching his hands. "What did Ian say?" His voice was calmer that it had any right to be.

"He swore that Sean was with you." I wanted to babble, to cry, to scream. I'd been wrong. How much of what I'd been seeing was real? How much was not?

Adam looked back at Sean's body. "I told Sean that the garden was one of the safest places to go. There's a bar on the inside of the seal that can keep anyone from entering. I told them both to come here if it was too dangerous." He moved to his feet and stood there, testing his balance and control of his legs. "It makes sense that Ian would be certain Sean was with me. I did try to protect him. "

His calmness and slow movement had a quieting effect on my brain. There was a puzzle here. "The three of you got separated... Sean came down here for protection. He must've run past you on the stairs... if you started at Level B. And Ian, panicked, didn't remember what floor you were on, hurt himself as he ran, thought—was sure—Sean was with you. You thought he was with Ian."

"But, he wasn't with anyone. We really did get separated." Adam gazed at Sean's body for a long moment. "Then who killed him?"

"Maybe Forester did. It makes the most sense. Someone stabbed Chambers to death. Probably Forester. Then he tried to kill me." I stopped and shook my head. "Wait. That's not possible. Lakshmi killed Forester before we got the panicked call on the radio that the Minkowski was chasing you." I sighed. "I don't know who killed Sean. Everyone's accounted for and David says that there's no one extra down here."

"Patrick was a good guy," Adam murmured. He turned away and walked into one of the nearest offices.

Jolene's voice erupted from my pocket. "Melissa, status? Over."

"We found Sean's body. We need to take it up to the security room. He was stabbed to death. Over." There was a long pause as I turned to the wall and pressed my forehead to the cool paint.

"All right. Block the stairwell doors before you come up. That's the most efficient course of action. Over and out." Jolene's voice crackled into static as she signed off.

I was tired. I wanted this all over with and done. I didn't want a monster trying to kill us. And I didn't want to be in PAR Laboratory anymore. "If wishes were fishes..." I whispered to myself. Straightening, I turned right into Adam's stun gun. I had a moment to marvel at the betrayal before the pain hit.

There are all sorts of pain and I'd experienced a lot of them: deep stabs, shallow cuts, acid burns, a bullet graze, menstrual cramps, migraine headaches, broken bones, and the list goes on. None of it prepared me for the pain of being stunned. Think of jumping into a very cold pool. There's the immediate shock of zero to ten. Every single muscle tenses and there is nothing you can do about it. It didn't hurt worse than a lot of pain I'd experienced but it was much more shocking—no pun intended—with a localized burning in my neck where he held the stun gun to me.

Then I was on the ground, shaking, and feeling like I'd just had the hardest workout of my life. I felt weak, like I'd never be able to get up again. But, even as I thought that, I pulled myself into a kneeling position, mimicking exactly what Adam had done. My head pounded. Literally pounded with every pulse of my blood. It was like the beginning of a migraine.

I didn't say anything as I looked up at him.

Adam held out the radio I didn't realized I'd dropped. "At least now we know we're both clean. Right?" He didn't smile. He looked like I felt—exhausted and heart sore.

But, he had a very good point. I nodded. "Fair enough."

He offered me a hand up. "I'm sorry."

As I accepted it, I realized he had a white cloth draped over his shoulder. It didn't take much for me to figure out what it, who it, was for. "Don't be. You're right. You couldn't know until you did. And I'd just admitted I'd been having hallucinations."

Adam shook his head. "I didn't do it because of that. Carrie showed me your file. Hallucinations under stress. I think all this qualifies. I did it because I needed to be sure. Just like you did."

"Doctor Giacomi had me stun her after… Lakshmi."

He didn't answer that. Instead, he said, "There's two doorstops on the table in there. I'm going to go get Sean."

The lab reminded me of the one I'd been in back in Oneida: covered work areas, a large sink, Bunsen burners, and jars of chemicals. The doorstops were on the table next to the door. The closet was open and there was another white cloth tarp on the floor. I stopped to get it as well. It would be good to show some respect to the other dead in the security room. I wondered what the people who'd have to clean up this place would think of what they found here.

Adam was waiting with Sean's wrapped body in his arms. I didn't blame him for not wanting to get blood on himself. We nodded to each other.

"Wait in the stairwell and watch me block open Level E. Then we use the elevator to go to Level A." I took the lead this time. The unspoken request was that we don't leave each other's side again until we lured the Minkowski into the trap.

"That's what I was thinking." Adam shifted Sean to a more secure carrying position and nodded to me.

I looked down the long hallway of cells on Level E. I couldn't tell if the last cell was open or not from the stairwell but I had to trust that Carrie knew what she was doing. Adam and I didn't need to talk on the way up to Level A. We kept near each other and watchful of the empty halls around us.

When we got to the security room, I let Adam go in first. He set Sean's body down next to the other four already there. Then he offered me a hand. I gave him one end of the tarp and unfurled the other end. Even as large as it was, the tarp wasn't big enough to cover them all. I grimaced at the hands and feet sticking out and turned away.

"Let's get to Level B and get this done." Adam gestured to the door, allowing me to exit first.

I nodded and silently prayed that this trap not only worked, but also killed the Minkowski dead for good. If it didn't work, a lot more of us were going to die and there weren't that many of us left.

THE REAL ENEMY

CHAPTER SIXTEEN

As Adam blocked the stairwell door to Level B open, I walked down the hallway to where Ian, Jolene, and Doctor Giacomi stood. They all looked serious and determined. Before I could say anything, Ian asked, "What happened to Sean?"

"Someone stabbed him. We think it was Forester. It's what makes the most sense." I lied to him—and everyone else—because we had bigger things to worry about: capturing a murderous alien. Then I would sit down and give the whole situation a hard think. Or hand the problem over to Carrie if she could spare the cycles. She was the smartest teen among us. There was something I was missing. Maybe in the telling we'd both figure it out.

"We?" Ian interrupted my thoughts, then gave Adam a sidelong glance before looking back at me.

"We," I confirmed as firmly as I could. I didn't need Ian worrying about Adam when he was about to do something monumentally stupid and dangerous. "Are we all ready?" I looked to Doctor Giacomi.

She nodded and pointed to a spot near us. "Yes. Ian will be right there." Then she pointed to the open meeting room opposite it. "We'll be in there. We've practiced a couple of times. We're as ready as we're going to be."

Adam, who had reached us, asked, "And you want us to run slowly, with the Minkowski following, past here and to the end of the hallway?"

"Yes. Ian will be on the ground, pretending to be unable to move."

Ian smirked. "I'll be screaming enough to put a scream queen to shame. There's no way it'll miss me if what Doctor Giacomi says is true—that it senses people by sound waves."

"Electromagnetic waves as well," Jolene added.

"I'll be a big, fat target. I'm ready. So... can we do this?" Ian's excitement shifted into something more nervous. "I'm on pins and needles here."

"Okay. Okay. We're going." Adam and I turned towards the stairwell.

Doctor Giacomi's voice floated after us. "Remember, if this doesn't work, stun guns. We know *they* work. Trigger them first, then stun the Minkowski."

Down the stairs to Level C, Adam and I waited by the stairwell door and listened. If the Minkowski was right there, we wanted to be ready to run away before it could hurt or possess us. Adam slid the doorstop out from under the door. It was a burnt wedge of wood. I didn't think it would've lasted much longer if the alien had kept at it.

I slowly turned the door handle and cracked the door. Adam peered through the opening. "Not here," he whispered. Of course it wouldn't be easy. "You want to split up and look for it?"

I shook my head. "Not really. Then we'd have to test each other again. I still have a pounding headache from the last time."

"Point. Me, too."

I considered the situation. "One of us could keep the door open and the other could go to the short corner and see if it's down the other long hallway."

"As Ian says, I volunteer as tribute." Adam half-smiled at the look on my face. "I'm faster than you and you know it."

"Right. Point conceded. But if you see it, you yell and come running. We both get out of here. No man left behind."

"Got it." He gave me a mock salute.

I ignored it as I opened the stairwell door wide and stepped in after him. Adam hurried down the short hallway. I pitched my voice low, "Remember to look inside the rooms, too. Don't get cut off."

I watched him stop at the corner and look down it until movement caught my eye. At the end of the long hallway, the Minkowski appeared. It was smaller than it had been the last time I'd see it. Condensed into a two feet pulsing ball of lightning and hate, it rippled red into green then orange, and shot towards me, going faster than I'd ever seen it move.

"Adam!" I yelled, backing up into the stairwell but still holding the door open.

The Minkowski was halfway down the hallway when Adam appeared and I pointed at it.

"Whoa!" Adam grabbed the door from me and slammed it shut with a bang.

I pulled him back from it just as the first strike of lightning crashed against the metal door, shaking it in its hinges. "I think it's pissed." Another crash of electricity shook the door then arcs of lightning coalesced around the door's handle and it began to turn.

"Shitshitshitshit!" I yelled as we bolted up the stairs and the door was flung open. The Minkowski rushed through. "It's coming," I yelled as we sprinted up the second set of stairs and onto Level B.

"Run! Go-go-go!" Adam pushed me in front of him. "It's fast!"

I could feel the hair on my arms and on the back of my neck prickle as the monster's electromagnetic aura radiated out from its condensed form. I hadn't known it could, or would, do that. I continued to yell as planned, keeping the alien following us. "Ian go! Go!" In truth, my panic wasn't faked. All of the sudden, I thought this was a very bad plan.

Adam grabbed me by the hand as we passed Ian to pull me faster. I stopped yelling and concentrated on keeping up with Adam. Ian took up where I left off.

"You want me, you bastard? Come and get me! I'm hurt. I can't run. Come and get me."

I threw a look over my shoulder. Ian was standing in the middle of the hallway waving his arms. The Minkowski had slowed as if sensing a trap. Ian waved some more. "I'm the one who got away! I'm the one you want. Come get me!" He backed up a couple more paces.

I missed the exact moment that Doctor Giacomi and Jolene burst out of the office and stabbed the Minkowski with their grounding rods because Adam pulled me around the corner of the hallway. I yanked my hand out of his and looked back just in time to see the most beautiful sight.

The Minkowski was immobile, caught between the two grounding rods. Electricity arced down the rods, harmlessly over the thick rubber gloves, and disappeared—only to reappear on the other grounding rod. All of the electricity was being fed back into the monster. It had worked. The alien flashed wild colors and morphed from a tight ball of gas and electricity into something almost man-shaped.

Ian pulled his stun gun from his pocket. "For my family, you bastard!"

"Ian, no!" Doctor Giacomi yelled.

He didn't listen. Ian stuck his hand in the middle of the Minkowski and triggered the stun gun. There was a huge crackle of electricity and a blinding flash of light as the world exploded in color and sound and pain.

I came to on the floor next to Adam. I have no idea what knocked me down or how long I was out. It didn't feel very long. I blinked, shaking my head at the blotches of afterimage light that swam in front of me, blocking my view. Adam stirred and shook his head as I pulled myself to my feet. I gazed at the destruction in the hallway.

The walls were scorched and the windows nearest the explosion were blown out, mercifully shattering glass into the rooms and not into the hallway. Jolene, Ian, and Doctor Giacomi all appeared to be unconscious. Sprawled in the hallway. It looked as if the explosion had thrown Jolene and Doctor Giacomi against the walls where they were slumped, and had slammed Ian to the floor.

I staggered down the hallway with Adam at my heels. I checked Ian first as Adam went to Jolene. Ian was already blinking his eyes and twitching his hands. "How do you feel?" I asked.

For about two minutes, Ian didn't say anything. He looked around, dazed and confused. Then he stiffened and grabbed my arm. "Is it dead? Did I get it?" He blinked at me a couple more times. "Did I get it?" His grip on my arm hurt.

I pried his hand off me as I looked around the hallway. There was no sign of the Minkowski—gas, lightning, or colors. "I think so. I think you did."

"I knew it would work." Ian closed his eyes with a sigh. "Oh god, I hurt. Really bad." He rubbed the side of his face.

I shook my head. "What the hell were you thinking? You, all of you, could've been killed."

He didn't open his eyes. "I had to try. It murdered my family. I had to do it."

"Melissa?" It was Adam. "They're not waking up."

I patted Ian's shoulder. "You rest, you idiot." I stood and moved to Adam and Jolene.

I hunkered down next to them. Jolene was pale and burned but she was breathing. Adam showed me his hand. There was blood on it—not a lot, but it was there. "They both hit the wall really hard. They're both bleeding from the head and are burned. I don't think we should move them. They may have spine injuries."

"You're right. We shouldn't move them." I stood. "But, we can make them more comfortable until they wake up and can move on their own. Or tell us how they feel at least. I'll go get some blankets and pillows. You stay here with them."

As I turned away, I saw Ian had propped himself up against the wall. He gave me a wave then closed his eyes. I shook my head again. Adam grabbed my hand before I could take off down the hallway. "What?"

He looked a little sheepish, then whispered. "Horror movie rules. No one goes alone."

I patted his hand. "The monster's dead. There isn't even a body to double-tap. It's okay. I think we're going to be okay now."

Adam gave me a dubious frown before he nodded. "Okay. You're right. The monster's dead. We're okay."

"I'll be back really soon. Just keep an eye on everyone. Make sure Jolene and Doctor Giacomi remain still."

"I will."

As I took the elevator to Level A, I radioed Carrie. "Minkowski dead. No need for the whole cell transfer thing. But, we've got three injured out here. The sooner you can get the stairwell door or the elevator unsealed, the better. Over."

"Is Ian…?" There was a pause, then Carrie added a belated. "Over."

"Ian's fine. Hurt. But fine. He did something really stupid but it worked. Over"

"Sounds like a story for another time. I'm working on it. I'll get us free yet. Over and out."

I smiled at the radio and stuffed it into my pocket as the elevator doors opened. I headed for my room and stumbled as several thoughts occurred to me at once. Something hadn't added up. A human had to have killed Sean. Everyone was accounted for during that time. Except Adam and Ian. I only had their words for what had happened to make them scatter and they disagreed on the facts. But, I had tested Adam. I hadn't tested Ian.

Ian. The one Adam, who'd spent his whole life observing people, just couldn't understand. Ian, who while he didn't actually change his clothes, only got a pair of shoes and a jacket, wouldn't let anyone into his quarters. Only Ian hadn't been frightened at the lockdown alarm. He'd shown up, excited, but without shoes.

Ian had pushed his hand into the Minkowski before he turned the stun gun on. That contact would've allowed the Minkowski to jump into him.

I stood there, my head bowed, my hand holding my cheek, thinking furiously. Ian had pushed the idea that Adam was dangerous and was lying about where Sean was. But, I had cleared Adam. He wasn't possessed and he hadn't been out of my sight until just this moment since I'd cleared him. And Adam hadn't gone off plan.

I turned towards Ian's room. I still had Doctor Dudetsky's access card if the room was locked. It would get me into any and every room. I didn't realize what I was going to do until I unlocked Ian's door and turned on the light. The room looked like a tornado had hit it.

I know he'd only been here a week longer than me but he had clothing strewn everywhere. I looked around the room. There was a pile of clothing next to the wall. Some clothing, half folded in an opened suit case, and some clothes kicked under the bed. Everything else seemed neat: toiletries by the sink and on the dresser.

I walked to the dresser and opened the drawers. There was nothing in them. Ian had been living out of the suitcase like he expected to leave at any moment. I glanced between the piles of clothes on the floor. I knew what I was looking for and I went for the pile that looked like it was trying to hide something—the clothes half under the bed.

I picked up a pair of jeans and saw blotches of red-brown stains on them. A t-shirt also had stains. There was a second pair of sneakers behind the bloodstained clothes. One of them had a darkening splash of blood on them. That would explain why Ian had shown up in socks. I laid everything out on the bed and tried to take a picture of it. I think it worked. It was hard to tell with my shattered screen.

I glanced at the time. 7:31am. I looked in my purse to make sure my pills were still there. Thank God they were. Again, that was a crisis I didn't want to think about right now. I decided it wasn't too early to take them. Because, what I needed to do next was going to suck so hard it almost hurt to think about.

After dry swallowing my morning dose—and a quick count to make sure I had exactly the right number of pills still on me—I thumbed my phone on and sliced the pad of my thumb open getting to David's number. Sucking on my thumb as the phone rang, I left Ian's room and moved to one of the unoccupied rooms. I would scavenge pillows and blankets from it.

"Tell me you've got good news for me." David sounded as tired as I felt.

"I've got news. Good… I think. And shitty news." I sat down on the bed and heard him sigh.

"Lay it on me."

"Good news. I think we've killed the Minkowski. Or, at least the main portion of it." I glanced at my thumb. It was still bleeding. I pressed it to my jeans. "Bad news… I'm really sure that Ian murdered Joe Chambers and Sean MacGregor. I've found bloody clothes in his room. I don't know if he's possessed, but I think he is."

"Okay. That *is* disturbing news. Why do you think he's possessed?"

"He went off plan and stunned the Minkowski while it was grounded, causing one heck of an explosion. But, he stuck his hand in it before he turned the stun gun on. I know from watching Lakshmi, that it takes just a touch to gather a piece of it." I took a breath. "I think he did that on purpose to make us all think everything was fine."

"All right. Explosion. What's everyone's status?"

"Carrie, me, Adam are all fine. Jolene and Doctor Giacomi are unconscious. Ian… suspect. He was moving after the explosion and he was at the center of it." I paused. "David, remember how I told you that you guys needed to quarantine us?"

"Yeah?"

"I think you need to knock us all out, then quarantine us in a way that no one touches us with anything that can conduct electricity. I think this whole thing has been about the Minkowski escaping. Nothing else makes sense." I listened to him consider this. The hubbub in the background was quiet. I didn't know how many people were listening in on the conversation and I really didn't care. "Also, Carrie says she's close to getting the elevator or the stairwell door open."

"Good to know."

"Got any bright ideas for me?"

Again there was a long pause. "Well, if you can capture or subdue Ian without touching him, do it. Otherwise, I'll call you back."

"Okay."

"Hey Melissa?"

"Yeah?"

"Stay strong. We'll get you out of this yet."

"Thanks. I appreciate the thought. Talk to you soon." I thumbed the end call button and left a blood smear on my phone. I didn't say what I was really thinking: that I couldn't see a way out for me—or for the rest of us—when the alien could jump from body to body and it killed the host when it was forced out of it.

I stood up as I shoved my phone back into my purse. Even as I gathered the blankets and pillows to help Jolene and Doctor Giacomi, my mind pummeled itself, trying to figure out something, anything, I could do if the worst had occurred. I finally decided that I needed to stop thinking about what could've gone wrong and get back down to Level B to see if my suspicions were correct. If they were and Ian infected Adam while I was up here, I was done for.

CHAPTER SEVENTEEN

I took the elevator down to Level B. I'd spent too much time running up and down stairs over the last few hours to ever want to do it again in this place. Adam, who had been kneeling by Jolene, looked over his shoulder. "Jolene is awake. Sorta. She laid herself down. I figured that was good enough for the moment."

"Yeah. I think so." I stood barely within arm's reach and handed him a pillow, then a blanket before looking up and down the hallway. Doctor Giacomi was still slumped over on her side. No Ian.

Adam tucked the blanket around Jolene's shoulders, knees, and ankles. "Rest now. We'll find out if we can get you to a bed." She didn't answer. She blinked at him a couple of times and was still.

He stood, moving slower than before. "I have no idea if there's a stretcher down here. Right now, I don't think we should move them without one."

"Probably a good idea. But, I don't know if the cold tile floor is going to do them any good. If they don't rouse themselves in a couple of hours, we may have to make do."

"I hadn't thought of that." He yawned. It was the first time I'd seen him affected by the all night crisis. "Maybe if we move a couple of mattresses down here. I don't know."

We both moved to Doctor Giacomi. I hunkered down next to her, giving her my best first aid once over. No fever or chills. She was breathing in long slow breaths. Her pulse was on the higher side of normal and she was totally out. No signs of eye flutters or of waking. "Did she move herself from sitting to her side?"

Adam nodded. "She twitched a couple of times, then slumped over. There wasn't much I could do. I kept checking on them, making sure they were still breathing and stuff."

As Adam tucked the pillow under her head, I saw the outline of an access card—Joe Chambers keycard—in her pants pocket. "Get the keycard. You'll need it." After he did, I handed him one end of the blanket and helped him lay it over the doctor.

Looking at the hallway again, I saw that Adam or Ian had cleaned up the grounding rods. "Ian? Where is he?" I asked as Adam stood. I continued to look around for the grounding rods until I found them just inside one of the office doorways.

Adam shook his head. "I don't know. Bathroom I guess. He was walking soon after you left. He looked a little shell shocked but all right overall. Talked to himself a little."

I beckoned Adam to follow me. I didn't have a plan. I didn't want to play Surprise: Stun Gun! with him again. "We have a problem," I said as we rounded the corner and stopped.

His face fell. "Problem? Oh, crap. What problem?"

I felt bad about ripping away the false hope we had that everything was going to be just fine. It wasn't and I needed to know if he was on my side or not. "I found bloody clothes in Ian's room. That's why he didn't want you or Sean in there. You might have seen it." I stopped and waited to see if Adam was going to pick up what I was laying down.

"He killed Joe… and Sean?" Adam's face contorted into a mask of pain and hate. "That son of… I'm going to wring his scrawny neck. We need to get him."

He took two steps towards me then stopped as I matched his steps, keeping the distance between us, and raised my hand. I shook my head. "There's no 'we' right now."

"What? What do you…" Adam stopped. He really looked at me and the expression on my face. For a moment, there was confusion, then his face cleared with understanding before it shifted into something closed to neutral resignation. "Shit. I was alone with him."

"Or I was. You didn't see him go. You have no idea if I'm running you a line of BS. Maybe I'm leading you into a trap."

"But the Minkowski is dead."

I locked eyes with him. "Is it? Can we be sure? It can jump bodies with a touch."

"For crying out loud." Adam pulled the stun gun from his pocket, lifted his shirt, pressed the stun gun to his stomach, and triggered it. His whole body clenched as he shook and fell forward with his mouth open in a soundless cry of pain.

"You idiot!" I grabbed for the arm holding the stun gun to his body and pulled it away. I tried not to wrench his arm out of its socket as I moved to break his fall. I only partly succeeded and he hit the floor shoulder first instead of doing a face plant. "What the hell were you thinking? You never stun yourself. Your muscles lock up and you can't let go."

When he could talk again, Adam swallowed hard and rubbed his head, "But I'm clean."

"Yeah. I guess you are." I let out a long sigh and sat down next to him. "Shit. I hate being stunned." I knew what I was getting myself into this time. My head was still pounding from the last time we'd played this game. But, I needed to prove that I was clean, too. "This is going to suck, but you can stun me again when you've got control of your body." At least this time, I wasn't going to fall over. I was already on the ground.

"No. That's cool." He lay there flexing his arms and hands, getting control back. "Just the fact that you're willing is enough." He paused, giving me a weak half-smile. "This time."

I nodded. "Thanks. Maybe a little too trusting, but thanks."

"Where do you think Ian is now? What do you think he's doing?" Adam sat up, then shifted into a crouch. He twisted his neck side-to-side and stretched the muscles in his neck.

I stood and offered my arm to steady him as he got up. "I don't know for sure but I've got a hunch we're both going to hate it." I pulled the radio from my purse. "Carrie, status report? Over."

We both heard my voice around the corner and down the hall. "You should get that radio." Adam nodded and went to retrieve it as I watched. I wasn't going to let him out of my sight again. I waited for the count of thirty to try the radio again. "Carrie, you there? Over."

By the time Adam was at my side again, he already suspected what I suspected: Ian was in the server room. We couldn't count on there being only two available access cards. Ian murdered Chambers but didn't take his card. That was the one Adam had now. I had Doctor Dudetsky's card. Forester either hid, destroyed, or gave Lakshmi and Doctor Giacomi's keycards to Ian. Jolene's card was still missing. Most likely, it was with the other cards.

"He's in the server room." I didn't know what else to say. If he was the human person behind all of this, it was the only thing that made any sense.

"Also, he has the pistols that Sadie had and you left behind. That means he has all three of them in there. All we have are these two stun guns."

"Carrie's in trouble. Or, she's working on getting the place unsealed and she doesn't know she's in trouble."

Adam shook his head. "She's smart. She probably knows. It's probably why she's not answering us. It's the only way to say that something's wrong."

"Or because Ian took the radio from her." I leaned against the wall. I was more than tired. I was exhausted. All I wanted was for this to be done and to sleep for a week. "I'm open to suggestions. I don't like the thought of attempting a head-on assault. It's one way in and one way out. He can shoot us coming through the door. Or shoot Carrie."

Adam thought for a long time, pacing in front of me with his head down. He'd come up with an idea but dismiss it before going back to pacing. He raised his head. "Actually, that's not quite right."

"What's not quite right?"

He gave me a small smile. "That part about one way in and one way out of the server room."

"What do you mean?" I felt hope blossom within and tried to stomp down on my sudden excitement.

"There are maintenance shafts. All that power and all those cords. I can do one of two things: pull the plug on everything that Carrie is doing. Or, try to sneak in through the ceiling."

"Dear God, don't pull the plug. That's probably the only thing keeping Carrie alive right now. I think this whole thing has been about helping the monster escape. If you pull the plug, you might as well shoot Carrie in the head."

Adam's excitement drooped. "Oh... He wouldn't, would he? I mean, they're in love."

"Maybe. Maybe not." I rubbed my head. "Maintenance shafts. Why didn't you mention them earlier when we were trying to figure out a way in without being attacked by the Minkowski?" Not that I think that would've stopped everything that happened, but I needed to know.

He shrugged. "I didn't think about it. You know? Crawling through the ceiling is never the first idea on my list for anything. I… I'm sorry. I just didn't think about it."

He had a point. I nodded. "All right. So, sneaking in through the ceiling…. That has merit. I could go through the front, pretending I don't realize he's the bad guy and distract him. You know?"

Adam looked like he wanted to argue the point but, to his credit, he didn't. Which is good. Because if he had pulled an "it's too dangerous" I think I would've stunned him for being an idiot. Nothing about the last twenty-four hours hasn't been dangerous to me, and everyone else, in one way or another.

"Okay. It's going to take me about five minutes to get into the maintenance shaft that goes to the server room and—"

I stopped him, curious. "Why do you know about the maintenance shafts anyway? They can't have you doing that kind of work. I don't care how many of them think of you as an intern or an assistant."

Adam chuckled. "No. Of course not. I think Lakshmi would… would've… had a fit if they'd tried to do that. I found the maintenance shafts while exploring when I was about seven, I guess. Remember, I was born here. For a long time, they were my… tree house… you might say.

"Then one of the maintenance guys caught me taking a nap in one of the maintenance alcoves. We made a deal. He wouldn't tell on me and I wouldn't mess with certain things—no pulling wires, no punching buttons, no crawling on the ceilings of rooms. Stuff like that."

He gazed off to the side, a faraway smile on this face. "I used to help them out from time to time. And one particular shaft became a refuge after my… when Eric left."

"I'm surprised you didn't run there during all this."

"I thought about it. It's not as easy to get in some of the spots these days, but I can do it." He gave me a direct look that said it was time for business. "Anyway, we're on the clock. Ian is in there with Carrie. I'm going to need about ten minutes to get in place to go through the ceiling. Okay?"

I nodded. "Yeah. I can do that. I'll go up to the server room and keep him focused on me."

He held out a fist. "See you in ten."

I bumped my fist against his. "See you in ten." At least, I hoped I'd be in a state to see him again in ten. I didn't know what I was going to walk in on or how Ian was going to react to my presence and he was the one with all the guns.

CHAPTER EIGHTEEN

I took the elevator to Level A and stopped by my quarters long enough to change out of my bloody t-shirt and sweatshirt and into a clean duplicate of the same, just different colors. If I was going to die, at least I'd have clean clothes on. It took a little longer than I wanted it to because of my injured shoulder, but it gave Adam the full ten minutes that he needed to get into position. I just wished that I had some of the painkillers I'd had in Oneida. I wasn't going to go down without a fight and something to dull the pain in my shoulder and head would be wonderful right about now.

Thinking of Oneida, and the injuries I'd gotten back then, reminded me that Mister Bat was still in the server room. Suddenly, I had another goal on top of rescuing Carrie and distracting Ian. I wanted my bat so bad I could taste it. It was my talisman, and practically my best friend.

At the server room door, I paused and took a breath. Then I swiped Doctor Dudetsky's access card, opened the door, and walked in. As I did so, I shoved the access card in my pocket and pulled the stun gun from my purse. "Pretty Penny, what's shakin'?" It was what Deroga always asked when he entered the office. It was a coded way of getting her status. Was she in trouble? Did she know she was in trouble?

Carrie's voice floated from the back of the server room. "Another day, another dollar."

Things are bad but I don't know how bad.

"You two realize I'm not stupid, right?" Ian's voice came from the same direction as Carrie's and held a note of contempt I hadn't heard before.

I stayed by the door, my heart pounding faster. I tried to keep my voice sounding level and unconcerned. "I'm not sure what you mean."

"I mean, I've read those books, too. I read every single one I could find when Carrie told me about them." He paused. "We had to have something to talk about, didn't we, babe?"

Crap. I shifted to the side, trying to get a glimpse of him through the server racks. Was he armed. He had to be. "How'd you get in here, Ian? I have Doctor Dudetsky's keycard and Adam has Joe Chambers' card. The server room is locked."

There was a long silence. Then Carrie yelled, "He's got a gun!"

"Shut up." There was the sound of flesh hitting flesh. "Keep working."

That did it. My fear morphed into rage. I picked one of the server aisles and moved down it. "What the hell are you doing, Ian? How could you hit her? Are you a monster now? Or have you always been one?"

"I'm doing what I need to do."

His voice was closer. He was moving, too. Stalking me. Where was Adam? My anger didn't let my fear return in force but it was there again, on the edges of my awareness. I found myself breathing too fast and worked to control my breath.

"What do you need to do, Ian? Are you trying to let the Minkowski escape? It killed your family. It tried to kill you." I ducked as I saw him turn down the aisle next to mine. He saw me and lifted the gun. I ran. The shot followed me, careening off one of the servers, causing it to spark.

"Careful. You might just kill our only way out of here," I called. "You don't know which one of these server's Carrie's actually working on."

"You just don't get it. For someone who thinks they're so smart, you are an idiot. You can't see what's right in front of your face."

"Then tell me." If I could keep him talking and keep him from shooting me, that should give Adam enough time to drop in and even the odds. I just hoped Adam didn't take too long.

"I let them in. The Coalescence." He barked laughter. "Minkowski is such a stupid name. It tells you nothing about them. They call themselves the Coalescence. They're a group mind and they've been visiting our dimension for ages. I've been talking to them for years, telling them all about humanity. They're going to fix everything."

The whole time he spoke, his voice moved away. I could tell that he had moved back to the workstation where Carrie was. Probably to use her as a hostage or maybe as a human shield. "What are they going to fix? They've killed everyone they've come in contact with."

"You're wrong. Not everyone. They needed to understand how we worked. Now that they know, they're going to fix us. Also, fix the mess we've made of the planet." He paused. "I'm going to be the first one they take to their home dimension. I'm going to be the first inter-dimensional traveler."

I heard the triumph in Ian's voice. I peeked around the server rack and saw him standing next to Carrie. She was focused on the screen in front of her. He held a stun gun to her neck and the 9mm pistol at his side. I pulled back. There wasn't much I could do. "You're going to be nothing. You're a traitor. To your family and to humanity. They murdered your family. They murdered Doctor Dudetsky and Lakshmi. How do you think they're going to treat the rest of us?"

Dammit! Where the hell was Adam?

"I don't care. My parents only cared about my brother and his scholarships. And my sister because she was the baby. The scientists here? They didn't care about us. All they wanted was their precious data. You saw how Dudetsky acted. He deserved to die. They all deserved to die. Besides, some people will have to die to pave the way for greatness. It's going to be a new age of mankind."

"As slaves, you mean."

Ian didn't respond to that.

Adam wasn't here and it was well past ten minutes. Something must have happened but I couldn't figure out what and I didn't have time to figure it out. I just knew I had to stop Ian and the alien from escaping. "Carrie, stop what you're doing. You can't break us out. It sucks. I know, but we have to do the right thing."

"If you stop, I'll hurt you again."

The menace in Ian's voice made me freeze and my breath catch in my throat. What had he done to her? I looked at the stun gun in my hand and wondered if I could get to him and stun him with it before he shot me to death. There was no way to sneak up on him. Twenty feet between me and him. He knew how to use the gun. He'd probably hit me two or three times before I reached him. Could I be shot and still stun him? Was that feasible?

"No."

I looked up at the sound of Carrie's voice. She could distract him while I charged him. That could work.

"Don't tell me, no. You don't get to say that word to me." Ian's voice was soft as he spoke. Carrie gave a soft moan of pain. Like she was trying to stifle herself.

I readied myself to rush Ian. To stun him and then maybe hit him with Mister Bat a couple of times. Then my phone erupted with "Secret Agent Man." It was David. He was calling back. I hesitated.

"Don't answer it," Ian said, his voice was soft and cold. "If you do, I'll punish her."

That settled it. If Ian didn't want me answering the phone, that's exactly what I would do. *I'm sorry, Carrie,* I thought as I pulled the phone from my purse and answered the call. I didn't wait for him to talk. "We've got a problem. Ian has Carrie under a gun. He wants her to break the lockdown. I've told her not to."

"And you? Are you okay?" David's voice was impossibly calm in the face of this outrageous thing I'd just told him.

I stuck my head around the server rack and saw that Ian had Carrie out of the chair. He was holding her by the hair with the stun gun pressed to her neck. I didn't see the pistol. I stepped out and let Ian see me. "I'm all right for the moment but I'm not sure how long that's going to go on for. Ian has a stun gun to Carrie's throat. He's been threatening her and hurting her to get her to finish breaking us out of here."

"You're looking at him?"

Ian and I locked eyes. "Yeah. I'm looking at them. David, when your people finally get through... shoot on sight. Every last one of us. No exceptions."

Ian triggered the stun gun and Carrie screamed. He let her go as her knees buckled and she dropped to the floor face first, twitching.

"I understand," David said.

If he said anything else, I didn't hear it. I dropped my phone and charged Ian. But he was ready for me. He knocked the stun gun aside and clocked me hard across the cheek. In the movies, people get punched and they don't react. This wasn't one of those times. It hurt. Pain radiated out in hot waves. I staggered and moved out of the way of his next hit.

I punched him twice in the stomach, the only place I could hit. I was rewarded with a double fist to my injured shoulder. I screamed and dropped to the floor. He kicked me hard in the stomach. I curled up and rolled over. Ian grabbed me by the hair and twisted my face to his.

"This. This is what the Coalescence will fix. People like you!"

Out of the corner of my eye, I saw Carrie moving. She rolled over and pulled herself into a kneeling position. I laughed at him, not much more than a couple of breaths in his face. "At least, now, I know Carrie's clean."

"Clean?" Ian shook me like a bad dog. "What do you mean clean?"

Trying not to yelp as he yanked my hair around, I forced more laughter. "You stunned her and it didn't force a Minkowski out of her. Did you know that I killed the one in Lakshmi? I stunned her and forced it out of her and then stunned it before it could run away. Poof. No more Minkowski."

"Clean? No. Defective. And their name is the Coalescence!"

He drove his thumb into my wounded shoulder, tearing the neat stitches Doctor Giacomi had put in. I couldn't stop my shriek of pain. Even when he stopped digging into my wound, bright spots swam in front of my eyes, and the taste of copper flooded my mouth. It was a race to see which would happen first: me throwing up or me passing out.

Ian slammed my head against the floor and stood. "Defective," he repeated, his voice softer. "Unfortunate." He moved over to Carrie's kneeling form. "That's part of the problem. The Coalescence couldn't bond to her. Just like it couldn't bond to my family. Or to Sean. Or Adam. I tried on all of them. We can't figure out why. Only some humans are suitable hosts for the Coalescence."

He grabbed her hair, gentler now, and pulled Carrie's head back so he could look her in the eyes. Tears streamed down her face but she didn't make a sound. "Poor, unfortunate, defective human."

Carrie didn't fight him, despite the fury in her eyes. She put her hands in her jacket pockets and waited, not saying anything. I wanted to fight him all the more for what he'd done to her.

"Defective," Ian muttered again. He let go of Carrie's hair and turned back to me.

I saw my phone just above my head and stretched out for it. I had no idea what I was going to do now but the idea of having my phone soothed me. I saw that David was still on the line and was listening to everything that happened. I smiled and held the phone up to Ian. "They heard. They know. The Minkowski have a plan but we humans are just too… too… different from each other to easily conquer. Like they did you. You've just told the world the monster can be beaten."

Ian's face twisted in anger, then smoothed over into something neutral, almost pleasant. "But you, Melissa, I haven't tested you yet." His smile froze my heart. "Maybe you can join the Coalescence. Then you'll understand what we're striving for."

I saw Carrie slowly pull her hand out of her jacket pocket and realized what she was going to do. I struggled to my feet to keep his attention on me. "Like hell, you murderous bastard. I'd sooner kiss a Fedora monster."

"No. I think it's time I test you." He held out a hand and electricity arced between his fingers.

I waved my hands at him as if to ward him off. "Stay away from me."

"I think," Carrie said, "you should go to hell." She pulled the syringe from her pocket and uncapped it. I threw my phone at Ian, striking him in the head as she stabbed the syringe filled with whatever it was into the back of Ian's thigh and slammed the plunger home.

Ian gave a roar of surprise and anger. He back fisted Carrie in the face. I heard the crunch of cartilage as she fell backwards. Then he turned and lunged for me, his hand crackling with electricity.

I ran.

Ian was right on my heels. Suddenly, we were in the most messed up game of tag I'd ever been in. If he touched me, and I wasn't immune like Carrie, I was toast. I couldn't let that happen. I needed to stay me.

Sprinting down the first aisle of servers, I turned the corner and sprinted down the next. Ian stumbled on the turn and crashed into one of the server racks, almost knocking it over. I paused at the noise, saw Ian stagger but he was still coming for me. I sprinted down the next aisle and went to turn the corner. Ian, realizing he couldn't catch me, retraced his steps. I gasped as I almost came face-to-face with him.

Ian swiped at me with a hand filled with lightning. I jumped back, his hand missing me by inches. Backpedaling down the aisle, Ian stumbled toward me like a drunken sailor intent on pounding my face in. But, whatever had been in that syringe finally did what it was supposed to do. Ian crumpled to his knees and tumbled to the floor on his side, his hand still arcing and still stretched out for me.

"Melissa?" Carrie sounded scared.

"Yeah." I half-sagged against the server rack then forced myself to straighten. I didn't want to knock it over. "I'm okay. What was in that syringe?" I gazed at Ian and watched the electricity in his hand disappear. I kept myself from kicking him in the head for good measure. Horror movies insisted on a double-tap to make sure the monster is down and out. In this case, touching Ian might be the worst thing I could do.

But Carrie could touch him. For some reason, she was immune to the Minkowski. I shook my head. The Coalescence. Now that I understood more about what they were, their chosen name made a lot of sense and reminded me what they actually were, that they were a hive mind that could break pieces of themselves off and infect others.

Carrie rounded the cornered as she spoke. "Some of the sedative that Lakshmi prescribed Sean after he got here. He had really bad, screaming nightmares. Sean had some on him. He gave it to me while you were on the phone before they all went out, looking for the missing people." She held a bloody rag to her nose. She looked down at Ian. "Asshole. I think he broke my nose."

"That is something I actually know how to help with. Let's get to the light. Then I'm going to need you to cuff him or zip-tie him. Whatever we've got on hand."

Carrie moved back to the workstation and sat down. I shifted until I could see her face. I saw the tear stained tracks down her cheeks and wanted to punch Ian all the more. Peering at her nose, it looked straight enough to me. "Look up and hold still. This might hurt a little."

I ran my fingertips down the sides of her nose and didn't feel any bumps or twists, just swelling. "I don't think it's broken. It's just bruised. He hit you a good one but didn't break your nose. You're probably going to look like a raccoon in a day or two." I nodded to her and she relaxed. "You're lucky. Setting a broken nose hurts and you sometimes have to adjust it more than once."

I dug a cold soda out of the mini-fridge and handed it to her. "See if you can stand the pressure of the can. We need to get some ice on it."

Carrie winced as she tried to do as I asked. She winced again and shook her head. "Not happening." She dabbed the edge of the bloody rag to her nose then looked at it. "At least my nose has stopped bleeding. What are we going to do with Ian? I don't know how long he's going to be out."

"Like I said, handcuffs or zip-ties. I'm pretty sure they have zip-ties in one of those drawers. But you're going to need to bind him. I can't touch—" I stopped as Carrie shook her head. "What? What's wrong?"

"I can't bind him with one hand."

I shook my head, not understanding. Then I remembered her left hand, that it wasn't whole. It still didn't make sense. It's not like she didn't use that hand. "You have two hands. You use them both without a problem. I mean, I've seen you. I barely notice that your hand isn't, you know, whole." I looked down at it and realized that she'd kept her deformed hand under the bloody towel.

Carrie looked down at the towel. "He knew it always hurt on some level. I'm good at ignoring the pain. I mean, there's not much else I can do. But, Ian used that against me." As she spoke, she let the bloody towel fall to the floor. "No one had ever done that before. Not even in the orphanage.

My hand was off-limits. I didn't realize how monstrous he was until…" She shook her head.

I caught my breath. The back of her left hand was bruised with raised, angry welts. Her fingers were so swollen she couldn't move them. As she turned her palm up, I could see that it was swollen and red, too.

"I didn't want to help him. I knew something was wrong when he came in without anyone else and asked how close I was to fixing things. He wouldn't answer my questions about what had happened or where everyone else was. Then I saw the electricity. I *knew* he was bad."

Carrie kept her eyes on her injured hand. "When I wouldn't do what he wanted, he hurt me. So, I pretended to work, to run command line code, and run scripts. The most I did was run more diagnostics. I planned to pretend to work until he was distracted enough for me to drug him. I didn't know you guys were still alive. He took the radio from me and broke it. I thought it was just me."

Rage boiled up and threatened to overwhelm me. "Tell me why I shouldn't just shoot him in the head?"

"He's got the only gun in the room and stunning him might free the Min… the Coalescence… from him."

I looked around for the other pistols. They weren't in sight. I wondered where he put them. My first guess was that he'd hidden them so he'd be the only one with a pistol. "I thought he took all the guns. We need to get that pistol off of him. Can you do that?"

Carrie nodded. "Yeah. Hold on." She jumped up and disappeared into the server stacks.

I spotted my phone where it landed after hitting Ian in the head. I walked over and picked it up. The poor thing had a cracked case to go with the shattered face. It refused to turn on. No more contact with the outside world. That wasn't happy making. The last thing David knew was me in a fight with Ian and my order that his people shoot us on sight. I really hoped he realized I meant with tranquilizer darts.

Carrie returned, holding the gun. "Where's Adam? Is he okay? And Jolene and Sadie? Ian wouldn't tell me." She put the gun down on the desk. "Also, there's like only two bullets in the magazine left."

"Good to know. I'm glad you checked." I pulled the radio from my purse and considered it. "Jolene and Doctor Giacomi were knocked unconscious from the explosion. They're safe enough on Level B. We even got them pillows and blankets." I raised the radio and showed it to her. "Adam was supposed to be clambering through the maintenance shafts to break in here through the ceiling. I was supposed to be his distraction. He was supposed to be the hero. I really don't know why he didn't show up. I just hope he's not stuck somewhere."

She gave me a skeptical look.

"Seriously." I smiled. Then I thumbed the talk button. "We've got things under control in here, Adam. Where are you? Over." I waited for him to answer. As the seconds stretched out and I felt the first inklings that all was still not right in PAR Lab. Carrie and I exchanged a worried look. "Adam? Can you hear me? Over."

Again there was silence. Nine counted seconds later, the radio came to life. It was Jolene and she sounded scared. "Melissa? Oh, thank goodness you're okay. You need to open—"

"Don't listen to her!" Adam's voice shouted over what Jolene was saying.

Carrie moved to stand next to me as I stared at the radio. "What the hell?"

I shook my head. My stomach did an all-too-familiar roll of fear and I knew it wasn't over yet. Every single time I'd thought we'd won, something else happened.

Jolene's voice crackled to life again. "Well now, that was unfortunate. Melissa, I think you should come to the server room door."

CHAPTER NINETEEN

Carrie and I looked at each other. "Shit," she muttered. "It got Jolene."

"When?" I paused and answered my own question. "When things exploded. It had to be."

"Doesn't matter when. Do you think it got Sadie, too?"

I shook my head, feeling sick. "I don't know, Carrie. I really don't." I took stock. I still had my stun gun. Carrie had the 9mm with only a couple of bullets left. "Okay. Seriously, how close are you to getting something open?"

"Pretty close, honestly." She rubbed the side of her face. "I think all I need to do is flip the bit on the automatic stairwell door locking timer scripts—all three of them—then compile and run them. I think. The code is archaic and intertwined like evil spaghetti."

"Evil spaghetti?"

"I'll show you if you want to see. There are linked variables in different scripts. Either the whole thing was hodge-podge together or it was designed by a shitty developer who thought he was being clever."

The radio came to life again. "Melissa, you really want to come to the server room door. *Now.*"

I shook my head. "No. Later. Listen, you don't run that script for anything if I don't come back whole. You let David and Tomas break in. Don't open the door if I go out. Keep the gun." I glanced back at the stacks where Ian was. "And if that sedative wears off? Shoot him in both knees. It'll keep him from moving and keep him alive with the Coalescence trapped within him."

Carrie nodded. "Don't do anything stupid."

"Too late. I'm here, aren't I?" I patted her shoulder. "I'll get us out of this if I can. Stay strong." As I walked to the server room door, I realized that I had repeated what David said to me. I wondered if he felt like he was lying as he said it, too.

I moved to the server room door from the side. I didn't want to stick my face in the little window, only to get it shot off. If Jolene was bonded to the Coalescence—and it sounded like she was—then there was a good bet that she had the other pistols. I wasn't sure who had what weapon and when they got them. My guess was that either she'd never put her pistol down or Ian gave it to her when Adam was looking after Doctor Giacomi.

From the left side of the door, I couldn't see anything. I ducked under the window and peeked out from the right side. What I saw made me forget my caution. I wasn't the one in danger.

Across the hall, Adam was on his knees with his hands behind his back. Jolene stood over him with one of the missing 9mm pistols at her side. Blood poured down the side of Adam's face from a fresh cut on his forehead. I know head wounds bleed a lot but this was terrifying. When Jolene saw me, she smiled. I know it was supposed to be a nice smile but it wasn't. It couldn't be. Not with her holding a gun on Adam.

She lifted the radio to her mouth. "It's nice to see you, Melissa. We should have a talk."

Any thoughts I had about that person still being Jolene fled. That was one of the Coalescence wearing a person suit. "What do you want?"

"It's more about what we each want. I'm sure you want Adam. I'm happy to give him to you. He's useless to me. In exchange, I want Ian."

Adam shook his head at me and mouthed the words, "Don't do it." He winced as she smacked him in the back of the head.

Anger rose as I watched her. "And if I don't give you Ian?"

Jolene pressed the pistol to Adam's shoulder. "I'll hurt him."

She sounded so much like Ian, shivers crawled up my spine. "The Coalescence is big on torture, aren't you? Why?" I was stalling and we both knew it. But I didn't know what I was stalling for. I needed some big idea to present itself in a hurry.

"You know our true name. That's good. As for hurting people..." Jolene paused to look at the hand holding the radio, to turn it over this way and that. Her tone took on a meditative quality. "We feel, but not as these bodies feel. We process pain differently. We are... testing its limits." She locked eyes with me. "Just as you are testing our patience." She ground the barrel of the 9mm into Adam's shoulder.

"Don't! You don't need to hurt him." I stopped thinking and let my mouth go. "You know I can't touch Ian's body and Ian hurt Carrie's hand too much for her to do it. We need a better way to exchange them. Send Adam in to get Ian. That's safe enough."

Jolene's face twisted in rage for just long enough to seem completely alien before it smoothed over into the fake sincerity she'd been showing. "What do you mean you can't touch Ian?"

I rolled my eyes and shook my head. "I know about people who can't be infected... oh, excuse me... 'bonded' with the Coalescence. I know Carrie and Adam are immune to you. I also know that I haven't been tested and there's no way in hell I'm going to let any of you test me."

"I see Ian got overexcited again." Jolene pondered for a moment. "Very well, I can let Adam retrieve Ian. But if you betray me, remember, I still have Sadie."

Hope rose as I thought about the good doctor who was more than just a doctor. Maybe we still had an ally on the outside. "Doctor Giacomi is still alive?"

"For the moment, but that will change if you don't do what I tell you to do." She gave me the sweet smile of a madwoman.

I looked down and considered the situation. It would be safer for me if Ian and Jolene were locked out while we were locked in. But, that would probably sentence Doctor Giacomi to death, and she didn't deserve that. Movement caught my eye and I glanced up. Carrie had appeared and was holding the gun. She mimed the door opening and her shooting out it. I nodded. I had no idea what kind of shot Carrie was but Jolene needed to be taken down.

There was a muffled yelp of pain from Adam and Jolene's voice came over the radio, less patient now. "Tick-tock. I want Ian and I want him now."

I looked out the window as Carrie crouched next to me and saw Adam was standing in front of Jolene. I couldn't see her face. If I couldn't see her face, she couldn't see mine. "Okay. Okay. I'm going to open the door. Adam will come in and get Ian."

"The handcuffs key is in Adam's pocket."

That explained why Adam had his hands behind his back. I looked at Adam and mouthed the word "Floor" at him. He nodded. I hoped he understood. I gave Carrie a soft count of "One… Two… Three!" and flung the server room door open wide.

"She's going to shoot you!" Adam yelled and bolted for the doorway. For a second, I thought he'd figured out what Carrie and I had planned. As Adam slammed himself into me, I got a brief glimpse of Jolene aiming her pistol at us. Then multiple gunshots exploded all around us as Adam and I went crashing to the ground.

Carrie jumped to her feet and slammed the server room door closed. A moment later Jolene slammed against it. She snarled at us, her face a mask of rage. Adam lay on top of me, pinning me to the ground. I tried to move but couldn't. Adam was limp against me. "Adam?" I shook his shoulders.

"Oh, shit." Carrie pulled away from the server room door.

Looking up, I saw Jolene look in through the window. She pointed her gun at me. There was nowhere for me to go. Adam wasn't moving. I was a sitting duck. I flinched as I saw her pull the trigger.

Instead of the window shattering and me being shot dead, the window cratered and cracked glass in a ripple effect. I saw the slide lock open and knew that Jolene had fired the last round in the magazine. "Carrie, help me. She's out for the moment."

Carrie hurried to me and we both pushed at Adam—her with one good hand, me with both of mine. Her better leverage gave us what we needed for me to wriggle out from under Adam's unmoving form. As I rolled to my feet, I saw he was bleeding and I was covered in his blood.

I couldn't do anything about that immediately. Right now, I needed all of us to get away from the server room window. I grabbed Adam under the arms and pulled. We inched back and away from the door until I couldn't see out the window of it anymore. If I couldn't see her, she couldn't see us.

Rolling Adam to his uninjured side, I saw that he had two bullet wounds—one in his right arm and the other in his lower torso. Both were through and through. Blood poured out of the entry and exit points.

"Get the first aid kit. We have to stop the bleeding." I lifted Adam's shirt to see how bad his wound was. He moaned low as I did so but didn't open his eyes. I saw that the bullet entered his stomach area about four inches to the side of his navel. Not good. The exit wound was slightly farther out, but instead of a neat circle, it was a ragged tear of flesh.

Carrie dropped next to me with the first aid kit. It was already open. She took one look at the exit wound and grabbed the largest gauze pad, ripping it open and pressing it to staunch the bleeding before I had to say anything. I looked at her face and knew she had seen some horrible things in that orphanage of hers. Someday, we were going to have to compare stories on how we learned first aid.

If we had more time, I'd try to sew up the entry wounds and the exit wound in Adam's arm. As it was, compression was all we could do until we were sure Jolene couldn't get into the server room.

"What are we going to do about Sadie?" Carrie asked as I packed more gauze on the wound and taped it down.

I shook my head. "I don't know. Jolene was out. Where do they keep the bullets around here?"

"Don't know. Security office most likely." Carrie pressed another gauze pad to the entry wound as I packed and taped it.

"I think she'll be fine. If Jolene hadn't killed her by now, she's not going to."

Before Carrie could answer me, another two bullets impacted and cracked, but did not break, the server door's window. I winced at the sound. Thank goodness for bulletproof glass and to whoever designed this room for being as paranoid as they were. I stood and walked a couple of steps towards the door. Just until I could see the window… and saw Jolene glaring daggers at me. She raised her radio up as I watched.

There was a moment of silence before my radio, forgotten on the floor next to the door, crackled to life and Jolene's pleasant voice said, "All right, you leave me no choice." With that, she disappeared from sight.

"Shit." I turned back to Carrie. She'd uncuffed Adam and was already working on patching up his arm. "She's going after Doctor Giacomi. You unlock the lab. Do whatever you have to. Adam's wound is too bad for me, or you, to deal with. My best guess is that the bullet tore through his intestines. If he doesn't get real help soon, it's going to get really bad. Like dead bad."

As I spoke, I checked my purse. My pills and my stun gun were still there. All I needed. I pulled Doctor Dudetsky's access card from my back pocket and handed it to her. "No matter what, don't let me back in. Let Agent Harrison's men do their thing. You still got your stun gun?"

Carrie nodded as she accepted the card and shoved it into her jacket pocket, "Ian took it. I put it on my desk. I got it back"

My eyes narrowed, I made the hard decision. "If he moves, stun him for a count of three. Force the monster out of him. Then kill it. I'm sorry to put this on you but it's the only way. "

Carrie clenched her jaw and gave me a curt nod. "I got it. Now go. Save Sadie. At least try."

"It's all I can do. Remember, don't let me or anyone else back in unless it's David or Tomas."

Carrie didn't respond except to make a shooing motion at me and to return to the workstation.

After stuffing the stun gun handle up in my purse and zipping it mostly closed, I realized those two things were not all that I needed. I ran back to the workstation area to grab Mister Bat. If I was going to go down, I was going to do it swinging for the fences.

Returning to the door, I didn't stop to check to see if Jolene was there to ambush me. If she was, she was smart enough to do it in a way that wouldn't let me see her as I came out the door. So, I went for the bull rush and slammed the server room door open as hard as I could. It rebounded off the wall with a loud, echoing crash.

The hallway was empty.

I bolted for the stairwell. I was beginning to really hate stairs. But, at least I could actually see them as I ran down them in a controlled fall. As I opened the stairwell door, I heard the shout of a woman and the sound of metal clang against tile. Doctor Giacomi was awake and fighting. That spurred me on and I almost tumbled down the stairs as I ran.

When I entered the hallway, Jolene and Doctor Giacomi were faced off against each other. Jolene had both hands up but not in surrender. More like a praying mantis ready to strike. I have no idea what happened to Jolene's gun but Doctor Giacomi was warding her off with the iron grounding rods. As unwieldy as those two rods were, the doctor was using them like she was half-ninja. If we got out of this, I wanted to know a lot more about her background.

Jolene lunged for Doctor Giacomi again and again, trying to touch her. But each time, Doctor Giacomi rebuffed her with a block or a returned lunge, stabbing at the infected woman. Then I realized that Doctor Giacomi wasn't doing as well as I thought. She staggered to the side and shook her head like she was trying to clear it.

Jolene grabbed both grounding rods and yanked them towards her, getting Doctor Giacomi almost within touching distance. "It's only a matter of time now. The rest of them are dead."

"Liar!" I yelled. "Get away from her, you bitch."

Jolene turned and smiled at me. I never want to be smiled at like that ever again. "Thank you for joining us." She dropped the rods and sprinted for me. But before she got three steps in my direction, Doctor Giacomi flipped the rods over and slung the rubber clad cable over Jolene's head and around her shoulders. She pulled hard, spinning Jolene's body in a half circle before she let go. Jolene stumbled down the hallway in the other direction, tangled up in the insulated copper wire and grounding rods in a great clanging of metal on tile.

Doctor Giacomi didn't hesitate. For an older woman, she moved like a track star. She rushed down the hall to me and grabbed hold of my bat. "May I?"

I let Mister Bat go. "Aluminum is conductive."

She tapped the rubber grip. "This isn't. Get the stun gun ready and don't let her touch you."

"Yes, ma'am." I had no intention of letting Jolene touch me. The idea of being infected with the Coalescence was born from my worst nightmares. Then there was no time to think. Jolene was coming.

"One or both of you will be ours." Jolene halved the distance between her and us in a saunter before she stopped. "And if you won't, you'll be an example. The Coalescence does not forget or forgive."

I took a step to the side, putting a little more distance between me and Doctor Giacomi. I didn't want Jolene to be able to touch us both at the same time. I raised the stun gun, getting ready.

Jolene sprinted at Doctor Giacomi, screaming as she did. Bat high, Doctor Giacomi didn't flinch. Even when Jolene feinted a grab at me, Doctor Giacomi kept her cool. Instead of swinging for Jolene's head, she swung low, cracking Jolene in the knee, before spinning out of touching range. Jolene's knee gave a crunch like stomping on frozen grass and bent in the wrong direction, cutting off her war cry.

I jumped forward with a war cry of my own before she finished falling to the ground and pressed the stun gun to her bare arm. I pulled the trigger. Her flailing arm knocked me away but I didn't stop. Stun gun still arcing, I pressed it to her neck.

Jolene stiffened, mouth open in high-pitched wail. I kept pressing the stun gun to her for the count of three. Then I stepped back arcs of electricity danced over Jolene's body and the Coalescence was forced out of her mouth. It was small. The size of a softball, hovering there. Its light rippled red and green and yellow and orange in fast rotation.

"Batter's up," I said, knowing it would track me by my sound waves. "I'm your last chance to live. C'mon. I'm right here."

This time, it didn't move slowly like it had when a piece of it came out of Lakshmi's mouth. But I was ready for the monster anyway. The

Coalescence zipped for my face and right into the live arc of my stun gun. It crackled then exploded into nothingness.

I looked down at Jolene, expecting to see her dead. She wasn't. She was burned and hurt but I could see her chest rise and fall in tiny, rapid gasps for air. "She's alive. It's her defibrillator." I considered her and found my empathy gone. "Should I shock her again?"

Doctor Giacomi gazed at her a long time before she looked me in the face. She didn't say anything. She just held out her hand for the stun gun. I gave it to her. I had gone too far. Both me and Doctor Giacomi knew it. But Jolene wasn't human anymore in my eyes. Then Doctor Giacomi gave Mister Bat back to me. Too far gone or not, I still had my best friend.

Doctor Giacomi leaned over, pressed the stun gun to Jolene's chest, and pulled the trigger. Neither of them made a sound. Not the doctor killing the traitor, not the woman willing to betray mankind. Jolene's body clenched stiff.

I held my breath, counting for as long as Doctor Giacomi held the stun gun to Jolene. I counted to ten. What was one more burned spot on an already damaged body? This time, while we watched, Jolene stopped breathing. While I watched, I couldn't tell if this was one of my nightmares or not.

I turned away, walking to the end of the hall. I started for the stairs, then changed my mind and pressed the elevator button.

Doctor Giacomi joined me while I waited for it to arrive. "Are you going to be okay?"

I shook my head. "No. I've been having hallucinations for the last twenty-four hours. Been attacked by an alien a couple of times. I know I'm going to go into quarantine after this, and my phone is broken. And I think… I think I might've been in a manic state for the last four months and having to come here has shoved me into a depressive cycle. No. I'm most definitely not okay."

She nodded. "Thank you for being so honest. I'll be right there with you in quarantine. Would you tell me who is still alive?"

I started to laugh. I couldn't help it. The laughter took an uncontrolled hysterical turn and then I was sobbing. Doctor Giacomi pulled me to her and hugged me tight. She was still hugging me as the elevator doors opened and she led me out of it.

I shook and cried for I don't know how long until my face hurt. She let me go when I pulled away. "Me: fucked up but alive. Carrie: hand half-mangled but alive. Adam: shot twice but alive and unconscious the last time

I saw him. But he's in a really bad state. He needs a hospital. Ian: infected with the Coalescence, admitted to letting the aliens in. Unconscious with a shit ton of sedatives last time I saw him. Everyone else: dead."

I stopped and gazed at her. My eyes felt gritty and sore. "Unless there's someone else hidden in the lab. In horror movies, there's always someone hidden and the monster can escape. Or kill the survivors."

Doctor Giacomi tilted her head then retrieved something from the floor. It was Chamber's keycard that Adam had taken from her. She touched it to the server door sensor. Nothing happened. She looked at a while longer then nodded to herself, muttering, "Magnetized."

I realized that Jolene hadn't made it into the server room because that key card no longer worked. Probably because of the explosion with the grounding rods. The card, or its chip, had fried along with Doctor Giacomi. It explained so much.

Dropping the card, Doctor Giacomi shook her head. "No. There's no one else in the lab. It was one of the things I asked David about. The entry system keeps track of that."

I smiled and pretended to believe her. Sometimes, it's easier to believe that everything will be okay, even when you know, deep down inside, it will never be okay again. I led Doctor Giacomi to the server room. "They're all inside there. I told Carrie not to let us in. I gave her my access card." I knocked on the door and waited. I could barely see over the craters in the glass.

Carrie came to the door the second time I knocked. "I can't let you in. You told me not to."

Her voice was muffled but I could hear her enough to know what she was saying. I raised my voice so she could understand me. "I don't want you to. I just wanted to tell you that me and Doctor Giacomi are… okay. Jolene is dead." That was mostly true. I wasn't possessed. That's okay enough for the time being.

Doctor Giacomi came forth and smiled at Carrie. She waved before she stepped back. "Did you get the lab unsealed?" I didn't know what I wanted the answer to be.

"We'll know in about five minutes," Carrie called. "I'm going to go check on things." She disappeared from the window.

I sighed and put my back against the wall across from the server room and let myself sink to the ground. All I wanted to do was sleep for a week. Sleep and never dream again. I knew I'd probably get to sleep—what else do you do in quarantine—but the nightmares were guaranteed.

Doctor Giacomi slid down the wall to sit next to me. "You know, if you like, you can call me Sadie. I don't mind."

"Maybe after we have our first session. I don't know how we're actually going to get on when not in terrified, crisis mode." Yep. I had no tact filter left.

She nodded with an understanding smile. "Fair enough. But the offer will remain open. Use it when you feel comfortable enough."

I closed my eyes and let my body relax against the wall. I hurt and I was covered in Adam's blood, but I dared to think that we might be all right after all. I shifted my hand until it was next to Doctor Giacomi's. She clasped it without comment and we sat in silence, waiting for those five minutes to tick by.

CHAPTER TWENTY

THE LOCKDOWN DRILL IS COMPLETE. THANK YOU FOR YOUR PARTICIPATION. REPEAT. THE LOCKDOWN DRILL IS COMPLETE. THANK YOU FOR YOUR PARTICIPATION.

The shouting robot startled a yelp out of me and I scrambled to my feet. Doctor Giacomi was right with me. She put a hand on my uninjured shoulder. "I don't think you need that."

I looked at Mister Bat. He was ready to beat down whatever came at us. I lowered it. Then set one end on the ground. "Sorry. A little… you know." It was more than that. I had fallen asleep and slipped right into a dream world filled with things chasing me.

"I know."

I gave her a sharp glance. Doctor Giacomi looked like she really did know. I wondered if I had been talking or whimpering in my sleep. I'm glad she didn't wake me up if that was the case.

Doctor Giacomi cocked her head in a listening posture. "That announcement can be heard throughout the building."

"So, they know." I looked at her out of the corner of my eye. "Just so you know, the last communication David and I had, I told him to come in shooting. To knock us all out and do the quarantine like you wanted. But not to touch us directly without insulation."

Doctor Giacomi looked down at me over her nose, her eyebrow raised. "You don't do anything halfway, do you?"

"No." I sighed. "I never have. I never will. I just hope he understood that when I said to come in shooting, I meant with tranquilizer guns. I wasn't really that specific."

"Ah." She looked up. "They're coming. You might want to put the bat on the ground."

Even I could hear the mass of boots on the echoing stairwell. I laid Mister Bat down and straightened. I didn't know if I should have my hands up or not. As soon as the first black clad, armored men came through the stairwell door, rifles pointed right at me, my hands shot up in the air. None of those rifles looked like tranq guns to me.

There were five of the armored men. I heard more booted feet pounding down the stairs. After the rifle bearing men lined up across the hallway, five people in bright yellow bio-containment suits came out of the stairwell. One of them stepped forward until he was even with the line. As far away as he was, I could still see it was David.

I relaxed a little but didn't lower my hands. "I told you to come in shooting."

"Do you still think I should?"

His voice was neutral. He was testing me. I nodded. "Yeah. As much as it's going to suck, you should. It's the only way to be sure."

"And you, Doctor Giacomi? What's your recommendation?"

"I recommend you get a status report, then let us sit down before you tranq us. We're injured and a fall to the floor won't do us any good. Then, yes, thirty day level E quarantine." Doctor Giacomi's voice was strong but rough. I wondered if she'd been playing tough to keep me calm.

David nodded. "All right. Status. You can put your hands down."

That told me that we'd given him the answer he had hoped for. At least, in my mind, that's what it was and that was enough.

Doctor Giacomi gave him our status—our locations, our known injuries, and Ian's status as sedated and a traitor to humanity. "As for Jolene Lake," she concluded, "her body is on Level B. If she is still alive, she has the same status as Ian Brown."

"Bodies," I said, interrupting. Everyone looked at me. "I'm sorry." I gestured behind me. "Everyone else who was murdered, we put their bodies in the security room. They're covered with tarps. We didn't know what else to do. We couldn't just leave them in the hallway." I pointed at the brown red stains.

"Ian killed Joe Chambers and Sean MacGregor. The Coalescence killed Doctor Dudetsky and Doctor Lakshmi. Doctor Lakshmi killed Forester. Jolene…"

"I killed Jolene Lake." Doctor Giacomi stood tall. Her posture said that she would do it again, too. In the blink of an eye, she shifted into readiness.

I looked around to see what had changed. The server door had cracked open. The entire line of riflemen shifted and prepared to fire. I saw Carrie's long dark hair. I took two steps forward, half-stumbling over Mister Bat, and held my palms out to keep them from firing. "Wait-wait-wait. It's Carrie. She's immune. She's okay. Don't—"

Pain blossomed in my chest as a rifle exploded and echoed in the hallway. Then David and Doctor Giacomi were shouting. "—shoot."

I looked down at the metal tube sticking out of my chest above my heart. "Ow. That hurt."

I reached for the tranquilizer dart and knew no more.

CHAPTER TWENTY-ONE

I woke up in a very white, sparsely furnished room. There was a bed. I was on it. A steel toilet stuck out of one wall to my right. The top half of the wall in front of me was a window. There was a door in the wall to the left. The only good thing about it was the fact that I wasn't on Level E of the PAR Laboratory. The room looked nothing like the cells the alien had been in.

I was dressed but in different clothing. White T-shirt, grey sweats, white socks. No shoes in sight. My left shoulder had been re-bandaged. While it was nice to be wearing clothes that I hadn't bled on, wearing a different set of clothes that I hadn't put on myself, freaked me out.

I sat up and my head felt like someone had stuck it in a vice that was squeezing for all it was worth. I put my hand to my head. "Motherpussbucket!"

Heather came to the window. "Well, hello to you, too." Her voice came out of a speaker on the wall. She appeared to be in some sort of receiving room attached to my prison. It looked as sparse as the room I was in and just as white.

Relief flooded through me. All of the panic that I was trying very hard not to acknowledge receded at the sight of my guardian. "Heather… you're here."

"Of course I am." She held up my purse. "I've got your purse and your pills. Mister Bat had to come home with me. I'm sorry. They just won't let you have it in quarantine."

I looked around at all the white. "Is this what I get for the next thirty days? 'Cause, if it is, it's going to suck."

"I don't know, hon." Heather shook her head. "I'll talk to David. In the meantime, I'll get Agent Harrison. He wanted to talk to you."

"Can you get me some painkillers, too? My head is killing me."

"Will do." Heather disappeared out the door, closing it behind her. I got a brief glimpse of pale green walls with a black floorboard before the door closed. Definitely not in the PAR Laboratory. I wondered where I was.

I shifted until I was sitting cross-legged against the wall at the head of the bed and contemplated the whiteness, the lack of privacy, and the utter boredom I had facing me. I wondered if there were cameras. I wondered if I was ever going to get out of here or if this was it. The thought of it made me want to cry but the pounding of my head was worse than the rest.

Tomas opened the door and came in. He had a file in hand. After closing the door and approaching the window, he pulled a chair out from against the wall and sat. "Hello Melissa. Heather told me your head hurts. You'll have pain meds momentarily."

A whoosh and a ka-thunk in the wall next to the door heralded the arrival of the meds. A drawer in the wall opened up with the soft hiss of hydraulics. I got up and found a can of Mountain Dew, my pill case, a new phone, and a small white cup with two small pills in it. I didn't hesitate. I gathered it to me, put the phone and pill case on the bed, opened the soda, and downed the pain pills. Turning on the phone, I saw that it was 7:30pm. I'd been out for hours.

"Is this headache from being tranq'ed or from being stunned?" I went back to where the drawer was and saw that its seams were almost invisible in the wall. It explained how I was going to get food and such in here.

"A little of both." He shifted in his seat. "You can press on the upper right corner to open it. Put your trash and such in it."

I touched the drawer's upper right corner and the same whoosh, ka-thunk sounded. Then the drawer opened. I put the little white cup in it. Stepping back, the drawer closed as soon as I was away from it. I turned to the window and crossed my arms. "You know, we've got to stop meeting like this."

"I would say, then you need to stop saving the world. But I'm not going to. It's where I keep my stuff."

I peered at him. He had a slight smile on his face. It made him look like a grandfather. The fact that he'd made a tiny bit of a joke made me feel better. "I don't know if I saved the world and I certainly didn't do it alone. Where is everyone?"

"Carlita, Adam, and Doctor Giacomi are in suites just like this one on this hall."

"Did you stun us all?"

Tomas nodded.

"Ian, too?" I turned away and went back to the bed. I had a feeling I needed to sit down for the rest of this conversation.

"Yes. Ian, too." His voice was dry.

At least Tomas didn't sugarcoat it. I didn't know why knowing Ian was dead bothered me so much. The guy was a traitor and he'd hurt Carrie. "That's why you didn't mention him. He's dead."

"No. Ian Brown is not dead."

I paused in my clamber to get back on the bed. Then I settled in. "What do you mean? If you stunned him, it would've forced..." I paused, my voice rose a notch in disbelief. "He wasn't infected?"

Tomas rubbed the side of his face. "We stunned him. Just like we stunned you all. Figured it was kinder to do while you were unconscious. The Coalescence came out of him, but it didn't kill him."

"I can't decide if I should be happy or furious." The enormity of this discovery filled my whole head.

"I'm worried."

"Lakshmi didn't have to die. It burned her up out of malice." My stomach turned over.

"Melissa, that's not your problem anymore. We've got it captured. Ian is incarcerated. You and the rest are only in quarantine on Doctor Giacomi's recommendation. You need to be debriefed. You need to be tested. So do Adam and Carlita." He nodded to the file in his hands. "Remember, we don't punish you for saving the world. But, we're now in a pretty sticky situation and we need to see how bad it is."

I drank my soda. I didn't want to think about the Coalescence, my possible vulnerability to them or what they might do to Ian. "How is Adam?"

"He needed surgery. He just came out. They have him in recovery."

"What's going to happen to him and Carrie?"

Tomas shook his head. "I don't know for sure. But PAR Labs needs a full cleaning, repair, and a security update. Neither of them can return to it."

"For the record, red light for lockdown mode is a terrible idea. You can't see well. The only thing that kept us from dying on the stairwells was the glowing paint lines—kudos to whomever thought that up. And it doesn't do anything to calm a crisis situation."

"You sound very adult."

"You go through years of therapy about 'working the problem' and dealing with trauma and tell me how you sound."

He nodded his head once, conceding the point. "We're going to get you some things to keep you occupied during the next thirty days. Heather will visit. David will debrief you. There will be doctors coming in. They'll be in full bio-containment suits, so you need to be extra good with them. Doctor Ferguson will come see you once a week. Also, all of you will get laptops that will allow you to talk to each other in quarantine. Doctor Giacomi has requested sessions with you as well."

I nodded, an idea forming in my head. "I'll be good. Take my pills and everything. All the tests. Even deal with that indignity." I pointed to the steel toilet.

"We'll get you a privacy screen."

"But, I want something in return."

Tomas narrowed his eyes. "What?"

I heard the caution and suspicion in his voice. "I want you to consider something. To talk to David and Heather about it. The next thirty days of confinement are really going to suck. Yeah, we all hurt and we need the rest, but I want you to give me, Carrie, and Adam something to look forward to. All I'm asking is that you guys consider this."

"I'm listening..." He put the papers down and clasped his hands before him in a listening pose.

I smiled. Tomas didn't cross his arms. That meant he really was open to listening to my crazy idea. I took a breath and laid out my plan.

CHAPTER TWENTY-TWO

"Welcome to Richland, Missouri, your new home, sweet home." David opened the door of the private plane and was first down the ladder to the municipal airfield. Heather followed. Then Carrie. Adam stopped at the entrance.

"What's up?" I leaned around him to look out. It was a bright, hot, muggy day. It was muggier than I was used to, and the heat felt like it would bake your skin if you stood still too long.

Adam didn't say anything at first. He glanced up at the wispy white clouds and faded blue sky. "No ceilings."

I knew what he was getting at. "I know. It's… what normal life is like."

"I'd rather be back at the lab."

"I know you would. But, it's closed."

"I know. I don't have to like it." Adam grimaced at himself. "Sorry. It's just… I've never lived anywhere else before. I feel out of control."

I slipped by him and onto the ladder. "Believe it or not, I understand. When I was under house arrest I couldn't leave my house. When the Fedoras… Mega Aphis… aliens killed everyone and I was the only one left, I was terrified of leaving the house. Not because of the aliens, but because I wasn't allowed to and hadn't left unsupervised in over a year. I knew my territory. I knew all the rules."

He shook his head. "I don't know what the rules are now. Only what I've read."

I stepped down off the ladder. "I'll help you. C'mon. Just to the truck."

Adam looked out at the black SUV with tinted windows. Heather and Carrie were already inside. David stood by the open driver's side door. "Yeah. Okay. I can do this." He clambered down the ladder and kept his eyes on the ground.

I walked beside him. "The trick is to remember that there *is* a ceiling. It's about eight hundred feet up. Lower with storm clouds. Higher when there aren't any clouds. Think twice the height of the whole PAR Lab from the tip of the pyramid all the way down to the bottom of Level E. Just know that there is a ceiling."

We walked fast and David opened the back of the SUV for us. I let Adam get in first. He relaxed as soon as he had a roof over his head and didn't seem to mind being squished in the middle between Carrie and me.

David put the SUV in gear. We drove down a crunchy gravel road past a golf course and a water treatment plant. I asked, "So… why Richland?"

"Richland. Population of about two thousand. Total of 2.29 square miles. Nice small, quiet town." Heather glanced at some papers in her lap. "And a five bedroom, four bath home on nine acres of land, fully furnished, with a thirty by fifty foot shop that I can turn into a dojo. All within the budget I was given."

"Damn," Carrie muttered. "Please tell me they actually have internet out here. Please? It looks like the freaking boonies."

"They do. Believe or not, they have a good communications infrastructure here." David glanced at us in the rear view mirror. "Cable and wi-fi is already set up at the house. This isn't the boonies. Also, we've got a greenhouse in the works for you, Adam."

Adam perked up at that. "That will be nice. A garden of my own that I can decide what to plant."

I saw some of the local teens staring at the SUV as we passed by. "Oh, yeah. We blend."

"Actually, we do." Heather looked over her shoulder at me. "Fifteen minutes down the road is Fort Leonard-Wood. Twenty if you're going the speed limit. It's another reason this home fit the required bill. Those kids are just trying to figure out what rank we are because a lot of the permanent military folk live off base."

"Do we have a rank?" Adam looked out the window with more interest now.

"Still to be determined," David said. "But you will have dependent military ID."

"How come I get the feeling you've been here before?" I addressed the question to both of them but it was mostly pointed at Heather.

She smirked. "Maybe because I have. But that's a story for another time."

Not twenty minutes later, we pulled off Highway 66 AKA Heartwood Road and turned onto Treeline Lane. Trees blocked one full side of the road. We turned down the driveway of a large ranch style brick home. There were no other houses to be seen on either side of the house. Just farmland and highway. I looked back down the driveway and across the road. Through the trees, I could see the barest hint of a blue topped house. They were our closest neighbor.

"It's really private." This was another new one on me. I grew up in a tiny town where everyone knew everyone else's business. Now, we were practically all on our own.

David led Carrie and Adam into the house as I continued to look around the property. I saw the shop in the distance and the foundations of the green house. Heather came up next to me and put her arm around me. "C'mon. You'll cook out here. Let's take a look at our new home."

I still had questions and worries about the Fedoras and the Coalescence, but they could wait for the moment. We were home. I put an arm around her waist and grinned. "So, when I can I get a driver's license?"

NEVER LET ME DIE

BOOK THREE

David would not look at Tomas as he spoke. "I don't know if I'm comfortable with this."

"This what? This test? This office? You need to be more specific." Tomas leaned back in his chair and watched the younger man for a long silent moment. He did not need to prod his protégé. The words would come.

This time, David did turn to his superior, glancing at the older man's face. "Everything. This test. How it's being done. Keeping Agent Shaker out of the loop. All of it." He paused before adding. "It's dangerous on a lot of levels. Especially for the kids."

"Of course it's dangerous. I planned it myself. If it wasn't dangerous, it wouldn't be a worthy test."

"What if they get hurt?"

Tomas caught and kept David's eyes with his own as he spoke hard truths. "They will heal."

"If they fail?"

"They fail and we start again or we… do what's needed. It really depends on why and how they fail, doesn't it?"

David scowled. "Heather will never trust you again."

"Agent Shaker doesn't need to trust me. She needs to follow orders. Which she'll do. She's an excellent agent."

"The kids won't trust you anymore either."

Tomas nodded. "Maybe. Adam and Carlita will forgive me. In time. It's in their nature."

"Maybe." David's tone matched that of his superior's. "But not Melissa."

The older man leaned forward. "She's not as broken or as fragile as you think. Either she will do this or she won't. If she hates me, so be it. Love is not required."

"I'm still not comfortable with this." David turned away, breaking their intense rapport.

"What you really mean is that you're not certain you trust me or… trust them to do what needs to be done."

David did not respond.

Tomas looked down at his memo. "Start the mission. Recall Agent Shaker and send the package." He knew that the order cost him something with David. At this time, that didn't matter. There was a bigger picture to consider. A global one.

"Yes, sir."

THE PACKAGE

CHAPTER ONE

Sometimes being crazy has its advantages. People walk on eggshells around you. They don't expect you to do as much. They leave you alone. They'd rather not accidently set you off. When people know you're crazy, they think about you and your moods a lot.

Most of the time, being crazy sucks. You can't trust your moods, your temper, or—in my case—your eyes. People don't trust you to control yourself. This is worse when it turns out to be true. Also, I hate it when they give you The Look. The one that says, "I've got you pegged," and "You're words don't mean anything," and "Oh, she's just having an episode." They can write you off without looking any further. Doesn't matter if you're wrong or right. You're crazy and because of that, you don't count.

I sat on my bed, looking at my sneakers for a long time. Long enough that I wondered if I *was* having a problem. I took a couple of breaths and examined my senses: no numbness—cloth against my skin; no bad smells—shampoo, perfume, cotton; no weird noises—the beating of my heart, everyone moving around in the house and talking; no hallucinations—only my, admittedly messy, room; no weird tastes—just my too-dry mouth.

It was my dry mouth that got me moving. Lithium seems to have dealt with the worst of what's going on in my head but the side effects were annoying. I popped a lozenge, ignored the slight tremor in my left hand, and avoided the mirror altogether. I knew what I looked like: a chunky blonde with acne. No matter how much I exercised, I'd never be as slender as Carrie. I knew it. I didn't need to see it.

A count to twenty at my bedroom door and I felt human enough to face the rest without exploding. In the six months we've lived in Richland, I'd come to love and appreciate the house Heather chose. It was big enough for the four of us and we each had our own space. Carrie set up an office with serious computer power. All of us used it but it was her domain. Adam had the garden and the greenhouse. That was mostly his area. I spent a lot of time in the basement dojo and I'd even started drawing again.

I almost felt good when I walked into the kitchen. That feeling dropped away and my heart rate sped up as everyone sitting around the breakfast table stopped talking and looked at me. There was a moment of silence as the free-floating anxiety and fear I'd been fighting with all morning came crashing down on me.

"Good morning, sleepyhead." Heather got up and poured me a glass of milk. "Your pills are by your plate. Scrambled eggs are still warm. You want some?"

I didn't move. "What's wrong? What happened?"

Adam and Carrie exchanged a glance, cementing my fears in place. "Told you she was going to freak." Carrie kept her voice low but I still heard her. She was dressed in her usual leggings, oversized shirt, and comfy sweater.

"No one is freaking out." Heather had that patient tone that told me something big had happened or was happening. "Mel, honey. Come sit. Take your pills. Have some breakfast."

This last was phrased as a request but I knew it wasn't. My grumbling tummy agreed with the breakfast part of things while my brain clamored for the safety of my morning cocktail—Abilify. Lamotrigine. Hydroxyzine. I nodded as I pulled myself from the doorway and slid into my usual seat at the table. "But, can I have the bottles, too? Please?" Despite trying to keep my voice as even and calm as possible, it still cracked on the word *please*.

Heather paused and nodded. "All right."

No one said anything but everyone knew I was going to count my pills. Just to make sure. I needed to be certain I didn't mess things up, that I'd taken all my pills at the right time, that I was going to stay sane. Doctor Giacomi said it was an appropriate coping mechanism.

I'm grateful they understood and didn't say anything. I was more grateful when Heather left the bottles of prazosin and lithium with the rest. She wasn't taking any chances and neither was I. I would count them all—morning dose and night dose alike—just to be sure.

I swallowed my lozenge whole before I took my morning dose in a single handful and left the bottles where Heather left them. I'd get to them before I left the table. This was my own private test of willpower. Could I eat breakfast, and enjoy it, before I counted my pills? I dug into the scrambled eggs Heather set before me. They tasted good. Really good. I could do this.

"Okay," I said as I took another bite. "Whatever it is, I can handle it. What's going on?"

"Heather has an assignment." Adam got up and served himself another heaping plate of eggs. His lanky figure had filled out in the last six months under Heather's "physical performance" program. His sweats and t-shirt did nothing to hide his muscles.

"Are we moving?" I watched all of them for signs of lies. I also noticed that my heart rate had dropped back to normal. Carrie and Adam were calm. It couldn't be *that* bad.

Heather took a sip of coffee. "No. I'm just going to be gone and out of touch for a bit."

I frowned. "Why am I supposed to be freaking out?" I ate in quick, small bites. It was a habit I couldn't seem to drop after the stuff that happened at the Lab. You didn't know if something bad was going to happen or when you were going to eat again. At least, that's what me and Doctor Giacomi thought. It was worse when I was nervous. I forced myself to put my fork down between every couple of bites.

I did not look at my pill bottles.

Carrie poked my arm. "You've been a ticking time bomb for months. Every change in routine has set you off. Even the change of no workouts on Sunday. Remember?"

I did remember. I didn't like change. Change usually meant bad things were coming. But, right now, I was still feeling pretty even. It was a relief to recognize the feeling. "Yeah. I'm okay now." I rolled my eyes at the round of exchanged glances. "Seriously. I feel all right. The meds are working." I turned to Heather. "How long?"

"Seven to ten days at a best guess. I expect all of you to keep up with your workouts." She pointed a finger at Carrie. "You, too, Miss I'm-Going-To-Make-Millions-With-This-App."

Carrie pouted. "I've got better things to do than sweat."

"Oh? Like what? It's not like you've got a beauty contest to go to."

"I don't know if you could win a beauty contest," I said. "Too many brains."

"Hey now. Some of those girls are really smart." Carrie jabbed her fork at me. "Don't be stereotypical."

She had a point. I didn't want to think about that too much. If I did, I might spiral into self-loathing. I turned my attention to Adam. "I know someone here who could definitely win a beauty contest." I gestured at him. "Look at those cheekbones."

Heather, Carrie, and I contemplated Adam's attractiveness while he squirmed under the attention. "I wouldn't win a beauty contest. They're for girls."

"Not so." Carrie grinned at him. "There are beauty contests for guys, too. You'd do well. I mean, you are tall enough, you have the right shape and, really, your cheekbones are to die for."

"She's got you there." I glanced at Heather.

She was watching me with a speculative gleam in her eye. "Mel, you're in charge of the workouts while I'm gone."

"Oh. Okay." This surprised but pleased me. I enjoyed some of the fighting exercises we'd been doing. Not all of them. Most of them actually kicked my butt. Still… I was in charge of them?

"Heather," Carrie groaned.

Heather smiled at her and sipped her coffee.

"I don't suppose you've let the authorities know? That you're going to be gone, I mean." Adam scowled at his plate. "Seriously, Officer Chapman can't seem to get it through his skull that we're homeschooled and are allowed out in public during daylight hours."

Carrie matched his scowl. "More likely, he can't get over the fact that you're black and I'm brown. This place is pretty white until you get to the military base."

I nodded, remembering more than one unpleasant encounter with the cop in question. In the last six months, we'd figured out which ones were in it for the community and which ones just enjoyed the power. Officer Chapman was one of the latter. I don't think he liked me either, but he was never as awful to me as he was to Adam and Carrie.

Adam put his fork down. "It's a serious question. I don't want to be stuck in the house for the next week and a half because he can't understand this. Or, if I do need to be stuck here, better to know now."

Heather nodded. "I did talk to them. I even have a case number for you three. You're all either fifteen or sixteen. Two of you have your driver's licenses. If you need to be out and about, you can. I had a long discussion with Detective Russell about the situation. It's well documented. I think he understands the situation a bit better."

I saw the tight, smug smile on her face and wondered what she did to make the Richland Police Department understand "the situation." It reminded me… "Who's our backup? David?"

Heather shook her head. "No. David's going with me. If you really need help on something, call Doctor Giacomi."

Adam blinked a couple of times and shook his head in slow, exaggerated arcs. "I think everything should be on fire before we call Sadie. The last time she was called for something that wasn't important, it didn't go well—for anyone."

"No kidding." Carrie shoved back from the table. "Okay, you're going away for a week and a half. Don't get in trouble. Exercise. Anything else?"

"Yeah. Don't burn the house down."

"When do you leave?" I'd finished my meal in record time, even though I tried not to rush. Now I was trying to keep it down. Some days my pills let me eat. Some days they didn't. Today, I think the nausea was my fault for eating too fast. "Also, is it going to be dangerous?"

"I leave tomorrow. No. It's not dangerous. Unless you count the boredom factor." Heather shrugged. "Just planning meetings. Could be exciting, actually."

"Yeah?"

"Yeah. I'll tell you guys about it when I get home. If I'm allowed."

There was nothing to say to that. After you've saved the world from an alien invasion scout force then stopped another alien from escaping its underground prison, you get used to hearing that things are classified and that you can't talk about the most horrific and exciting moments of your life to anyone but a very select few people. Most of whom were sitting around the table with me.

Adam watched me count my pills as he cleaned up the kitchen. He didn't say anything until I was done. "You want to help me haul dirt to the greenhouse?"

Glancing over my shoulder as I put my pill bottles away, I saw he was looking at me in that specific way that said he wanted more than help. He wanted to talk. Might as well get it over with. "Sure."

We bundled up for the unpredictable February weather. So far, there'd been snow, sleet, rain, thunderstorms, and beautiful blue skies. The temperature ranged from below freezing to the mid-60s. Sometimes all in the same day. In weather like that, layers were your friend. We were lucky. Overcast skies and lower 50s kept the hauling of dirt from being too gross and sweaty.

The greenhouse was a marvel of technology. It was huge, with green glass walls and an irrigation system built in, and was a good ten degrees warmer than the outside—despite the lack of insulation. Tomas had asked Adam what he wanted… then gave him everything he'd detailed out. When the government pays for their special kind of special kids to be happy, they spare no expense.

Part of me still wondered what all this was going to cost us in the end. No matter how kind and generous our guardians were, they still worked for the United States government. In my experience, people in power always want something in return.

I shed my hoodie once inside and helped Adam place the bags of dirt where he wanted them. It was soothing work but I knew that wasn't why I was here. When he handed me a small garden cultivator, I accepted it but said, "All right. What's up?"

He pointed me to one of the raised garden boxes and waited until I started breaking up the dirt before he answered. "So, you really okay?"

I pulled a couple of tiny weeds from the broken dirt and cast them aside before I answered. "Yeah. I think I am. It's the sanest I've felt in months." I couldn't blame them for walking on eggshells around me. I've always had a temper. This last Christmas was hard. Really hard. I'd been fighting with anger and depression. I missed my family—all of them. I'd lashed out at my new family and at myself. Doctor Giacomi decided I needed lithium when I started doing stupid things like hitting the punching bag until my knuckles were bloody.

I thought about last December and the incident that had Carrie and Adam calling Doctor Giacomi for help. I remembered hitting the punching bag and how each blow hurt, but it's not real to me. More like me watching someone else hurt themselves. I looked at the knuckles on my right hand, scarred from the bag. I remember thinking the pain proved that I was still alive and I shouldn't be. Not after everything that had happened.

I shook my head. This wasn't a thought spiral I wanted to get into. It was a habit I needed to break. I pulled myself out of the past and back into the present.

I realized Adam hadn't responded and looked up at him. He was wrist deep into his garden box and he seemed content. But there was small furrow to his brow. I couldn't tell if he was thinking or concentrating. "What about you? You okay? I mean, with all this and Heather leaving?"

He met my eyes. "Yeah. I guess. I mean, I'm getting used to the sky. As long as I don't focus on it, I'm good. If I have a place to go—from here to the house or into the car to go to the hardware store or Gerty's Green Thumb—I'm fine. Just don't expect me to be doing long runs up and down Heartwood Road with you."

I smiled. He had come a long way for someone who'd lived in an underground laboratory his entire life. "Trust me, I don't want to be doing any long runs up and down Heartwood, either. But you know Heather's going to start that as soon as the weather gets normal. Or less schizophrenic."

Adam scowled and dug into his garden box.

I also focused on my garden box, breaking up clods of dirt, and preparing the box for the new garden soil. I knew he didn't actually expect me to prep this box to his satisfaction. It was just an excuse to talk. "So, what'd I miss before I got to breakfast? Is she leaving us pizza money?"

"Yeah. We can have pizza twice and she's leaving movie money. Anything else, we have to pay for out of our personal stipends. Also, you have to drive to the movies. Or anywhere else we go. You need the practice."

I gritted my teeth. I already had my driver's permit but when things went to hell in my head, I stopped caring about driving and reverted back to my general dislike of all things with four wheels. That was something Heather wouldn't allow. In case of emergency, everyone in the house needed to be able to do all the jobs and that included driving.

I probed my brain like I was questing for a sore tooth. It was a pleasant surprise to discover that I'd become ambivalent about driving once more. Still, the movie theater was like an hour and a half away. That was a lot of driving to do. But, no longer hating the idea, I was gritting my teeth out of habit. I forced myself to relax and unclenched my teeth. "Okay. I can do that."

Adam gave me a sharp look. "Really?"

I nodded. "I really am feeling better. The brain meds are working again."

He relaxed. "Good. Cranky Mel is a cranky pain in the ass."

"Fair." I shrugged. "What about you? Are you good with Heather going away?"

"I guess. I mean, what's a week and a half? I'll stay home most of it. Doesn't matter if we have a case number. I really don't want to deal with Richland's Police Department. Besides, what—"

I tried to cut him off. "Don't say it. Don't you dare say—"

"...could go wrong?" Adam finished with a grin, eyes flashing with mirth.

"—it."

I was a master at *What Could Go Wrong*. "So many things! The last time there was a special mission, I went crazy and you had to call in the cavalry. The time before that, I met you and Carrie and we all almost got possessed by a murderous alien. We," I gestured between us, "both got shot. Then, all of us ended up in quarantine for a month and I ended up with a new psychiatrist because the old one didn't have the clearance to deal with what we'd gone through."

All of the kids had Doctor Sadie Giacomi as their shrink now. Not only had she gone through what we'd gone through, she had the training to help us with everything brain related *and* had the security clearance to help. Of course, it meant nothing was sacred. If the government wanted to know what went on in our talks, they knew.

Also, I'm pretty sure she was a super spy or something like that before she became a psychiatrist. I've asked, but she's not talking. She just smiles at me. I wonder who her shrink is. I mean Doctor Giacomi had to talk to someone, right?

I shook my head and put the cultivator down. "Don't ever ask 'What could go wrong?' because I can think of at least ten terrible things and none of them include us being dead. Which is still way up there on the 'things going bad' list."

He sobered. "You think about us dying?"

Looking at the half-finished garden box, it was too easy to see it as broken ground for a coffin. I'd seen enough broken ground to last me a lifetime. "Yeah. I do. I've lost a lot." I shrugged, not looking at him. "So have you and Carrie."

"I'm sorry." He looked around the greenhouse. "I forgot to bring out water. You probably should go in and get some. You know?"

Dehydration is one of the main side effects of lithium. Everyone in the house knew to make sure I was always drinking something. I half-smiled at him. It was both a dismissal and an escape for me. The conversation had turned too dark for both of us and Adam wanted out. I didn't blame him. I was happy to go. "Okay. See you later."

I had the treadmill and my latest audiobook calling my name anyway. I could safely get lost in another reality for a while. Sometimes, my own reality was too dangerous for comfort.

CHAPTER TWO

Two mornings later, I went out to get the mail. Our mailbox was at the end of the long driveway off a short road that had only two houses attached to it before it came to a dead end. Obviously, there was almost no traffic at all on Treeline Road. In the winter, when the leaves were gone, we could see the blue metal top of the house across the way if we looked for it. In the summer, it would be hidden by the trees surrounding the property. We were isolated and that was the way we liked it.

Mrs. Janice Palmer lived across the way. She was an older, widowed woman with kids and grandkids. We knew this because we'd met each other in that way that locals have to come check out the new people—with a plate of homemade brownies in hand. As it happened, she liked her privacy as much as we did. However, she was pleased to see that there were now kids nearby old enough to babysit if needed. Not that I wanted to babysit but there you have it. Small sacrifices make for good neighbors, and as Mrs. Palmer went, she was a very good neighbor.

I pulled magazines and bills out of the mailbox and sorted it as I walked back towards the house. A detail out of place made me freeze for a half a second before continuing back to the house, the hairs along my arm standing at attention—and not because of the cold air. To the side of the front door, half under a bush, was a plain manila envelope.

I hadn't noticed it leaving the house. I could already hear Heather scolding me. "Always be aware of your surroundings. You never know what's going to try to kill you next." I knew I needed to make a note of this for when she got back. Awareness tests could be a pain, but they're needed in Heather's world. My world. Like it or not, me and my adopted siblings were part of a secret world that kept things quiet so nobody panicked.

I didn't speed up my walk and I continued to pretend to look at the mail in my hand. At the same time, I tried to look at the grounds around me for a watcher. We had nine acres of land—all of it surrounded by trees and bushes. There was nothing in the open and I didn't see anything standing out. But that didn't mean something wasn't there. It was way too easy to hide a monitoring camera in a tree. I should know. We had some ourselves. Maybe one of them picked something up.

The hairs on the back of my neck stood up when I bent over and retrieved the envelope. It was heavy and had more than paper in it, but I didn't exam it out in the open. I hurried inside, closing and locking the front door behind me.

I took one look at the envelope and knew there was a problem. Discarding the rest of the mail on the kitchen table, I hurried towards the basement door, calling for the others.

"Adam! Carrie! C'mere! It's important. Dojo!"

The basement dojo was one of the best places about the Richland home. It was a huge, single, finished room that took up the entire length of the house. We'd covered the faux tile floor with padded mats and exercise equipment. One corner had the treadmill, rowing machine, and bike. The other had the speed bag and the heavy bag. Next to them were free weights—all the implements of torture a girl could never want. The far mirrored wall had a table and a computer to keep track of our progress. There was even a small half-bathroom next to the table. Best of all, there were no windows and I could be sure no one was eavesdropping.

I stood by the table with the manila envelope next to me, and watched my adopted siblings come down the stairs at a slow trot. They grumbled until they saw the look on my face. Then they hurried up.

"What's wrong?" Carrie reached me first. She had Khalessi, her favorite laptop computer with her. She hugged it close to her chest.

I pointed to the envelope. It was a plain, ordinary, 8 x 11, manila envelope with a single word written on it. "This arrived sometime in the last day. It was left on the porch. I found it while getting the mail. This is a problem."

Adam peered at it. "Who's Elise? Maybe whoever it was got the wrong house."

"No. Elise is Heather." I gazed at the name written in marker. "You guys know that she did other stuff for the government before she turned into a glorified babysitter, right?" They both nodded. "She used to run safe houses in Europe..."

Carrie sucked in a breath. "Elise Dehousse? Heather was Elise Dehousse?"

"Yeah. She told me about it before I met you guys. It was part of our trust exercises." I made a face but continued on. "It was a bad time for her."

Adam touched the name on the envelope. "Who's Elise Dehousse?"

Carrie pushed her hair from her face. "A few years back, an undercover agent was revealed on national TV by an idiot politician... Belgium, wasn't it?"

"I don't remember..." Adam frowned. "I don't watch a lot of TV. I mean, I stream stuff, but I'm not really that much into the news. Never have been. Especially years ago. You know?"

"It was a thing. It was dangerous. It ended that part of her career." I waved an impatient hand. "That's not important. What's important is the fact that someone who knows who she was left her something and she's not here."

"How come we didn't hear them leave it?" Adam frowned at the envelope.

"I don't know. But, we should check the security footage for last night." I gestured at Carrie. She was the one in charge of that sort of thing.

"I'll have to do that from the office. The security server isn't connected to the internet, only the house's internal network." She didn't look at me as she spoke. She only had eyes for the envelope on the table. "It's oddly shaped."

I picked up the envelope and shook it. We all could hear the soft metallic clink of metal on metal. "There's more than paper in it."

"We need to open it." Carrie's eyes shone with anticipation.

"I don't think so..." Adam shook his head. "This isn't for us."

"I agree with Carrie. We need to open it and then figure out if we need to tell Doctor Giacomi." I didn't wait for another yea or nay, I ripped open the top of the envelope and dumped its contents on the table. An orange and black handled weeder hit the table next to a small metal key. A stiff card fell out last and fluttered next to the rest.

Adam picked up the long slender garden tool. "What the...?"

I picked up the small key. "This looks like it goes to a lockbox."

Carrie pulled the arm of her sweater down and picked up the card with covered fingers. "Fingerprints, guys." Adam and I put down the strange objects in a hurry as Carrie read the card. "It's a poem. *Stolen Child* by Yeats."

Peering over her shoulder, I looked at the neat handwriting. I didn't recognize it. "What are the blotches at the front and back of the sentences?" They looked like dots and dashes stacked on top of each other.

Carrie put the card down and stared at it. "It's familiar."

After a moment, Adam said in a soft voice, "Morse code. But stacked, instead of written out normally."

"Of course." Carrie sat on the chair in front of the computer and pulled up a blank page. Looking between the card and the computer, she typed out the dots and dashes in order.

"Don't tell me you know Morse code by heart." I looked between the two of them. "Because that would be weird."

Adam grinned and took off up the stairs without a word. Carrie winked at me in a way that said she and Adam had used Morse code at PAR Lab for nefarious purposes. "Not by heart, but enough to know a lot of these are numbers. I'm just going to run them through a Morse code converter. Much easier than doing it by hand."

By the time she was done, Adam had returned with a plastic baggie. He pushed the card into it with a fingertip. "So we can handle it without mucking up the fingerprints. Not that we have any way of getting the fingerprints off of it."

"We don't but I'm sure Heather or David or Sadie will." Carrie sounded perplexed.

I turned back to the computer and frowned at what Carrie had typed.

Help N37975825 W92770338

"Well, the first word is clear. But, the rest?" Carrie tapped her lip, thinking.

It was familiar to me. "What if you put a period after the first two numbers? Like this? N37.975825 and W92.770338?" I leaned over and typed in two periods. "Looks like GPS coordinates to me."

Carrie didn't answer. Instead, she typed the coordinates into Google Maps and blinked at the results. "There's a castle in Missouri? Really?"

"What?" I leaned forward. "Ha Ha Tonka Castle? Hell of a name for a castle ruins."

Carrie typed more, then spoke as she skimmed the webpage she'd pulled up. "On Wikipedia, it says that Ha Ha Tonka Castle was started in 1905 by Robert McClure but he died in 1906. His son finished the castle in the 1920s. It was a hotel, then it burned down, then it got bought by the state of Missouri and turned into a state park. Now the castle is mostly in ruins. It's called Ha Ha Tonka after, um, huh. Says it means "laughing waters" for the springs under the castle. But, really, that doesn't seem right to me. Can't believe a lot of things on Wikipedia. But… there's a castle ruins in Missouri. Who woulda thunk it?"

"Seriously? We need to go to a castle ruin to help someone?" Adam raised his hands in surrender. "Count me out. This is the beginning of every horror movie ever."

"That's my line." I elbowed him with a grin.

He ignored me, looking more alarmed.

Carrie shook her head, skimming over another webpage. "It's not a real castle. It was a manor house built in the style of a European castle. That's why they call it Ha Ha Tonka Castle."

"I don't think we're into horror movie territory, yet." I pointed at the weeder and the key. "Whoever sent this wanted Heather to find and unlock something. Plus, they need help. Says so in the note."

Adam crossed his arms. "Still sounds like a horror movie to me. I can't believe you guys want to do anything with this. Also, you can kill people with that weeder."

Glancing at the long, slender metal garden tool on the table, I knew he had a point, but I wasn't willing to let it go. "Point conceded. You sound a lot like me. Maybe I shouldn't have instituted movie night." I picked up the little key and examined it. "Whatever this unlocks, it's nothing major."

"Fingerprints," he scolded.

"Not like we're going to get prints off this. Besides, we're going to need to use it anyway."

"Geocaching." Carrie turned to us. "This is a geocaching site. It has to be. They're not usually locked but they are given coordinates like this. You have to search an area until you find it. It's usually a box or a tub or something waterproof. You take something from it and you leave something in it. Sometimes just your name. Sometimes a toy or a token or something."

I shook my head. "I've never gone geocaching before. Is it hiking? Or dangerous?"

"There's hiking and no, it's not dangerous."

Adam shook his head. "We need to call Sadie and let her know."

"Let her know what?" I pointed at the coordinates on the computer screen. "We got a puzzle to a geocaching site located in castle ruins? How is that 'everything is burning down'? I wouldn't go to her with just a puzzle. Not after what you said."

Carrie shrugged at him. "Yeah. I gotta agree with Mel. Besides, I've gone geocaching before. I can narrow this down. Let's find out what this is before we bring in the big guns. Who knows, maybe 'Elise' is a coincidence."

The three of us looked at each other. Not a single one of us believed that to be true.

"I'm out. This is wrong. It is a trap. We should call Sadie. If you do this, you do it without me." Adam turned and left the dojo, stomping his displeasure all the way up the stairs.

CHAPTER THREE

Carrie turned to me. "In or out? Adventure or sulking in your room like normal? Because, I can go and do this on my own if I have to."

"No need to challenge me. I'm feeling better and I'm in." I touched the weeder then looked towards the dojo stairs, still seeing Adam's angry stomp. "Just don't do anything yet. Let me talk to him. You know? We all need to be onboard. Normally, he'd do this, wouldn't he?"

She crossed her arms but still nodded. "Yeah. I'm kinda surprised he took that route."

"So, something's up, yeah?"

"Yeah." Carrie agreed but her focus was once more on the note.

I realized that something was up with her, too. I grabbed one of the office chairs and pulled it over to her, sitting in it. "I know I've been kinda in my own world and I haven't been so easy to live with but… I do know how you are usually. This isn't it."

"What do you mean?"

I bit my lip, forcing my brain into some semblance of coherent thought while booting the paranoia—*she's not Carrie, she's something else, she been replaced*—to the side. "You're the one who really likes routine. I mean, I know I've been obsessing on it for a bit but one of the things you wanted, to be comfortable, was a weekly routine so you know where you were supposed to be at any given time, and where we all would be at that same time. Remember?"

Carrie frowned. "I still want my routine."

I gestured to the note in her hand and the strange items that came with it. "This is not routine. This is definitely strange… Also, Adam could be right. It could be a trap. So, what gives?"

She was quiet for a long time. I didn't push. I waited. I've gotten good at waiting. Even my beloved Deroga says, *"Sometimes, ya just gotta shut your trap and let them do the talking."* So, that's what I did.

I smiled down at my hands, marveling at my ability to think rationally. When you're crazy and in the throes of a weeks long—hell, months long—bout of insanity, it's amazing to be able to think again. To feel even and sane. To recognize it for what it was. I liked the feeling of sanity. I wanted to remember it. I hid the smile from Carrie. I didn't want her to think I was laughing at her.

Looking away from Carrie unlocked her thoughts.

"In the Lab, there was always something going on. I was always being tested. I always knew the rules and how to get around them. All my life, I lived by getting around the rules: rules of the orphanage, rules of the bullies, rules of the government, rules of the Lab. I liked the challenge of it. Getting caught by someone who didn't just toss me away to rot in juvie, or prison—that was a real possibility—was the best thing that happened to me."

Carrie lifted her diminished hand. "In the Lab, no one cared about my hand. The first time I tried to use it as an excuse for something, I got dressed down one side and up the other. I was never to let something like my hand stop me from using my brain. Here…" She stopped, looking at Khalessi as the screen went dark.

I bit my tongue. I wanted to jump in and defend Heather, defend our home, defend everything I, we, had. But, Doctor Giacomi's words came back to me. *"When someone is talking about how they're feeling, remember that* they *are the hero of their own story and* you *are a bit player. It's not about you. That is your armor. That's your shield. Their pain is not about you. You don't have to defend yourself or your actions. Unless, of course, you punch them in the nose—physically or metaphorically."* She was right. This wasn't about me.

"Here, we have a routine. We're training to be a team. Training like crazy. More than I ever wanted to. But… I'm not challenged. Not like I was. I feel like I need to *do* something. Anything to make me feel like I'm not stagnating." She raised the coded note. "*This* is a challenge. *This* is something I can do. *This* is interesting. Routine is only good if you can break it once in a while. Do you understand?"

I glanced up. She was staring at me, willing me to see things her way. I did. I nodded. "I do understand. But, I want to ask you to wait until tomorrow. I want you to sleep on it. To think about it. Adam has one point right: It wasn't meant for us. It was meant for Heather."

Carrie's face settled in that familiar stubborn frown. "Heather isn't here. We don't know for sure when she'll be back. It might be time sensitive."

"If it was that time sensitive, they wouldn't have stuffed it in our bushes instead of putting it between the front door and the screen door. Right? Or knocking? There's a lot of questions we can't answer. So wait until tomorrow. Please?"

Her expression softened a little. "Okay, I won't run out today. But only because I want to comb through the security feed for the last couple of nights. Maybe I can see who delivered the package and when. Then do a search on their face. More information is good." Then she added, "and because I want to know why Adam doesn't want to do it. But I *am* going to go tomorrow. With or without you."

"I'm going with you. You need someone to help you dig the box up." I stood. "Maybe we'll have Adam with us. I don't know. I'll go see what's up with him."

Carrie grabbed my arm as I turned to leave. "I'm really glad you're feeling better. It was hard there for a bit."

I put my hand over hers. "I know. I'm sorry. I'm glad I'm better, too." I didn't want to leave it on that. Me being broken shouldn't be the focus between me and Carrie. "Any advice on what to wear for geocaching? I might as well dress for the occasion."

"I'm going to go with warm and Wellingtons. It's going to be cold and mucky."

"All right. I'll let you know what Adam says."

I hurried up the stairs, hoping Adam was in a receptive mood.

After grabbing a couple of sodas on my way through the kitchen, I tiptoed up to his bedroom door and listened. Either he wasn't listening to music and was sulking. Or, he was and had his headphones on and had his music up loud which meant he was actually angry.

"You can come on in, Mel. I can see your shadow."

All right, he was sulking. I opened the door and stood in the doorway. I held up a soda. "I come bearing gifts."

"A Trojan horse?" He spun in his desk chair to watch me.

I shook my head. "A Trojan soda, maybe."

He gestured for me to come in. "Nah. It can only be a Trojan soda if you set it outside my door, told me it was in worship of Heather, and that I couldn't claim it as my own tribute to Heather. And if you fit inside it."

I had no idea what he was talking about. The fact that Adam was raised by a bunch of scientists and doctors made him seem very much like a weird adult rather than the teenager he was. It also warped his sense of humor into something incomprehensible. "Uh…" I handed him the can.

"Never mind. I've been reading history again."

I sat down on his bed and looked around. I didn't come in here often. The room was starting to look like what I imagined a normal teenage boy's room would look like. Piles of clothes, books, and games everywhere, old soda cans on his desk. When we first moved in, his room could've passed a military inspection every day. Apparently, a lot of the scientists liked to have conversations with him in his room. He had to keep everything just so or Lakshmi or Doctor Giacomi would scold him and remind him the importance of appearing neat and clean at all times. Every conversation was a test after all.

It was nice to see him relaxing.

"How'd you know it was me?"

We both popped open our sodas. Adam took a long swallow before he answered. "Carrie wouldn't have waited or listened. She would've just barged in. I have to lock my door if I want to make sure I'm not interrupted."

I looked away, blushing at that thought. I knew what guys did that they didn't want to be interrupted. I glanced at him and he was flushed, too.

"Why are you here?"

He didn't sound angry. Just wary. Maybe a little tired. I shrugged. "I wanted to see if you were, you know, okay. I mean…"

"What? Because I don't want to go running off after a fool's errand that wasn't meant for us?"

"Well…. yes?"

Adam shook his head. "I'm not doing it. I'm not breaking the rules again. I lost everything last time."

I blinked at him, surprised, then remembered our conversation a couple days back. I must've opened a can of memory worms that wouldn't let him go. But, I wasn't sure where breaking the rules meant you lost things. "I don't understand what you mean."

"Every time someone breaks the rules, I lose. I lost my... Doctor Vandermeek because he broke the rules. Then I lost Lakshmi and my home, because Ian broke the rules." He scowled at my blank look. "The rules of humanity. The rules of morality. The rules of society. They keep being broken around me and I'm the one who pays for it. Hell, I'm a broken rule and I'm going to pay for that for the rest of my life."

"You can't think like that. Mistakes happen. Rules are broken. It's a fact of life. But you are not a mistake. Broken rules aren't going hurt you. Also, this thing that Carrie's going to do, it's a plea for help. Not a broken rule."

"Carrie's still going to go look at those coordinates?"

I nodded.

"You going with her?"

I turned from him to study the plant poster on his wall. It was filled with native plants to this region of Missouri, what they were, what their scientific name was, and when they grew. "I can't let her go alone. But, I asked her to wait until tomorrow. To really think about it. You know. To act instead of react."

"That's just it. I don't think either of you is thinking." Adam paused long enough to gulp half his soda, then continued. "Look, you know the training Heather's been teaching us? The blind fighting one where one of us is blindfolded, one is the attacker, and the third is guiding the blind one?"

"Yeah."

"I feel like I'm shouting "Left. Left. Block left." and you guys are ducking right. You're not listening and you're going to get hurt."

I sat back and thought about what he was trying to get across to me. I was so used to being the one who jumped last. I'd taken to following Adam and Carrie on almost all activities. I'd never had siblings my own age. It was nice not to be in the lead. But that wasn't what was happening now and I wasn't sure what was going on with Adam. It was time to pull out the universal pokey stick and ask some questions.

"You're afraid? For us?"

"Yes." He paused, grimacing. "Yes," he repeated. "I'm afraid. For you, for me, for all of us. For this." He gestured to the room. "For Heather. I hate it every time she goes away. Last time, you freaked out and we had to call in Sadie."

It was my turn to grimace. "'Freaked out' is a nice way of putting it." That was the day that I'd punched my knuckles bloody on the punching bag. There were still reddish-brown stains on the leather that I couldn't get out no matter how much I tried. It was almost a metaphor for my life.

"The point is, we followed the rules then and you got help."

"What rule aren't we following if we go get what's at those coordinates?"

"I don't know, but I don't want to lose what I have here. What *we* have here. I don't want to lose my home again. I like it the way it is now."

There it was. Adam had lost as much as me and it was still raw for him. I'd reminded him of that. Of the three of us, Carrie had lost the least, losing only her home. She'd kept her sibling and one of her mentors. Adam had lost the only home he'd known, his surrogate mother, his whole world. Carrie was one of the few keystones he had left.

I bowed my head to hide my own grief and guilt. When I had my face under control, I looked at him. "I'll make sure we don't lose anything. I swear it. Not our home. Not Carrie and her need for adventure."

"Are you still going to go? If you don't go, Carrie will stay. Won't she?"

Adam's eyes begged me to say yes, but I couldn't. I'd seen that stubborn look on her face. "If she decides to go, I won't let her go alone. I think she'll go. Heather's not here to answer that plea for help. We are. Can you understand that?"

He slumped and nodded. "She's stubborn, isn't she?"

It hurt my heart to see him like that. "Yeah. And I've got to have her back, you know?"

"It's always you girls against me."

I shook my head. "No. If it was you who wanted to go and her who wanted to stay, I'd have your back, too. I wouldn't let you go alone. Ever. I'll always have your back. You're the only family I've got. You know?"

"Yeah. I know." He looked away. "Promise me you guys will be safe."

"I promise. Nothing is going to happen."

"Fine. I won't stop you. But I'm not going." Adam continued to look at his hands.

I tried to soften the defeat in his shoulders. "We're just going to go geocaching and then we'll come home. That's it. I swear. Everything will be okay."

I really hate it when I accidentally lie to people. Especially to myself.

CHAPTER FOUR

The free-floating anxiety that had been plaguing me for months returned like a bad habit as I put on my Wellingtons. I recognized it for what it was: fear of change and the unknown. As I named my demon, I felt it lessen and relax its stranglehold on my heart. Everything would be fine. I could do this. This was going to be nothing more than geocaching. I was there to back Carrie up, find something that was probably a prank....

I smirked at myself in the mirror. "You are such liar."

Adam was waiting for me as I left my bedroom. "You're going to be careful, right?"

"Yeah. Promise. I'm the one with the anxiety about leaving the house, you know. Not you. You just have agoraphobia."

He didn't smile. "This isn't a game, Mel. Seriously. Whoever left that for Heather knows she was an operative. They're going to be expecting a person with those skills."

"What am I? Chopped liver? Or Carrie? She's the smartest person we know. Not to mention we've both held our own against bad guys. You, too. If you're so worried, you come with us." It wasn't a fair shot. I knew he disliked open territory and that was where we were going.

I softened at the distressed look on his face. "It'll be okay. I swear it. We'll go see this castle, be disappointed at how small it is, and find what there is to find. Besides, it's best if someone stays here and keeps an eye on home base, you know? Just in case this is a ruse to get us out of the house so someone can ransack it."

"I didn't think of that." He looked down the hallway as if there were already intruders in the house.

I shrugged. "Welcome to my life. Tell me about anything and I can tell you what horrible thing could happen." It's true. In my mind, we'd already had one car accident, been eaten by a bear, got caught in a pit trap, and fallen off the edge of a cliff. If I think about things, my mind is filled with nothing but disasters. So, I don't really think about them if I can get away with it.

Adam followed me to the front door and watched as Carrie and I shrugged into our coats. "I'll watch the house but you need to call when you get there and when you leave."

Carrie rolled her eyes. "Yes, dad."

I pushed her out the front door. "We will."

As soon as the door closed, she offered me the car keys. I didn't take them. "What's this?"

"You're driving. Heather says you need to practice. You're driving to wherever we go."

I looked at the black SUV. I didn't like it. It loomed its presence to one and all. "But..."

"No. I pulled it out of the garage for you to make it easier." Carrie shoved the keys into my hands. "You need to practice. I need to be able to see if I can narrow down where in the ruins we need to look. It's a big place." She patted her bag for emphasis.

I scowled and nodded. "Fine. Whatever."

"Hey, if a half-handed girl like me can not only learn to drive and pass the test on the first time in *this* city, you can, too."

I didn't answer as I clambered into the SUV. She had a point. I needed the practice and I needed to face my fear.

As soon as we were on the road, Carrie opened her laptop. "Also, I found the footage of the guy dropping off the envelope. Not much to see. He was in all black from head-to-toe, even mesh or something over his eyes. Came around from the side instead of up the driveway to shove the envelope into the bushes. He did it quick, like he knew where the cameras were. The envelope fell to the ground not five minutes after he left. I don't think it was supposed to. In any case, I need to add more cameras. I didn't think anything would come in from the field. I was wrong."

I focused on the road, remembering that the few other cars were not out to get me. "How do you know it was a guy? I mean, if they were covered from head to toe..."

"No boobs. Granted. It could've been a really skinny woman, but my gut says man. Center of balance and all that."

"Okay." Made sense. We picked up on a lot about a person just based on how they walked, stood, and gestured.

Tom-Tom said that Ha Ha Tonka State Park was about thirty miles north of the house. We were about thirty-five minutes out. Carrie was deep into her laptop, flipping through images, zooming in and out.

After too many minutes of silence, I asked, "What are you doing?"

"What I need to do. You keep your eyes on the road."

"But..."

Carrie scowled and snapped, "Right, you with the anxiety. Good in a crisis. Annoying otherwise."

Hurt, I gripped the steering wheel tighter and fastened my gaze forward. "Sorry." I didn't try to hide how much her comment stung.

For a long moment, Carrie didn't say anything. She scrolled through images. "Don't be sorry. I'm impatient. I don't like the lack of routine. If you hadn't freaked out about the change in the Sunday schedule, I would've. You did me a favor. But I like a challenge and I forget that, for other people, challenges are scary rather than exhilarating."

I didn't say anything. I was still mad at her, but Carrie had taken on the tone of someone in a reluctant confession. I loosened my grip on the wheel and took a couple of slow breaths. Being angry wouldn't help anyone right now.

As I replayed what she'd just said, I realized Carrie was as scared as she was excited by what we were doing. I glanced at her. She was squeezing her laptop hard. That meant my job right now was to listen. It's funny and annoying. Doctor Giacomi and Deroga Darrington agreed on this point. I didn't want to listen but everyone and everything around me kept telling me that was what I was supposed to do.

"I hate exercise. I'm in good enough shape. The team exercises don't make any sense, not for me anyway. I mean, I understand them and all, but it's not like I'm going to be out in the field with you guys ever. Whether I want to be or not. No one in their right mind is going to let me." Carrie waved her left hand around. It was the one with a congenital defect. She was missing the top two knuckles on all of her fingers. I almost never noticed it anymore.

"Besides, my strength is right here." She tapped the edge of the computer. "Also, I think I've figured out where we need to look when we get there."

The whiplash topic changes were hard to keep up with. I think she had apologized without saying "I'm sorry." I wasn't sure. Either way, my anger was gone and I was running even again, thinking about her possible want to "go into the field" with me and Adam. Was that what this was all about?

After about a minute of silence, I figured it was safe to ask a question. "Where do we need to go?"

"Well, we're going to have to walk a bit from the parking lot up to the castle. But, looking at the GPS coordinates, there's a path on the west side of the castle to an overlook area. It's on the edge of the cliff but I'm really sure that's where we need to go."

"How do you know?" I didn't doubt her but I had no idea how she'd get such information.

"Google maps. I plugged in the coordinates and then switched to Earth mode. You'd be amazed at what kind of information is online these days."

"Like what?"

Carrie shrugged. "If you've sold a house in the last five years, anyone can take a virtual tour of it. Zillow.com is not your privacy's friend. Seriously, look up any address you know and see if it's listed. Sure, the decorations won't be the same but the layout is there. Whenever any of my online friends tell me about moving, and I get the address, I always take a virtual tour. But, I've learned not to tell them about it because they think it's creepy. I suppose they're right. I'm just curious."

Fear tiptoed back into my brain. If Carrie could do that, what could other people do?

She continued on, oblivious to my growing fear. "It's the same with any public building. People put up building layouts on their websites in the name of posterity. Or, if not on public websites, in private archives that are really easy to get into—if you know anything about reverse engineering."

"Is our house...?" The question popped into my head as my stomach took an elevator ride straight down. Even as the nausea rose to replace it, I forced myself to unclench my hands and my teeth.

"Yep. It is. And there's nothing we can do about it."

We'll see about that. A comment to David or Heather might make a difference. Then again, if Carrie couldn't get it pulled off of the realtor's website.... The idea spun around in my head for too many minutes with no solution that wouldn't get someone in trouble. But I couldn't stop myself. My only relief came when another car passed by or we had a turn.

Then I had to kick this new terrible fact—and all my useless nattering—to the curb because we were there. I needed to get my head in the game. There was plenty of time to have nightmares at the idea of strangers peeking into the house over the internet, later.

I parked the SUV in the castle's lot. The sign on the way in said that the park was in its winter hours and there weren't any scheduled staff on site. But there was an emergency number. I was relieved. I thought the park might be closed. As it was, we were the only car in the lot.

Carrie took another look at her computer, snapped it shut, then put it under her seat. "C'mon. It's not that far. I've got the key and the weeder."

I shook my head as I unbuckled myself and got out of the SUV. I had forgotten about the weeder and the key. If Carrie hadn't brought them, we'd be up a creek. Maybe. Then again, this was her show. I was, as David once said, just muscle. I was here to escort her, dig out whatever it was, and make sure nothing went wrong.

Too bad I sucked at my job.

The two of us looked around, then headed up Natural Bridge Road. A quick look at the historic sign told us that no one was allowed to drive up to the castle but this used to be the long driveway there. It was quiet around us. I looked at the mostly naked trees with some trepidation. I wasn't used to tree lined roads yet. These looked like skeletons to me.

Carrie shifted closer. "It's a good thing Adam didn't come. He'd be a wreck." She kept her voice hushed as she looked around us. Her breath came out in puffs of warm air.

One look at her face told me that she wasn't doing so well, either. She'd put on a brave face for me. "Yeah, it's not like any of us are country folk." I kept my voice as quiet as she did and also kept looking around us. I didn't want to say anything but the hairs on the back of my neck told me that someone or something was watching us.

Or I could just be crazy.

Or, it could be both, my cynical mind added. *Just because you're crazy doesn't mean they aren't out to get you.*

This thought made me smile and shake my head.

"What?" Carrie didn't look at me as she asked. She was looking ahead to the castle ruins.

"Nothing. Just me being me." The ruins showed just how large the castle had once been. I wished I could've seen it in all its glory. I bet it was really pretty. Now, it was a shell of stone walls and archways with a front courtyard that overlooked the water.

Carrie led me around the backside of the castle until we reached a stretch of walk barred by a small black iron fence. It wasn't much of a barrier. Mostly, it was there to tell the tourists to stay out. But anyone who actually wanted through could just clamber over it. She and I exchanged a glance and a smile. I took the dare and climbed over it first. I helped her on the way down.

We continued down the walk until we got to the lookout platform. It was beautiful. The view of the valley and water below could be a postcard. The rounded viewpoint had a stone railing to keep the clumsy from falling. To the side were trees and bushes. While I admired the view, Carrie moved to the bushes and looked under them.

"Here." Her voice was muffled but it held a note of triumph.

I hurried to her side and knelt next to her. "You find it?"

She handed me the weeder. "There. You see?" She pointed under the bush at half-buried box.

I did see. "Are geocaches usually hidden like this?"

"No. But this isn't a normal one, you know?"

I knew. I wriggled down and used the weeder to pry the small metal box out of the ground. It came easier than I thought it would. Then I used the tool to lift the handle and pull the box to me. Just enough until I could pull both of them out from under the bush. Something in the box clinked against the sides. I handed it to Carrie and shoved the weeder into my anorak pocket. I pushed up from the cold rock and dusted myself off.

Carrie shook it, listening to the sound of paper and hard plastic rattle inside, and grinned at me. "I told you. It's just like geocaching."

I stopped her as she pulled the small key from her bag, shaking my head. "C'mon. Let's get back to the car. Whatever is in that can wait. I don't like being out in the open." The hairs on the back of my neck were at attention again.

She looked around and nodded. "Right. The car. In a secure area." She put the key and the small box into her bag and resettled it across her body.

We retraced our steps along the backside of the Ha Ha Tonka Castle ruins, our heads on swivels. I could tell that Carrie was feeling just as paranoid as I was, now that the excitement of the search was done.

A pebble skipped against stone.

We froze in place and listened. Silence. For about a count of ten we didn't move. Then, with sheepish grins, we headed down the road towards the parking lot at a fast clip. Both of us were panting at the fast pace.

The bullet cracked the asphalt next to us just as we'd started to laugh at our fear.

"The trees!" Carrie swung that way and I followed, crashing into the undergrowth. It wasn't as easy going as the road but it did put obstacles between us and the shooter. Stifling cries of fear, we bolted through the forest as pop after pop of a handgun sounded behind us, the bullets striking the trees and ground near us.

"Which way?" I ducked away from a tree as its bark exploded in splinters that scratched my face. My breath came out in gasps and I wasn't sure she heard me until she pointed and took the lead. Carrie may have hated exercise more than me but she was still in better shape. Or at least faster. Part of me hated her for it.

We thrashed through the forest like frightened deer, banging into trees, and stumbling on the soft, wet earth. I could hear someone chasing us now. They stayed on the road, shooting at us through the trees, but their shoes pounded hard against the pavement. It was the only reason they hadn't hit us—whoever they were. Carrie yelped as a tree branch splintered next to her.

I wanted to shout with relief when I saw our black SUV through the trees. Then I realized that we'd be out in the open and the shooter would have a clear shot. "Left… side… of… car!" I was trying to tell her to go for cover. I have no idea if she even heard me.

We burst out of the forest and onto the pavement. Its sudden stability was a relief. I slowed just long enough to dig the car keys from my pocket. Pointing them at the SUV and pressing the key fob, it gave the reassuring chirp that it was unlocked.

Carrie cried out in pain and tumbled to the ground. She'd been shot. I didn't know where and I couldn't stop to find out.

Coming around the corner from the road into the parking lot was a man in all black. His pale face was uncovered and he pointed a long barreled pistol at us. The chamber was open. He was out of bullets. I had to get Carrie into the SUV before he reloaded. Calm descended, I stopped thinking, and moved with that goal in mind.

Carrie was struggling to her feet as I scooped her up from behind by the waist. She was as slender as I was stout. I was stronger than her by a mile. "My leg," she said through gritted teeth, tears on her face. "He shot my leg."

"I got you." I pulled her around the front side of the SUV to the passenger door, yanked it open, and pushed her inside. I winced at her yelp of pain but that wasn't my focus. "Stay down." I closed the door with a slam and peeked out from behind the vehicle.

The shooter held his pistol before him but was hovering near the tree line. He watched the SUV, moving towards the passenger side of the vehicle with slow, measured steps as he aimed the gun in the general direction of us. I couldn't figure out what he was waiting for. He was the one with the weapon. Why didn't he rush us? Maybe he thought we had a weapon in the car. Maybe we did—somewhere in the vehicle. I didn't know.

I saw the driver side door pop open a little. Carrie was trying to help me. It was enough. I pulled the weeder from my pocket and threw it as hard as I could away from the vehicle in the direction the shooter was headed. As soon as it hit the ground with a rolling clang, I sprinted the last couple of feet to the car door and pulled myself in.

Carrie had flattened herself against the seat. While her face was still wet from her tears, she wasn't crying anymore. "Go!" she urged. "Go! Go! Go!"

I didn't need any more encouragement. I started the SUV and watched the shooter—I had a clear view of him: white male, brown hair, clean shaven, upper 20s, black fatigues—and he had a clear view of me. He aimed his pistol at the SUV. Cold anger descended and I slammed the gas to charge him. His calm demeanor turned into a look of surprise. He backpedaled hard into the forest. I whipped the SUV around, spraying him with rocks, and sped down the road, out of the parking lot, and away from immediate danger.

The SUV beeped its shrill admonishment at the lack of seatbelts on the part of its passengers. As Carrie struggled into her belt, the beeping shifted to a single, angry tone that drilled into my head. At the nearest cross street, I stopped long enough to put mine on and silence the pain.

"Calm down. Calm down. Drive normally." Carrie's face was drawn tight and her light brown skin was tinged grey.

"Holy shit. We have to get you to a hospital." I kept my eyes on the road, white-knuckling the steering wheel.

"You want to get us taken away from Heather?" Carrie turned the GPS on and set it for home. "Because that's what'll happen. She's not here.

I don't care what she told the Richland Police Department or Detective Russell. I've been shot and they're going to assume gang violence or terrorist threat."

"What? How could they? You've been shot."

"Look, Blondie. You can get away with stuff I can't. I've got brown skin. Chapman already thinks I'm Arabic. We go to a hospital and a police report will be filed. It's mandatory with gunshot victims. No hospital. No police. You obey the damn rules of the road and get us home. I am *not* going back into an orphanage or the foster system."

She made too much sense. Also, she was on the edge of hysteria. "Okay. But you get to call Adam and tell him." I glanced at her, then into the wheel well. I didn't see any blood. "Where were you shot?"

"Calf." Carrie laughed, half hysterical, half sobbing. "I'm filling my boot with blood. I can feel it. At least I won't have to clean up the inside of the car."

CHAPTER FIVE

Adam was just as freaked out as I thought he would be. As soon as I pulled into the garage, taking care not to go beyond the hanging tennis ball, he burst out the kitchen door, armed to the teeth, and wearing a bulletproof vest. "Situation?" He asked as I got out of the SUV. His voice was calm, too calm considering how much his hands shook.

"Carrie's hurt. Get her inside." I took the rifle from him. "I got to check something."

He gave me a nod and moved around to the passenger side of the vehicle. Carrie didn't protest as Adam picked her up and cradled her in his arms. "Dojo," she commanded.

I wasn't surprised. We were in crisis mode. The dojo was where we trained, and it was underground. I waited until the door shut to put the rifle down. I didn't think we'd need it. At least, not yet.

Gazing at the SUV, I grabbed one of the bottles of water we left in the garage and downed half of it, then swished some around in my mouth so I didn't feel like I was sucking on a cotton ball. I took stock of myself to make sure I was still on an even keel. I was. My heart wasn't racing. There were no hallucinations, yet. I was still thinking clearly. Lithium was a godsend after all I'd been through. Without it, right now, I'd be a complete basket case. Instead, I could rely on my senses and my intuition. That intuition told me there was more to do here.

With my hindbrain on alert, I don't know why, but I knew something was wrong with the SUV. I dropped to my already dirty knees, and peered under it. Little by little, I inched along the side of the vehicle until I saw what I didn't know I was looking for: a small device on the underside of the back bumper. It was about the size of my thumb, had a small stiff antenna, and a little red light. The light was solid. I didn't know if that was good or bad.

I pulled the tracking device from its spot, put it on one of the work tables, and hammered it into tiny pieces of black plastic and sharp bits of metal. I considered it for a moment then shrugged. The damage was done. If the tracking people didn't already know where we lived, they knew now. I left it there, not wanting to bring it in the house. I retrieved the rifle and went inside.

After I put the rifle back in the gun cabinet, I got myself a back holster and my favorite pistol. I put them in my room before I went downstairs. Carrie was stretched out on a pile of the padded mats, her boots off, and the jeans of her left leg missing from the knee down. Adam swabbed at the wound with a gentle hand as Carrie gripped the mats. At every touch, she screamed through a mouthful of terrycloth towel.

It took all my willpower not to push him away from her. I knew he'd had some medical training, but it wasn't as extensive as me. "Did you give her painkillers?"

Adam shook his head. "She wouldn't let me. Not yet."

I looked over her leg and saw only one wound. "Shit. No exit wound. The bullet's still in you."

Carrie took the towel out of her mouth and looked at me over her shoulder. "I need to know what's in the damn box. I need to know."

I looked between Adam and her and nodded. "All right, but I can give you a local painkiller."

Adam looked at the large medical kit next to him. "We have that?"

I knelt next to him, shooing him out of the way, and lifted the inside tray of the medical kit. There were half a dozen syringes and bottles of clear liquid. I chose good old novocaine, loaded the syringe with a hundred milligrams, and said, "This is going to hurt."

Carrie turned away and stuffed the towel back in her mouth. I'm glad she did. I only sorta knew what I was doing. I knew a hundred milligrams in the lower legs was fine. I didn't know for sure how long it would last or if it would work at all. I didn't let that stop me. I pretended she was just like the kid I had to give diabetic shots to in juvie. Fifty milligrams on one side of the bullet wound. Fifty milligrams on the other.

I knew it had worked when Carrie stopped making pained noises and relaxed against the mats. She sighed with pure relief. "That's better."

I took the time to cover the wound with a sterile gauze pad and wrap her calf with an ace bandage. It was all I could do at the moment. I knew we needed to get professional help for her—and soon. "It isn't going to last for long. After we know what's in the box, you *will* need to take some codeine... and I don't know how to get a bullet out of your leg. That's way beyond the training I had."

I made a mental note to ask for more emergency medical training. It wasn't used a lot but when it was, it was really needed. I also wondered if there was a medical book in our supplies I could use.

Carrie turned over once I was done. "Yeah. I know. I'll call Sadie soon. But first..." She pointed at her discarded bag. Adam got up and retrieved it for her.

I moved to one of the chairs. "One more thing..." They paused and looked at me. "The shooter put something on the SUV. I found it and broke it."

Adam frowned. "A tail?"

I shrugged. "Maybe. Probably a tracking device."

"But why?" He looked to the side and answered his own question. "Ah, to know where we go. I read a lot about the government doing that."

"Maybe. They already know where we live. Maybe they just want to know where'd we go next."

Carrie pulled the small metal box and the key out of her bag. "Doesn't matter." She opened it and I saw that it actually was a small metal cash box. Inside were a couple of note cards and a USB thumb drive. Carrie picked up the card and frowned. "Another code." She showed it to us.

"Looks like a simple letter replacement cipher to me." Adam took the note cards and stared at them.

I looked over his shoulder. He was right. The note cards were covered in a gibberish of letters, punctuation, and numbers. It looked like someone had written a letter, then turned all of the letters into other random letters. Still, there was a definite pattern that made the random letters look like a coded message. Especially the 217 in the middle of the message.

"Heather told me about one of those. It was a Caesar shift cipher because Julius Caesar used it. She used to use them when she ran the safe houses. That and code phrases." I offered my hand. "Lemme see if I can figure out if it is one."

He gave me the note cards. I stared at them, looking for a clue to which one it could be. Unfortunately, it was gibberish and there was no neat "use this code here" marked anywhere.

Carrie gave me about two minutes before she huffed. "Give those to me. I'll break it. Better yet, help me to the computer." Adam offered her a hand up and helped her hobble to the computer at the table. She sat with a wince, then pulled herself together. "I need my old black laptop. The one I call 'Brick'. Also, I need my silver laptop, Khalessi. I'm sure it's still in the car."

I'd totally forgotten about her laptop under the passenger side seat. "I'll get Khalessi."

"I'll get Brick." Adam said. We pounded up the stairs as Carrie tapped at the dojo computer in front of her.

While I was upstairs, I made a point of checking all of the windows and doors, making sure they were locked. It was a coping mechanism to make me feel safer. By the time I got back, Carrie had typed the coded message into a document and the dojo computer was busily going through all twenty-six combinations of the Caesar shift cipher with a neat little graphic turning the dials. On Brick, Carrie had the thumb drive plugged in and open.

"There's nothing here," she said, pointing to Brick. "Empty flash drive."

"Maybe we're supposed to put something on it?"

"There's no 'we'," Adam said, tromping down the stairs. He carried a pair of crutches in one hand and placed them to the side of the table where Carrie could reach them if she wanted to. "This message is for Heather. Not us."

"Hah! ROT-23." When neither Adam or I responded, Carrie pointed at the screen. In one window was "BIFPB." In the other window was "ELISE."

Adam and I exchanged a glance. Carrie sighed. "Look, ROT-13 means the alphabet was shifted down thirteen characters. A becomes N, B becomes M, and so on. This one is ROT-23. A is X. B is Y. C is Z. D is A. Get it?"

"Oh. Yeah." I nodded. "What does ROT mean?"

"Rotate. Rotate by 13. Rotate by 23."

"Right. Right. Heather told me that." I rubbed my face, feeling dumb. "So, they wanted us to solve it."

Adam shook his head. "Not us. Heather."

We ignored Adam. Carrie nodded. "I imagine if you wanted to get a message to someone, you'd want them to be able to decode it..." Her eyes went wide. "Do you think that guy who shot at us is the one who sent it? He was trying to stop us because we weren't Heather?"

I took a breath and nodded. "Maybe."

"Now, we call Sadie?" Adam asked.

"No." Carrie and I said at the same time. We exchanged a knowing look. She gestured for me to go on and pulled Khalessi to her.

I turned to Adam. "We can't go to her, yet. We need to see what the message is. Also, we need to see if there is some way to make this right. It may be nothing. It may be something we can't do. We're in this far. It's not time to stop. Not yet. We might not have to bring Sadie into this at all, and only need to give Heather an after-action report. She's the one who keeps telling us to "think for ourselves" and to "be proactive"."

Emotions rolled over his face: fear, understanding, reluctance and acceptance. He glanced at the computer with some curiosity before he looked away. "All right. Let's see what the message says."

"It's kinda a doozy." Carrie pushed away from the desk to let us see Khalessi's screen. She hissed a little as she bumped her leg.

"We're going to have to do something about that." I pointed at her leg. Blood was already seeping through the ace bandage.

She gave me an impatient wave. "Read."

Adam read the message aloud. "*Elise. Sorry to interrupt your domestic bliss. I need help and only you can help me. I'm on a mission and need files from the General Leonard-Wood Army Community Hospital. Easiest place to get them from is the server room on the third floor. I need all of the files on Project Yenmil. It's important. Put them on the USB device and bring them to 217 West Camden Ave, Richland, on Sunday. I will be there all day. Please. This is important. Do this for me and I will consider Belgium paid for, fair and square. Be careful, Elijah.*"

"Project Yenmil? That's not creepy at all." I turned back to Carrie. She pulled Khalessi to her, pulled up Zillow.com, and typed in the address. "What are you doing?"

She gave the resulting page a disgusted look. "Nothing. Looks like that address is a business or something. Or hasn't been sold in the last five years." She thought for a moment longer then pulled up Google Maps. She set it to street level. "Huh. An auto upholstery store. Odd place for a secret meeting."

"We have to do this." Adam's voice was soft and concerned.

Carrie and I looked at him. "Uh, what happened to 'we need to tell Sadie'?" I examined his face. It was unreadable. A complete blank. Like he was thinking very hard or was hiding his feelings.

"I recognize this name, Project Yenmil." His voice still had that far away quality.

"What is it?"

"I don't know. I just know that I know this word: Yenmil. I think I heard it before." Adam shook his head. "I know I've heard it before."

"At PAR Lab?" I asked.

"Had to be. It's the only place I've lived before here."

Carrie closed Khalessi and Brick with a purpose. "All right then. You two need to go to Fort Leonard-Wood, break into the hospital, and get those files."

I jerked back to her. "Wait, what?"

"You heard me. This needs to be done and now. We've got less than two days."

"But..."

Adam interrupted me. "I'm in. What's the plan?"

After a moment of silence, I realized that both of them were looking at me. *Well, shit.*

CHAPTER SIX

I stalled for time. I walked over to one of the other office chairs and sat down on it. Keeping my eyes on the ground, I thought as hard as I could as I crab-walked the rolling chair over to where Adam leaned on the table and Carrie sat. I could feel their eyes on me. I was always the one with the plan. They've never realized that I made it up as I go along.

Like I needed to do now.

"All right." I looked up, exchanging glances with them. "We can't go into this blind. First," I nodded to Carrie, "I need a map of the hospital and anything you can get me about it. Next," I turned to Adam, "you figure out a reason we're going to be there tomorrow morning..."

"Tomorrow?" Adam shook his head. "Why tomorrow?"

"Because it's too late today." I squinted at the computer's clock. "It's 1620. It would be 1700 before we got to the base. I doubt the hospital is going to be open for dependent appointments for much longer after that. Especially on a Friday night. Plus, we don't know how long we'll be there. Not to mention, with the tighter security we've seen over the last couple of months just to get to the commissary... No, we need to go in tomorrow when we've had some sleep and we're not going to do something stupid because we're tired. Plus, we go in during weekend commute time. The checkpoint will be too busy to be curious. If we go in now..." I shook my head.

All of this was true. But, the main reason I didn't want to go today was the simple fact that I wasn't ready. I hate having things sprung on me. I like to have a plan. I like to know what I'm doing. I need to think about things. Plus, I really did want the information I was asking for. I set my face into a "no arguments" expression and waited.

Adam gnawed his lip then gestured for me to go on.

I looked at Carrie.

She didn't look happy but she still nodded her agreement. "Okay. Tomorrow."

"Right. Adam, you need to figure out why we're there when we're stopped at the checkpoint. Also, you'll be driving. We don't need the MPs to get shitty about my permit." I stopped and thought some more. "Next is the problem of the server door lock."

I got up and started to pace.

"I don't know what kind of locks they have. It could be keycards or punch locks or..."

"It's punch locks," Carrie said. "At least, most of the locks I saw were. Keys or punch locks."

"How do you know?"

She raised her diminished hand. "The physical therapy I had to do after... you know."

I knew. Ian, her boyfriend and traitor to humanity, had hurt her pretty bad, trying to get her to help him and the Coalescence escape PAR Lab during the lockdown. He had mangled her hand, thinking it was a weak spot. He'd been wrong, but she'd needed extra physical therapy to bring it back to its normal abilities.

"Anyway," Carrie continued, "The physical therapy room is on the third floor and they had a bunch of locked rooms for their equipment. All of them had these ten-key punch pads." She paused. "That gives me an idea. Let me do some research."

"Okay. But what about when we get in? What then? I mean, I figure I can leave Adam on lookout while I'm inside and I know my way around a computer enough to play games but... I don't know how to break into a locked computer."

"Maybe Carrie should come..." Adam shifted and touched the crutches. "Here's a good reason to be at the hospital."

Carrie shook her head and her tone had a note of hysteria to it. "No way. If you think normal hospitals get excited at gunshot wounds, can you imagine what would happen at a military hospital? The MPs would be there in a heartbeat. No. No hospitals. I can't go. Period." She paused then added in a calmer tone, "But that doesn't mean I can't be with you. We've got phones." She turned to me. "I can walk you through whatever you face. Besides, most computers in a server room are super easy to get into once you're in the actual room. A lot of their security is based on keeping people out of the room to begin with."

I leaned back in my seat. "Yeah, as much as I want you there, I agree. You can't be there. You can't run if something goes wrong. It's got to be me and Adam. But you need to figure out how to get us past the door lock."

Carrie opened Khalessi and tapped on the keys until she smiled. "Simple. We use an infrared app." She turned the laptop around and showed us a video.

I couldn't stop myself from smiling as I watched. It was one of those warning videos about how thieves can steal your pin number at the grocery store by using an app that lets them see heat signatures and how, if you can get a look at, or a picture of, the pin pad within a minute, you can see which buttons were pushed, and in which order based on the heat trace left behind. The video also showed how to prevent this.

I couldn't believe that they posted stuff like this on the web. "Don't videos like that just show people how to be bad guys?"

"They're supposed to inform the public of a threat and how to mitigate it." Carrie shrugged. "I'm sure they didn't think that people would use it to break into places. I'll find the app and put it on your phones. Then you two can practice using it while I look up the other stuff you guys need for tomorrow."

Over the next hour, Adam and I practiced with the punch lock on the gun locker. It was the only punch keypad we had access to. When we both could walk by and get a picture of the punch pad that we could read, we called it good. Adam disappeared into his room, saying that he needed to think. I knew he was going to wrack his brain to figure out what he knew about Project Yenmil. I didn't blame him. I wanted to know, too, and I wasn't the one who recognized the name.

I brought Carrie dinner and painkillers an hour after that. She had moved to the office and had her leg propped up. I saw she was sweating and she gave me a strained smile as I handed her the pills. The fact that she took them without a fuss told me how much she hurt.

"We really need to get you to a hospital." I tapped her shoulder and made her look at me. "Or to call Sadie. You don't know what damage you're doing to yourself by leaving the bullet in your leg."

Carrie nodded. "I know. I know. As soon as you have the files, I'll call. I swear."

We locked eyes. I searched for the lie and didn't find one. I didn't expect to find one. Carrie always was a better liar than me. I sighed. "All right. What do you have?"

"You want to get Adam?"

"No. He's thinking."

"Brooding, you mean."

I shrugged. "If it helps him remember what Project Yenmil is, I don't care. Besides, we'll have to go over this again in the morning, just to be sure. Might as well let him brood. Maybe he'll come up with something."

She pointed at the computer. "Okay. I have a lot for you. Almost too much information. General Leonard-Wood Army Community Hospital has a website. I'll have it narrowed down for you by tomorrow. But here are the basics: There's a main first floor where Emergency and the main clinic are. That's this pizza-box-looking part of the building. The rest of the hospital is the six-floor building tacked onto the middle of it. I couldn't get deep inside the actual layout of the place but I did find some online schematics of it. Even the military has to file permits."

"Especially the military, I'd think."

Carrie shrugged. "In any case, you've got the first floor to get through. Avoid the second floor. That's surgery. Probably a lot tighter security and people apt to ask questions of strangers. Floors three to six are medical offices and doctors' offices. So, you're going to have to figure out how not to stand out. I'm pretty sure, looking at this, there are central waiting areas next to the elevators."

Frowning, I studied the floor plans. "It's a weird looking building. But it seems straightforward."

"On paper, yes. Once you're there, in those copycat hallways, less so. Also, some places may be for employees only. You may have to pretend to work there."

"Like a candy striper? Do they even have those in a military hospital?"

Carrie laughed. "No. They do have volunteers, though. They wear these bright blue vests. Mostly they escort people in and out of the hospital or from department to department. Like wheeling someone to radiology. Otherwise, they're glorified gophers. Go for this. Go for that."

"Sounds thrilling. Maybe I'll just be stealthy."

"Right." She gave me a skeptical look.

I peered at the overhead images of the hospital and compared them to the permit schematics she'd found. "Looks like we need to go through the clinic, up the elevators to the third floor. Wait for someone to go into the server room, get the code, wait for them to leave, and profit."

"Probably." Carrie pushed her long dark hair from her face and nodded. "I'm going to narrow this stuff down for you. By tomorrow, I'll have your actual path and maybe even a room number. It should be what you need. I just want to make sure I don't have any better resources. It'll be fine."

"I hope so. I'm only along for the ride."

She frowned at me. "Don't do that."

Taken aback, I blinked at her. "Do what?"

"Talk yourself down. You do it way more than you should. You need to be positive. You're running this operation. Remember that. So, don't do that."

I was startled by her words. I hadn't realized me making fun of myself bothered her. I nodded, not really understanding but willing to do what I needed to do to keep the peace. "Yeah. Okay. Sorry. It was just a joke."

Carrie gave me an irritated huff then turned her focus back to the multitude of computer screens in front of her. I knew a dismissal when I saw it. I also knew I should think about that whole talking myself down. Doctor Giacomi was going to use her universal pokey stick on it and ask some really uncomfortable questions. I should probably start preparing myself for them.

I shook my head. It was too much trouble. I'd burn that bridge when we got to it.

THE HOSPITAL

7

CHAPTER SEVEN

Adam and I drove towards the hospital. The GPS said it would take about forty-five minutes with the traffic. I noticed just about everything of interest was always about forty-five minutes away from where we lived. Probably because we didn't live in the heart of Richland. Not that Richland was a busy city. It barely qualified as a town. Then again, we liked the quiet. It was a suitable compromise.

We didn't talk much on the way. Both of us had long thoughts to think. I bet that Adam was reliving many memories from his time in PAR Lab.

Carrie had gone over the map to the base—even though it wasn't needed because of the GPS—and the basic route into the hospital and up to the third floor. She hadn't found any more schematics, but she had found some personal blogs with pictures of the hospital from one of the new doctors on staff. Fortunately, floors 3, 4, and 5, all had open offices with medical specialties on them. There was no information about what was on the 6th floor. Probably administration offices for the hospital.

I shifted, trying to find a more comfortable position. The 9mm pistol I had tucked into the back holster dug into my spine. I couldn't bring Mister Bat with us. It was an obvious weapon in the thick of things. Tossing a ball and glove in the back wouldn't be enough to camouflage it. Instead, I'd put Mister Bat by the front door in case someone went for a frontal attack. Not that I thought anyone would.

As we turned from Highway H onto Missouri Avenue, Adam cleared his throat and said, "Not long now."

I looked at the GPS. Seven miles. I could feel tension creep into my shoulders and took a couple of breaths, trying to calm myself. I saw that Adam clenched the steering wheel in a death grip. His tension forced me to calm down. I asked, "You okay?"

He shook his head. "No. Not really. Not enough clouds in the sky."

I hadn't noticed the pretty day. "It'll be fine. You know where the ceiling is. Eight hundred feet up."

Adam didn't respond.

"You're going to have to relax a little. The MPs at the checkpoint will notice."

He barked a little laugh of dismissal. "S'ok. I've got that covered. They'll understand if they ask me why we're here."

"Why am I here?"

Adam relaxed and a tiny smile crept across his face. He glanced at me. "Women troubles."

I sat back, regretted it, and shifted to the side. "Really? Women troubles?"

"I've seen scientists and doctors blush and clam up when Lakshmi..." His voice broke a little on her name, then he pushed on. "...when she would say something like, 'I need to go. Women troubles.' Or, 'Sorry, that time of the month. I'll be back.' She and Jolene made a game of it. Sometimes, they used it to get out of meetings that dragged on too long."

Adam loosened his hands on the wheel and cracked his neck with a jerk to the side. "What I'm saying is, no guy ever questions a girl with women troubles. I bet you five bucks the guard can't even look at you after that."

Having grown up an only child, and never heard of such a thing, I was mystified. Then again, only my mom and Sharon had dealt with me when it was that time of the month. Still, Matt was perfectly okay going to the store to get tampons and stuff. In fact, he'd been a master at producing chocolate at just the right time. "Deal. Five dollars. After you say those words, the guard won't look at me."

He didn't shake my hand but we grinned at each other.

We were silent until we came to the line at the checkpoint to get onto Fort Leonard-Wood. There were five cars in front of us. It looked like the MPs were taking their time despite the backup, looking at IDs, and talking to the people in the cars. My heart leapt to my throat when they pointed the fourth car in front of us to the side and began a search of the vehicle.

"Oh, shit. Did we make sure that there wasn't anything in the SUV?" I tried to keep the panic out of my voice.

"Yeah," Adam breathed. "Did it last night. Wanted to make sure there wasn't any blood. There wasn't. Cleaned up the bit of trash. There's nothing to worry about."

I watched the MPs search the white Cadillac. Everything seemed to be going all right. Then, one of the MPs pulled a fencing foil and mask from the trunk. The driver bowed his head and started talking. More MPs came out. I'm not sure what the guy said, but it was the wrong thing. There was a flurry of movement and the driver was pressed up against the Cadillac and being searched. One of the MPs had a pistol drawn and pointed at the driver. Then he was cuffed and hauled away.

I looked down at my hands. They were shaking more out of fear than the essential tremor I had to deal with. "Oh, mother of pearl, son of a gun, what the flying fig am I going to do?" Part of me marveled at how I could drop into "proper" habits of "not-swearing" in the face of authority. Part of me gibbered in fear.

Adam put a hand on my forearm. It was very dark against my pale skin. I latched onto the contrast and stared. He had nice hands. Long, slender fingers. Well-formed nails. His hand was warm and seemed to glow against my arm.

"It's going to be okay. You need to be okay." His voice was quiet and firm.

"What if we get searched?"

"The SUV is clean. I made sure. I told you."

"But I'm not." I looked up at him then forward. One car between us and the checkpoint.

Adam withdrew his hand and looked ahead. "What do you mean?"

"I've got a pistol on me." Both of us spoke low with our lips barely moving.

He opened and closed his mouth a couple of times. Surprise and fear warred for a second before he shut his emotions down. I wondered how often he'd had to be neutral at the lab. A lot, it seemed, from the way he could control himself. Adam let out a breath and asked, "Do you have your concealed carry permit?"

I nodded. "Well, yeah. It's in my wallet." I patted my purse, tucked cross-body, under my coat. "I always keep it with me." Heather had insisted that all of us train for and earn our concealed carry permits.

We didn't run around with concealed weapons but she wanted us to be prepared for such a possibility.

He nodded. "No worries then. I got this. You chill."

This last was a command. It surprised me. Weirdly, it also made me relax, despite the grip of the pistol digging into my back. I wondered why the hell I'd brought it with me. It had been an impulse. One that I now regretted.

Adam drove us up to the checkpoint, rolling the window down as he did. We'd put our dependent IDs in one of the cup holders for easy access. Adam grabbed them and held them out to the MP on duty. I tilted my head forward so I could get a look at him. Blond hair, freckled skin, average height. Three flat bars on the shoulder and "KLEIN" on his name tag. A sergeant. I never thought Heather making us memorize military ranks by service would come in handy.

"Morning," Sergeant Klein said, flashing his black light flashlight over our IDs to illuminate the ultraviolet symbols. "What are you kids doing here today?" His voice was formal and alert.

Adam said something that sounded like "Dob-meer exam today." But, I couldn't be sure. He held his head up high and proud. Whatever he said, it was right thing.

Sergeant Klein gave him a second look and quirked a half-smile at him. "Good luck with that, son." He looked over at me and asked, "What about you, Miss?"

I didn't have time to panic. Adam, still with his head high and proud voice said, "My sister has women troubles. She's got her own appointment."

"Oh God." I put my face in my hands, blushing from the roots of my hair right down to my chest. "Did you have to say that?" My reaction wasn't faked. I was completely mortified. I didn't want to see the look on the sergeant's face. In my mind's eye, he smirked his amusement at me.

"You two have a good day."

Out of the corner of my eye, I saw Sergeant Klein give Adam back our IDs. Adam dropped them in the cup holder as I turned my head to the right, refusing to look at him or Sergeant Klein. Adam grinned the whole time as he drove through the gate and down Missouri Ave.

"From here, it's a straight shot. Six and a half miles." Adam relaxed into his driving, taking care not to speed on base. You never sped on base. Ever. It was just one of those things. "I guess I owe you five bucks. He blushed, almost as much as you but he still looked at you. Made of sterner stuff than doctors, I guess. Also, I saw him look at the GPS. I'm not sure what happened but they've really tightened things down a lot since I was here last."

"I earned that five bucks."

Adam shrugged. "You did exactly what you needed to do. Be a girl."

I had no response for that. I think it was a compliment. If not, I knew he wasn't being mean. Sometimes, Adam was hard to read, but he wasn't malicious about anything. Not that I'd ever seen. "What's a dob-meer exam?"

"Department of Defense Medical Examination Review Board. D.O.D.M.E.R.B. It's the medical exam that ROTC scholarship candidates have to get. I read that it's pretty tough. Every part of you poked and prodded. It's a big deal. Means you've gotten enough good marks and recommendations that you're a serious candidate. That's why the MP said good luck."

"ROTC?"

"Reserved Officers' Training Corps. Your college is paid for and while in college, you take classes on being an officer. After college, you graduate and you become active duty as a 2nd Lieutenant."

I gazed at him. "You're not thinking of actually doing this, are you? Joining the army?"

Adam furrowed his brows in disbelief as he glanced at me. "No. But I told you that I'd take care of the reason of why we'd be on base. Fort Leonard-Wood is an Army training base. It makes sense that scholarship candidates would be sent here for their medical exams. Doctor Dudetsky always said that proper research saves time and money and that you needed to do it right if you were going to do it at all."

I nodded. "Well, Dudette taught you well. I believed you."

"That was the point."

"I'm still taking that five dollars you owe me."

Adam flashed white teeth as he navigated a curve in the road and pulled into the parking lot. "Worth it. You're still blushing."

I felt my cheek. It was warm against my hand. I felt my face flush all the more. "Jerk."

He laughed as he parked the SUV. "Maybe."

The hospital was unmistakable. It loomed over everything around it as we pulled into the half-full parking lot. It seemed even bigger than the pictures made it look. That was saying something. It was built from the same red brick that all the other buildings around it were built with, and had the same white-edged windows. At first glance, it looked a little like a big dorm building. Or school.

The people walking to and from the main hospital entrance where in both uniform and civilian clothes.

I shifted, putting my hand to my back, intending to remove the pistol and the holster, when Adam said, "You need to leave that thing in the car."

Scowling at him, I unsnapped it from my belt. "Way ahead of you."

"Why did you bring it?"

I ignored the accusation in his tone as I put the holster and its lethal cargo in the SUV's glove box and closed it with a firm click. "Because, I couldn't bring Mister Bat. And I'm glad I didn't. You saw what happened with Mister Fencer. Also, because we got shot at on the first part of this mission. Excuse me for wanting to be prepared."

"Are you sure we're doing the right thing?"

Something about the tone of his voice made me look at him. He had his head down, looking at his lap. Grimaces of fear and scowls of anger warred for dominance. The two emotions usually just cancelled each other out. Instead, Adam looked like he was in a mental tailspin. I didn't understand his sudden shift in attitude. He had been so confident.

I didn't know what to do. I did the only thing I could do. I put my hand on his leg. "You okay?"

Adam shrugged and gazed at the hospital. "No. Not really."

"You're the one who backed Carrie on this. Because of Project Yenmil. Did you remember something?"

Adam shook his head. "No. That's the problem. I can't remember why I know it. I just... I know it's important."

I followed his gaze as I pulled back into myself. "We're here now. We're going to go into unknown territory to do something that is technically illegal to help out a friend of Heather's from back in her espionage days. It's probably stupid and it's definitely dangerous. I need to know you're with me on this. I need to know you've got my back. Otherwise, we need to just go home."

He bowed his head and stared at his black and orange sneakers. I took a lozenge out of my pocket, unwrapped it, and popped it in my too-dry mouth while I waited for his answer. If he didn't have my back, this whole thing was a bust. Adam raised his head. "Yeah, I'm in. I've got your back. You can trust me. It's just that... I've been following some very strict rules all my life. It's not easy to break them, you know?"

I didn't. I nodded anyway. "I know." I pulled my phone from my jacket pocket and looked at the time. "Carrie's got to be having a cow right now. We're fifteen minutes past the time we said we'd call."

"Just tell her we had women troubles."

Adam flashed me a grin as I blushed. I put my Bluetooth earpiece in and thumbed her contact number.

"Mel? What the hell have you two been doing?" Carrie sounded pissed and worried. "I thought you got stopped at the gate. What took you so long? Are you okay? What happened? Are you there?"

Women troubles indeed.

CHAPTER EIGHT

After I hung up, Carrie called us both back on a conference call. I don't know how she managed it. I'm not a complete doofus about technology but some of it was like wizardry. If I asked, she would tell me what she did, but I still wouldn't understand it and then I'd have a lot more things running around my head, confusing me. I already had enough panicked ferrets up there. I didn't need to add to the chaos.

"It should be simple." Carrie's voice came over my Bluetooth earpiece. "You just—"

"I know," I interrupted, looking at Adam. He gave me a hurry-it-up gesture. "Down the main hallway, through the clinic area, to the back where the elevators are. Up to the third floor. Wait until someone goes in, get the code, wait until they leave, break in, profit. We got it."

Carrie was silent for a moment. "Yeah, that's about it. I can monitor things from here but if an alarm goes off, all I can do is tell you. I can't stop it."

"Keep an ear on the police banner. It's the MPs who'd get the call, but who knows what else would happen." Adam shoved his hands in his jacket pockets then yanked them out again, snapping his fingers. He unlocked the SUV and dug in the backseat.

"We'll be fine," I told her and myself. "We'll keep the line open. Just assume we're not talking to you. You're going to listen to a lot of heavy breathing, I think."

Carrie chuckled. "Oh, baby."

I watched him come up with a manila folder filled with about a dozen pieces of paper. "What's that?"

"It's part of my DODMERB exam stuff. ROTC information about the scholarships and such. It's something for me to look at while we're waiting. Anyone walking by will see me looking at military forms and will make assumptions."

I held up my phone. "I'm just going to play a game or surf the web like a normal person."

"There are cat videos waiting to be viewed," Carrie added.

I grinned, trying to hide my fear. Then I made a show of getting serious by lifting my chin and squaring my shoulders. "Okay. Let's do this."

Adam and I walked into the hospital with our heads high. I was half a step in front of him, making it look like I knew exactly where I was going. No one gave us any notice. At least, not at first. However, after we took off our jackets, it felt like every other person looked at me. It was the paranoia talking. It had to be. But it made me glad that I left the pistol back in the car.

The hospital seemed even bigger on the inside with various sections color coded by wall paint. Emergency was to our right as we entered. Its walls had a two foot stripe of red paint about five feet from the floor, running horizontally around its edges. The left side of the hallway was blank until it hit a cross hallway. Signs on the sides of these openings declared what part of the general clinic was down them: dentistry (yellow), ophthalmology (green), radiology (purple), pediatrics (blue), and so on.

I wondered where they kept the overnight patients. ICU appeared to be part of Emergency. Perhaps they were up on the second floor. I couldn't be sure and I didn't want to ask because a helpful person might try to find out exactly where the person I was looking for was—and who was that again—and everything would go wrong. I kept my wonderings to myself. I also didn't want Carrie to know she was right. Inside the hospital was a lot more confusing than I remembered it being. Then again, I always had Heather to lead me to where I needed to go.

The transition from the generally open to the public part of the hospital to the multi-level part where the specialized doctors' offices—like physical therapy—and administration lived was a sudden break into white walls, white and brown tiled floor, and many lined signs indicating where various places and doctors were. I was surprised to see a separate "women's care" facility on the third floor but grateful at the same time. It would give me a reason to be there. I also saw a sign for in-patient care pointing past the main bank of elevators. Apparently, the back half of the pizza box was for overnight and long-term patients. That was one less thing to wonder about in my chaotic brain.

While we waited for the elevator, I felt more people staring at me again. I looked around and looked at Adam. He looked as calm as ever, like he visited the hospital every day of his life. Then I realized that he probably felt at home here. It was a structured military-based facility with doctors, scientists, civilians and military all smooshed together. Just like PAR Lab had been.

The elevator doors opened and the soldier standing there stared at me for a moment before brushing by. Adam and I entered. As soon as the elevator doors closed and we were alone, I whispered to him, "Why is everyone staring at me? I'm not crazy. They are."

Adam nodded. "Yep. They totally are. It's your shirt."

I looked down, looking for a stain or a rip. "What? Why?"

"It's pink. In a military hospital. Took me a couple of minutes to figure out. Once I did..." He shrugged. "You can't miss it."

I had dressed up for the visit. More than a t-shirt anyway. I was wearing a baby pink tunic and blue jeans. Heather had gotten the shirt for me before she realized that I'm not big into pink. I hadn't wanted to hurt her feelings. I'd kept it and worn it off and on. Once the doors opened on the third floor and I looked around at the beige walls, then the few uniformed people I could see, then a doctor in a white coat, I realized that I hadn't seen any pink at all in the hospital. Not even smatterings of it as we passed by Pediatrics. It had been color-coded in blue. Adam was right. I stuck out as if I were wearing neon orange in the forest.

"Too late to do anything about that now," I muttered. "C'mon, let's find the server room."

Despite the multi-level part of the building looking like a giant rectangle from the outside, it was a labyrinth within. It took us two full rounds up and down the hallways of the third floor to understand that there were three sections in a square 'S' shape. There was a main waiting area in the middle, just outside the elevators. Then two-thirds of the S was a series of doctors' office suites with smaller waiting areas within, including physical therapy and the larger women's care suite.

The server room—or at least what we guessed was the server room—was on the other third. It was one of three non-descript doors we'd found on this part of the floor and it was the only one with a punch lock. There were no open doctor's offices nearby. This was both good and bad. Less people to see us. But less reason to be hanging around.

"Carrie, we found it," I said. I pitched my voice low but not whispering. I'd already learned that a murmur was quieter than a whisper.

"It's about time. Get a picture of the door."

I looked at Adam and he shifted towards the door with a nod. Leaning against the wall near me, he looked at his phone and started tapping on it, like he was playing a game. I smiled when he nodded at me again. I hadn't noticed him taking the picture. He was subtle about it. I guess all our practicing paid off.

For good measure, I did a quick walk by and took a picture of the keypad. I made sure there was no flash and no click of my phone. As I walked down the hallway, sending the picture to Carrie, I almost ran into a man coming around the corner. I stared at him, startled.

He was tall—really tall—with a grey beard and balding head. He wasn't dressed in a military uniform. He was dressed in the civilian tech's uniform of a buttoned up shirt and khaki pants. He had a hospital badge hanging around his neck. It read "D. Barker" under a picture of his smiling face.

He wasn't smiling now. "What are you kids doing here?" Barker emulated his namesake as he barked the question at me.

"I was looking for the bathroom. I can't find it in this place." It was the first thing that popped into my head. It wasn't a lie. I really did need a bathroom.

He scoffed an annoyed huff. "Well, maybe if you looked up from your phone, you'd see it was just around the corner." Barker pointed back the way he'd come.

I looked around the corner and was surprised to see restrooms for men and women there. "Oh."

Barker looked at Adam. "What about you?"

Adam pushed himself off the wall. "Following her." His voice had a sulky tone I'd never heard before. "She was leading the way."

I rolled my eyes and pushed past Barker, hurrying to the ladies room.

Behind me, I heard Adam mutter, "Girls."

Barker laughed. "Get used to it."

Moments later, Adam's voice came over my earpiece. "Bingo."

I didn't answer because that would've been weird. In fact, being in the restroom and using it while on the phone was really weird.

Then Adam muttered. "Well, damn."

"What? What happened?" Carrie, like me, didn't like it when things didn't go according to plan.

"Let me send this to you."

My phone vibrated with the text message. I pulled my phone out of my pocket and thumbed it open. The image of the keypad was a blob of heat. There were no neat button signatures. My heart sank. Something was wrong. This wasn't like when we tested the keypad at home. I kept silent and listened to Adam and Carrie.

"Shit." Carrie sounded distracted as she typed in the background. "Are the buttons metal?"

"Yeah. What's wrong?"

"Hold on. ... Yeah. Dammit. The infrared thing doesn't work with metal buttons."

"What do we do now?"

I didn't know who Adam's question was for. I didn't have an answer. My first thought was knocking on the server room door and bull rushing Barker, but the man was huge. Plus, there's nothing stealthy about clubbing a man in a server room. No doubt, there would be cameras and we'd be caught.

"Anyone?" Adam asked.

"Ask him out for coffee," I snapped. "I'm thinking. Carrie, if you have an idea, we're all ears."

Carrie did not respond. I didn't think she would. We didn't think this through. There was no Plan B. Now, Adam and I were stuck in a hospital with no idea how to get into a server room. I thought as hard as I could. My mind whirled and scampered and the only thing I could come up with was beating Barker over the head. Even if we pretended to work here, we wouldn't have the code to get into the room.

Maybe we could slip into a doctor's office when they went out to lunch and get to the server files that way. It couldn't be that hard as long as there weren't too many permissions set up, blocking doctors from the Project Yenmil files. *Hah.* I thought. *Fat chance of that.* But, still it was a different idea and Carrie could help. Maybe it would work. Maybe...

I jerked at the sound of someone knocking on the door. I was dressed and waiting inside the stall before I realized that I had heard the knocking over the earpiece. "What was that?"

Instead of Carrie or Adam answering, I heard Barker's muffled, and still cranky, voice. "What do you want?"

Adam had knocked on the server room door. I held my breath and waited. What the hell was he doing? I listened to them over the phone and wished I could see their faces.

"You're a tech guy. I thought I saw computers in here. Can I talk to you? I'm gonna be an ROTC cadet. I'm going to do computers for the Army."

"Um. All right. I'm in a maintenance window. I got time."

"A maintenance window?"

"Supervising a few virtual machines downloading updates. We've had bandwidth issues lately and those updates are massive."

"Wait… those computers in there are connected to the internet? In a hospital? Couldn't someone just hack into them and, like, kill a guy during surgery like in that movie… or something? I mean, that's why I'm getting into computers. To become a white hat."

Adam's voice sounded so shocked and prim, I put a hand over my mouth to keep from laughing in his ear.

Barker did laugh. "Nah, those movies are bullshit. Things don't work like that. There are dangers involved with the internet connection, but none of them involve the kind of hacking shown in the movies. You can't believe any hacking things on TV. Here, lemme show you." He paused. "You can't come in but you can look in."

"Ok. … Whoa. That looks nothing like what I thought it'd look like. Not like in the movies."

"Yeah, they're older computers but it stops the 'hackers' as you call them—mostly the hackers are actually malware, trojans, botnets. That sort of stuff. That's what we have the firewall for. See that ugly box right there on the bottom? That computer has two antivirus engines that scan the incoming and outgoing data streams for known patterns and a cloud-based zero-day protection feature. This means it uploads unknown executables into an offsite sandbox, executes it, and does a few tests before it's allowed to pass. We have a few other separate security appliances for email security and other things."

I blinked at the gibberish Barker unloaded and wondered if he was making up words and terms to impress Adam. Then again, Carrie wasn't snarking off about it. I had to trust she understood what he was saying.

"Dude, you're amazing." You could hear the hero worship in Adam's voice. "But, if things don't work like in the… I mean… Can the Army teach me to be a white hat?"

"It's not as simple as that, kid."

"Can you tell me?"

"I..."

"I got time. Please? Will you talk to me? No one will tell me the truth. You're on the inside. You know the *real* story. You can tell me what it's *really* like. Can I buy you a coffee or something, man? Please. I need to know before I sign away my life to the army."

"What about your stepsister?"

Adam made a disgusted noise. "She's going to be in the bathroom forever. Plus, she's got her doctor's appointment. I'm just hanging until she's done. She doesn't have her driver's license. I'll text her and tell her to wait in the waiting room for me. She'll be mad but whatever."

"Gotta teach her some patience. All right."

"Hold on."

My phone vibrated. I read the text message. It was to both me and Carrie. *Going dark. Will stall him. Key code is 7946. Will warn when he's coming back.*

Holy crap, Adam did it. He got the key code. I held my breath and silently counted to thirty. During that silence, I heard muffled voices and the sound of fabric rubbing against plastic. Adam must have put his earpiece in his jacket pocket. I peeked out of the ladies room. No one was there.

"Mel?"

I squeaked as Carrie's voice startled me. "Dammit. Yeah. I'm here."

"You in?"

"Not yet. Heading that way now." I took a quick breath, let it out, squared my shoulders, and walked out of the ladies room with my head held high. I walked like I belonged here and I was just headed into the server room to do a quick errand.

"Did he really just go ask the tech guy to coffee?"

"Yeah, he did. I didn't expect that. Hey, that computer stuff that Barker said, it was real?"

"Yeah. He wasn't blowing smoke, if that's what you mean."

"Good. I didn't understand a word of it."

"That's why you have me."

"I know."

I stopped at the door and punched the server room code on the keypad. There was an audible click and the door handle turned under my hand. I entered the cool room and closed the door behind me.

I was in.

CHAPTER NINE

This server room was completely different than the server room in PAR Laboratory. At the same time, it felt exactly the same.

There were eight server racks in two rows. All of them stood away from the walls to allow easy access to networking ports on both the front and back of the servers. Instead of identical sleek, black server blades, they were older gray machines, varying from one server high to the thickness of four servers in one. Fans and machines whirred, hummed and clicked. The whole room had a cobbled together feeling.

Along the two side walls were crates and shelves filled with eclectic machine parts, cords, keyboards, mice, and monitors. There was a rack against the left wall next to a door. The rack was stuffed full of boxes, wires, and computers.

It looked as if nothing was ever thrown out, just stored. Against the back wall was a single long table with four monitors, four keyboards, and six rolling office chairs. One of them was broken, listing to the side like a drunken solider. Glancing up high, I saw two dark glass camera domes—one above the door, one in the back part of the cold room.

I put my jacket back on and pulled up the hood. "Carrie, there are cameras."

"Ignore them. Keep your head down. If all goes well, no one will want to dig through the video to see you inside. Focus."

"Okay." She was right. My face was already on the cameras in here, and all of the cameras all over the hospital. I needed to do my job and get out before anyone discovered that something was wrong.

I walked to the back of the room to the computers. All of the monitors were live. One of them showed a black window with neon green text scrolling. "Old school," I muttered. Then I realized... all of the computer screens were open and unlocked. I wriggled each mouse on the table to keep them live. I didn't know how long before the sleep cycle locked them.

"We're in," I said.

"In?"

"The computers are all unlocked. From Barker's maintenance window."

"Awesome. Get me the IP address of one of the computers like I showed you. Also, check on the bottom of the keyboard for a post-it note for a password."

I pulled up a command window, typed in "ipconfig", and read her the numbers as they came up. "192.0.2.255."

"Good, good. Password?"

I picked up the keyboard I was working on. Nothing. I refused to let the hovering panic descend. Instead, I picked up each keyboard. Of course, the post-it note was on the last keyboard I looked at. There were three passwords written there. "I'm going to text them to you so there's no mistake."

I typed them in with a smile. I recognized each one:

Baby1on5

Battlest

*

Avenger8

"D. Barker is definitely a geek," I said.

"Yep," Carrie agreed. "All right. Just watch the computer screen. I'll tell you which computer to plug the USB into. Then you'll have to actually download the files."

I didn't answer. Instead, I went to the next computer over and opened the "Apollo" icon. I didn't know what I was looking for, but I had a hunch I was looking for something, anything that was familiar to me. I clicked the network file then the server called "Doctors."

Part of me wanted to know if there was a doctor named "Payne" here. I still missed Darcy. There wasn't, but I did find a subnet called "Visiting

Doctors." I clicked on it and saw a very short list. I recognized one of the names: Vandermeek.

I froze, not sure what to do. It was possible that there was more than one Doctor Vandermeek working for the military. It was more than possible, it was very likely. But the hair on my arm, and on the back of my neck, stood up. Adam recognized the name "Yenmil" and it was probably part of something Doctor Vandermeek had worked on.

"Carrie, there's a Doctor Vandermeek working here."

"Oh. I'll work on that as soon as I finish up with this. One job at a time. Okay. Find the computer named Sinclair." Her tone was distracted.

I walked over to the two columns of computers. They were sorted, mostly, by different TV series or sci-fi books: *Dune, X-Files, Battlestar Galatica, Babylon 5*, and more. As soon as I found it, I said, "Got it."

"Okay. Plug the USB thumb drive in and go back to that other computer. Once the device is recognized, drag and drop the folder I have highlighted. It'll fit. It's only 5 gig. The thumb drive is 32 gig."

I did as she said, then I asked the question I didn't want to ask. "What if this Doctor Vandermeek is Erik Vandermeek, Adam's..." I stumbled over the word, "cr-creator? And he's part of Project Yenmil?"

"We'll burn that bridge when we get to it." She still sounded distracted.

"What are you doing?"

"Finding out what this Vandermeek has on his share."

I was silent for a long moment. "Do we tell Adam?"

"No." Carrie's answer was final and did not invite discussion.

I didn't like the answer, but I had to wait until we got what we needed to satisfy my own curiosity. If it was Erik Vandermeek and not some other Doctor Vandermeek, that would unpack a whole lot of emotional baggage. I had abandonment issues because my parents died. Then my guardians died. Even my dog and my favorite nurse died. Adam's dad didn't die. He just left.

I thought about it. I couldn't even call him "Adam's dad" and be accurate. Vandermeek didn't let Adam call him anything other than "Doctor" even though he gave Adam the last name of "Erikson." Talk about a good way to mess up a kid and ensure he needs therapy. Well, that was what Doctor Giacomi was for.

I paced around the server room as I waited for the files to download. The longer I had to stay put, the more likely someone would find me here. I was sure there was more than one tech guy in a hospital this size.

Adam's voice broke my train of thought with terrible news. "I hope you two are done. I couldn't stall Doug any longer."

I hurried back to the computer. The file transfer was only 78% complete. "Just tell me where he is." I watched the numbers tick over then remembered to close down all the other files I'd opened.

80%.

"He's talking to another tech guy."

"Let me know when he gets to the elevators by the vending machines. Or looks like he's headed up here by the stairs." Barker had the lanky look of someone who took the stairs as often as he took the elevator. I needed to know when and how he headed this way.

"Okay."

"Carrie, are you going to be able to close everything on this computer, to make it look like no one was here?"

She scoffed. "Of course."

"He's getting in the elevator."

I looked at the number. 83%. "We're not going to make it."

"Lock all the computer screens and get out. We can get back in."

"How?" I tried not to panic.

"Window key and "L" at the same time." One by one I did as she said. I looked at the thumb drive file transfer. 88%. I cursed and locked the last screen. Then I hurried to the server room door and froze.

Barker was talking outside the server room. It was muffled but sounded like, "Yeah, yeah. I know. Let me check on this first."

Someone else said. "You know? How do you know?"

I needed to hide and now.

I ran to the door next to the wall rack and pulled it open. It stuck for a moment, then squealed as it let go. Subtle it was not, but there was enough room inside the little closet amongst the cables, pipes, racks, and little used cleaning supplies. Not a minute after I pulled the door closed with another one of those metallic squeals, I heard the click of the server room door unlocking. I couldn't see anything but could hear Barker and he wasn't alone.

Pressed against the closet door, I was afraid to move. Every breath seemed to cause me to shift, making something else shift in the confined space. Everything sounded like an avalanche even though I knew, logically, that was my fear speaking. I couldn't see where things were to steady myself. All I could was stand there and wait, listening.

"Everything seems to be looking good," Barker said in his deep voice. He still sounded cranky. "Ah, Christ. Starbuck's still eating RAM like crazy. I don't get it. "

"Hard reset?" the other voice asked.

"Maybe. Hold on."

I remembered the thumb drive sticking out of Sinclair and wanted to die. If they found it, we were done for. Why hadn't I grabbed it?

Because, it wasn't done loading the files. Besides, pulling a USB device out of a computer without ejecting it might damage the data.

I hated that calm, know-it-all voice even though, right now, it sounded a lot like Carrie.

"Yeah. Turn it off and give it a twenty count."

There was a pause.

"Wait a minute. That's strange."

Ohshitohshitohshit. I bit the inside of my mouth as hard as I could to keep the fear at bay. I tasted blood as I kept myself from shouting in pain. Tears sprang to my eyes and gray descended. I swallowed convulsively, my stomach doing a slow roll. I didn't know what was worse—the pain or the taste of blood.

"Mel?" It was Adam. "Do I need to come get you?"

"No," I whispered low, realizing that if I panicked, both me and Adam were in for it. "Can't talk. Shhh."

"... moved the Starbuck from her spot."

I missed the first part but, apparently, whatever was strange, it wasn't about the thumb drive sticking out of Sinclair.

"That was me." Barker's voice came close, then faded as he passed the closet. "Here he is."

"Old school."

"Yeah. Starbuck and Boomer will always be guys to me."

"I don't know. I liked the new version a lot, too."

Barker didn't answer that. Then there was silence for at least ten thousand years, before Barker said. "All right. It's booted up fine. I'll keep track of the RAM. Just note it for the AAR."

"Will do. I got to go deal with Doctor Tappard's email problem."

"I'd like to deal with something else of hers."

"You got that right."

I made a face at the dirty old men leers I could hear in their voices. Ew. Just ew.

The sound of the server room door opening and closing allowed me to relax. "Oh, geez." I bowed my head and relaxed my aching muscles. I wanted to rinse out my mouth. I wanted to be home. I wanted out of this suffocating, dusty closet.

"Mel?"

"You all right?"

Adam and Carrie. They both sounded really scared. As much as that just sucked for me, it had to have been worse for them. All they probably could hear was my panicked breathing and maybe some muffled voices. Everything else had been waiting without knowing what was going on.

"Yeah. I'm in the server room closet. I'm okay. They just left. I'm waiting for a moment to be sure they're gone. The closet door squeaks."

"Okay. When you get the thumb drive, remember to eject it first." Carrie paused. "And I got those other files, too."

"Adam," I said, wanting to keep him from asking about *those files*. "Meet me at the SUV. I'll be down as soon as I can. Ten, fifteen minutes. I've got to check something."

"You sure?" He asked, his voice doubtful.

"Yeah. I'm sure. Grab me a soda from the cafeteria?" I didn't know where the cafeteria was but there had to be one in a hospital this size. Me and Heather had never been here long enough to want to get anything to eat. Finding it would keep Adam occupied.

I opened the closet door and peeked out. It was empty. The door squealed as I pulled myself out of the closet, but less so. I doubted the closet was used for much more than a place to forget useless things. A little oil and a little working of the hinges would make the squeal go away.

"Will do."

"Thanks." I breathed a sigh of relief. In truth, I didn't think he had forgotten about *those files*. Instead, I'm pretty sure Adam had decided to deal with it at home. He didn't miss much of anything, but he did bide his time. Again, another lesson from the Lab. I should keep track of them. Some of them were useful. When he asked about *those files*, I would spill my guts. I just didn't want to do it here and now.

I hurried to the fourth computer, wiggled the mouse, and shook my head when the screen popped up, no passwords needed. Doug Barker, and the other hospital tech people, needed to have a conversation with Carrie about computer security. I ejected the USB flash drive, locked the screen again, then retrieved the drive on my way out the door.

I didn't stop to think about things. I just kept moving. Turning the wrong way, I walked down the hallway to the stairwell. I didn't want to meet Barker at the elevator. Once in the stairwell, I headed up on impulse. I wanted to see if I could find Doctor Vandermeek's office. That was the thing I was going to check out. I was going to start on the sixth floor and work my way down.

As I ran up the stairs, my heart sank. The higher I got, the dirtier and more damaged the stairs got. First, it was only cracks in the cement, then chunks of stairs were missing. By the time I got to the sixth floor, I had to stick close to the wall to make sure I didn't fall. The railing was gone. The military must have run out of money to keep the stairs up. Either the sixth floor was abandoned or these stairs were one heck of a code violation.

I was surprised to find the sixth floor as bright and as clean as the third floor. Shaking my head, I figured I'd tell Heather when she got home or I'd put an anonymous complaint in to whomever takes care of things like hospital stairwells. Broken stairs are a hazard at the best of times and lethal in the worst.

Walking down the hallway, I saw that it wasn't set up like the third floor was. Instead of an "S" shape, it was more like a square eight: small offices on the outer walls with group offices and meeting rooms on the inner rings. It was much quieter up here, too. Probably because it was a weekend.

I started on the outer ring. Somehow, I couldn't see the man who created Adam, then abandoned him, sharing an office with anyone. From what little Adam told me, Doctor Erik Vandermeek was smart, vain, and arrogant. He would want, maybe even need, his own space. Especially if he was working on something he wanted to keep secret.

I tried to be subtle. Weekend or not, a number of the offices were still occupied by doctors and administrators—both in uniform and not—and my pink shirt attracted their attention. It was too hot outside of the server room to keep my black jacket on. All I could do was put on my best "I'm supposed to be here" look and keep going.

"Sprite okay?" Adam asked.

The question startled me. I wasn't used to having the phone on in my ear all the time. Every time we had a long pause, I forgot I was connected. Every time either Adam or Carrie spoke up, it was all I could do to keep from flailing in surprise. "Yeah." I kept my voice low. I didn't want people thinking I was talking to myself.

"Excuse me. Can I help you?"

I turned, cold with fear, at the voice right behind me. A small Asian woman with short curly hair gazed at me with her head cocked. She had a doctor's coat on and a name tag with "Doctor Kawai."

"I, uh, I'm sorry." I didn't know why I apologized. It was instinct. "I'm looking for Doctor Vandermeek." I saw her lip curl with distaste then disappeared into that pleasant neutral expression all doctors seem to have mastered. I guessed he wasn't the most-liked guy around. "I need to talk to him."

"Does he know you're here?"

I shook my head and stuck partly to the truth. "No. But I need to talk to him."

Doctor Kawai peered at me. "Are you in trouble? Do you need help?"

"Boy-howdy, does she ever need help," Carrie muttered in my ear.

I bit my tongue to keep from laughing and shook my head.

I guess she believed me. Doctor Kawai pointed in the direction I was going. "Around the corner, two offices down on the left."

I smiled. "Thank you so much." I turned and walked away fast as I could without running.

"Doctor Vandermeek?" Adam asked.

Crap and double crap. "I'm sorry, Adam," I murmured low, keeping my head down. "I didn't want to tell you until I knew for sure. It's possible he isn't your Doctor Vandermeek." I turned the corner and saw the name on the door: Doctor Erik Vandermeek.

Or maybe he was exactly who I thought it might be.

"Dad?" Adam asked, his voice was full of wonder and hope. "Holy shit, my dad is here."

"We don't know that for sure," Carrie said, trying to mollify him. "We're still checking."

"No! He's right here, walking out of the cafeteria."

CHAPTER TEN

"Are you sure, Adam? Really, really sure?" Carrie's voice had taken on the careful, calm tone that is used to sooth upset animals and kids. "It's been more than eight years since you've seen him."

"It's him. I recognized his walk. He was always walking away from me. It's Doctor Vandermeek."

I didn't say anything. I didn't know what to say. It was like listening to a tense podcast where something terrible was about to happen. Carrie and Adam had been pseudo-siblings and friends long before I came into the picture. It was best if I kept my mouth shut. Besides, I had other things to investigate. I stepped to Doctor Vandermeek's office door.

It was unlocked.

I slipped in, closed the door behind me, and lowered the office shade. It was a small office crammed full of books, binders, folders, and stacks of papers. But it was clean and semi-organized. It looked a little like someone who had just moved in and shoved all their stuff on every available surface and had been putting things in their correct place as time allowed. The desk, in the back left corner, faced the outer window. There were two filing cabinets to the right and hanging shelves on both side walls.

I went to the desk and looked at it. Standard computer set up with two monitors. Stacks of folders overflowing the file basket, papers spread out with incomprehensible titles like: "Analysis and Composition of Myelin Protein Zero" and "The Peripheral Myelin Protein Gene PMP-22 Problem." None of it made any sense to me.

I had no fear of Vandermeek showing up unannounced. Adam was following the man he thought of as "Dad." The word poked at me, breaking open the scab of grief at the death of my parents that would never heal. My mind kept wanting to follow that train of thought, to remember my parents and all I'd lost.

I shoved all that aside and looked around the office while Adam and Carrie continued to talk in my head.

"I want to talk to him."

"Don't. We're not ready. You're not ready."

"He's heading towards the clinic. What if he leaves? What if I don't see him again."

"You'll see him. We know he works at the hospital."

"How do we know?"

I had to answer Adam's desperate question. "I'm standing in his office right now." I looked around and found a picture of Doctor Vandermeek with two older people I assumed were his parents. "I'm looking at a picture of a white man with black hair and pale skin. He has light colored eyes." I picked up the framed picture and squinted at it. "I can't tell for sure but I think they are blue."

Adam didn't answer me at first. Then he asked. "Is the man in the picture wearing jewelry?"

"Yes." I tilted my head for a better look. "Class ring on his right hand. Silver with a green stone. Thin silver band bracelet on his left wrist. It's tight. I don't think he could get it off if it doesn't have a clasp."

I put the framed picture back on the desk in the same place it had been. I tried to shift it to the same angle. I didn't really want Vandermeek knowing anyone had gone through his office. Not that I thought he'd notice.

"That's him. I'm not going to lose him. Not again."

"Adam, think about this. He left you. What do you think will happen if you suddenly get in his face?"

"I just want to talk to him. He owes me that much. He didn't say goodbye. He was just gone and he let other people tell me that he was gone. He owes me."

I stopped listening and sucked in a breath as something caught my eye. Sticking out one of the many folders on the desk was the corner of a picture. In this picture, I saw the bottom half of Adam's leg and his ugly black and orange high top sneakers. I slid the entire folder out from its spot in the stack and opened it.

On top of a small stack of paper, more than a dozen pictures of me, Adam, and Carrie stared up at me. I scanned the pictures. All of them were after we'd lived in Richland for a while. There was a picture of Adam carrying stuff from the Gerty's Green Thumb to the SUV. Another one was of me and Adam sitting in The Ugly Mug, the one coffee shop in the little shopping center that pretended to be a strip mall. One was of Carrie at Best Buy. Most of the pictures were of Adam. The last picture was our house.

"He knows." My voice cut across the argument Adam and Carrie were having. "He *knows*. He's got pictures of all of us. He's got a picture of our house."

"What?" Carrie's voice was small and shocked.

"I'm holding the pictures in my hand right now. Pictures of us. You, Adam, me. Our house. Us at Gerty's and The Ugly Mug. Vandermeek knows we're here. He's known for a while. None of Heather though."

I shoved all of the pictures back into the folder with the papers, closed it, and held it close. I wasn't letting go of this for anything. I needed more time to look at the pictures and to read whatever else was in the file.

"He knows I'm here? He knows where I live?" Adam's voice, though soft, was full of fury. "He knows and he didn't even try to contact me? He can't get away with this."

"What are you doing?"

Adam didn't answer Carrie's question and I knew bad things were coming. I hurried out of Vandermeek's office, not caring that he would know that someone had been there. He'd been spying on us—all of us—and that was unforgivable.

As I ran for the stairwell, Adam yelled "VANDERMEEK!" in my ear. I yelped in pain and pulled the earpiece from my ear. I heard another shouted "Vandermeek!" as I shoved the stairwell door open and thanked the stars above that this side's stairwell was in good order. I paused to put the earpiece back in, steeling myself for another shout, and bolted down the stairs at a dead run.

"Mel, what is he doing?"

"I don't know," I panted out as I took the next set of stairs. "I'm not there."

"You've got to stop—"

Carrie shut up as an unfamiliar voice said, "I was wondering how long it would take you to get the courage to confront me."

"You knew I was here?"

I couldn't tell if Adam's question referred to us at the hospital or us living in Missouri. I put a burst of speed on as I ran down the stairs, but not so fast that I couldn't keep up with what was being said or lose my balance and fall on my face.

"Of course I knew. You're one of my successes. I never didn't know where you were. I always kept track of how you progressed."

I didn't like the tone of Vandermeek's voice. It was slimy, like a used car salesman.

"Why didn't you come see me? Why didn't you just ask me?"

Adam sounded so hurt that I wanted to punch Vandermeek's face in for him. I knew Adam had issues but didn't realize just how hurt he'd been. I should've, but I didn't. Too wrapped up in my own problems, my own grief.

"I wasn't ready. Now I am. Take him."

"What? Wait! Lemme go!"

Oh fuck. I jumped down the last of the stairs and slammed out the side exit of the hospital. I sprinted around the building and ran for the parking lot as fast as I could. All the while, I listened to Carrie shout, "Don't let them take your phone. Keep it on." as I heard Adam fight and struggle. Then I stopped hearing him.

As I reached the parking lot, I watched a black SUV, that could be the twin to Heather's, drive away from the sidewalk in front of me. I sped up and read the license plate aloud, panting as I did. "464-XWF." I stopped running and repeated myself as I watched the SUV turn the corner. "464-XWF. 464-XWF. The plates. Black SUV. Took him. Write it down."

"464-XWF," Carrie repeated.

I gulped in air as I walked back to the spot where I saw the SUV pull away from the curb. I found Adam's earpiece. It was still on. "They took him. I've got his earpiece. I don't know if they threw it away or if he lost it when he was fighting with them." I turned it off and shoved it into my jacket pocket.

"They took him?" Carrie sounded incredulous and on the edge of hysteria. "Vandermeek actually kidnapped Adam?"

"I know. It sounds crazy but, yeah, he did. There's no way I can catch up to them."

"Don't try. Calm. Calm. Come home."

I didn't know who she was trying to calm down. I returned to the car and was really glad Heather had one of those 'locked out of the car' magnetized boxes under the front bumper. I hunkered down and retrieved it. "Also, Vandermeek has been spying on us. All of us. The pictures prove it." I put the folder on the passenger seat as I got into the SUV. "I've got them and everything else in that folder."

"I can't believe it."

I turned on the GPS and set it for home. In the back of my mind, I added yet another mental note to my growing list. This one was to get familiar with the area because I didn't actually know how to get home from the base without the GPS device and that just wouldn't do. Technology always failed at the worst time because that's when you noticed it failing.

"I don't care if you can't believe it. It just happened. Look up those plates and see who they belong to, yeah? Get me an address or something." With an effort, I softened my voice. "Please?" I didn't need to make an enemy of the one person who could help me find Adam. Not that I thought she wouldn't help me.

"All right. Come home first. I want to see those pictures and whatever else you found."

"Okay." I didn't argue with her. I needed to see how she was doing with her leg. I needed her to figure out why Vandermeek would kidnap Adam instead of just coming by for a visit. There were too many questions and no answers.

I knew I'd been sharp with Carrie, but I'd just lost the only brother I'd ever had and I wanted to get him back. Still, I didn't let my emotions show in my driving. I drove like I was teaching a driving class, obeying all of the rules of the road until I got off base. Then I sped up.

We didn't say anything for a good ten minutes. I couldn't stand the silence. "I'm sorry. I didn't mean to yell."

"It's cool. Not mad. Just researching."

I sighed in relief. I owed her one for that. Then, I asked her the biggest question on my mind. "Carrie… you don't think this whole package thing was to get me and Adam to the hospital, do you?"

She didn't say anything for a long, long time. Finally, she said, "No. I don't think so. Vandermeek didn't know Heather when she was in Europe, did he? I mean, he was in the Lab and then…"

"Then, who knows? Heather got ratted out about three years ago. There's an overlap period."

"No. That doesn't make sense. If Heather knew Vandermeek, she would've told us, wouldn't she? Or, at least, told Adam. And he would've told me. You know? As part of the trust building exercises we've been doing."

I wasn't sure. I didn't like the fact that Carrie was questioning whether or not we could trust Heather. I didn't like the direction that would take us. If we couldn't trust our guardian and adopted mom, who could we trust?

I shook my head. I knew I could trust Heather, even though she once told me that every person working for the State Department, or any agency with a three letter acronym, always had secrets. Always. She had admitted to keeping things from me. Mostly because I didn't need to know them. They didn't affect us. Now, I wasn't so sure.

I didn't say any of this. Instead, I said, "Yeah. I guess. I just can't get over…" My phone chirped its low battery signal at me. "Well, crap. Phone dying."

"It's the Blu-tooth. It's why I never keep mine on."

"Well, that and we've just spent the last hour and a half on the phone."

"That would do it."

"If we get cut off, I'm on my way now." I looked at the GPS for reference. "ETA in twenty-five minutes."

Carrie didn't answer. Instead, she sucked in a breath that was almost a gasp.

"Carrie? Are you okay? Are you hurt? Carrie?"

"Mel, I think you'd better hurry. There's someone snooping outside the house."

My heart sped up and I pushed the pedal until I was ten miles over the speed limit. I wasn't comfortable going any faster. If Officer Chapman came along, he was just going to have to follow me to the house. I wasn't stopping for anyone.

"Hang up and call the police."

"I can't. Bullet wound."

"Screw the bullet wound. Heather and David will sort things out. They can't do that if you're dead."

If Carrie answered me, I didn't hear it. My phone gave another chirp and shut down.

CHAPTER ELEVEN

For the next twenty minutes, I sped down the highway, terrified for Carrie, terrified for Adam, terrified for myself. The only thing that kept me from going any crazier than I already was, was the knowledge that I could deal with one of my fears first: I was in control of my driving. Yes, I was driving fast. As fast as I could go without having an accident. I could control that. Get home as fast as possible and see what we will see.

Unfortunately, while I drove a straight highway, it was easy for my mind to chase itself into knots, wondering who was snooping around the house. We lived on nine acres in the middle of farmland. We had one neighbor we'd only seen a few times. Otherwise, the only people who came by were the postman and the FedEx guy. In this area, we liked to keep ourselves to ourselves.

The people I could think of were the person who dropped off the manila envelope and the brown haired guy who'd shot at us at the castle. Maybe the shooter had come back to finish the job. I didn't think they were the same person. I didn't think "Elijah" would shoot at two teenage girls. At least, I hoped that Heather hadn't worked with someone like that in her past.

As I turned onto the frontage road, I abandoned my questions and focused on getting home. Carrie had better be all right or there was going to be hell to pay. I'd killed before. I'd do it again.

Part of my mind put a black mark next to that last thought. I knew I needed to unpack it and examine what I really meant and why it didn't disturb me as much as I thought it should. I stopped thinking as I pulled up my driveway. Thinking was done. I needed to save Carrie.

I parked in front, not willing to wait for the garage door to open. I grabbed the file of papers and pictures as I slid from the SUV and ran for the front door. Punching in the key combination, I plotted out my next moves: folder on the entry table, grab Mister Bat, and find Carrie.

What I actually did was put the folder down, grab Mister Bat, then stop and listen. I listened hard. The house had an occupied feel to it. Someone was still here. Hopefully Carrie and no bad guys. I closed the front door with a near silent click then stalked through the house, listening, and trying to sense where people were.

There was a small cry of pain from the dojo below.

I sprinted for the basement stairs, yelling, "Carrie! Carrie!" As I burst into the dojo, I saw three things: Carrie lying on the mats, a gray haired person leaned over her, and blood. Lots of blood.

I rushed forward, Mister Bat held high, shouting, "Get away from her, you bastard! Or I'm going to knock you into next Tuesday!"

At the same time, Carrie raised a hand, "Mel, no!"

The person didn't move. But she did say, "Is that any way to be neighborly?"

I lowered my bat as I recognized her. "Mrs. Palmer?"

Now that I was closer, I could see her… and see that she was kneeling next to Carrie because she was sewing up Carrie's leg. Instead of a small bullet hole, Carrie's calf now had a four inch gash that was mostly sewn closed with black thread. Next to them was a pile of bloody gauze wrappings, a paper plate with a bullet on it, a couple of bloody medical tools—scalpel, forceps, tweezers—an open bottle of disinfecting alcohol, and a pair of scissors that Mrs. Palmer used to snip off the black thread. Next to all that was our large medical kit. It needed to be restocked as soon as possible.

"This is going to hurt," Mrs. Palmer said as she lifted the bottle of alcohol.

Carrie stuffed the towel she was holding back in her mouth, then screamed a muffled scream through cloth and gritted teeth.

"What are you doing here?" I couldn't get my mind around it. Mrs. Palmer was almost a stranger. I couldn't believe it, even as I watched her sew up Carrie's leg. The possibility of something like this never entered my mind.

Mrs. Palmer cleaned blood off of Carrie's leg with a practiced hand. Then she wiped her own hands clean before she went to work bandaging up the surgery wound. "Well, I just dug a bullet out of your sister's leg. No, she wouldn't tell me how she got it, but I've worked in enough trauma wards to know that nothing good ever came of a bullet left in the body."

Her gentle, aged hands lifted Carrie's calf to wrap the whole thing in a medical bandage, and then an ace bandage, as she spoke. "Now, I don't know what you kids have gotten yourselves into but I'm a big believer in not sticking my nose in places it don't belong. But, your adopted momma asked me to keep half an eye on the house while she was gone and that's what I was doing."

When Mrs. Palmer was satisfied with her work, she tapped Carrie on the thigh. "You can sit up. Carefully." She looked over her shoulder at me. "Get me a trash bag, would you?"

I couldn't not obey. Her quiet assurance and words had command of the room and I knew it. I hurried into the small half-bath and dug out a fresh trash bag from under the sink. While I did so, Mrs. Palmer continued to talk.

"I've been expecting you three to have a party. Nothing too crazy, but a party nonetheless. You haven't had one. It's been quiet. Too quiet to a mother's senses. It wasn't normal."

I came out of the bathroom wondering what the heck we were going to tell her. I decided to keep my big, fat mouth shut. I had no idea what Carrie had said before I got here. I handed Mrs. Palmer the trash bag.

Mrs. Palmer accepted it and gave me a frank look. "But you three aren't like normal teenagers, are you? You've been through some rough times, I warrant." She started cleaning up the results of her impromptu surgery and let the silence grow.

Carrie and I exchanged a look. I shrugged. I didn't know what to say. I gestured to Carrie. She had been here from the beginning. She was going to have to lead this one.

"We..." Carrie started, then stopped.

The old woman shook her head. "It's all right. I don't need to know unless you think I need to know." She gave Carrie a firm look. "Now, no weight on that leg for at least a couple of days. Get that brother of yours to..." She paused at the panicked glance Carrie threw me.

"Ah... There's something going on with the boy. All right. Well, either you'll figure it out or you'll ask for help. In any case, use the crutches. Keep your leg elevated. When your momma gets home, you get her to take you to whichever doctor you feel safest going to."

She got up and handed me the now full trash bag. I looked at where she'd been kneeling. The place was spotless. No one could tell that she'd just cut open Carrie's calf and pulled a bullet out of her.

Mrs. Palmer gazed at me, watching my face. "The bullet, a .22, is in the bag. Good thing, too. Anything bigger would've done a lot more damage to the leg. I don't know if you have a reason to keep the bullet or not. If you do, you can dig it out. I gave Carrie some oxycotin and the local to her leg will wear off in about an hour. She needs food, liquids, and sleep. You need to make sure this happens. Got it?"

I nodded. "Yes, ma'am."

She continued to gaze at me. "Whatever you kids have gotten yourselves into… I'm not going to ask… but if you need help, I'm across the way. You just have to ask. I won't say anymore. But, I am going tell your momma about this when she gets home. I want us to have an understanding."

"Yes, ma'am." I glanced at Carrie.

She gave me a weak smile. "We understand."

Mrs. Palmer nodded to herself. "I'll see myself out. Good luck with what you're dealing with." With that, she headed up the dojo stairs.

Carrie and I listened to her walk across the house then heard the front door close with a firm click. I turned to Carrie as I put the trash bag on the floor next to me. I wasn't willing to toss everything away. That bullet was going to be important. It was evidence. "What the hell happened?"

"Give me the crutches, would you?" Carrie pointed to the stairs. The crutches were leaned up against the wall. I did as she asked. "After your phone cut off, Mrs. Palmer knocked on the front door. I realized she wasn't snooping in a bad way."

"But she was snooping." I followed Carrie as she made her way to the stairs with slow, precise steps and started up them.

"Yes. In any case, I couldn't not let her inside. Couldn't hide the pain I was in. She insisted on looking at me. Did you know she was once part of Doctors Without Borders? That woman's got some history on her."

"No, I didn't know. But I think, after all this is done, I'll see if maybe she can teach me some of the medical stuff she knows." I paused and directed Carrie to the living room. "In the comfy chair," I ordered. "Leg up. Also, I've got stuff to show you." She didn't argue with me. That was a clue as to how much she still hurt or was drugged. "I'll go get it."

Carrie grabbed my arm. "Get me Khalessi?"

I nodded.

"And more painkillers?"

I nodded again.

"And a drink?"

I smiled. I could see where this was going.

She smiled back. "And a cabana boy? Or girl? I'm not picky."

"I'll see what we've got in stock."

I turned away, then stopped. I was still carrying Mister Bat. I didn't want to put him down but I didn't have enough hands. I leaned him against the door frame as a compromise. The house was locked and the one person who might have been a threat turned out to be a savior. Just thinking about it set my head spinning. When all was said and done, I was going to see if Mrs. Palmer would tell me a few stories. I bet she had some good ones.

By the time I got back with everything Carrie wanted, plus a few extra things, Carrie looked better than she had. She was bright-eyed, alert, and no longer had that gray-ish undertone. I was surprised. It showed in my face.

"The bullet had really been hurting me. It doesn't hurt like that anymore. I mean, it still hurts, but it doesn't hurt-hurt." She flapped a hand at me. "You know what I mean."

"You sure that's not the oxycotin talking?" I handed her Khalessi, a can of Sprite, and a sheathed Smith & Wesson M&P 9mm pistol, 11 rounds. It was just like the pistol I used. She liked this one better because it had a smaller custom grip.

"I'm sure." She hefted the pistol. "Loaded?"

I nodded as I plugged my phone into the power strip on the table next to the comfy chair. "Loaded and ready." While I watched, Carrie took the time to look at the magazine and to open the chamber before she set the pistol aside—ready but with the safety on.

"Okay." She opened her laptop. "What do you have for me?"

"Scary stuff." I dropped the folder of papers and pictures in her lap. "What do you have for me?"

Carrie glanced at her computer. There was a map showing with a moving red dot. "Adam hasn't stopped moving yet." She opened the folder and sucked in a breath at a picture of her and Adam in the grocery store. One by one, she looked through the pictures. "None of these are more than two months old. You got your black jacket in late November. Same time Adam got the world's ugliest shoes

I nodded. "That was my guess. Someone has been watching us for two months. And we didn't notice. Not them following or taking pictures. I don't know if that's because Heather wasn't with us or what. But why would Vandermeek do this? Why wouldn't he just come talk to Adam. I mean, most of these are of him. Doesn't that say something about his feelings for Adam?"

Carrie pushed the pictures aside and picked up the papers. I looked over her shoulder and saw what I'd been avoiding. There were notes about when and where we'd been. The fact that we went grocery shopping on Wednesdays. That Carrie and I got our hair done at Hair Designs. That Adam had an open account at Gerty's Green Thumb. That we all went shooting on Thursdays at the local range.

The more I read, the sicker I felt. I shifted away. Someone… no, Doctor Vandermeek… had been spying on us for months and we hadn't noticed. *Heather* hadn't noticed. Had she? At least some of these times, Heather had been with us and she hadn't seen anyone taking pictures of us. That meant either she knew about it or the photographer was really sneaky.

"I think we need to call Sadie."

I jerked back so I could look her in the face. Carrie flinched away from my expression. I worked to smooth whatever was there into something more normal and less angry. "You can call her if you want. But she's not going to be able to help Adam. Not in time." I looked at her computer. "As soon as he stops moving, I'm gone. I'm going to go get him and bring him home. This is my fault."

She shook her head. "It's mine. I insisted."

"It's both our faults. You insisted. I wanted to go. But, worse, I didn't follow my own rules. I split us up when we should've gotten back together. I told him to go ahead. I kept why to myself. I messed up."

"Maybe. Or, maybe both of you would be in the back of that SUV right now. Remember… there's a report on you here, too." She shuffled papers until she came up with the one that had my name on it. She offered it to me.

I thought about that for a moment, ignoring the paper. I straightened and pulled the thumb drive out of my jeans pocket. "Maybe. Either way, I'm going to go get him. I promised that I'd always have his back. I'm not going to break my promise. Not to him. Not to you. You need to see what's on this flash drive. See if it's linked to Doctor Vandermeek."

Her computer binged as she took the thumb drive. "He's stopped. He's been in the same place for more than five minutes now."

I moved so I could see her computer again. The dot wasn't moving. It was next to the Gasconade River. "Where are they?"

Carrie frowned at the computer, moved the map around, and zoomed in on the area. "Doesn't look like it's above ground. Ah, I'm not surprised. It's near the Cave Restaurant and Resort off of Rochester Road. Underground is a good place to hide someone." She typed some more. "It's about thirty minutes away. Maybe a little more in traffic. I'll text you the address."

"Is it in the Cave Restaurant?"

"No. I don't think so. It's a bit too far away. Unless they have all kinds of tunnels off that place no one is talking about." She pulled up a website. "Also, both the restaurant and resort are closed for the season. A really good place to hide someone."

"All right. That's where I'm starting. I'll move out from there."

"Keep your phone plugged in. I'll let you know if he moves. I can get you close but not exact. If he's underground, you may have to backtrack and find a tunnel entrance."

I picked up Mister Bat, my phone, and its charger. "Okay. I'm gonna bring him home. Promise."

"Mel?"

I stopped. "Yeah?"

"Be careful." She looked tired and scared.

I probably looked the same way. "I will." I did a bit of quick mental calculation, then said, "If you don't hear from us in three hours, call Sadie. She's our cavalry. You be careful, too. I've got to have my home base to come back to."

Carrie looked back at the red dot on her computer screen. "All right. I'll be here and on alert." She touched the pistol without looking at it. "I'm ready if anything happens here."

I should have told her to call Sadie as soon as I left. That would've stopped a whole lot of pain that was yet to come. Wishes and fishes and all that jazz.

THE CAVES

CHAPTER TWELVE

I drove in silence with my phone charging. Carrie and I were on the phone with each other but we didn't talk. She searched through the files I'd brought her and the ones she'd downloaded to find anything that could help us. I thought long thoughts about what could be happening to Adam, and I also made sure I didn't get into an accident or pulled over. The main reason we stayed connected was to make sure I was headed in the right direction. If Adam was moved, Carrie would tell me and I'd follow her instructions. She was my navigator in this.

As I drove, I wracked my brain, trying to remember everything Adam had actually said about Doctor Vandermeek. The first time we'd talked about him was in the kitchen area of PAR Laboratory.

"It's okay," Adam said. "Ask what you want to ask. It'll be easier that way. Carrie's got the right of it in that regard."

I bowed my head and watched the hot pocket turn in the microwave. "That obvious, huh?" I saw him shrug out of the corner of my eye.

"Anomalies are always interesting."

The way he spoke reminded me of the doctors and scientists I'd visited. I guess when you lived around them all your life, you emulated what you heard. "What's it like being genetically perfect? I mean... how...?"

"Like? I don't know. I'm never sick. My physicals are well above average." He took a bite of his hot pocket and paused. "As for how, Doctor Erik Vandermeek broke some laws, put together the exact genetic makeup of what should constitute

a perfect human, grew me in an artificial womb, and birthed me at the nine month mark. I honestly don't know any other way to be than me."

I pulled my own hot pocket from the microwave and sat down, freeing it from the cooking sleeve. "Did you grow up here? In PAR Lab?"

"Yep. I've had a bunch of different caretakers but, Lakshmi – Doctor Gowda – has been my most consistent parent, I guess you could say."

"What happened to Doctor Vandermeek?"

He furrowed his brow for a moment, then smoothed his face into something neutral again. "He left when I was eight. I don't know if he left willingly or not. I think yes. He called me Adam Erikson. He didn't give me his last name. Never let me call him 'Dad' or 'Father.' I think..." Adam shrugged, "it was because he was white and I'm not."

From that first conversation, I knew that Doctor Vandermeek wasn't a good guy despite Adam's love of the man. He was the type to treat people like things or resources instead of people. He was willing to break the law. This afternoon proved that again. Also, he was probably racist on top of everything else because he gave Adam the last name of "Erikson" but wouldn't let his creation call him anything other than Doctor Vandermeek.

At the same time, he was proud enough of his creation that it didn't make sense that he'd abandoned Adam eight years ago. I thought about a conversation I'd had with Adam in the kitchen back in December.

Adam stared at the chicken noodle soup in his bowl, not eating.

"Promise, it's not poisoned," I said as I joined him at the table with my own bowl. "It's not even homemade. Just canned." I slurped the broth, sucking a noodle in after. "See?"

"It's not that." He gave me a distracted smile as he began to eat. "I was just thinking about my... about Doctor Vandermeek. The last real conversation we had was over a bowl of chicken noodle soup. Not the canned kind. He'd made it. He was an amazing cook when he took the time. I guess most scientists are." He stirred the soup. "I thought he was a wizard."

I didn't say anything. I took another mouthful of the soup. He wanted to talk about things. I just wanted to eat. But this was one of those things Doctor Giacomi and I had talked about: I needed to be more aware of my surroundings and the people in them. Especially their needs.

She wanted me to listen to Carrie and Adam. They would want to talk about stuff – probably about their pasts. To let it go. The best thing I could do was listen, even when I didn't want to. That way, I would learn that I wasn't as alone as I sometimes felt.

That's what I did now. I listened and made sure he saw I was listening.

"We ate together in his quarters. That didn't happen often. I remember he said to me, "I've got big plans for you, my boy. Big plans. We're going to change the world. We're going to make a new world. A better world." The whole time, he waved and pointed his soup spoon at me." Adam gestured with his spoon, mimicking the motions Doctor Vandermeek had made. ""We're going to change the world." But then he left. I don't know why, and no one would tell me anything other than he had important work to do and I couldn't be with him."

I continued to eat, waiting for Adam to say more. He didn't. He brooded over his soup, scooping up spoonfuls then dribbling them back into the bowl.

"Did you ever get the impression that people lied to you about him?" I'm not sure why I asked the question. It just felt right, like having hold of the universal pokey stick to poke what needed poking.

Adam flicked a glance at me then focused on his soup again. "Yeah. I did. A lot of times, after they told me he was doing something important, they would look at each other. I recognized that look as confirming with each other that the story told was the agreed upon story. Even Lakshmi would cut her eyes away from me when I asked about him. Sometimes I think, maybe, he did something really bad and they sent him away."

"Really bad?" I gestured to him.

Adam shook his head. "Nah. Not me. Or to me. He'd been pardoned by someone important for breaking the laws with me. At least, that's what I think happened. Not that anyone in the public found out. It was a behind-the-scenes thing. It always made me wonder that if he had been sent away, what was worse than breaking the laws of nature?"

He put his spoon down. "But, whether or not they sent him away, I think he wanted to go. I think he had other things on his mind. Other projects. He was proud of me but I wasn't enough. I don't know why I wasn't good enough. I don't know what's wrong with me." Adam paused and looked at me, pain naked on his face. "He didn't even say goodbye."

I pondered the idea of "breaking the laws of nature." I didn't consider Adam something immoral or abnormal. He was stronger and faster than the average guy, but so were Olympic athletes. He didn't ever get sick, even when the rest of us all came down with something. He was smart. I shrugged to myself. Created or not, Adam was just another teen with a whole lot of baggage. He was also a guy in trouble because a man he loved as a father—who didn't love Adam back—had used that against him.. That was the worst cut of all.

I pulled my focus to the present and my driving as the GPS had me turn right onto Rochester Road—which seemed to be not much more than the local name for Highway W. The Cave Restaurant and Resort was less than half a mile away. With trees—mostly skeletal but some with the beginnings of new growth—crowded around the road and the river to my left, I realized that I hadn't seen another car in ages. I felt very much alone.

"Okay. I'm..." The rest of what I was going to say was cut off by Carrie's yelp of surprise. I tried to stifle a giggle. That giggle turned into a laugh as I made my way to the parking lot. I was glad that I wasn't the only one startled by the voices in my head.

"Not funny," Carrie grumbled.

"It kinda is. You laughed when you scared me. In any case, I'm almost there. It looks like the only place to park is going to be at the resort."

"Well, Adam hasn't moved. He's about a quarter mile from where you are. I had hoped he'd be in the closed down resort but it doesn't look like it." As I pulled into a parking spot, Carrie continued, "It looks like you drove right by him. Practically on top of him."

"I think I would've seen that."

"I know. I'm just saying that the GPS is close but not close enough and you're going to have to hunt around for an entrance."

"Right. I've got the coordinates. I'll use my phone. But once I get underground, don't expect me to stay connected. In fact, I think I'd rather hang up and focus and save my battery. I want to have enough power to call you back when I've got him."

Carrie was quiet for a moment. "All right. We both have work to do."

I know she didn't like the idea of not being in contact but it was safer for me not to be distracted by real voices in my head. "If you don't hear from me in two and a half hours, things have gone horribly, horribly wrong."

"Okay. Stay safe."

"You, too."

I waited until Carrie disconnected the call. I didn't want to feel like I was alone but I did. Mostly because it was true. Adam had only me to depend on right now. Worse, I was back in horror-movie country—going into unknown territory against an unknown number of bad guys to save my brother by myself. I leaned across to the glove box and pulled out the 9mm pistol I'd left there. I checked it for ammo. It was still full. After clipping the holster to my belt I grabbed Mister Bat and slid out of the SUV. It was time to get Adam back.

If I could find him, that is.

I glanced at the phone. He—*or just his phone,* my mind warned—was southwest of me. If he was underground, the entrance was probably down by the water. I walked towards the edge of the parking lot, the sun high overhead. It was pretty but still cold.

Something shiny on the edge of the lot to the right caught my eye. As I walked over to there, I hurried my steps. I recognized what it was: the SUV car keys with the large silver "H" keychain I'd bought Heather with my first government allowance—excuse me, stipend—she had negotiated for me. My idea of retail therapy is to buy stuff for other people to make them happy. She'd used it ever since.

I picked them up and looked around. There were only two ways the keychain could've gotten here: they were thrown by the bad guys or dropped by Adam. After shoving them into my purse, I peered into the forest from the edge of the asphalt and knew that Adam had dropped them on purpose. He knew me. He knew Carrie. He knew… he *trusted*… that we would come for him.

He left a trail in the forest that a blind person could follow. I mean that literally. After a massive flattening of the loamy ground, there were clear marks that someone had been walking the deer trail: broken branches, heavy foot falls, even a couple of buttons from a shirt. I couldn't remember what Adam had been wearing, but I bet it included a button-up shirt. He'd even managed to scuff arrow marks into the dirt with a dragged foot for the line and a stomped foot impression for the arrow.

In other words, he did everything wrong he could think of in counter to what Heather had begun to teach us about tracking game and hiding our own trails. Looking at the many footmarks, I don't think he needed to do as much as he'd done. None of the footfalls looked like they'd attempted to hide their trail. None of them looked down as far as I could tell. Whoever was behind Adam had walked on his arrows without a pause.

This told me one of two things: First, none of the people with Adam were experienced in the woods. Second, they didn't care enough to hide their tracks. This second idea scared me. It meant either they weren't going to be here long or they were confident in their security.

I stopped at an area where a scuffle had taken place and shoved the phone into my purse. I'm not sure why, considering the trail markers but the struggle made someone bleed. I hunkered down and touched the blood smear on a leaf. It was dry. I shivered and wondered whose blood it was.

From where I was, I could see down the trail back the way I'd come. I looked in the direction the deer trail went and saw that it didn't look anything like what I'd been following. I frowned and stood, looking around. From what I could tell, the group disappeared from the forest right where I was.

"No one just disappears in a forest," I muttered, then winced at the loud sound of my voice in my ears. I walked about ten feet back down the trail and stared at the struggle area. To the right were trees, fallen leaves, some plants. To the left was the same with the exception of a larger tree broken off at about the seven foot mark.

The more I looked at the broken tree, the more I realized that it didn't fit into the surrounding forest. It had the correct coloration but not the correct bark. I walked closer and saw a hole in the wood that should have been a tree knot but was just black. All of a sudden, like one of those 3D pictures coming into alignment, I realized what I was looking at: not a tree but a hunting blind.

CHAPTER THIRTEEN

It was one of the best hunting blinds I'd ever seen—and I'd seen a lot of them in Onida. The largest as well. Four grown men could stand or sit in perfect comfort without crowding each other. As I walked around it, looking for the entrance, I saw more and more covered peepholes. Once I knew what I was looking for, it was almost impossible not to see them. I knew the entrance into the blind had to be on the side facing the scuffle. I put my hand in the small lookout hole and pulled. The front third of the "tree" opened in a soundless, smooth arc. I stepped inside and closed it behind me.

The blind was dark but not black. The one open peephole brought in some light. The rest came in through the mesh top of the blind. It didn't appear to be waterproof, just water resistant. In the dim light, I could see the wooden hatch into the ground. It had an iron handle poking up. I wondered how long it had been here. Its worn look, aged wood, and rusted handle said it had been here a lot longer than a few months.

I opened it up and knew it had been used recently. The hinges made no sound and didn't fight me. They were well oiled. Within the hatch, I saw iron rungs disappearing into the darkness. As I slid down into the hole and closed the hatch above me, I thought about the last time I'd been underground. This was completely different, but no less terrifying. I hated being scared. I let my anger carry me into the darkness.

Each step down came with a quiet ting of Mister Bat clinking against the rung as I braced against it. I wasn't putting my bat down for anything. I knew it might not work in tight quarters but it was the only quiet security

I had. One more rung and I hit the floor with a jarring step. I'd only come down about fifteen, maybe twenty, feet.

I stared around me. It wasn't as dark and black as I'd expected it to be. The tunnel leading away from the ladder rungs was much wider than I'd thought it would be. There was faint light at the end of the tunnel. As my eyes adjusted to the dimness, the shape of the tunnel system became clear. It was a light-colored stone shored up by wooden beams. The tunnel was as wide as a one-way street and split off in two directions about fifty feet down. None of it looked new.

My steps came back to me, soft and muffled against the hard packed dirt. I hugged the right wall unwilling to walk in the open towards the light. It seemed much brighter now. Either my eyes had adjusted quicker than I thought they would or my paranoia was in high gear—with good reason. With my heart thudding in my chest, I knew it was both.

The light came from the left. Not a lot but enough to allow me to see in the tunnels. I watched it for a long couple of moments. It did not move. It did not flicker. It was not a candle. Was it possible to have electric lights down here? That would indicate a lot more was going on down here than hiding a kidnapped teen.

With Mister Bat before me, I moved down the tunnel staying close to the wall. I wished that I'd had a marker or even lipstick to mark my way. I was going to have to use the right-hand or left-hand rule to find my way around.

Turning to the left, I saw my first lamp. It was a small, rectangular LED thing about two by four inches. While it wasn't super bright, it was enough light to illuminate a good twenty feet in either direction. Every thirty feet or so, there was another light. It gave the tunnel an undulated appearance. Stepping close to it, I saw that it was wired and the wire—long, black, thin—ran along the ceiling of the tunnel.

The tunnel system was wired. I was amazed at its presence. It meant people spent a lot of time down here in the tunnels and wanted it a little less dark. My amazement turned into fear as I heard steps coming up behind me.

I hurried forward and peeked into a room. It was filled with stuff but empty of people. That was the important part. I ducked inside, careful not to knock into the crates of empty brown bottles with labels like "Dance Cave Beer" and "Two Johns Brewing" on them. They were old and dusty. There were other crates in here but I didn't have time to exam them. The walking feet stopped.

"You have your orders. I need to get back before the agents miss me."

"Yes, sir."

"And Gavin, make sure Doctor Vandermeek doesn't need anything. He's got his hands full with those kids."

"Yes, sir."

There was a pause then the footsteps resumed. One set receding. I listened for the sound of the hatch and for the sound of the second set of steps while my mind reeled over the idea of "kids." Had they taken Carrie after all? In the last twenty minutes? They couldn't have. They couldn't have captured her and then gotten her here in time to be included in the idea of "kids." It wasn't possible.

The second set of footsteps, presumably Gavin, started up again. I shifted farther back in the room, trying to remain absolutely silent. In front of the room's entrance, I could see a man's shadow approaching. It paused and I held my breath.

In the movies, when anyone senses someone in a place that should be empty, they call out, "Who's there? Anyone?" If they are a bad guy, they listen, shake their head, and go on, walking right past the good guy intruder.

This wasn't like that.

I held my breath and waited for Gavin to continue on past the cave storage room. It looked like he was going to do just that. But instead of walking past the room entrance, he jumped in front of it with his arms wide and a loud "Ha!" It wasn't an angry sound like he was trying to attack me. It was a playful sound and he had a huge smile on his face.

I still panicked, moving on instinct and terror. I jammed him in the solar plexus with the end of Mister Bat. His "Ha!" turned into an "Oof!" as he bent over. I followed up with an overhead whack to the back of the head.

Gavin crumpled to the dirt and I jumped over him to keep from being trapped. He rolled deeper into the room, his arms splayed wide, and his foot hitting a wooden crate of empty bottles. They jangled a discordant tune that had me looking for more bad guys. He didn't move again and a small puddle of blood spread out from his head.

Looking at him, the guy didn't look much older than me. He had a shock of red hair that reminded me a little of Sean MacGregor. I grimaced. This Gavin was a bad guy. I couldn't put him on the level of Sean. This guy had kidnapped at least Adam, probably other kids from the sound of it. But I hoped he wasn't dead. If nothing else, so he could be questioned later.

I stepped to him to see if he had a pulse.

A tiny trickle of lightning ran from his left temple, across his face, and down around the right side of his neck.

I backpedaled until I hit the wall opposite the room entrance. Then I was running back the way I'd come. I had no control of my thoughts or my feet. Slamming into the wall next to the rung ladder stopped my panicked flight. Heart pounding, breath gasping, I tried to get hold of myself as my mind yammered, *"The Coalescence! They're here! They're here! They're here!"*

I counted to ten. That didn't work. Everything in my body begged me to flee far and fast. Even though I knew I'd be abandoning Adam who had been abandoned by his creator father, who had lost his whole family, who was in trouble, who *trusted* me to come save him. I counted back from one hundred by seven and got tangled up after seventy-two. Mentally falling over myself helped calm the panic.

I pressed my forehead to the cool metal of Mister Bat and forced myself to think. "Stop. Stop." I murmured, not doing much more than moving my lips. "Think. It's a hallucination. You're scared. You're stressed. Think. It's not real. Not real."

I did think and a memory blossomed in my head that made me realize that I had hallucinated the Coalescence. "The stairs. The hospital stairs weren't broken. They were fine. You didn't realize it. You were hallucinating then. You're hallucinating now. You just knocked out a goon. Just a guy."

My pounding heart and gasping breath slowed. My dry mouth was so bad, my tongue practically stuck to the roof of my mouth. I wished for a lozenge but didn't have any left in my pocket. Calmer, I worked spit into my mouth as best I could. Adam needed me and I needed to not let either of us down. I counted to ten then counted backward from ten to zero, promising myself everything would be fine at zero. It worked.

Back in control, I retraced my steps, much quieter this time. I barely looked at Gavin, who lay still unmoving in his puddle of blood. Once I got past the storage room, I snuck down the tunnel, following the left-hand rule. With every step, I saw Gavin and the puddle of blood, wondering if I'd just killed him. The urge to go back was stopped by the memory of the lightning that squirmed across his face like a worm. I shuddered and stopped where I was, frozen once more with the thought that the Coalescence might be somehow involved.

No, I'd hallucinated it. The broken stairs in the hospital proved that. My mind threatened to run around in circles until it burned itself out. Fear warred with rage. Panic hung out on the sidelines waiting to be tagged back in.

I decided not to think about Gavin anymore. Hallucination or not, I couldn't touch him to find out if he was dead. He wasn't important anyway. Adam needed me. He had to be my focus, my only focus. I followed the tunnel around to the left, sticking to a modified left-hand rule. If I could see into a room, I just looked from the doorway.

I worked hard to control my breathing, sneaking along, peeking into rooms. The tunnel system was extensive. There were a lot of rooms and I knew there was a whole other half to the underground complex. It had been here a lot longer than the few months that Vandermeek had been watching me and my adopted family. From the scant, regular lights showing a dirt and rock floor smoothed by age and use, the tunnel had been around for decades, maybe even centuries. I discovered by whom, at least most recently, in one dimly-lit, short tunnel.

Turning into it, a sickly sweet and rotten smell wafted up from the back of the darkened hallway. I stopped and looked around, wondering if I was hallucinating again. I bit my lip and did a quick senses sweep: still in a cave, no numbness, no weird sounds, dry mouth, and no bad taste. Just the smell of death. It was real. It had to be… as much as I didn't want it to be.

There were three room openings. I knew the smell for what it was: death. Hadn't I smelled enough of it in Onida? I wanted to not look but I needed to be sure Adam wasn't among the dead. I needed to see what had happened.

The first room showed me why the tunnel system had so much use. There was a small cardboard table with a folding chair next to a small pile of wrapped packages. One of the packages had been cut open, revealing a double handful of dried marijuana buds. The table had a sheaf of papers that I didn't bother looking at. The tunnel system was once used by drug smugglers. Probably had been since smuggling was invented.

The next room was filled with crates. The third had several cots. Three of the cots were full of unmoving bodies. The bodies were covered with sleeping bags. From the blood on the floor, my best guess was that they'd all been killed while they slept. I wasn't sure how. I didn't see any bullet holes. I wasn't willing to get close enough to find out.

One of the bodies had a shock of very blond hair poking out from under the sleeping bag. Another was fully covered but from its curves, I guessed it was a woman. The third had a black hand sticking out and crumbled against the floor. I stared at the hand, trying to convince myself it wasn't Adam. It couldn't be. They'd just taken him and this hand had a longer than two hours dead gray tinge to it.

I backed out of that room, feeling like a coward. "If I don't find him, I'll come back here and make sure." Even as I promised this, I wasn't sure if I was lying to myself or not. Turning, I hurried away as my stomach did a slow roll and resumed my search, thinking it couldn't get any worse. I was wrong.

I hadn't gone more than another thirty feet to the entrance of another small tunnel, when I heard the hard, clicking steps of a person with hard-soled shoes coming up behind me at a rapid pace. Since no alarm sounded, this person had to be coming from one of the two long tunnels I hadn't investigated yet.

I ducked into the tunnel, then backed into the one room off it. I kept my eyes on the main tunnel, trying to get a glimpse of who was going past. As the tall man in a white doctor's coat clicked by, I realized something loomed behind me. I didn't move or give any indication that I knew someone was behind me. I waited until the clicking steps faded before I did anything.

I turned, ready for an attack, and found myself almost face-to-face with a Fedora monster.

Between a man and the Fedora monster, I'd rather be caught by a human man. I struck out at the Fedora with several wild swings before I realized that it wasn't fighting back. As Mister Bat crashed into its carapace, there was nothing more than a dry cracking sound like walking through dried corn husks. The monster jerked and twitched under the blows but did not fight back.

I stopped reacting in panic and lowered my bat. I hoped to whoever was listening out there that I hadn't screamed. I didn't know if I had or not. I kept my eyes on the alien as I listened for those clicking steps to come hurrying back.

There was nothing but my gasping breaths and hammering heart.

I stared at the Fedora. I'd seen this monster in my nightmares off and on for almost a year. It was about six feet tall with four sets of inward curving mandibles that were as black as the rest of its head. Its eyes were oblong and three times larger than a human eye. Its eyes were no longer the glossy black of alive but a grayish charcoal color of dead and dried. It had no nose and its head was hairless.

I stepped a little closer. It hung by thin cords from the cave's low ceiling. The Fedora's body—excuse me, *Mega Aphis* body—had segmented iridescent blue-green sections with a fuzzy black and blunted stinger. Its upper arms were jointed like human arms with discernible shoulders, elbows, and wrists that ended just above the serrated spearhead hands. It had its middle set of limbs curled close to its body and its legs had two sets of knee joints.

There were bullet holes in its chest and abdomen. I recognized them. I should. I'd put them there. I'd woken in Onida with it hanging above me. I'd shot it twice with a shotgun.

Someone had taken that exact monster, brought it here, and hung it up. I couldn't figure out why. Without thinking about it, I reached out a hand and touched the creature. There were stitches all over its body. Like someone sliced it open then sewed it shut. Someone had cut up the creature, then stitched it back together. Had to be for a medical reason. Had to be.

I looked at the bullet holes in the monster's chest, then at its eyes. If it was the one I shot, it shouldn't have eyes. David shot those out when it'd grabbed my wrist as I retrieved my pills. This thought made me open my purse and look to see if my emergency stash was there. It was, a small pillbox wrapped in plastic.

I frowned at the Fedora. Either this was a brand new one or someone had taken bits and pieces of several Fedoras and sewed them together. I shook my head. It made no sense. I couldn't figure out why they would do this or why it would be hanging up here.

The fact that it was here, when I knew Tomas had taken control of the bodies, and what? I didn't know what he'd done with the bodies. I'd assumed they'd been shipped off to some big brains for dissection and study. All the bodies should've been under lock and key. And accounted for.

My stomach dropped at the implication. The thought that Agent Tomas Harrison might be working with Doctor Vandermeek, might have known about and approved of Adam's kidnapping…

A slow burning fury shoved away the fear that had been threatening to overwhelm me. I trusted Tomas. Trusted him. If he had anything to do with this, I'd kill him.

I left the Fedora behind and hunted for both Adam and Vandermeek with a renewed purpose. I had some questions for Vandermeek and he was going to answer them whether he liked them or not.

The deeper I got into the tunnel system, the more sounds seemed to echo and bounce. I wasn't alone, but I couldn't make out the murmur of words—if that was what they were. It took me two more short tunnels to realize that the murmur I thought I was hearing was actually the sound of a fan or several fans.

I stopped in the middle of the main tunnel and listened. I wanted to find them. Part of me wanted to be found. I heard the whoosh of fans and the humming of a machine. I wasn't sure what kind or machine but it had a distinctive sound that I recognized but could not place. I wished, not for the first time, that Carrie was here. She was the one with the near perfect memory.

I closed my eyes and listened harder. Fans, humming, footsteps, voices in the distance. At the footsteps, I pressed myself to the cave wall in an instinct to hide, despite my want to be caught so I could stop searching and just be brought to where I needed to be. I felt a faint thrumming through the rock. Whatever was making the noises was close. Opening my eyes, I knew I needed to find the source of the noise. If Adam was here and alive, that was where he would be.

I straightened, touched the butt of my pistol to make sure it was still in its holster, and looked up. My eyes traced the line of the electrical wires from the lights. Until this point, they'd run in one direction along the main tunnel. "New plan," I murmured. "Follow the power."

Keeping half an eye on the wires, I moved quietly through the tunnel, Mister Bat at my side. I was surprised when I felt a breeze and smelled the scent of water as I got closer to the noise. I saw the light grow as I turned a corner and heard the splashing of water. Either someone was running a bath or there was a small waterfall nearby.

The tunnel bent to the right and opened up into a huge cave that made me catch my breath.

CHAPTER FOURTEEN

The cave was so large that two of Onida High School's gymnasiums could fit in it with room to spare. Wide and open, there were at least two passageways off the sides of it and I could see a pool with a small waterfall in the back. The splashing water echoed around the cavern. There were lights strung up along the outsides of the cave that revealed its beautiful stone walls with colored striations. None of that mattered. What mattered was the horror sitting in the middle of the cave.

It was a makeshift medical office in a horseshoe configuration open towards the tunnel I hid in. There was a table filled with computers and medical equipment I'd only seen on TV. A machine whirred and turned, spinning something at high speed. There was a refrigerator full of bottles, vials, and boxes. All of it was labeled in black and white. Next to that was a four-level wire rack loaded down with all kinds of mechanical parts that I couldn't begin to tell you what they did. Within the horseshoe were two rolling office chairs. Both were shoved under the table. Behind the table was a single large fan circulating the air in the cave. This was the fan I'd been hearing all along.

The office became something medieval with four cages and a portable restroom lining its left side. From under the cages came a thick bundle of cables that ran the fifty feet right up to the side of the main tunnel opposite me. It looked like they all connected to a huge fuse box. While covered with a light coating of dust, everything had the sleek look of newness.

Two of the cages had people in them. One was a white girl of seven or eight with black hair. She was sitting next to the bars, dangling her skinny legs out, pressing her face against the metal. She seemed to be resting. In the other, Adam paced like a pissed off metronome.

I didn't see Doctor Vandermeek. I hadn't expected to come upon Adam like this. I didn't know what to do. Pressing myself to the tunnel wall, my mind filled with heroic ideas and then discarded them as not possible: sneak in and get Adam out of the cage—no keys; pull the fuses out of the fuse box—still no keys, blinding everyone, and a good chance of electrocuting myself in the process; wait for Vandermeek to get back and force him to unlock Adam's cage—doable but I didn't know how many more people were down here. It was the most likely of my ideas to work.

My mind kept coming back to the girl in the cage. Where did she come from? Was she another created person like Adam?

Approaching clicking shoes pulled my attention from the girl and towards the sound. Out of the right-hand passageway, Doctor Vandermeek returned, his hands full of a white box about nine inches square. "Now we can get to work," he announced.

Adam stopped pacing. "You assume, Doctor, I'm going to cooperate." Despite the cold anger in his voice, Adam's face was calm. His eyes showed his emotions: fear, anger, and disgust.

The girl said nothing but watched everything with guileless, dark eyes.

I shifted Mister Bat to my left hand, unsnapped my pistol holster, watched, and listened.

"Of course you will cooperate. You have no choice." As he spoke, Doctor Vandermeek opened the box and pulled out both vials of liquid and syringes.

"There is always a choice. You taught me that. Don't you remember?"

Vandermeek shook his head. "Can't you see what we're doing is for the best of the human race?"

"No, I can't."

"Evie can. Why can't you be more like her?"

"Evie." I'd never heard Adam speak with such contempt. "She's your new version of perfect? You decided to use your own DNA for her? Don't look surprised. I can see the family resemblance."

Doctor Vandermeek paused in his work to gaze at the small girl who smiled at him. "She is your half-sister. I will admit that. My DNA had something I needed that the original cellular template did not."

"She isn't my half-sister. She's nothing to me. You were the process by which my DNA was combined but you aren't my father. None of my

DNA belonged to you. You were barely a creator. You left. I was raised by Lakshmi. Now, I'm my own man with a real family."

I saw Doctor Vandermeek fill the syringe with the clear liquid. He didn't hide his actions. But, what he did do was palm the syringe once it was filled. He turned to Adam with a disappointed look on his face.

"This teenage rebellion does not credit you or your upbringing."

"What would you know about it? You weren't there. You don't know anything about me." Adam shot back. He began to pace again.

"I know everything. I've known everything about you since your inception. Then, from the moment I left to fulfill my real duty, to what happened in PAR Laboratory, to the events that got you transferred to this place with those people you call your family. I know everything there is to know about you."

Vandermeek moved closer to the cage, the syringe cupped away from the cage. I realized that the good doctor was baiting Adam, getting him angry so he couldn't think. Then what? To get in range and hope Adam grabbed him? Or to just try to spring the needle full of whatever onto him? I didn't know and I didn't like it. I was going to have to do something soon.

"You're lying. You don't know anything about me or my family."

"Oh, we have people close. So close you wouldn't believe it. They dance to our tune. All of them dance to our tune. How do you think we got all of you in PAR Laboratory at once?"

All of us? What did he mean by that? Was he talking about Tomas. Had Tomas been compromised somehow? Or, was it David who was compromised? It would explain the Fedora carcass in the tunnel. And PAR Lab? My skin prickled with goose bumps as my thoughts spun. *Was Vandermeek somehow involved with the Coalescence? Had I actually seen the Coalescence earlier?*

Adam grabbed the bars and scowled at the man he'd thought of as a father for years. "You're going to regret this. Mel and Carrie will come. There's no doubt they know where we are. I hope Mel says hello with her baseball bat upside your head before they cart you off to jail."

I bared my teeth in a vicious grin at the idea. If anyone deserved a bat upside the head, it was Doctor Erik Vandermeek.

He ignored Adam's threat. "Of course they will. My people have already picked the girls up. They'll be sharing those cages next to you. Within minutes." The whole time Doctor Vandermeek edged closer and closer to Adam with that palmed syringe.

Fear for Carrie spiked. Then I realized Doctor Vandermeek was lying. He had to be. I wasn't captured. Not to mention they'd barely be on their way back if they'd gotten Carrie the moment we got off the phone. That wasn't likely considering I'd left her armed. Also, I suspected that Mrs. Palmer had other skills than just medical if she heard weapons fire from her one and only neighbor. Especially after that impromptu surgery.

Doctor Vandermeek was almost within striking distance of Adam's cage. I saw Adam shift. I knew he was going to grab the man and that would be the perfect opportunity for Doctor Vandermeek to stab Adam with whatever it was. I had to stop it and now.

I pulled the pistol from its holster, walked out into the light, and said. "Adam's right. You are *such* a liar."

Doctor Vandermeek barely gave me a look. He lunged for Adam's arm. Adam was faster. So was I. The gunshot was incredibly loud in the echoing cave. As Adam jerked back from the bars, the syringe missing him by a mile, Doctor Vandermeek stumbled backwards into the refrigerator, bleeding from his upper chest. The syringe dropped from his hand but didn't go far.

"Daddy!" Evie yelled and reached through the bars towards him.

I barely looked at the little girl. I kept my eyes on the downed man. In horror movies, you never look away from the monster. The blood was bright against his white coat. He was still alive and breathing hard.

"You're going to unlock the cage and let Adam go or I'm going to kill you. I've killed before. I'll do it again." I kept my voice and my hand steady. Too much fury ran through my system for me to feel any fear. "Now. Get up and get those keys."

In the movies, the doctor would've crawled over to the cage and let Adam out. That didn't happen here. "You little bitch. You shot me. Do you realize what you've done?" Doctor Vandermeek's hand groped for the syringe and found it.

Lightning ran across his face and down to the wound.

"Holy shit." Adam scrambled to the back of the cage, getting as far away from his creator as he could go.

I didn't move. I stared at Doctor Vandermeek, lightning arcing from eye to eye as he pulled himself to his feet. I didn't know if I was hallucinating or not. From the way Adam had reacted, I didn't think I was. My fury dribbled away in a river of cold terror. "Adam…" I stepped back. "Adam, can you see that?"

The doctor steadied himself against the refrigerator, blood spreading down his chest. He raised the syringe up like a knife. "You. Little. Bitch."

"Yes," Adam yelled. "Shoot him. Shoot him!"

"Daddy!" Evie's scream mixed with Adam's terror and disbelief.

I shot Doctor Vandermeek two more times. This time, I aimed for his legs. My mind worked fast. *Don't kill him. If you kill him, the Coalescence will come out and get you. Hurt him, don't kill him.* Each bullet hit their mark: one in his right knee, one in his left thigh.

Vandermeek hit the ground with a cry of pain. This time, when the syringe went flying, it went a long way. He gasped in breath and bubbled out blood as he pushed himself up and leaned against the refrigerator. "You… can't… stop… us." Hate burned in his eyes with every word. "It's… too late. Too… late."

I stepped towards him. "For you, maybe. Not for us." Part of me wanted to shoot him again and again.

"Mel, behind you!"

I whirled at Adam's warning and backpedaled from the sight of Gavin, bruised and bloody, lumbering towards me with his hands outstretched. Lightning arced all over his body.

CHAPTER FIFTEEN

I fired a wild shot at Gavin, trying to scare him off, to keep his head down. It didn't work. He kept coming, faster than I backpedaled. Too many more steps backward and I would be trapped within the makeshift office and within range of Doctor Vandermeek. I turned and ran. I needed to get things between me and the possessed goon. I needed time to disable him.

Around the backside of the office horseshoe was a tangle of wires and more supplies as well as the fan. I ran around these, jumping over and dodging through the obstacles. My fear made me agile. I shot over my shoulder, not looking where I was firing. A grunt of pain was my reward.

As I passed the cages, Adam made a swipe at Gavin, catching the man's jacket and pulling him into the bars. Gavin flailed, off balance, as lightening arced towards the teen. Adam didn't have to be afraid of the Coalescence. We'd all discovered that back at PAR Lab. Neither did Carrie. Me? I was still an unknown. No one knew what allowed the Coalescence to possess some and not others. I didn't want to find out.

"Run, Mel! Get help." Adam had hold of Gavin by the arm.

I stopped and hesitated. "But..." I didn't want to leave him. If I left him, they could take him and I'd never find him again.

He met my eyes. "Do it." An understanding crossed between us. He knew the risks and was willing to take them.

Gavin turned and punched Adam hard in the stomach. I heard the whooshing sound as Adam lost his breath and collapsed to the metal floor of his cage. Gavin rushed me.

I pointed both Mister Bat and the pistol at him. I shot again and missed. I tried to hit Gavin with the bat but he caught it in both hands and used it to throw me into the cages. I crashed into metal with an explosion of pain and sound. I'd let go of the bat but not the gun.

Gavin threw Mister Bat to the side and advanced.

Panicked, I raised the pistol and shot him until the pistol wouldn't shoot anymore. Three of the remaining five bullets struck true and Gavin stopped, stumbled backwards, then half-sat, half-crumpled to the stone, bleeding from his chest, stomach and leg. My heart sank. If I'd killed him, I didn't have a thing to keep the Coalescence from attacking me.

I holstered my pistol, then grabbed the bars of the cage next to me to get to my feet. I found myself looking Evie in the eye.

"The girl," Adam gasped, still trying to suck in breath. "Get away from her."

It was far too late for that.

"Hello Melissa," Evie said, sounding much older than her years.

I looked down at her hand on mine, the lightning already squirming into my skin and up my arm.

"We've been waiting for you."

It was a slow spreading of warmth, like lowering your body into an almost too-hot bath. There was pleasure, but it was on the edge of pain. *This is what possession feels like*, I thought as I closed my eyes.

"Not possession. Joining. Bonding. Becoming one."

"No. I won't."

"Don't use your words. Words aren't needed anymore."

Inside, I felt Evie—Evelyn Joy Vandermeek, he'd claimed her as his own—as she moved to Gavin and hovered over him. I didn't have to wonder how she got out of the cage. For her, it hadn't been locked to begin with.

"No. I will not." I forced my body into a standing position, still gripping the bars of the cage. This particular cage had been meant for Heather. Relief flooded me. Heather was still... still what? Not safe. But she was still true to who she was. I had not lost her.

I also felt the Coalescence's surprise at my ability to still move.

"It's better this way. With the Coalescence, you never lose anyone. Ever. You live forever within. You will never be alone. We are family. We are all."

I shook my head. The Coalescence stiffened my neck, halting the movement. "No. Don't believe you." I didn't hear my voice anymore but I still had control of my lips.

"Fight them, Mel. You can do it. Fight. Please." Adam was desperate and despairing at the same time.

I forced my eyes open and looked at Adam from the corner of my eye. "Am," I said. My eyes closed. The Coalescence worked its way through my body, my mind. I knew so much more now. I could feel the other Coalescence in the room. Gavin, body dying. Evie, so strong and powerful. Doctor Vandermeek, still alive and in pain.

"We will show you."

I felt more than saw, though I could see through the eyes and senses of the Coalescence. Evie reached out and covered Gavin's nose and mouth. I felt his fear then his acceptance. The part of him that was human gave up its hold and let the Coalescence do as it will. I felt Gavin die, but I didn't feel his body's pain.

"I am still here," Coalescence Gavin filled my mind for a moment before receding into the hivemind. In that instant, I knew things about Gavin: He had been married. He had killed his wife when she couldn't be possessed. He felt sad but relieved. And he was angry his dog, a German Shepherd, couldn't join with the Coalescence. No animal could. Evie pulled the orphaned sliver of Coalescence into her. I felt the pleasure of the Joining.

"We are more than the sum of our parts. We grow with the Bonding. We need you. You need us."

I pushed all of this away. It meant nothing to me. "Memories. Just memories," I whispered. I felt Coalescence Lakshmi come to the forefront. *"I let you have your phone because you needed the security of it. All I ever wanted to do was to keep my children safe."*

"You have her memories. That's not her." I thanked the stars above that Adam was immune. The thought of reuniting with Lakshmi might be enough to turn him.

The Coalescence grabbed onto this thought and held tight. It dug into my memories, my observations. I fought it as best I could by building a mental wall, brick-by-brick. This blocked them but I knew it wouldn't last long. I would lose myself. I couldn't blame Lakshmi for turning… or even Ian. He wouldn't have been strong enough to fight this.

"Bond with us. No pain. No loss. Ever again."

Even as I realized this, the Coalescence punched holes into that brick wall and let the fear of pain, of being alone, of being insane, crash into me. It pulled up the memory of the Fedora monster stabbing me with its blade-like hands and made me relive the memory. I screamed in remembered pain, feeling my blood course down my body.

But with that memory came the understanding that the Coalescence had conquered the *Mega Aphis*, had possessed them, had sent them in as part of a scout force to test our defenses. The Coalescence had stopped using them after they'd realized that the *Mega Aphis* had killed so many potential hosts. I reeled at the thought that the Coalescence had been behind the creatures who had murdered Sharon and Matt. I wondered if they'd had anything to do with Sean's Nehrings.

The Coalescence stopped the assault on my mind and offered me a hand. *"What do you wish to know? We can tell you of the worlds, of the universes, not yet known by man. You can deliver our message of other life. Come to us. Bond with us. Be one of us."*

The sudden change in tactics jarred me. For a moment, I was actually tempted. Then the memory of Sharon's body, cold and stiff under my head, bubbled to the surface. "No." I gritted my teeth and dug in. I would not lose myself to these creatures. "I am Melissa Jean Allen. I will not join you."

"You will when Adam does." The warm pleasure in my body turned painful. My joints throbbed and ached. There were spikes of pain even though I wasn't moving. It was like something stabbed me with a needle over and over.

"Adam is immune."

"Not for long."

I seized that smugness and followed the thought to its origin. Doctor Vandermeek. As the Coalescence had tried to dig into me, I dug into him. I discovered that he was the one who had had the Fedora monster brought to the cave. Several of them. He cut them open, examined them, sewed the most uninjured parts into that Frankenstein creature hanging up in the cave. It was a trophy.

I dug deeper. The Coalescence did not block me. It did not know how to. It was Doctor Vandermeek, the human part of him, that did. He shoved me out, but not before I understood that he believed he'd found the source of humanity's immunity: Infection by the Coalescence was based on the nerve protein myelin sheath. There was a genetic variation that allowed the Coalescence to bond with humans. Most human protein myelin nerve sheaths were incompatible with the alien. Vandermeek had been working on a gene therapy that was part virus and attacked the myelin protein, breaking it down like multiple sclerosis. The other part was a cure that rebuilt the myelin protein sheath into something compatible with the Coalescence.

I didn't understand what a 'myelin nerve sheath' was but I did understand that he had pretended it was a preventative and a cure for multiple sclerosis. He had called his work Project Yenmil.

"You cannot stop us. You are too late. No one can stop us. We are all. We are everywhere."

I pulled back into myself, realizing the horror of the Coalescence's plan. They would use gene therapy to make humans compatible and then take over the world, one possessed person at a time. They were going to test this out on Adam, Carrie, and Heather. After they used me to see if Heather was immune.

I could not allow that. I needed to be free. I needed electricity. I bared my teeth in a smile despite the pain it caused me. I knew where I'd get it.

At my triumph, the Coalescence did everything they could to try to lock me down. Movement came at a cost. My joints were on fire, every step was on shards of glass. They pulled at my memories of being shot and made me relive them. They pulled on my memories of hallucinations—holes in the floor filled with lava, black webs wrapping me up, of the ocean filling the cave to drown me.

"Don't you see what we offer humanity? Immortality, knowledge, hope."

I pushed it all away and focused on what I wanted. I was the most important thing in the universe at this moment. Me. Melissa. No one could take that from me.

Behind me, I knew Evie had patched up Doctor Vandermeek, keeping him from dying. His research was important enough that the individual human needed to live. His innate knowledge of human physiology could not be replicated by the Coalescence. I felt her making decisions for the whole. I knew when she turned her attention to me.

"You will stop fighting. Now."

The Coalescence flared pain throughout my body and I screamed, "No!" I forced it back behind that brick wall, building it again. Pain was my focus. Anger, my energy.

My eyes on my goal, the fuse box, I ignored the Coalescence, stumbling forward on what felt like bloody stumps instead of my feet. Then Evie's small body—impossibly strong for her size—crashed into me, knocking me over but knocking me that much closer to the electricity I needed. She grabbed my foot and pulled me away, back towards the cages.

I gripped the thick bundle of wires tight, adrenaline surging, pushing the Coalescence's control and pain back. I knew they were afraid of electrocution. Fixing the idea in my mind, I bit down on the bundle of wires as hard as I could, I fiercely *believed* that I would bite through and be electrocuted. With that, Evie would be electrocuted and the Coalescence would die. I believed it with all of my heart and soul.

Evie let go of my foot and scrabbled backwards with a small cry of fear. The fear, not mine, almost overwhelmed me.

The bite did nothing. I surged forward, regaining my feet. I stumbled to the rock wall, ripped open the fuse box, and grabbed the two large fuses within. Sparks flew. The pain was enormous. Worse than being stunned by a factor of a million. My body jerked tight and I screamed, wild and high, as the electricity coursed through me and my skin burned. Something kicked me hard in the chest.

Then there was blackness and I knew nothing more.

CHAPTER SIXTEEN

There was darkness. There was pain. Someone leaned over me.

I flailed, yelling "No!" Or tried to. A thin whine of exhaled breath joined my twitching hands. I couldn't move.

"Mel? You're alive? Mel?" Adam shook me, his hand squeezing tight on my shoulder.

"Stop," I whispered, my throat raw and burned. My chest hurt bad. I felt like something hard and jagged was sitting on it. My hands throbbed as I curled them to my stomach. "Where?" I couldn't see anything. It was pitch black.

"We're still in the cave. You blew the fuses."

I tried to think. I shifted up on my elbows. It was a mistake. I just had time to roll to my side and my knees before I vomited up everything I'd eaten in the last two weeks. At least, that's what it felt like. Next to me, Adam used his phone as a flashlight.

I winced away from the light, trying to think. I was afraid, but I couldn't figure out why. I didn't know where I was. The raw, thudding pain in my chest radiated out in waves of hate. Small rocks bit into my hands and knees. I shifted to a kneeling position and looked at my hands. My palms were red and swollen. The burn marks brought it all home to me.

"The Coalescence. Where? Where?" Adrenaline mixed with fear, dulling the pain, and giving me the strength to kneel. I searched for the enemy in frantic jerks of my aching head.

I could see Adam now, my eyes adjusted to the cell phone light, and his face was drawn. "You killed the one inside you. It was an explosion of light before everything went… went out. It was like what happened with the trap and Ian. There were tiny motes. Evie tried to collect them, but she couldn't. I heard her and Doctor Vandermeek go. He insisted on taking something when they left."

"There are more." I didn't know what I was talking about. At the same time I did. My mind was too scattered to be coherent. My instinct knew we needed to leave. This place wasn't safe. "We gotta go."

Adam stood. He caught me as I tried to stand and failed. With his arm around my waist and my arm over his shoulders, we moved in a herky-jerky three-legged race. It wasn't fast or graceful, but we moved. The light from his phone swinging around in wild arcs with every step. I kept my eyes on the ground, trying to keep from throwing up again.

After a few steps he stopped. I waited, leaned against him. "Mel?"

"Yeah?"

"I don't know the way out. I had a bag over my head. Do you know…?"

Anger rose, pushing back the nausea. I had not imagined him black-bagged while he was leaving me clues on where to find him. I realized just how scared he must have been and not the confident, trusting guy, sure he'd be rescued. Anger gave me focus. "Follow the lights."

"I don't understand."

I couldn't figure out another way to say it. "Follow the lights," I repeated and pointed up.

With a doubtful look on his face, Adam pointed his cell phone up. There wasn't a light fixture above us. The electrical cord was. I fastened on the word.

"There. Cord. Light." My mind worked in single syllables and I couldn't make it go any faster. I gestured for him to give me the phone. He did. Moving hurt. All I wanted to do was lie down and sleep forever. Instead, I forced myself to keep looking up and pointed the cell phone up and forward so we could see where we were going.

"Follow the lights," Adam said, nodding. "Okay. I can do that." He shifted his grip on me and helped me along.

We walked like that, stopping every once in a while for me to keep from losing the lunch I didn't have in my stomach or for my chest pain to die down to a dull roar. I don't think I'd ever been so tired or hurt. All my hurts before had been sharp things and localized but this was different, an all-over throbbing ache with spikes of pain in my hands and chest. Somehow, together, we moved down the tunnel, listening for the Coalescence that had to still be back there.

As we passed the tunnel with the Fedora in it, I stuttered to a stop. Adam shifted into that patient waiting posture while he half-supported my weight. I waved the cell phone light down the short tunnel to the single room entrance. "Fedora. Get pictures."

"Fedora?" Adam sounded mystified.

I wanted to scream at him. I'd woken the whole house up from enough nightmares about them that he should know what I was saying. "Fedora. Fedora. There. Get pictures. Proof."

I handed him the phone and pulled away. Then stumbled to the wall, using it as support, and waited. Adam gave me an "Are you crazy?" look, then walked towards the room entrance. I finally remembered the proper name for them just as Adam turned into the room. "Mega Aphis," I whispered after him.

My words were lost in his cry of surprise and shock. Adam backpedaled out of the room, swearing up a blue streak that ended with him looking at me, "What the hell?" His arms were up in a defensive pose, as he looked between me and the alien monster.

"Mega Aphis. Dead. Get pictures." I slumped against the wall. "Not supposed to be here."

"Holy crap." Adam looked into the room and stared at it with a careful eye before creeping forward to get the pictures. "Jesus," he muttered, taking more than a dozen pictures and a once-around video of the hanging creature.

He came back, his face gray with an emotion I couldn't identify. "You fought those?"

I nodded. "Me. David." I forced my brain into gear. "Me and David. Yes. We fought them."

Adam handed me the phone again and slipped his arm around my waist. "Damn," he said as I put my arm over his shoulder. "We don't have any more of those to stop for, do we?"

"No." I thought about the dead drug dealers. He didn't need to know about them right now. They were dead, yes, but only human. Thus, not as important. Something twitched in my brain at that last thought. More things to unpack with Doctor Giacomi. I wasn't sure I liked the direction my brain was moving in.

"Good. I don't know if I could deal with something else like that."

He wasn't shaking but his voice had a strange, subdued quality. Maybe I shouldn't have made him get the pictures of the Fedora. We both had had one hell of a shock. Me literally. The two of us hurried up the main tunnel, following the lights, and the wires until we came to the exit tunnel and the last light.

I pointed down the hallway. "There. Up the rung ladder, into a hunting blind."

"A what?" The two of us hurried to the ladder.

Part of me wanted to smack him for his dumb questions. Except, I knew he was just trying to regain control of the situation by asking for information. It was something I did, too. It's why I recognized what he was doing. That didn't make it any less annoying. "Hidden tent you hunt from." It was the best I could do while suffering from the dumb.

Adam looked like he wanted to ask me another question. I shook my head. He pointed to the ladder. "You go first. I'll catch you if you fall."

I thought about arguing but I couldn't think of any reasons he should go first other than the fact that one of them could be up there. Adam was immune. I was not. But I was tired. I didn't want to argue. Also, I would know if something was wrong with the blind. I was the one who'd seen it.

I climbed the ladder one slow rung at a time. Holding on was an exercise in pain. The jagged bar across my chest felt like it was sawing through my sternum. I tried to keep from gasping out my hurt but I failed.

"Almost there," Adam said.

He was right under me, overlapping my legs a little, keeping his shoulder almost level with my butt. I think he thought he'd just let me sit there if I couldn't keep going. As gallant as the idea was, the thought that I might have to sit on his shoulder kept me moving. My pride propelled me up, knowing I'd have to lift the wooden hatch to get out. I raised my arm, braced it against the hatch and shoved hard.

It didn't move. Not at all.

My heart jumped to my throat and I shoved again, pushing with my legs. The wood bowed but the hatch didn't open.

"What's wrong?"

"I don't know. I think… I think they locked the hatch. It won't move." I looked down at him, barely seen in the cell phone light. "I think we're trapped."

Adam, already climbing back down the rungs, said, "Come on down. Let me at it."

I did as he asked. He helped me the last few rungs, and I slid down the rock wall until I was sitting again. Dirt floor had never felt so comfortable. I didn't want to move again.

He handed me his phone and I nodded, pointing it up towards the hatch.

"Do you know how it's locked?"

I thought hard, my mind still swimming through mush. "There was an iron handle. It was rusted. I didn't see a lock or anything that could be a lock. All I remember is wood and the handle."

Adam was quiet, his head bowed in thought. He nodded to himself. "If that's the case, there's two things that could keep it closed: another iron handle or hook you didn't see and they tied the two together with rope or chains… but I didn't hear metal on metal… or, they put something heavy on the hatch." He looked up, his face a mask of determination. "Either way, I'll deal with it."

I believed him. With his anger and his superior strength, he would get us free. I wouldn't allow myself to think of any counter arguments. For the moment, I knew I could trust him to do what needed doing.

I leaned back and watched Adam go. He climbed the rungs with fast, sure movements. When he got to the top, he mimicked what I'd done, put his arm over his head then pushed with his body. The hatch didn't move. Adam stepped up two more rungs until his shoulders and part of his back pressed against the hatch. He was hunched over. He tried to stand. I heard him straining.

"All right," he said, nodding to himself. I knew he'd taken the whole situation on as a challenge and he wasn't going to stop until it, or he, was broken. He shifted his body until he was comfortable, then *heaved,* pushing with his legs as hard as he could. Something cracked. Adam grunted long and loud as he gave the hatch another hard shove. Something scraped over wood.

"Please," I half-whispered, half-prayed. "Please." I knew one of three things would happen: Adam would succeed and get the hatch open. Adam would fail and break something within him. Or the rung he stood on, and braced against, would fail and all sorts of badness would happen.

I held my breath.

With a final loud grunt, Adam stood, flinging the hatch up and over. He pin-wheeled his arms, looking for all the world he was about to come tumbling down on top of me. I was up and moving out of the way as he grabbed the sides of the opening to keep himself from falling. My heart thudded too fast in my throat. That was closer than I wanted to think about.

"C'mon," Adam threw over his shoulder as he clambered out of the tunnel.

He didn't have to tell me twice. Fear is a great painkiller… or at least pain-delayer. I climbed the ladder as fast as I could, ignoring every last one of my body's complaints. I took Adam's offered hand and let him pull me out. As he closed the hatch behind me, I saw the huge stone rock that had been on the hatch. It had to have weighed at least a hundred pounds. Bastards.

I looked out the peephole and didn't see anyone. "Okay. Should be a straight shot from here to the parking lot."

He stopped me before I opened the blind's door. "Thank you. For coming for me."

I looked up at him. I could see that the kidnappers had punched him in the eye and the lip. Both were swollen and bruised. "You're welcome. You're family. We couldn't… leave you. And I promised you I'd always have your back. Just yesterday, I promised." We stared at each other for a moment before I led us out of the blind. "Besides, we're even. You saved me. How did you get out of the cage?"

We followed the tracks he'd left through the woods. I kept looking around, expecting an ambush.

"When you blew the fuses. The cage was electrically locked. It opened." Adam looked like he wanted to say more, but he didn't.

I didn't press it. My head hurt. My stomach hated me. My chest felt like I'd been hit with a bat. I let out a soft gasp.

"What?" Adam's head was on a swivel. "What's wrong?"

I shook my head. "Nothing." Nothing I could do anything about anyway. Mister Bat was still back in the cave. I'd forgotten him. That was the second bat I'd lost to the monsters in less than a year. I knew it was stupid, but the loss of my bat—again—was it. I stopped where I was and started to cry.

I couldn't help it. Mister Bat had been my singular friend for years. I didn't want to keep replacing him. There was something about that, about losing Mister Bat *again*, that made me feel like I'd never be able to hold onto anything in my life ever again. I would always lose. It was stupid, but I couldn't stop thinking that.

Adam put his arm around my shoulders, turned me, and hugged me in a firm but not too-tight hug. I sobbed into his chest for a short while. Until I could get my emotions back under control. His shirt, missing several buttons, was wet.

"Sorry," I mumbled. I kept my head bowed to hide my face. I didn't want him to see my red eyes and blotchy cheeks.

"Don't be. Sadie says that crying is a healthy release of stress and tension. We've both earned a good cry."

I glanced up at him. "Thanks."

He smiled at me. Then he scanned the forest again.

The two of us walked in silence until we reached the parking lot. I pulled the SUV keys from my purse and offered them to him. "You drive."

"Yeah." Adam took them. "You need to call Carrie, right?"

"Right. But I don't know if I can… My phone." I pulled it out of my purse and it was dead. I showed him the blank screen.

He pulled his phone out of his jeans pocket and checked it. "Low power but it works." He handed it to me.

"Ok. I'll call." I knew I needed to do more than that. I needed to bring in the cavalry. Unfortunately, with both Heather and David gone, and the possibility that Tomas was compromised, I didn't know who that was.

CHAPTER SEVENTEEN

Despite my assurances that I didn't need a doctor, Carrie insisted on sending Adam over to get Mrs. Palmer. I honestly didn't know if my heart, my ego or my paranoia could deal with being poked and prodded by someone I barely knew, much less trusted.

It seemed I didn't have a choice. I was still arguing when Adam arrived with Mrs. Palmer in tow.

"I'm fine. I took a nap on the way back. Yeah, I hurt a little but… it's fine."

"No, it's not fine," Carrie glared at me. "You were electrocuted."

"I concur with Carrie and Adam," Mrs. Palmer said as she entered the kitchen. She looked like she had before—jeans, comfortable chambray shirt, and sneakers—but she also had a large bag slung over a shoulder. "Now come over here and don't argue with me."

I recognized that tone of voice. Nurse Payne used to use it on me when I didn't want to take whatever medical test she was about to give me. "Yes, ma'am." I trudged over and sat in the chair she indicated.

"And you, Adam," she pointed a lethal finger at him, "...don't go anywhere. You're next. I'm not blind. I can see you've taken a beating." She put her bag on the table and opened it up, digging into it.

Adam stopped as if hooked by a cane. He headed to the kitchen table and sat down.

Mrs. Palmer glanced at Carrie who raised her hands in surrender. "I've been keeping off my leg and keeping it elevated." She pointed to the chair her leg was propped up on. As she did, her sweater fell open to reveal the holster clipped to her belt. "I've been good."

Mrs. Palmer gave Carrie's pistol a long, considering look. "All right then."

She turned back to me. "Let's start with the basics." Mrs. Palmer pulled out a small flashlight and looked at my eyes, flicking the light into and away from them. "Tell me what happened."

I swallowed hard. I didn't know how I was going to keep our secrets in the face of that determination. I decided I would tell her the facts of what happened but nothing about why. I licked my lips. "I grabbed the two main fuses in a fuse box."

"Open your mouth, please." I did as she asked. She looked at my mouth then put the flashlight aside. "I'm going to check your glands." She waited for my nod before she began. "What happened before the fuse box?"

I thought about all the things I could say, but most of it would give too much away. "There was a fight. I got thrown into some metal."

"With him?" She jerked her chin towards Adam. Her hands were gentle as they moved around my jaw and down my neck. It was strange contrast to her clipped and cool tone of voice.

"No. No. I… We… he helped me. I helped him."

She ran her hands down my right arm and I winced when she got to my hand. "That hurt?" I nodded. "Where else does it hurt?"

"My chest hurts a lot. It feels like a seatbelt pressed into it. It's sore." I turned my hands over, looked at them. "The palms of my hands are a little uncomfortable. My back…" I shrugged. "Achy." Looking at my hands, I could see they were more than a little red and swollen. My left hand had some black marks that hurt when I rubbed at them.

Mrs. Palmer shook her head. "I'm not sure how you're not dead. You were electrocuted."

"She was dead." Adam's voice cracked as he spoke. "I brought her back. I don't know how."

Everyone stared at him.

"Adam?" I knew my eyes were like saucers in my face. I couldn't believe what he'd just said. *I was dead?* The thought made no sense.

"It went black after you grabbed the fuses. I got…" He flicked his gaze at the older woman before it returned to me. "out," he decided. "After I got out, I used my phone to find you. You were thrown back from the wall. I gave you CPR. You didn't… you weren't…" He furrowed his brow. "Then you were."

"What was the last thing you did before she regained consciousness?" Mrs. Palmer's voice was dry, matter-of-fact.

"I hit her." Adam looked at his hands. "She wasn't breathing. I was scared and mad. I pounded her chest." He mimed a downward hammer motion with one fist. "Then she was gasping and making hurt noises. It was… bad."

"Ah. Well, you did the right thing to bring her out of afib. Congratulations. You saved her life." Mrs. Palmer's voice didn't lose that factual quality.

I stared at Adam. I hadn't realized I'd died. If he hadn't gotten to me. If he hadn't done what he did, I wouldn't be here. I wasn't sure how I was supposed to feel. I knew I was glad to be alive and that was a relief. A real relief. I didn't want to die.

But, I *had* died. I couldn't wrap my head around it. There was no tunnel of light at the end. Nothing like what they talk about with near-death experiences. No one meeting me to take me further. No sense of peace. It was just nothing. Like sleeping really deep. No dreams. I wondered what that meant.

Mrs. Palmer ran her hands over my left arm but was careful not to make me wince when she got to my left hand. "Short term effects of electrocution include exhaustion, dizziness, headaches, and inability to use the limbs the electricity passed through. Are you having any trouble seeing?"

I tore my gaze from Adam. He wouldn't look at me. "No. I can see."

"Good. Long term effects, that can happen in a week, a month, several months or even years from now, include: cataracts, weakness, spinal cord injuries, chronic pain, headaches, irritability, depression, chronic exhaustion, and inability to use the limbs affected."

Carrie muttered, "Headaches, irritability, depression… how is that different than now?" She winked at me.

Mrs. Palmer frowned at my trembling left hand. "I recommend you go see a doctor and soon. You should look into neuropsychological testing as well as a full exam. In the meantime, do you have any sports drinks in this house?"

Adam nodded and jumped up. "I'll get some."

She put two fingers in my left palm. "Squeeze."

I did and realized why she was worried. "Oh, the trembling. It's okay. It's a side effect from the lithium."

Mrs. Palmer stopped moving and considered me. There are certain times when you're with a doctor, any kind of doctor, they get the hint that something is really wrong… or that you're lying to them… when they get still and their face goes neutral like they don't want to give you crappy news. Her face was like that now. I watched her jump through the mental hoops to get to the point she needed to ask me something I didn't want to answer.

"Lithium," she said. It wasn't a question.

"Yes."

She rubbed a wrinkled, age-spotted, rock steady hand over her cheek. "Melissa, please tell me the truth, did you try to commit suicide?"

I blinked in surprise. She went all the way there. I thought she was going to go with the "are you crazy" question, but no, she took it to the worst logical conclusion. I shook my head, "No."

The problem was, the answer was sorta yes. I'd rather be dead than possessed and put Heather and David and the rest in danger. But I couldn't say any of that. I shook my head again and repeated, "No."

Mrs. Palmer nodded to herself like she expected no less. "Melissa…"

I grabbed her hand. "Seriously, no. It's why I'm on the lithium. I was self-harming but I'm not anymore. This is the best I've felt… I've been… in ages. Mentally. I can't tell you what I was doing but I wasn't trying to commit suicide."

Adam moved up close, putting his body halfway between me and Mrs. Palmer as he put the Gatorade on the table. "She wasn't trying to kill herself."

I could've cried. Even as upset and hurt as he was, Adam was still trying to protect me. I didn't think he realized what he was doing.

Mrs. Palmer did. She pulled her hand from mine then looked between Adam and Carrie's faces. Her gaze settled on Carrie. "What do you think?" Her voice was still as neutral as glass.

Carrie chose her words carefully. "I know what she was doing. She wasn't doing it to hurt herself. She was doing it to protect… us, Adam. I can't tell you any more than that."

Mrs. Palmer looked up at the ceiling. "Please tell me that you are going to call someone with the security clearance to know what's going on. Please? Or that you've already called?"

The three of us looked at each other. They nodded to me. I turned to Mrs. Palmer. "We will be calling someone. Someone who can know. You know?"

"And help?" she pressed.

I nodded. "And help." I hoped like hell I wasn't lying. I hoped I *could* call Doctor Giacomi, but I just wasn't sure. I needed to talk to Carrie and Adam about it.

"All right. I'm going to listen to your breath and make sure your airway and lungs are clear but you need to see a doctor. As soon as you can. In the meantime, hydration, electrolytes, eat a decent meal, and keep track of how you feel. Every ache, pain, fuzziness, weakness, all of it. Agreed?"

I nodded and opened up the Gatorade, suppressing a wince as the cap rubbed against my hurt hand. I took a couple of gulps—they tasted divine—before I answered. "Agreed."

Mrs. Palmer pulled her stethoscope out of her bag and looked up at Adam with a sardonic half-smile. "May I?"

Adam looked down and realized he was standing almost between us. "Oh, yeah."

We spent the next couple of minutes going through the routine of breathing heavy, breathing normal, of her knocking on my back and my chest until I felt lightheaded and a little dizzy. I did everything I could to hide my pain and fuzzy head from her. I wasn't going to give her another reason to do what she thought she should do—which was call an ambulance, I was sure.

Then Adam took my place in the chair. She looked him in the eye, then gave him a good visual examination. "What can you tell me about what happened to you?"

He thought about it for a few of long moments. "I was punched a couple of times. Then kicked in the head."

I blinked at him. "You didn't tell me that."

Adam shrugged. "Then I fell about fifteen feet. I hit my shoulder, but it's okay."

Carrie and I exchanged a look. We both had the same question in our eyes: Why hadn't he told us? Then I knew why. I shook my head and mouthed the words, "No time." She nodded to me.

"How do you feel?" Mrs. Palmer walked around the chair to look at the back of his head. From where I was sitting, he looked fine. "I'm going to touch your head."

"Okay."

She ran a thumb over part of his skull and he winced. "How bad does that hurt?"

"It's fine until you touch it. And touching it is more of … I'm aware of it and it's not comfortable."

She returned to her seat in front of him and gazed at his face again. "There's not much I can do about your bruises. Ibuprofen, if you can take it, and a cold compress for the swelling. Tylenol for the pain if you can't take the ibuprofen. You also should get looked at. Head injuries are no laughing matter. Mind if I check your shoulder?"

Adam nodded and Mrs. Palmer got up and started manipulating his arm. I liked the way she told us when she was going to touch us and asked if she could do so. I could tell she was thinking very hard and trying to decide something. I wished we could tell her everything. But we couldn't. We couldn't put her, or us, in that kind of danger. She didn't have the clearance to know. Even if she did, there was always the question of what she would do with the information.

When Mrs. Palmer was done she packed up her bag, and looked at each of us in turn. "To tell you the truth, if I didn't already know that you three aren't normal teens, I'd be calling the authorities. But I know, and that makes me stay my hand. For now."

Carrie frowned. "What do you mean, we're not normal teens?"

Mrs. Palmer gazed at her. "I'm aware when a security check is done on me. Retired or not, I still have contacts. I've had two done on me since you guys moved here. I also know that you three are home schooled. I know the four of you go shooting every week and that's a little unusual. I know that Officer Chapman doesn't really like you guys because he doesn't understand you." She sighed. "He means well but he can be a real putz."

"Contacts like Google Alerts contacts or contacts like red phone contacts?" Carrie's eyes gleamed with interest.

"Never you mind, youngin'." The corner of her mouth twitched upward before hiding away again. "In any case, when Heather asked me to look in on you, she asked me to call her before I called anyone else if *anything*, anything at all, happened. I have an emergency number for her. She was very specific about the fact that you three are important to important people. I don't know who. I don't want to know who. At least, not yet. So, I'm not going to call anyone. Not even Heather."

She raised that lethal finger and pointed it at each of us in a sweep back and forth. "But if any of you get hurt again—at all—I'm making that call. I figured I should let you know where I stand. Maybe the thought of me calling this emergency number will make you three a little bit more cautious in the future. Am I understood?"

"Yes, ma'am." Adam and Carrie said in unison.

My snarky side just wouldn't let things go like this. "Even a stubbed toe?"

Mrs. Palmer gave me a look that said I was treading on very thin ice. "Even a stubbed toe. So, either you deal with your own stubbed toes or you don't stub your toes at all. Got it?"

I smiled at the fierceness in her eyes despite her calm voice. "Yes, ma'am. Got it. No more stubbed toes."

Mrs. Palmer looked heavenward and shook her head. "I'm going now. All of you, eat and drink, and painkillers. I've got an AAR to write up for Heather when she returns." She took her bag and stalked out.

I followed, locking the door after her. I watched until I couldn't see her anymore. Returning to the kitchen I asked, "What's an AAR?"

"After action report. Military term." Carrie sighed. "It's been a day. What's for dinner?"

"Frozen pizzas okay?" It was the only thing I could think of that wouldn't take a lot of brainpower to make.

Carrie nodded as Adam got up and turned on the oven.

CHAPTER EIGHTEEN

"Not that I think you were wrong, but why did you want us to wait to call Sadie?" Carrie sat at the kitchen table while I pulled the pizza from the oven. I was starved, despite drinking two bottles of Gatorade. Adam hovered nearby, trying hard to look like he wasn't just waiting for me to fall over. I couldn't blame him. He'd just found out he'd brought me back from the dead. I think he wanted to make sure it stuck. I didn't let it bother me. Or, at least, tried not to.

"Truth is, I don't know if we can trust her." I waited for the explosion of confusion and denial. It didn't come. Adam and Carrie gazed at me and waited for me to continue. Their expressions were guarded and told me I'd better have proof or a good reason for my statement.

"Well, I... Okay. Here's the deal. When I was possessed, the Coalescence said they had someone close to us, really close, making sure we did what they wanted. Doctor Vandermeek has been having someone watch us for at least two months, possibly longer."

"Longer," Adam said with a sigh. "He said so."

"The only people who knew where we were are Heather, David, Doctor Giacomi, and Tomas. Before that, in the underground tunnels, I heard one of the goons say that he needed to get back to "the agents" before they missed him." I finger quoted "the agents" so they knew I was quoting the person speaking.

"Did you recognize the voice?" Carrie kept her own voice neutral.

I shook my head. "No. But, I wasn't listening to recognize a voice and I was in an underground tunnel. Sounds were all messed up."

"It's true." Adam shrugged. "I don't know if I would've recognized voices either."

I turned back to the pizza and cut it up with long swipes of the pizza cutter. "Heather is the only one I'm sure isn't compromised. They wanted me to test her. David works for Tomas. Doctor Giacomi reports to Tomas. One of them is compromised."

"I think you're right." Carrie drummed her fingertips on the kitchen table as she gazed at her laptop.

I turned to her. "What do you mean?"

"I found some personal notes from Doctor Vandermeek. They were about Adam." Carrie turned Khalessi around for us to see. "This is the interesting one. The rest are academic, mostly."

Adam went to the table while I brought paper plates full of pizza over. He read the note and frowned before reading it aloud. "It says, *"I've requested permission to see Adam but have been blocked by Agent Shaker. This isn't right. I am his father. His creator. I've escalated my request to Agent Harrison and to Doctor Giacomi.""* He turned away with a sneer of disgust. "This is fake. It's not real. It can't be."

"Why not?" I asked as I sat down.

"First, Heather would've asked me. Second, Sadie would've talked about the subject with me, asking me if I wanted to see him. Third, he *never* called himself my father. Ever. Fourth, if you look at his other notes, none of them are that personal. I'll bet all my pizza on that." Adam ticked these off his fingers as he spoke.

Carrie blew out a breath. "Yes. That's what I thought. I'm glad I don't have to convince you. I think this was planted to make you want to go find him. To make you distrust Heather, Sadie, and Tomas."

I nodded. "Yeah. I don't think he knew we would run into him at the hospital. I think that was a fluke. He saw you before you saw him, then he lured you out."

"Probably." Adam chewed thoughtfully. "But, I think we can trust Sadie."

"Because she's immune?"

"Yeah. Because she went through what we went through. The lockdown. The attacks. And because she killed one of the Coalescence."

I considered this and remembered the fear Evie had at the thought of being destroyed. "Okay. We need someone to deal with the underground lab. Get everything they left behind.... If they haven't cleaned up already.

I'm going to ask her about Vandermeek's request. That will settle who the cavalry is."

"Call her on speaker. We'll listen. We know her a little better than you." Adam looked to Carrie for confirmation. She nodded her agreement.

"Fair enough. But I do the talking. Don't let her know you guys are listening."

We moved into the office for better acoustics and used my phone. Miracle of miracles, it still worked. After Carrie reset it to its factory settings that is. She figured that its lack of power is what mostly saved it from electrocution. That and multiple layers of fabric and leather between electrified me and it.

I dialed Doctor Giacomi's number and waited.

The phone picked up. "Melissa? Is something wrong?"

I licked my lips and steeled myself. "Yeah. There's a question I need to ask you and I need you to tell me the truth whether or not you think I should have the truth. This is really serious."

Doctor Giacomi paused. "All right, I'll try, Melissa. That's the best I can promise."

I glanced at Carrie and Adam. They nodded acceptance at this. "Okay. The question is this: Has Doctor Vandermeek sent a request—official or otherwise—to you for permission to visit with Adam?"

She was quiet for a long couple of moments. When she spoke again, she sounded concerned. "Doctor Vandermeek? Doctor Erik Vandermeek?"

"Yes, him. Has he?"

"No. I've received no request. I have to say, this really surprises me. I would've spoken to Adam about this. Why are you asking? I need to know." This time, Doctor Giacomi almost sounded alarmed.

I looked at Carrie and Adam. Carrie nodded. Adam mouthed the word, "Truth." at me. That made my decision for me. "All right. There is a lot going on. A whole lot and it's really dangerous and you *cannot* tell Agent Harrison."

"Melissa?" More wary concern.

"We think..." I stopped and considered. "We think someone close to Agent Harrison is compromised." I didn't want to say that I thought Tomas was compromised. Not aloud. Not yet.

"Explain."

"Doctor Vandermeek was Coalescence. Is Coalescence." I was gratified at her soft inhalation of breath. "I saw it with my own eyes. Promise me you won't talk to Agent Harrison. Not yet. Not until you do the thing I need you to do."

"What happened? When did you see Doctor Vandermeek?" She paused, then asked, "What do you need?"

"Doctor Vandermeek had a hidden laboratory. He kidnapped Adam. He was going to do experiments on Adam to make him susceptible to possession. I rescued him. I need you to go get what he left behind. If there's anything we can use against the Coalescence, you've got to get it before they clean everything up. We can't. There's something important we need to do first."

Doctor Giacomi was silent for at least half a minute but I could hear her typing. "You kids don't do anything halfway, do you?"

I exchanged a smile with Adam as I said, "No ma'am."

"I'm going to have to bump all of your appointments up to two hours each next week, aren't I?"

"Yes ma'am. And, Doctor…?"

"Yes?"

"There's a Fedora monster, a *Mega Aphis*, corpse in the tunnel system as well as some dead people." I hoped Doctor Giacomi understood what I was trying to tell her. I couldn't just come out and say that the Coalescence had possessed the Fedoras. I didn't want to think too hard about that because of the nightmares I knew I'd be having, but she needed to know.

There was more typing before she answered. "All right. You three have forty-eight hours to do whatever it is you think you need to do. Then I'm going to have the whole story. For now, I'll use… other resources. Tell me where this lab is."

Carrie, Adam, and I relaxed. Doctor Giacomi might not be telling the truth but we were all willing to believe her for the moment. She had not let any of us down yet. "Ok. I'll text you coordinates. Plus, Adam and I left a trail a blind person could find. The trail leads to a hunting blind…"

After we hung up with Doctor Giacomi, Carrie said, "Now, we need to get ready for tomorrow."

Adam shook his head. "It's a trap. Just like that personal note. Just like you going to the castle to get the package."

"It might be, but we'll be ready this time. Stun guns and pistols. I want to see who Elijah is. If he's a real person."

Carrie nodded. "I'm going this time. Besides, if we use pistols… the police station is about half a block away. So, if we have to shoot someone, that *will* bring the police."

"Good to know," I said. "If I'm shooting someone, I probably need help."

"I'm in but I'm not carrying any weapons." Adam looked at us. "I'm immune and I don't want the police mistaking me for the bad guy."

"If there is a bad guy."

"There is always a bad guy," Carrie said. "Always."

Adam shifted his chair closer to Carrie. "What was in those Yenmil files anyway? Doctor Vandermeek's personal notes?"

Carrie shook her head. "That was in the personal files I downloaded from his share. Maybe he was practicing. I don't know. Project Yenmil is something completely different. It doesn't look that important to me. I mean, it is about a medical breakthrough to help MS victims and to identify the specific protein that causes MS. It looked like Doctor Vandermeek wanted permission to test the Army recruits for the protein and to administer his gene therapy as a preventative measure."

My skin went cold. "Did he get permission?"

"No. Not yet. But he did have permission to start testing his cure on current MS patients who were active duty. They were just setting all that up now. That's why he's at Fort Leonard-Wood."

I looked back and forth between Adam and Carrie. They were so unconcerned. How could they be so calm? "You do realize that's how they're going to fix it so immune people can be possessed, right?"

Carrie's eyes went wide. "No. Why didn't you tell me?"

"I thought I did."

"No! You didn't. That changes everything."

I glanced at Adam. He looked as confused as I felt. "I don't understand."

"Look, if these files tell you all that, the person who wants them can't be Coalescence. They already know this. The person who wants these files is someone we can trust. Someone who is already fighting against the Coalescence."

Adam shook his head. "I don't… No. Doctor Vandermeek's name is all over this. It was supposed to draw me out."

"But this wasn't for us. It was for Heather. Heather was supposed to get these files for Elijah. Maybe he's trying to bring her in on an anti-Coalescence thing and he doesn't understand that she's already anti-Coalescence."

"Or maybe he does and he's trying to warn her that Tomas is compromised," I murmured and stared at my fingers, trying to puzzle it out. "Maybe he knows she won't believe him unless she figures it out for herself." I looked up. "Makes sense."

Carrie glared at me. "Tomas isn't compromised. He's too smart for that."

"I don't know..." I looked to Adam for support but he shook his head and shrugged.

"He is *not* compromised. He is *not* Coalescence." Carrie snapped her laptop shut.

I shook my head. "Someone close to us *is* compromised."

We all sat back and thought about it for a moment. I didn't say anything else but I thought that, maybe, "Elijah" was actually David. Maybe he already knew that Tomas was compromised. I don't know why I thought this. I just did. I couldn't decide if I wanted it to be true or not. But Carrie wouldn't believe it and I didn't want to argue with her about it.

"It's not Tomas. I'm going with you tomorrow. To see for myself." Carrie's face settled into her stubborn expression. "Besides, you're going to need me. If nothing else, to drive the getaway vehicle."

CHAPTER NINETEEN

Carrie shoved Khalessi into her cross-body bag then struggled to her feet. She grabbed her crutches and hobbled out of the kitchen. I knew it was because she didn't want us to fight with her over her going to the meeting tomorrow. Adam and I exchanged a look. I jerked my chin after Carrie. Adam nodded. He was going to take first crack at trying to make Carrie see sense. She couldn't go with us.

I waited to see where they'd have this fight before I cleaned up the kitchen. Either it would be in the office, and I'd be able to hear everything or it would be in her room and I'd have to abandon the kitchen to eavesdrop.

"I don't think you should come tomorrow." Adam's voice was clear.

It was the office and I was in luck. I moved quick and quiet, cleaning up the kitchen as I listened.

"I don't care what you think." Carrie's voice was softer but I could still hear it.

"It's going to be dangerous and you can't run."

"I don't have to run if I'm driving. Also, I don't have to move to shoot. You need backup of some kind and I'm all you've got."

"But..."

"Adam, you're not going to change my mind. Stop trying."

I winced. She sounded pissed. I shoved the paper plates into the trash and put the dirty dishes into the dishwasher. It was still quiet when I ran the water for the sponge but they were talking again when I turned it off.

"... Coalescence?"

"If you say that again, I'm going to throw something at you." Carrie's voice was cold with fury. "You know what? Just go away. I don't want to talk to you."

"Carrie..."

"No! Shut up and go away!"

I blinked at that. I'd never heard Carrie sound so mad. She cared about Tomas more than I realized. Then again, he did save her. I wiped at the countertops, pretending I hadn't overheard almost everything, as Adam returned to the kitchen. "How'd it go?"

He shook his head.

"What'd you do?"

"Asked her what she'd do if Agent Harrison was actually Coalescence." Adam grimaced. "She didn't like the question."

I mimicked his grimace. "Yeah. That was a bad move."

Adam shook his head. "No, it wasn't. It was a good question to ask. If she's coming with us, we need to know how she's going to react. Do you think she'd shoot Agent Harrison?"

"I don't know."

"I mean, you'd shoot Agent Hood if he was Coalescence, wouldn't you?"

I shook my head. "David's not Coalescence."

Adam shrugged. "Yeah, probably not. But you'd be able to shoot him if he was, wouldn't you?"

I scrubbed at a non-existent stain on the countertop, fighting with my rising temper. I knew Adam wanted an answer but I really didn't want to think about David being possessed. "David is *not* Coalescence."

"How do you know?" Adam pressed.

"I know." I refused to look at him. Truth is, I didn't know. It was something that had been hovering on the edge of my mind since we'd gotten back from the caves. When I was possessed, the Coalescence hadn't mentioned anything about David or Tomas. Only Heather.

"How?"

Anger spiked and I whirled to him. "Because David is Elijah." He had to be. He couldn't be Coalescence. He had to be the one who was doing all of this.

"Do you have any idea how dumb you sound right now?" Carrie stood, propped on her crutches, in the kitchen doorway. "This is exactly why you two need me."

My face flamed hot. I felt like she'd slapped me. "What do you mean?"

Adam stepped away from us both. I knew he was trying to stay out of the crossfire. He'd seen some of our fights.

""David is Elijah." Sometimes I wonder if you actually use that brain of yours." Carrie hobbled her way back to the kitchen, sat down, and propped up her leg. When I didn't say anything, she continued. "Seriously. You're smarter than that."

I turned back to the kitchen sink and squeezed the sponge hard. "Just say what you mean."

Carrie gave a disgusted sigh. "Fine. David was called away at the same time Heather was. Do you really think he came back and shoved that envelope into our bushes? No. It wasn't him. I would've recognized his walk."

"He could have sent someone."

"Right. I suppose he also sent that someone to the castle to shoot at us? No. If David is Elijah, he could've just had a conversation with Heather in the car as they went to wherever it is they are. He wouldn't have picked her up then sent her a message. *That* doesn't make sense."

"Unless the message wasn't actually for Heather." Adam froze as we both looked at him. "I mean, maybe it was for you, Mel. You knew about the Elise identity."

I scowled at him. "You're the one who's been saying all this has been for Heather the whole time. Whose side are you on, anyway?"

Adam shrugged. "Both Agent Harrison and Hood knew about the Elise identity. What Agent Hood knows, Agent Harrison knows. Both of them knew Heather had this assignment. It really doesn't make sense that the letter came from either of them unless… it was never really meant for Heather… but for you."

I wiped my hands dry with a dish towel then continued to mangle it as I thought about what he said. I hated how much more logical both of them were than me. "How did this become about me? We were supposed to convince her to stay home tomorrow." I gestured to Carrie.

She shook her head. "Not going to happen. Even more now than ever. You guys need me. I am the smart one."

"Smart ass," I muttered. "But what will you do if we need to run away?"

"I'm going to stay in the SUV. I'll run away on four wheels." She paused. "What will you do if David is Coalescence?"

I scowled at her. "Low blow."

Carrie crossed her arms and waited. Adam shifted closer to her. Traitor.

I took a breath, let it out, and hoped I wasn't about to lie. "Stun him. Force the Coalescence out of him. Kill the Coalescence. Can you say the same thing about Tomas? Could you do that to him?"

She huffed, annoyed, "Yes. If I had to. I could."

"They can kill as they are forced out of the body. We've seen that." I dug the knife in deeper. "And make it hurt. They did that to Lakshmi."

"That's enough." Adam voice was sharp and hurt. "Stop it. We're not the enemy."

Carrie and I both jumped at Adam's shout. I realized what I'd just said. "Oh, God. I'm sorry. I didn't—"

"You didn't," he interrupted, "but you did. So stop it. We've got a job to do. We can't do that if we're all acting like idiots. Just stop." Adam stomped out of the kitchen but not before I'd seen the tears in his eyes.

I sighed. "Shit."

Carrie nodded. "Yeah."

"I'm sorry."

"Me, too."

I put the towel down and sat at the kitchen table. "Okay. You don't want to think about Tomas being compromised. I don't want to think about David being compromised."

"No." Carrie agreed.

"But one or both might be. So… we do what we have to do if it comes to that. Incapacitate, stun, free them from the Coalescence. Agreed?"

Carrie looked me in the eye. "Yes." Then she looked away. "You will need me. I'm another point of view. I'm the getaway driver. I'm the one who can call in Sadie."

"Call in Sadie?"

"If you don't think she's already here or on her way, you don't know her very well. She's probably got a small army with her. When she says "other contacts" I bet she means all kinds of trained special ops people. The cavalry."

I nodded. "You're right. She probably has them on speed dial." I tilted my head. "I don't like the idea of you coming with us but, yeah, I guess we do need you."

Carrie smirked at me. "You'd better hope you don't actually need me. If you do, that means everything has gone horribly, horribly wrong."

THE MEETING

CHAPTER TWENTY

Even though Adam and I both tried to get Carrie to stay home, I was glad she was here. Now, as she drove us through Richland, I realized deep within we did need her. We were at our best when all three of us were working together. Her driving let me and Adam scout the lay of the land from the safety of the SUV without being obvious about it.

Carrie drove around the block in question, twice, before parking several blocks away. The first time, Adam had looked left and I looked right. We'd switched sides on the second drive by. Carrie shifted in her seat so she could see Adam next to her and me in the back. "All right, what did we get?"

"On the side with the auto upholstery store, we've got three buildings and the side of the Highland Center. It goes house, upholstery store, house, then side of the strip mall. Both houses seem empty. No cars, no lights. There are people at the strip mall, in the laundromat, I think. Our target is dark. No cars, no lights." I tapped my lip. "Behind, from what I could see, it was just cars and a parking area. There were other houses back there but nothing close enough to worry about." I looked at Adam. He nodded his agreement.

Carrie tapped her fingers on the armrest. "As expected. It's Sunday. All good people are in church." She turned her attention to Adam.

"The other side has the police station—two cars there—and it's active, lights and all. Next to it is the car wash. Next to that is a house. It might be abandoned. The front door was open. Behind it all, fields, the water tower, other houses." Adam shrugged. "Only the police station had movement."

I didn't have anything to add. "It looks like it's a go," I said. "Carrie, you drive us up to the front of the upholstery store and park. You'll stay in the car as agreed. Adam and I will go up and walk in like normal customers. If it's locked, we'll go around back and force the lock. We'll be in constant contact with the phones."

"I'll let you know if I see other people coming—including cops."

"Keep your pistol handy."

Carrie nodded and looked at Adam.

He raised his hands. "No way, no how. Not this close to the police station. I'm better unarmed."

She gave me a doubtful look and I shrugged. "He's better at hand-to-hand. I'm better at pistols."

"But what about a stun gun? There might be Coalescence in there." She looked at me. "Seriously. You're vulnerable. They know that now. If you get possessed again, he needs to be able to free you. Plus, we agreed… if anyone is Coalescence, we free them."

Even if that freedom meant death. Carrie didn't say that but it was implied. We all knew it.

I looked at Adam. He looked uncomfortable. "I don't…" He shook his head.

I knew it was his decision but if it was needed, it would be to save my life. Or Tomas or David's lives. "Just have it in your jacket pocket, okay? It would really suck for me to get possessed and to be the only one with a stun gun."

Scowling, he nodded. "Fine, but if I get shot by a cop, it's your fault."

"I hope it doesn't come to that."

"Me, too." Carrie dug into her computer bag and came up with the small stun gun. She offered it to Adam. "Thanks. It makes me feel better knowing you have it. We still don't know who you're meeting. Elijah could be a friend or an enemy."

"Or, someone who isn't involved at all," I added.

We stared at each other for a moment after Adam hid the stun gun in his jacket. I touched the USB thumb drive in my pocket for the tenth time this morning and nodded. "Phones."

The three of us put our earpieces in and Carrie called me, then bridged Adam in. "Test, test," she said.

"Yes. I hear you." Adam gave her a thumbs up.

"Loud and clear." I smiled, scared to death. I couldn't believe we were actually doing this. I saw that Adam and Carrie looked a little green, too.

I knew I couldn't show my fear. I needed to be confident for everyone. "Okay. Let's do this." With that, there was no turning back.

As planned, Carrie parked the SUV in front and turned off the engine. Adam and I got out and walked up to the unassuming green and white building.

My first thought was that it had been a home converted into a business. I was wrong. It looked more like a converted barn or warehouse. It was one long, single level with a garage door to the left, a regular door in the middle, and a window with the shade pulled down to the right. There was a clean, green and white vinyl couch under the window that had once been the front seat of a truck. It was a nice touch. As garages go, from the outside, this was a nice one.

Adam took the lead and opened the door. It wasn't locked. I was right behind him. We walked into the waiting room of the business. There was a door to the left side—probably into the work area of the garage, a long counter towards the back, several chairs, a magazine rack in a little waiting area, and a hallway leading to a couple of back rooms. From where we stood, I could see three doors: one on the left hand side in the back and two on the right hand side. At the very back of the hallway was a door with windows that let the light in.

"We listen at the doors," I whispered to Adam. He nodded.

I lifted the flip countertop to let us in. Adam headed to the far back left door as I closed the countertop without a sound, then turned to the first door on the right. We both walked with a soft step, making as little noise as possible. I listened at the first door. Nothing. I glanced at Adam. He shook his head. I pointed at the right hand door. Adam stepped to it and listened. His eyes got wide. He beckoned me to him.

I pulled my pistol and moved to his side then I cocked my head and listened at the door.

"... how long we'll have to wait."

"As long as we need to. All day, perhaps."

"No, they'll be here. Sooner rather than later."

There were three voices speaking. Two men and a woman. I recognized every one of them.

Adam mimed kicking the door in and me going first. I nodded, raising my pistol to the ready position. I made sure the safety was off, but that I also kept my finger off the trigger. Heather was big on trigger discipline and now, as my heart pounded and my hands shook, I understood why. I took a long slow breath to steady and focus myself then nodded to Adam.

The sound of the door slamming open was a shock in the quiet of the hallway but I didn't let that stop me. I entered, scanned the room, and pointed the pistol at Agent Tomas Harrison.

The room turned out to be a break room and kitchen area. There was a single, round table in the middle next to a small couch. A countertop and sink ran along the backside of the wall and stopped at a refrigerator. Three chairs sat at the table. Only one of them was filled with Agent Tomas Harrison. Agents David Hood and Heather Shaker sat on the couch.

Tomas, to his credit, froze where he was, in a half-standing position, then slowly sat back down, and put his hands on the table in front of him as Adam positioned himself at my side.

"Heather, get away from David. Now." I was surprised at how calm and assured my voice sounded.

"What?" Heather gave David a startled look.

"If you trust me at all, trust me now."

Heather got up and walked to the other side of the table. She walked behind me and Adam to get there. I didn't move from pointing the pistol at Tomas. David didn't try to move. "Mel? What's going on?" He sounded confused and almost wounded.

"Tomas knows."

Tomas gazed at me without flinching. "I trust that Agent Shaker has taught you the four rules of gun safety?"

I knew what he was talking about. There were four main lessons of gun safety: Act as if every firearm is loaded. Never point a gun at something you're not willing to destroy. Always be sure of your target and what's beyond it. Keep your finger off the trigger until you're ready to fire. I was doing all four right now.

"I'm sure of my target and I'm prepared to destroy it." The words popped out of my mouth without hesitation. Inside, I wondered if I could shoot him. I'd trusted Tomas. Really trusted him until the last couple of days. Also, I really didn't want to shoot him.

He pursued his lips and nodded to himself. "Then we should hear what you have to say."

David shifted, "Melissa, this isn't a—"

"Stand down, Hood." Tomas didn't raise his voice but the command slapped David in the face. He kept his eyes on me but flicked his attention to Adam from time to time. I saw him zero in on Adam's bruised face.

"First," I said, "Heather, who is Elijah?"

Heather, who had been watching Adam and me with a concerned frown, shook her head. "Elijah?"

"Did you ever work with an Elijah from Belgium?"

"Oh. Oh! Yes. Elijah Barrowman." She leveled a glare at David. "It was in my file. He died four years ago."

"Okay." I focused on Tomas. "Why did you ask for the Project Yenmil files?" His brow crinkled a little as he glanced at David. David shook his head. I didn't know what to make of it. I tried again. "Project Yenmil. Run by Doctor Erik Vandermeek. Why did you ask for them?"

Tomas shook his head again. "We didn't. That's not what the letter said."

"Bullshit. You asked for them." I tried to calm myself. This wasn't what I'd expected. They were in on it but they weren't telling the truth.

Adam cleared his throat as Tomas shook his head. "You did, sir. I quote, *"I need all of the files on Project Yenmil. It's important. Put them on the USB device and bring them to 217 West Camden Ave, Richland, on Sunday. I will be there all day. Please. This is important. Do this for me and I will consider Belgium paid for, fair and square."* Told us to get them from the Fort Leonard-Wood hospital… where Doctor Vandermeek is working."

Tomas, his hands still plastered to the table in front of him, asked, "David?"

David shook his head. "That's not what I wrote. Mel, please, put the gun down. This was just a test."

Anger and confusion rose. "A test? A test that got Carrie shot and Adam kidnapped by Doctor Vandermeek? A test against the Coalescence? I died! I was dead. Adam brought me back. How the hell is this just a test?"

"Did you know Doctor Vandermeek was here?" Heather's question was to David. It was soft and as full of fury as I felt.

"No." David shook his head and looked at Tomas. "I didn't."

Tomas had a glimmer of sweat across his brow and his cheeks flushed a hectic red. "Is Carlita all right? Is she alive?"

The soft click of a door was all that heralded the arrival of a stranger bearing a cardboard carrier filled with four coffee cups. He was a white, clean-shaven man in his upper 20s with brown hair. He wore a casual blue suit and a white button up shirt. Despite the fact that he wasn't wearing black fatigues, I recognized him at the same time he recognized me.

"Him! He's the one who shot Carrie while we were at the castle."

The man threw the hot coffee at Adam and me as he turned for the back door. Adam, ignoring the coffee onslaught, tackled him into the opposite wall, and the two of them went down, fists swinging. I yelped as the hot liquid scalded my arm and raised the pistol to the ceiling to keep from accidently firing it.

Just as Adam pinned the coffee guy to the ground, electricity sparked out from him, running over Adam. He was Coalescence. And he worked with Tomas. He was the infiltrator, the one they talked about as close to us. The back of my head buzzed with unheard static.

"I'm immune, you asshole." The electricity died away and the coffee guy struggled all the more. Adam held on with both hands. "Mel! I can't stun him."

That meant me. No matter how much I was in danger of being possessed again, I had to be the one to stun him. I didn't know if anyone else in the room was vulnerable or not but it didn't matter. None of them had fought the Coalescence like me and Adam.

I handed Heather my pistol and jerked my head towards Tomas and David. "Don't let either of them move." I had to trust she would do what I said. I knew I could trust her because the Coalescence had wanted her tested.

I turned from Heather and pulled my stun gun from my pocket. "Adam, hold him."

Adam grunted his response. He sounded out of breath and straining to keep the traitor down on the ground.

I waited until I saw exposed skin on coffee guy's ankle and shin. I dodged his wild, blind kicks as I moved in close. I couldn't grab him. Adam saw me shift and trapped coffee guy's leg in a scissor hold. I had my target, the man's exposed calf. With a lunge, I pressed the stun gun to his vulnerable flesh. Coffee guy screamed as I stunned him for a count of five, forcing the Coalescence out of him.

CHAPTER TWENTY-ONE

Coffee guy stiffened, his undulating cry of pain cutting off as the small glowing orb of gas and electricity forced its way out of his mouth. Coffee guy slumped to the ground and Adam let go of him. I didn't know if he was alive or not. For the moment, I didn't care. I only had eyes for the Coalescence seeking a new host.

Standing, I backed away. "No one say anything. No one move. It tracks by sound wave." I held the stun gun up, keeping it level with the alien. The Coalescence was in a small glob about twice the size of a tennis ball and pulsed different colors with lightning streaking through it. If it wasn't a murderous, mind-controlling creature, it would be beautiful.

"That's right. Come for me." I let my voice drop into a sing-song tone, exactly as Doctor Giacomi had done in PAR Lab the first time I saw one of the aliens. "You need a new host. And I'm susceptible."

The Coalescence hovered nearer and nearer. I heard Tomas and David shifting in their respective seats, and Heather take a breath. I couldn't look to see if she was still covering the men. I focused on my target. Adam stood in a silent motion behind the Coalescence, his stun gun out. Our eyes met and we nodded to each other.

"Come get me!" I shouted.

It did. It was fast. So fast. It came right for my face.

But Adam and I were faster. We both triggered our stun guns and stuck them into the Coalescence at the same time. There was an explosion of light as electricity from the arcing stun guns overwhelmed and killed the monster. We both winced back from this as David whispered, "Christ Almighty."

I looked to Heather. To my relief, she still had Tomas and David covered. I smiled my gratitude at her.

She didn't smile and nodded to the table. "You should pick that up."

I turned and saw a small holdout pistol in a sheath on the side farthest away from Tomas. I frowned at it and him.

Tomas shrugged, his hands on the table. "I figured it was better to disarm myself. Clearly there are reasons for your trust issues."

I gazed at David as I took the holdout pistol from the table and put it in my jacket pocket.

He shook his head. "I'm not armed."

"Here," Heather said behind me. I shifted back, standing even with her as she held out a couple of zip ties to Adam. "You want to secure the prisoner."

"Melissa?" Tomas spoke soft and concerned. "Is Carlita alive? Please tell me."

I didn't get a chance to answer him as a shot rang out in the hallway. Coffee guy yelled and dropped the knife he had raised to plunge into Adam's unprotected back. He fell over, clutching at his leg. It hadn't occurred to me that coffee guy was still a threat.

"Gotcha," Carrie's voice said over my ear piece. "Mel, tell Tomas I'm alive before he has a heart attack."

I twitched at the sound of her voice. She'd kept so quiet I'd forgotten she was there. I looked to Tomas. He was tense and watching as coffee guy held his knee, making pained noises in the back of his throat. Adam kicked the knife away from him.

"Did you hear that?" I asked Tomas.

"The gunshot, yes." He and David exchanged a glance.

David shook his head. "I already talked to the police about this exercise. They won't come."

Exercise? We needed to have a long talk and soon. "No. Carrie. Yes, she's alive. She's the one who shot coffee guy."

Tomas relaxed and bowed his head, letting out a shaky breath of relief.

"Mueller," David said, watching Adam zip tie the guy. "His name is Sergeant Don Mueller."

Heather shifted her stance as Adam stood, leaving Mueller and Carrie in the hallway. "Well, now what?"

I looked at the stun gun still in my hand. "Before we do anything, Agent Harrison and Agent Hood need to be tested for Coalescence possession. Then we can have a real conversation about what's happened in the last three days."

"Not me?" Heather tilted her head. "How do you know I'm clean?"

"The Coalescence wanted me to test you. They didn't mention either Tomas or David."

Tomas shook his head. "No. Agent Shaker, too. For my peace of mind." He glanced through the doorway at Sergeant Mueller. "Clearly, I have not been keeping my house as clean as I thought I had."

Heather nodded. "Yes. This is needed before we do a full debrief. Based on what I was told would happen—and I didn't know until well after me and David had gone," she leveled her gaze at David, "—didn't involve shootings, kidnappings or Doctor Vandermeek."

After we determined that Sergeant Mueller wouldn't die from blood loss, we locked him in the small bathroom. I felt bad leaving him on the cold floor with a bullet in him until he whispered, low enough that only I heard him, "We will succeed. You cannot escape us." Then, I used my willpower not to kick him in the head.

I covered each agent with the 9mm as Adam used the stun gun on them to make certain that all three of them were clean. It was not a fun experience to watch the three people who'd kept me from going to juvie, and from going crazy, and from dying, go through the stunning process. There was something heartbreaking in watching the adults I'd trusted go through something that made them so vulnerable. I couldn't look at them the same way again.

However, once it was done, we all breathed a sigh of relief that a minimum of trust could be re-established. Then the six of us crammed into that break room for what turned out to be the first of many debriefings over the coming weeks.

Tomas, David, and I sat around the table. Adam and Carrie sat on the small couch with Carrie's legs propped up in Adam's lap. Heather had pulled one of the office chairs in and was sitting behind and to my left.

Adam and Carrie flat out said that I was going to do the talking for them and they'd only chime in as needed. That left me to make sense of what was supposed to have happened versus what had happened.

Tomas, David, and I stared at each other for a moment. I didn't know what to say. Heather leaned forward and put a hand on my shoulder.

Warmed with gratitude, I relaxed and thought about everything I'd learned from my beloved Deroga Darrington, from Adam and Carrie, from Heather.

I needed to establish what the baseline was. I raised my chin and locked eyes with Tomas. "What was this test? What was supposed to have happened?"

"It was a test of teamwork, of improvisation, and of getting around the rules." Tomas didn't look away from me but I knew he was talking to all of us. "The three of you are not normal teenagers. Two of you are experienced in extraordinary acts of defiance and rule breaking. The third is physically superior in almost all ways. The three of you have been training together as a team. You have reasons to be loyal to each other and you've all gone through fire together. We wanted to see what you would be willing to do."

Tomas gestured to David who took up the answer. "I devised the test. Got Heather out of the way…" He glanced over my shoulder at Heather and mouthed "Sorry." to her. "… and then set an easy enough task: Have an old friend of Heather's request help. We used the name Elijah because, if you hadn't found the envelope—which would've told us something—and Heather did, she'd know it was a ruse."

David wouldn't look me in the eye as he continued to speak. "I had decided on the financial records of the Fort Leonard-Wood hospital. It was one of three targets Sergeant Mueller and I narrowed down. Then, Tuesday night, I had him deliver the envelope with the first stage of the test. There were four parts: One, decrypt the first note and decide what to do. Two, find the second note and decrypt with the short timeline. Three, break into the finance office and download the records. Four, meet here."

"What would've happened if we'd called Doctor Giacomi on the discovery of the first letter?"

"Nothing. She would've come for it and that would've been that. We'd know that Adam had influenced the two of you to follow the rules. It would've been information for the future. All of this was data collection and teamwork."

I tapped my fingers against the table. "So she did know about this." I nodded to myself. It made more sense now. "That's why she was willing to do what I asked and didn't fight me on it. I should've known there was more to it."

"You called Doctor Giacomi?" Tomas tilted his head in surprise.

"Yes, and asked her not to contact you. I'll get to that in a moment." I glanced over to Carrie and Adam. "What would've happened if we'd been caught?"

"We had a flag on your names with the Fort Leonard-Wood MPs," David shrugged. "It would've been a frightening experience, one you would've learned something from, but we would've gotten you out within four hours."

"So, all you wanted was to test whether or not we'd open a package not meant for us…"

"But with a name you'd recognize as Heather in her field agent days."

I ignored David and continued. "Break a code. Go geocaching. Break a second code. Then break into the finance office of the Fort Leonard-Wood hospital, download financial records, then bring them here to this place? That's it?"

Tomas and David exchanged a glance. "Yes."

Adam, Carrie, and I shared a disbelieving laugh. "That so did not happen. That would've been a lot easier."

Carrie shook her head and pointed at her leg. "That would've been a lot less painful."

"Yeah. A lot less painful," I agreed. I still hurt from being electrocuted and punched in the chest by Adam. Even though I hurt less than yesterday, I would probably hurt for weeks to come. "This is what happened…."

I talked for a good twenty minutes straight, trying to keep to just the facts and not bring in the arguments the three of us had. David started taking notes when I talked about Carrie being shot and Mrs. Palmer fixing her up.

Tomas murmured, "Remind me to reread the background check on Palmer."

"No need," Heather interrupted. "Former army nurse. Combat medic in various unnamed wars for a couple of agencies. Purple heart. Officially retired, going on five years. I reviewed her file before I asked her to check up on the kids. I do my due diligence."

Tomas nodded. "Accepted. Continue."

"She knows we're not normal and that someone did a background check on her." Carrie added with some admiration. "She's still got connections. And she's not afraid of speaking her mind."

The three adults exchanged a glance before Tomas gestured for me to go on.

When I was done telling him everything that had happened—the kidnapping, the underground lab, the Fedora monster, the rescue, the possession, the escape, and getting to this point, Tomas said, "Please tell me you told Doctor Giacomi about the underground lab."

I made a face at him. "Yes, of course. I was hurt and cranky but not dumb. If there was still valuable information there, we needed it. They've figured out—or think they've figured out—how to make immune people susceptible to them. We need all the information we can get. Maybe it'll lead to a clue on how to make those of us who are vulnerable less so."

"Why trust Doctor Giacomi in all this if you didn't trust me or Tomas?" David sounded casual but I could tell he was still hurt at my lack of trust.

I thought about my answer, knowing it would probably hurt him more but he needed to know the truth. "Because she didn't work closely with you two. Because she was there with us in PAR Lab. I knew she was immune. I knew she would understand. She killed them. She was there. She went through the same thing we did."

David nodded, "You have a point. Maybe with Doctor Vandermeek's research, we can find the marker to figure out who is vulnerable and who isn't." He kept his emotions close to his chest. I couldn't tell if my words hurt him or not. I hoped they didn't.

"Even if Doctor Vandermeek makes a run for it, I pulled down all his files from the hospital share." Carrie considered for a moment. "Then again, he planted that note in there for Adam. So, maybe we can't trust it too far."

Tomas waved a hand at her. "We've got medical experts who will figure that out. For now, if you all don't mind, I need to lock down Vandermeek's office and contact Doctor Giacomi." His gaze lingered on Carrie, turning soft and paternal, "I think the three of you need a full medical exam to make sure you're all right."

"We will be," I said, looking at them. "We survived it together."

Tomas nodded. "That you did."

David got up as Tomas stood. "I'll go get Sergeant Mueller. We'll take him in for questioning."

"I'll do it," Tomas said. "You get the car. I don't want to carry a trussed up traitor down the street. I don't think anyone in Richland would understand.

"Yes, sir." The two of them walked out together.

I spun in my seat to Heather. "When we get home, are you going to tell us what this test was *really* all about?"

She tilted her head. "What makes you think we're going home now? Medical first. For all of you."

"It's Sunday. The hospital's probably on emergency calls only. Can't we go tomorrow?" I wrinkled my nose. "I don't want to sit in the emergency room for hours for not-an-emergency. You know?"

"It's a military hospital. 24/7." Heather flicked her glance between Adam, Carrie, and me before she nodded. "But, all right. It can wait until tomorrow."

"Home and the truth?" I pressed.

"Yes, the truth from what I've been told." She winked at me. "There are some big plans being made."

Outside the break room, I heard. "Well shit." It was Tomas and he sounded annoyed.

I jumped out of my chair and moved to the door with Heather and Adam following. Tomas stood in the bathroom doorway. I slipped to his side to see what he was looking at. The white tile floor was covered in blood. So was the sink, the wall, and the now-open window. But the bathroom was empty.

Sergeant Mueller had escaped.

I looked at Adam and Carrie. I'm sure my face mirrored their wide-eyed look of fear. I shook my head and patted the air in what I hoped was a calming gesture. "It'll be fine. He can't get far. They've got his name and face on record."

Heather and Tomas stood to the side, their heads together with their backs to me, speaking so low I couldn't hear what they were saying. David was on the phone, giving Sergeant Mueller's information to someone. I stepped back into the break room.

"Shit," Adam said.

I nodded. "Agreed, but this doesn't change anything. Evie and Vandermeek already escaped. Unless Doctor Giacomi—Sadie—got them. Mueller escaping doesn't mean anything."

"Except that they know we know about them." Carrie twisted her hands around each other, then clasped them tight. "Wish I could do something."

I knew she wanted her laptop. It was still in the car. I shrugged. "Me, too. But wishes and fishes and all that."

"What does that even mean?" Adam scowled at me. "You say it all the time. It doesn't make sense."

"Oh. Something my mom used to say. 'If wishes were fishes, then beggars would feast.' It just means that wishes don't come true. Only action." I shrugged. "Sorry." I didn't know why I was apologizing. Maybe because Mueller got away.

"Okay kids, here's the deal," Heather leaned into the break room. "Situation as planned. We're going to head home. High alert. We know they're out there and they know where we live. Nothing's changed in that."

I gave Adam and Carrie an *I-told-you-so* look.

"Food and rest tonight. Medical exams in the morning. Then we have a talk. A real one. Off to the car. There's nothing more we can do here."

Carrie shifted to her feet and grabbed her crutches. "So, it's SNAFU, huh?"

"Yep," Adam followed her out and down the hallway.

I watched them go, then glanced at Heather.

"Situation normal. All f'd up." She gave me a fake smile. "Go on now."

I already knew what SNAFU meant. I had wanted to see if she agreed with it. She did, but didn't want to say so. Tomas and David stood next to each other, looking into the bloody bathroom as they spoke. Tomas must have felt my gaze. He looked up and nodded at me. No smile. He wouldn't forget I'd held a pistol on him. I nodded back. I didn't know what this meant for me and him but everything had changed somehow.

Yeah, situation all fucked up indeed. Nothing I could do about it now. I followed Adam and Carrie out to the SUV with Heather right behind me.

CHAPTER TWENTY-TWO

"… get you a new baseball bat tomorrow after we get back from the hospital," Heather said as she drove us home.

I sat in the back with Carrie. She played a game on her computer. Sometimes, I don't think she could function without it. I glanced up at the review mirror. Heather was watching me. I smiled at her. "That's good. I don't like the idea of Sergeant Mueller running around free and me without my favorite weapon. Maybe we should get half a dozen. You know, just in case."

Adam looked over his shoulder. "Yeah. I hope Sadie caught the other two while securing the underground lab. That's going to bother me for a long time."

I knew which "other two" he was talking about: Doctor Vandermeek and Evie. The fact that Adam didn't want to name them concerned me, but I didn't have enough knowledge of psychology to know if it was just his way of coping with the fact that his creator was a possessed traitor to humanity who wanted to experiment on him or what. I noted it to ask him later and to maybe tell Sadie in my next session.

Sadie. I thought of her as Sadie now and not Doctor Giacomi. I pondered that. I guess I thought of her as a person rather than just a doctor. Well, that was interesting. Probably because she hadn't let me down yet. Trust, hard won and easily lost. That led me to thinking about David and Tomas. A lot there I didn't want to face. I went back to thinking about the conversation in the hallway after I watched her kill the Coalescence. She'd asked me to call her Sadie back then. I refused because I didn't know her. Then, I didn't because of, I don't know, habit I guess.

I smiled and wondered how she'd take it if I started calling her by her given name—as she'd requested so many months ago. She was right, too. The next couple of sessions were going to be long ones. Too much to unpack.

Carrie poked me. "Whatcha thinking?"

I shook my head. "Nothing really. We're alive. I'm happy about that."

She closed Khalessi with a decisive click. "Heather, what are we going to do now?"

"You need to be a little bit more specific. I mean, right now, I'm turning on Heartwood Road. In ten minutes, we'll be home and someone will figure out dinner..."

"Mel will," Adam jumped in. "She's the best cook of us."

"Only if you clean up." I tried to smile but something caught my attention. I shivered like someone walked over my grave. I looked around, out the windows of the SUV, trying to spot what my paranoid hindbrain was trying to tell me.

"Deal." He didn't seem to notice my disquiet.

"No." Carrie frowned, shaking her head. "I mean, our position is compromised. They know where we live now. Are we going to move?"

That was a somber thought. I liked where we lived, despite the lack of a decent local mall or movie theater. The house was great. We'd just settled into a routine I liked. I didn't want to change up everything again.

Heather was slow to answer. "Well, relocation takes a lot of resources. If they, the Coalescence or their human allies, could infiltrate Agent Harrison's people so close to him, who knows where they already placed themselves? Finance and Accounting would be a good place. Following the money tells you a lot. So, I'm sorry, Carrie. I don't know. What do you kids want to do?"

I glanced over my shoulder, then turned around at movement in the distance. It was probably nothing but it didn't hurt to keep an eye on it. The movement became a white vehicle of some kind. It moved faster than I thought it should.

Carrie's answer was immediate. "I don't want to move. I like this house."

"Same here," Adam added. "I don't want to leave my garden." He paused. "Mel, what about you? Stay or go?"

I didn't answer. I looked out the back window, watching a rapidly approaching, white truck coming right up our backside. There wasn't much traffic on the frontage road in general and this guy could be an impatient local or could be something else. "Uh, Heather? I think we got a problem."

"I see him. Almost home." Her voice was tight with concern. This put all of us on high alert. Seatbelts checked and eyes open. Carrie stowed her laptop in her bag.

There was an arsenal at home that we could use to fight off whatever this was. I had my head craned to figure out who was driving the truck. I didn't recognize the truck, I probably wouldn't recognize the driver.

"Hang on kids, I'm going to take the corner hard."

"He's coming in fast." I tried to keep my voice level but it rose on the last word.

The truck put on a burst of speed and I recognized the driver's face just before he slammed into us. Even with sunglasses on, I knew who he was. "It's Mueller!" We were slammed forward in the impact.

Even though I was jerked to the side and my seatbelt bit into my waist, I kept my eyes on the truck as it backed off. I pulled my pistol from its holster. Focus descended. "Warning," I said. My voice was far calmer than I felt. "Gunshot." I took careful aim and hoped Heather wouldn't be mad at me shooting out the back window of our vehicle, but I figured she'd understand. Just as I took the shot, something crashed into the side of the SUV, tumbling us off the road.

The world became a spinning, painful whirl as the SUV did a full barrel roll down the shallow ditch. I lost my pistol as my body flailed about, belted in only at the waist. I smacked myself hard in the nose with my own fist just before I cracked my head against the door. Everything went black and grey as the pain cascaded through my head, down my neck, and into my already bruised chest.

I heard Adam yelling as I blinked away the fog and winced as the pain in my nose warred with the pain in my head. I blinked more as Carrie shook me. "Mel, you've got to help Adam. Mel!"

I looked at her, dazed. "Adam? Heather?"

"Heather's unconscious but alive. There's three of them out there. Adam's fighting them."

Shaking my head and blinking all the more. I had no idea how long I'd grayed out. Adrenaline covered and dulled the pain as I realized just how much danger we were all in. "Protect Heather. Mueller's there." I unbuckled my seatbelt and looked out the back of the SUV. Mueller was still in the truck. There was a bullet hole in the truck's windshield, but it was nowhere near its intended target.

Through the front of the SUV, I could see Adam in combat with three men. They were trying to dog-pile him rather than trying to hurt him. Fury rose as I understood that Doctor Vandermeek had not given up on his desire to experiment on Adam.

I had to slam my way out the side door, half crumpled from the accident. As I got the door open, Carrie shoved one of her crutches at me. "It's not a bat but you can still use it." She had blood running down one side of her face but her eyes were clear.

"Yeah. Thanks." I pulled it out after me and used it to keep me from falling on my face as I moved around the SUV, over the uneven, slippery ground, to get to the fight.

Adam held his own against the three of them; young looking men with crew cuts. He showed his superior physical strength and speed. As one would come in to be knocked away, the other would follow suit. Adam's goal was to keep them from the SUV. They wanted to wear him out so they could beat him down and take him with them.

I wondered if they were all military. That would not bode well for anyone if the Coalescence had infiltrated so far. Then I realized that I hadn't seen any electricity. Not when Adam punched, kicked or threw any of them. I didn't think they were possessed. That meant observation time was over.

"Coming in right," I called to Adam as I stepped forward and used the crutch like a battering ram against a man with a tattoo on his forearm. Tattoo fell back with a grunt and focused on me.

Adam and I shifted until we were almost back to back, just like Heather taught us in training. That kept the danger to our front half and kept our backs relatively safe. Tattoo rushed at me, making a grab for the crutch. I dropped my weapon, grabbed his arm, and pulled him over my hip. He landed hard on the ground, but I didn't let go of his arm. Instead, I twisted and pulled as hard as I could, adrenaline giving me strength.

I don't know which bone broke, but the sound of it was audible, even as Tattoo screamed his pain

"Down!"

At Adam's command, I dropped next to Tattoo and felt something fly over me. I think it was one of the other guys. Flat on the ground, I didn't have much leverage. Tattoo was howling and holding his arm, but he wasn't out. I throat punched him. His howls turned into choked gasps and gags. After a hammerfist to the nose, Tattoo was out. He still gagged and gasped for breath, but it was in soft twitches and moans. Between his nose, his throat, and his broken arm, I determined he was no longer a threat.

Behind us, there were two measured shots. I looked to the SUV. Heather was still slumped over the wheel. I didn't see Carrie and I didn't see Sergeant Mueller. I also didn't see the guy who kicked me in the back of the head.

It wasn't pain so much as stunning agony. I fell over, still conscious, but unable to get my body to do anything I demanded it do. My helpless twitching matched Tattoo's. As I lay there in the muck, wetness seeping into my clothes, I tasted blood. It must've been from when I hit myself in the nose with my fist. It made me glad that I had lost my pistol first. Things could've been much worse.

A man jumped over me from behind. He was probably the one who kicked me in the head. I watched him scramble up out of the ditch and run towards Heather and Carrie in the SUV. I flailed my hands in a futile gesture to get up, to run after him. There was nothing I could do to stop him or help Adam and the rest.

There was another measured gunshot. It had to be Carrie. I prayed it was. She had her pistol, plus the one I'd lost, and she was a solid shot.

Then there was the sound of a cocking 12 gauge shotgun. It's unmistakable. Also, I knew we didn't have one. The shotgun exploded and hit something metallic. Wheels burned rubber as that shotgun cocked and fired again. I caught a glimpse of the white truck speeding down the road in the direction of away.

I didn't know where anyone was. I didn't know who was alive and who wasn't. I needed to move if I wanted to live. I forced myself to a kneeling position and looked around. Adam stood over the body of one of the men, his fist bloody. He looked back the way we'd come, watching the truck go.

Next to me, Tattoo fluttered his eyes open and moved to roll over. I put a stop to that with a double hammerfist to the forehead. It wasn't pretty, it wasn't strong as I wanted it to be, but it worked. That was the whole point to winning a fight. He subsided into twitches and nothing more.

I put a hand to the back of my head. It came away sticky with blood. That wasn't good. "Adam?"

He waved me to quiet as he hunkered down and sidled up to the SUV. I realized he didn't know who had shot the shotgun. Neither did I. He peeked around the corner of the SUV then backpedaled fast, his hands raised. "Whoa! It's me, Mrs. Palmer. It's me, Adam."

"And me, Mel," I yelled as I struggled to my feet, my balance not agreeing with me or me standing—especially not on sloped ground. I pinwheeled my arms, falling again, but Adam lunged to me and stopped my fall.

"You two look like hell." Mrs. Palmer lowered the shotgun. "What did I tell you about not hurting yourselves anymore?" Her voice was sharp, but there was a kindness and concern written all over her face. She eyed the downed men. "Are there more on the way?"

"We don't know." I was grateful Adam helped me climb out of the ditch. My head and my face hurt more than I cared to think about. I was covered in muck. All I wanted was a bath and to sleep. Not necessarily in that order. But, Mrs. Palmer had the right of it. There might be more coming. We needed to be ready.

"How did you know we needed help?" Adam gestured to the shotgun.

"After my last two meetings with you kids, when I hear a car crash outside my house, followed by gunshots, I know there's trouble. I wasn't born yesterday."

Carrie hobbled out of the SUV on one crutch. "I called for backup. David and Tomas know. They are on their way. I gave the license plate number and description of the truck. Wouldn't be surprised if it was stolen. But, I kept that bastard in the truck. He tried to get out a couple of times."

"More details I don't need to know." Mrs. Palmer pursed her lips and looked between the three of us then focused in on Adam. "Do you know how to use a shotgun?"

"Yes, ma'am."

She held the shotgun out to him. "You're on sentry. I need to see to Heather."

Wonder of wonders, Adam didn't argue. He accepted the weapon and moved to stand next to Carrie. She still had her pistol.

Mrs. Palmer turned to me. "After Heather, I'll look at you. You're bleeding pretty bad. Sit and tilt your head back."

I didn't have the energy to fight. Sitting sounded like a wonderful idea. I sat on the edge of the road and did as Mrs. Palmer commanded. It allowed me to keep half an eye on the incapacitated enemies. The asphalt felt better than it had any right to.

That was how David and Tomas found us—in front of our house with a crashed SUV, Mrs. Palmer looking an unconscious Heather over, Adam and Carrie standing sentry, and me trying to keep my blood inside my body.

CHAPTER TWENTY-THREE

Mrs. Palmer pointed that lethal finger at me, Carrie and Heather in turn. "You will take your medicine in one hour and fifteen minutes—after you eat everything on your plates."

"Yes ma'am," came the subdued chorus from the three of us. We were arranged around the living room in various states of pajamas and bandages. In our laps were trays of grilled cheese sandwiches, chips, and water. Next to each plate was a small cup of pills. The pills were different for each of us.

As Adam entered the living room with his own tray of grilled cheese sandwiches and chips, Mrs. Palmer turned on him. "You will make sure they do so."

He half-smiled at her and blew a breath. "Have you met them, Mrs. P.? I'm lucky I have my own bathroom. I can't tell them to do anything." He settled in his seat on the couch next to Carrie.

"Ah, but you have a not-so-secret weapon." She flourished a walkie-talkie and handed it to him. "You have me." She glanced over her shoulder at us to make her threat clear. "I may be deployed as needed."

Adam chuckled as he pocketed the walkie-talkie. "All right."

"Now, I'll check on your protection detail. Agent Baldwin is a good one. I haven't decided about Agent Lenaghan. I'll be back in..." she checked her watch. "Three hours and forty-five minutes."

"We'll be fine," Heather said with a tired smile. "Promise. I may be a delicate flower right now but I am also an agent." Her bruised face made her look a lot more hurt than she was. She had a bandage around her head and a sling to keep her cracked collar bone in place.

Mrs. Palmer returned the smile. "Oh, I know. It's easy to get back into the habit of pushing obstinate soldiers around, making sure they do what they need to do to mend. As obstinate as that Agent Harrison of yours." She gave us a half-wave. "I've got soaps to watch."

I watched her go with a smile. She was the only one I'd ever seen go toe-to-toe with Agent Harrison and make him follow her orders to have the four of us taken to the hospital immediately because she didn't have the equipment to make sure none of us would die from internal bleeding or cranial hemorrhaging. I could believe that she'd chewed military officers up one side and down the other to get what she needed for her soldiers in the field. She had a way of suddenly being bigger than life.

Silence descended on the living room. This was the first time all of us were up, coherent, and in the same room together since the attack three days before. I looked around the room as I took a bite of my sandwich. I might be a better cook than Adam but he made a mean grilled cheese. Adam still had the remnants of his black eye and that was it. Otherwise, he was fine—physically. Carrie was in a new set of leg bandages. She'd elected to keep the forthcoming scar and not have her leg cut open again. She also had a long scratch down the side of her face. It looked worse than it was, still crusted over with a thick scab. No one knew if it would scar. She had joked that it would give her character and make her seem mysterious. I admired her confidence and wondered if I'd ever feel that strong.

Heather returned my gaze when it rested on her. I smiled out of reflex, trying not to show how worried I was for her and my siblings. Her blackened eyes and bandages made her look like the worst of the bunch. I had a pair of black eyes as well, from almost breaking my own nose and a bandage around my head because of the stitches where that guy kicked me. I still didn't know his name.

I took another bite of food at the same time as Heather and giggled into the silence. Adam and Carrie glanced at each other then at me, smiling. My giggle turned into laughter. It was infectious. The three of us tried to stifle our laughter but laughed harder at Heather's perplexed look.

"All right, I'm game. What's so funny?" Heather took another bite of her sandwich.

This sent us into another bout of hysterical laughter. I tried to speak. "No beauty contests!"

Carrie squeaked long, shrill laughter at that. Even Adam laughed, mouthing the words I'd said.

Heather watched us for a long moment, smiling. "Okay. Yeah, I don't think any of us is going to win a beauty contest anytime soon." She chuckled, then winced with a soft gasp and put her hand against her collar bone, trying to stop the pain.

That sobered me up quick. Carrie and Adam stopped laughing, too. We stared at each other. I smiled and shrugged. "I'm sorry. I just. The last conversation we had over a meal… it was about beauty contests." That seemed so long ago.

"I know," Heather said. "I know." She looked at the three of us. "All right, the last thing I promised Melissa was that I'd tell you what that test had really been about."

Carrie and Adam shifted, leaning forward. I found myself mimicking them. I was just as eager as them to find out what was going on. I knew, right now, the one thing I could count on was Heather telling us the truth.

"Here's the deal. I've been training the three of you to fight and work together because I think the three of you have the talent and skills we, the government, need. Also, because I was under orders to." Heather shrugged. "And, because I teach what I know. I've been training agents off and on for decades."

Her expression took on a neutral cast I couldn't quite read, but I think she was more in duty mode than personal.

"Those of you who need to get your GEDs will get it this year. Then what? Traditional college is out for all of you." She glanced at Adam and gestured to him. "Except for maybe you." Then she looked at me. "After you're eighteen, you can go to college if you want but that's a couple years off." She smiled at Carrie. "I already know what your answer to college is."

"Boring. Not interested." Carrie spoke in a firm, dismissive tone.

Heather nodded.

Adam shrugged. "I don't think I need to go to college to learn about working the land, do I?"

Heather returned the shrug. "I'm sure there is some kind of schooling for that. I don't know what it is. Feel free to look it up. Maybe a mentorship. Maybe formal education. I don't know."

I raised my chin. "I don't think I really want to go to college. I was kinda thinking EMT or paramedic." I paused, then pushed on. "We kinda need that around here. It's something I'm pretty good at, but I don't want to be a doctor. The idea of eight years in school...." I gave a mock shudder that wasn't feigned. I couldn't stand the idea of that kind of formal education.

Heather nodded. "I think EMT training might be good but I know you can't take it until you're eighteen. Not my rules or under the official rules of your supervision. EMT training rules. I've looked into it already, given your interest in trauma medicine."

"Maybe Mrs. Palmer?" I tried to keep the hope out of my voice. It wasn't often that I actually wanted something like this. It was hard to keep my emotions inside.

"Maybe. I'll run it by Agent Harrison. She did bully him into making sure we were all cared for. Also, she's officially hired as a nurse for us for the next ten days. After that, you guys can help me. I'm the only one who got really hurt."

Carrie crunched a potato chip then waved half of it at Heather. "But, what was the point of the test? Really?"

Heather gazed at her plate and took a moment to gather her thoughts. "We need to hunt down every last Coalescence and deal with them. We also need field teams who can investigate strange goings on. Unofficial field teams, especially ones who understand what we're fighting—how and why. Who can improvise, work together, and trust each other. Teams that can take care of themselves. Like you guys."

"I think we need a bit of help on that last one," Adam said.

"You're inexperienced in some ways but years ahead of our best agents in other ways. You know, really know, what we are fighting. Especially you, Mel. You've been inside their head." Heather furrowed her brow. "So to speak. You know what I mean."

"Wait." I tilted my head to the side. "You want us to become an alien hunting team?"

Heather paused, considered my statement, then nodded. "That's about the size of it. You all know what to look for. Two of you are immune. We've got Doctor Vandermeek's research and an idea on how to inoculate those vulnerable against possession. Also, you three understand what we're fighting against. How dangerous they are. And that this has been going on for longer than we thought." She nodded to me, "It wasn't until you linked the *Mega Aphis* to the Coalescence that we realized they were linked by more than the fact that they were alien invasive forces. The Coalescence was behind it. How many other incursions are they responsible for?"

"Do we get any say in this?" Adam asked at the same time Carrie said, "But we don't really know how to do this. We'd need training and covers and money and… stuff." She tapped her ever-present laptop. "Better hardware and software."

I didn't say anything because both of them had articulated my whirling thoughts. It was a lot of responsibility but, in a very strange and weird way, the world needed us. I couldn't figure out which was scarier—the responsibility or the need. Or the fact that I kinda liked the idea of it.

"I'll answer Adam first." Heather gazed at him, open and frank. "Of course you have a choice. You always have a choice. If you want to have nothing to do with this and to become a private gardener, maybe own your own horticulture business, then that's what will happen. We'll help you get set up. This is not a requirement or a mandate. But, you, your skills, and your experience would be appreciated."

Heather gazed at me. "You are not required to do this. Yes, you are under the official care of the State Department but you are not a slave. After you turn eighteen, your case will be reviewed and, I suspect, dismissed. You have a choice. You always have a choice."

I didn't know what to say. The cynical part of me wanted to laugh in her face. The hopeful part of me believed her and believed that she had my best interest at heart. If she was lying, she did an excellent job of it.

Heather turned to Carrie. "You all will be considered good citizens of the United States of America. No matter what your past is. This whole thing is your choice. The test was to see if it was even a viable choice. I think you've all proven that it is. The test, and the fight. You worked so well together…"

Heather took a breath. "As for training, I know what Tomas and David would like for you three. If you choose to do this, there's a full-on training course that's part boot camp, part, well, espionage and infiltration training. Each with a focus on your particular talents as well as general talents."

She looked at Adam. "Strength, infiltration, and field work."

Heather nodded to Carrie. "Research, communications, and ops. Some field work."

She turned to me. "Leadership, ops, and field work."

"Whoa," I murmured. This was more than I ever expected.

"No one has to decide now. Basically, you've got a couple weeks to figure out what you'd like to do. If you want to try this out, then we'll move forward on it." Heather tilted her head. "Me? I think you three make a great team. If I can, I want to continue being involved. I know too much not to want to work to win this covert war."

The three of us exchanged glances. No one said anything but from the looks we were exchanging, and the excitement I saw in each others' eyes, I thought we all were going to say yes. Despite everything that had happened, we were ready to sign on and do something about this subtle invasion.

I shook my head. Imagine that: Melissa Allen, Alien Hunter.

EPILOGUE

Sergeant Don Mueller was on his knees before Doctor Erik Vandermeek and Evelyn Vandermeek. "Please. I didn't know she'd be there so soon. I thought… I was going to be gone before they came for their meeting. That she wouldn't know – "

Evie cut him off with a gesture. "Your job is not to think. It's to obey. You failed."

Erik noted how the hard, adult words coming from his young daughter's mouth shocked and demoralized the sergeant. The juxtaposition of it warranted future study. It may make dealing with his wayward experiment easier in the future.

Erik glanced at Evelyn. He wanted to get closer to her thoughts but she'd shut him out after the debacle in the cave. So used to near constant contact with the other Coalescence around him, the limited contact worried him. Especially since all he could feel from her was a simmering anger.

"An interesting idea," *his Coalescence commented.* "The study of human reactions is as fascinating as it is vexing. You do not react as any of our other hosts do."

Erik could not agree more. We are human, *he thought.*

"Not only did you fail at gaining Adam's confidence, you let your Coalescence be murdered. Then your foolhardy attack on the SUV lost us two recruits and injured a third."

"Please, Evelyn. Please. I'll do better. I swear." Sergeant Mueller groveled, pressing his forehead to the ground.

Evie shook her head, her dark hair waving. "You are not worthy of Bonding."

Sergeant Mueller sat up, a stricken look marring his already bruised face.

Erik knew his cue when he heard it. He raised his pistol and shot the sergeant twice in the chest. He stood and fired a third time, destroying the failure's brain. Erik put the weapon away and turned to Evie, awaiting her pleasure.

Evie whirled on him. "And you." She spat the word out with venom. "You're lucky you still have the skills we need."

Erik stepped back from the small fury as she advanced, her fists clenched. "What..? I'm sorry…."

"You know what you did."

"You know what you did." Evie's voice matched his Coalescence's tone perfectly. Of course it would. They were in Sync while he was not. "You destroyed our plan to lure Adam to us. To have him come to us willingly. To make him distrust the others. To make him an ally. No. You saw him and you acted without thought of consequence. You set our plans back an incalculable amount. You will be punished."

"Evelyn, please…" Erik knew he sounded just like the late Don Mueller but he couldn't help himself.

"Goodbye for now. Perhaps for all time."

He realized what was about to happen a moment too late. Erik screamed as his body arched in agony, burning pain crawled out of his lungs, up his throat, and out of his mouth. The Coalescence could join or separate from their hosts with pain or not as they chose. They could kill or not at their whim. His Coalescence added the insult of pain to the injury of its separation.

Lying on the floor, his torso in flames, he watched his companion of decades hover over and sink into Evie. She smiled as the Coalescence joined within. Her smile faded and she gazed at him, dispassionate and cool. "You will remain Unbound until we feel you've learned from your mistake. Until then, contemplate your solitude, Outcast. Figure out how to undo your mistake."

For the first time in as long as he could remember, Erik was alone with his thoughts. The emptiness inside deafened and dulled him. He realized that Evelyn had never been his daughter. She belonged only to the Coalescence.

"I swear, I will make this right." Erik meant every word. He would do anything to make sure he could Bond with the Coalescence, and his daughter, again.

NEVER LET ME FEEL

BRAND NEW SHORT STORY

"Is what Heather says about John Lolen true?" I picked at the cracking leather on the car door's arm rest. David's car, an ancient four-door sedan known as the Fedmobile, had seen better days.

"I don't know. What'd she say?" He glanced over at me. "Mel, stop that. The old girl has enough troubles without you helping."

I put my hands in my lap. "You should get another car."

"Not until I run this one into the ground. Besides, she's got a few more miles in her." David gave the steering wheel an affectionate pat. "Mister Lolen?" he prompted without looking at me.

I tilted my head at his careful tone. Maybe this guy I was going to see really was a high mucky-muck. I shrugged. "Just that Tomas only calls him by his last name even though he's younger. That the man has "seen some things" and, well, that he's important and I needed to remember that. I mean, I know I have to talk to him about my experiences with the *Mega Aphis* and the Coalescence—that he has clearance—but I'm just not sure what's the big deal with him. Why do I need to be careful around him? You know?"

David didn't say anything as he turned into the parking lot of a three-story brick building. It was an unassuming thing. Just one more administration building on Fort Leonard-Wood. There was a bronze plaque to the side that was too far away for me to read.

Once he parked the car and turned it off, he sat there, not moving, silent for long enough that I felt my heartbeat speed up. I took a breath and waited, though the urge to shake him was strong.

"Mister Lolen *is* an important man, Mel. He's Agent Harrison's boss. It's not a secret but it's not advertised. He's also the man who has to decide if the government is going to officially lift the quarantine on South Dakota. He traveled all the way from DC to speak with you. You *need* to be on your best behavior."

He continued to talk but I wasn't listening. It'd been thirteen months since the day South Dakota Died and with it, my whole life. As far as I knew, I was the only survivor of what happened. If there were others, they, and the government, weren't talking. The idea of being able to go home, if only to get some small keepsakes, hit me like a bus.

"Melissa?"

A hand on my arm.

"Mel? Are you okay?"

I shook my head. "No, but when has that ever mattered?"

David pulled back. "It matters to me. It's always mattered." He frowned a wounded look I'd seen too many times since that day in the upholstery shop. The fact that, for a little while, I didn't trust him hurt him more than I'd ever really know. I still don't know why. Maybe because he came for me in a quarantine zone against Agent Harrison's orders.

I took a breath, anger warring with my need to keep the peace. "I'm sorry. I lashed out. I didn't..." I shook my head. "I need a moment. Shrapnel effect."

He nodded, his face smoothed back over to neutral. "Okay." Without another word, he unbuckled himself, got out of the car, and shut the door with a gentle click.

I put my face in my hands and waited for the tears. They didn't come. That was probably the lithium. One of its side effects. I popped a lozenge to combat my dry mouth and thought about Onida. This Mister Lolen was going to talk to me as part of his determination of whether or not they would open South Dakota again. Officially, anyway. No doubt, there were people sneaking in. Lots of valuable things left lying about.

What I didn't understand was why someone so important wanted to talk to me first. I'd told David everything I could think of from back then when he first interviewed me. I'm sure it was in the reports. My stomach flipped and flopped. Was I in trouble again? Had this Mister Lolen decided that I was too much of a danger to be on the outside?

I squeezed my eyes shut tight. That was the paranoia talking. I was a good person. Heather was a good guardian. I didn't need to be locked up. I didn't need to be afraid.

I looked out the car window. It was a blustery day with gray clouds flying by. David leaned again the Fedmobile. He looked like he wanted to be anywhere but here. For the moment, I wasn't sure what I wanted. I needed to know why Mister Lolen wanted to talk to me and I needed to know if I was going to be able to go home and get some of my old stuff.

I nodded to myself as I unbuckled my seatbelt. "Let's go meet The Man."

*

Government buildings all have the same feel of utility and bare bones necessity. Well-built, blocky, dull. Like all the others I'd been in, this one was decorated with pictures of high-ranking military people from all over. It was all at a familiar height and setting. I'm sure there's a regulation for how to decorate military buildings. It made me wonder about the person who wrote the rules on that.

After walking the halls and up the stairs to the third floor, we came to a much nicer area. The hallway was still regulation tile but the offices were all carpeted. We entered the office suite at the end of the hall. I stopped myself from whistling at the change. It was a full waiting room with a receptionist's desk and a second, window-enclosed, office filled with more military pictures and two flags—the American flag and the Fort Leonard-Wood flag—set behind and framing the large desk.

A pleasant looking Hispanic woman in an army uniform stood as we entered. "Hello. You must be Agent Hood and Melissa Allen. I'm Sergeant Alisha Santos. Please," she gestured to the leather couches, "make yourselves comfortable. I'll let them know you're here."

I was too keyed up to sit. I turned to the back wall and looked at the pictures of the uniformed men and women there. I couldn't focus long enough to read who they were or why they were framed. Behind me, I heard Alisha speak.

"Sir? They're here." Pause. "Yes, sir."

I glanced over my shoulder.

Alisha hung up her cell phone and pocketed it. "They'll be right out."

I turned and waited. I wasn't sure where "they" would be coming from until Tomas and Mister Lolen walked out past a large, potted tree against the left office wall. Smiling, I wondered if the tree was put there on purpose to hide the fact that there was another way out of the office. I bet it was.

David straightened. "Wait here." He walked into the main office and shook hands with the two men.

I eyed Mister Lolen. He was a bald, white man dressed in dark slacks with a matching vest and a maroon shirt. From what I could see, he had the worst case of resting bitch face I'd ever seen. Either that, or he frowned a lot. But, he smiled when he shook hands with David. The smile was attractive and made his severe face lighten up into something friendly and engaging. Either way, I got the sinking feeling that I wasn't going to enjoy this interview.

"Are you all right? Would you like a cup of water?"

I jerked out of my thoughts and realized that Alisha had left the confines of the desk and had approached. She was still about ten feet away from me. I shook my head as my spidey-sense crawled up the back of my head. I realized I didn't like Alisha and I didn't know why. I shook my head. "No. Thanks."

"Don't be nervous. Mister Lolen is a good man." She tucked one side of her short bob behind her ear. "But, it's fine if you are. After what you've been through."

"What would you know about it?" I knew that was rude but I couldn't help myself. I rubbed the back of my neck, trying to get rid of the creepy-crawlies.

"Everything. I *am* Mister Lolen's personal assistant. It's my job to know. It can't be easy losing your family—twice—then having to come here to talk about South Dakota. It must be lonely." She glanced at the trio of men. "I just wanted you to know that it's okay, that I understand, and if you need to, you can talk to me after the interview."

I grimaced as she hit a nerve. She had the worst bedside manner ever. "Thanks," I mumbled and backed away, into the wall. The picture next to me clattered. I whirled to catch it but it was still secure.

"Melissa?"

David beckoned me to him. It was show time.

*

David patted me on the shoulder and left as I entered. I wanted to pull him back in but Tomas stepped forward. "Melissa, this is Mister Lolen. He's here to talk to you about South Dakota."

I stopped where I was, just inside the doorway, and eyed Mister Lolen. Up close, he was as striking as he was severe. A little taller than me but not as tall as Tomas, he had gray-blue eyes with crinkles at the corners. His suit was well made but didn't look expensive. With his gray and black paisley tie, he had a European feel that made you want to pay attention to him. The man had charisma. I guessed he was about the same age as Heather, early forties.

After a moment, I realized that we were staring at each other. As much as I was examining him, he was examining me. I fought the urge to cross my arms. Instead, I shoved my hands in my coat pockets and thought, *I am Melissa Jean Allen. I've fought monsters and won. I'm not afraid of you.*

Liar, the other side of me smirked.

We stood like that for another thirty heartbeats, each of us refusing to back down. Mister Lolen kept his face in that small, severe frown. I wondered if I should say something. I decided I shouldn't. I didn't know what to say anyway.

Tomas cleared his throat. "Perhaps we should have this conversation sitting down."

Mister Lolen gave him a slight, amused half-smile. "Of course."

That broke the stand-off as everyone shuffled to their seats. Mister Lolen behind the large desk, Tomas and me in the comfortable seats across from it. As we sat down and I read the name plate sitting on the desk, I realized that we were in the camp commander's office. I blinked a couple of times and gave Mister Lolen another look. Who was this guy that he could boot the camp commander out of his own office?

Mister Lolen steepled his hands before him and asked, "Why should I open the South Dakota quarantine zone?"

The question was a battering ram. It made me want to run far away. Instead, I opened my mouth and let the words come tumbling out. "Because it's safe. I killed the euthanasia field. Those people need to be put to rest." I winced at my words. They were already at rest. They all died in their sleep. "Because it's the right thing to do."

"What's to stop the *Mega Aphis* from coming back and killing everyone in that region again?"

"The Coalescence won't let them. They killed too many potential hosts."

"You know this how?"

I frowned at him. "Because I was possessed and I killed the Coalescence in me. I didn't kill the information I got. I told David..." I looked over my shoulder to gesture to David out in the sitting room and paused. Alisha was by the doorway. I stopped talking and gazed at her. My spidey-sense was tingling again. There was something familiar...

"Yes, Alisha?"

"I just wanted to see if you needed anything. Coffee? Tea?"

Mister Lolen shook his head. "No. That will be all." He waited until she sat back down then prompted, "David...?"

I blinked and shook my head, trying to clear it. "David. I told David all this. It had to be in a report."

"Yes. It was in a report but I wanted to hear it from you. Why should I trust you? You just admitted to being possessed by an alien."

Heat rushed to my cheeks. "And I've been stunned multiple times since then. I don't have a Coalescence in me. I still know what I know. You can trust me if you want to or not." I scowled. "It looks like you've made up your mind."

"Convince me."

"Of what?"

"That I can trust what you have to say."

"How?"

Mister Lolen sat back, his eyes narrowed. "That's on you. Convince me that opening the quarantine zone is the right thing to do."

I looked at Tomas. He nodded to me then turned his attention back to Mister Lolen. There was no help there. How the hell was I supposed to convince this stranger that South Dakota was okay? Especially when I had no proof except for my memory? I bowed my head and thought hard.

I raised my head and locked eyes with him."Because you've already got men inside South Dakota. You've already made sure that whatever sensitive material is in there has been dealt with. Because if we live in fear of what might be, that's not living. I broke the transmitter. I know you guys have it. I know you know what to look for. Besides, what's to stop them from doing something like South Dakota over New York? Oh, right. I know, because the Coalescence wants to possess us. That's how they're invading. They don't want to kill potential hosts."

"That's not good enough."

I stared at that scowl for a moment, feeling like he'd slapped me. When the anger rose, I let it. "Screw you and your "good enough." I don't know why you brought me here. You've already made up your mind." I stood. "Do whatever it was you were going to do and leave me the hell alone."

"Melissa..." Tomas put a hand out.

"No. He's already made up his mind. I don't know why I'm here." I whirled and stomped out of the office.

I continued through the reception room to the far door. David intercepted me. I let him stop me and pull me into a hug. I owed him that much. I pressed my face to his chest, trying to stop my treacherous tears.

"It's going to be okay." David pet my hair. "I'm sorry this hurt so much."

My spidey-sense went off before Alisha spoke. "Can I get you anything?"

"No, Sergeant Santos, I've got this." David kept his back to the woman.

As soon as he said the word "Sergeant" I knew what had been bothering me about her. David felt me stiffen and pet my hair again. "It'll be okay. I promise."

I didn't look at him as I whispered, "She reminds me of Sergeant Mueller."

It was David's turn to stiffen. "You sure?"

"Yes. I can feel her." I kept my voice low. "It's a tingle like when Mueller showed at the upholstery shop."

"Are you sure enough to bet my career on it?" His voice was as low as mine.

Was I sure? Could I trust my senses with all that was wrong with me? My hallucinations weren't consistent. Three times she came near me and the back of my head tingled. It wasn't all in my head. It wasn't a hallucination. I had to take the chance. Heaven help me, and David, if I was wrong.

I twisted to look up at him and nodded.

He nodded back. "My left inside pocket."

I snaked a hand to that pocket and found a stun gun. I pulled it to me and hid it in one of my inner jacket pockets. I took a breath and straightened. "I'm okay now." I wiped at my tears. "I'm sorry. It's hard. I could, maybe, go home."

David patted my shoulder. "I know. I know." He raised his voice a little. "Sergeant? I think we could use that water now."

"Of course, Agent Hood." She stood and walked to the sideboard next to her desk. She poured two glasses of water and brought them over to us.

As soon as my spidey-sense went off, I backed away from her. It lessened. I stepped forward as if to take the offered glass, and the creepy-crawly, tingling sensation came back. It got stronger the nearer we were to each other. I let my hand drop as I looked at David and said, "I'm sure."

David didn't hesitate. He pulled his stun gun from behind his back and tagged her with it in the neck. Both glasses of water went flying as Alisha gave a high wail of pain. She continued to scream as lightning arced over her body and the Coalescence came out of her mouth. David lunged for it as a man's yell of pain came from the main office.

Everything moved too fast. I was aware that Tomas had stunned Mister Lolen. I saw that Alisha was still alive. I gave a gasp as David killed the Coalescence. I didn't feel the alien die but I did feel the abrupt lack of tingling at the back of my head.

"I'm sorry. I'm so sorry." Alisha twitched on the floor, crying. "I couldn't stop it. I couldn't control myself. I wasn't me. I'm sorry."

I stared at her. This was the first time I saw a freed person—who wasn't me—who seemed like they were grateful that the alien possessing them was dead. I didn't know what to make of it.

David stepped forward. "You okay?"

I nodded. "You?"

He sighed. "Yeah but you know the rules. You need to stun me." He put his stun gun back in his jacket pocket. As he started to take his jacket off, two MPs burst through the office door with their weapons drawn.

I dropped my stun gun and raised my hands.

*

"The rules suck." We were back in our previous positions: David paced in the reception area. Me, Tomas, and Mister Lolen sat in the camp commander's office. The sitting room had the addition of two MPs standing by the door. "There's got to be a better way to test for possession. I'm sure repeated stunning does bad things to the body. Especially to me. I was electrocuted, you know." The essential tremor in my left hand was at a rock concert, playing the drums. I had to sit on it to keep it from distracting me.

"I know." Mister Lolen eyed me like a scientist eyes a particularly interesting bug. "Tell me about this "tingling" you feel."

I shook my head. "I don't how to describe it without sounding stupid."

"Try."

I wanted to glare at him but I was too tired and my head ached with the adrenaline crash. "It's a spidey-sense. It shows up at the back of my head near the neck. It's like… you know when you're doing something and you suddenly realize you're being watched? It's kinda like that. But stronger. The closer I got to Sergeant Santos, the stronger the sense was."

He nodded, seeming to accept my explanation. "You felt this with Sergeant Mueller?"

I shrugged. "I thought I did. I felt something. I didn't know what back then. We'd been fighting."

"Interesting. Interesting." He gazed at me with a gleam in his eye he didn't have before.

A dawning horror blossomed. "You suspected the sergeant was possessed." It wasn't a question. Mister Lolen didn't contradict me. Rage flared. "You asshole! That's why I'm here. Not about South Dakota. It was all about Sergeant Santos."

He tilted his head and watched me with no emotion at all.

I surged out of my seat. "You motherpussbucket bastard. Was I bait for her or was she bait for me?" I looked at Tomas. "You knew about this?"

Tomas shook his head. "No." He watched the two of us with a calculated gaze.

"I can't believe this."

"Sit down." Mister Lolen's voice was quiet.

I scowled at him. "No."

"I said: Sit. Down."

He didn't raise his voice but something in the way he spoke had me sitting before I knew what I was doing. I crossed my arms, mostly to tamp down on my left hand, and watched him with wary anger. I really wanted to punch him or someone.

"First, I did want to hear what you had to say about South Dakota. Second, I did want to see how you reacted under pressure. Third, I did suspect something was wrong with Sergeant Santos. She was acting out of the ordinary. Little things. Adding sugar to my coffee. Forgetting to close my office door. Things, I think, she knew she could do to tell me she was no longer her own person. As for you, yes… you both were bait for each other. I wanted to see how the two of you interacted."

I shook my head, my face hot with anger and lingering fear. "How could you do that to me? Knowing I'm vulnerable to possession?"

"It was a calculated risk." He shifted and looked at his hands. "I'm sorry, Melissa, but I needed to know. We're at war. The world is at stake. I needed to see what would happen. Now, we know you can sense them. We didn't know that before. Now, we can test Alisha, Sergeant Santos, to see if she has the same sensing ability. We have some of them captured."

"You could've killed me."

"Yes."

I didn't expect such blunt honesty. It sapped the anger out of me and a cold fear grew in my roiling stomach. I didn't know what to say.

"I know you've decided to train with Adam and Carrie to help hunt down these alien infiltrators. You'll be risking your life every day of every mission. You've got to realize that. If you can't handle it, better to know now."

"But you set me up." I wanted to pace but I didn't dare move from my seat.

"I took a calculated risk in a controlled environment and I'd do it again. Both Agent Harrison and I will be sending you into known and unknown danger. That's the job you've signed up for. We can't always tell you the reason why. A lot of times, it's best if we don't. You will need genuine reactions and plausible deniability. That's part of the job."

There was nothing I could say to that. I looked at Tomas.

He nodded once. "It's true. We do what we must when we're at war. You'll want to talk to Heather, Carrie, and Adam about this. They need to understand what you've all signed up for. Otherwise, this is a non-starter."

I dropped my eyes and grimaced. I hate it when assholes are right. Mister Lolen was an asshole but he was an asshole in charge. I *did* sign up for the job of hunting and fighting the aliens. I *knew* that government people never tell you everything—Heather flat out told me so. The worst part about it, I couldn't not fight the Coalescence. I could sense them now. That would drive me crazier than I already was. I let out a heavy sigh. "Fine. You're right. I don't like it though. You should've trusted me."

Mister Lolen shifted in his chair. "As for South Dakota, you are also right."

I looked at him, startled.

"We do have people in there. I needed to see if the only survivor of the South Dakota Massacre thought we should return. You and Agent Hood were the ones on the scene and he deferred to you. Now, as a thank you, what do you want from South Dakota?"

As I watched, he pulled a small notepad and a pen from the desk drawer. He waited with the pen at the ready.

"I want to go there." The words blurted out of my mouth. "I want to go home and choose what I keep. I want to make sure Sharon and Matt have a decent burial next to my parents. That's what I want."

Mister Lolen gazed at me for a long silent moment. My heart sank. I'd asked for too much. Then he nodded. "All right." Raising his voice, he called David into the main office. "Agent Hood, a moment, please."

David stopped at the doorway. "Yes, sir?"

"You have the authorization to escort Miss Allen to her home in South Dakota. She may bring back whatever she wishes—within reason. Also, arrange for the burial of her guardians in the cemetery her parents are buried in."

David nodded. "The paperwork will be on your desk in the morning."

"Thank you." Mister Lolen turned back to me. "Is there anything else?"

I shook my head. "No. Thank you."

"Then I think you have some travel plans to make."

We all heard the statement as the dismissal it really was. I stood. Tomas remained seated. David held out a hand to me. I walked to him, feeling stunned. He smiled. "Let's go make some plans."

I returned the smile. "Okay." My heart wanted to beat out of my chest but not out of fear for once. I was going home.

ACKNOWLEDGMENTS

No novel is written in a vacuum. Especially not a series. Many people help in little in big ways. These are just some of the people I would like to thank.

Jennifer "Radar" Wylie for all the medical behind the scenes reason everyone died in *Never Let Me Sleep*.

Bob Sessions for the law enforcement facts in *Never Let Me Sleep*.

Lily Cohen-Moore and *Shane Gilber*t for the details on the psychiatric condition, symptoms, and reactions. I appreciate everything you shared and helped me understand.

John Pitts for a being a point of sanity when all was chaos.

Emily Pitts for being the perfect target audience and my main alpha reader.

Jay Lake for always encouraging me. He died three days before I got the series offer but I know he'd be so pleased for me.

Maura Glynn-Thami for being my medical expert for the medical facts and help. I put my characters through a lot. Thank you for making sure I didn't make a fool of myself in the process. I particularly appreciate the behind-the-scenes on how the Coalescence possess people.

Oliver Creutzner for being my master of the technobabble server room scenes in *Never Let Me Die*. I needed assistance in making those scenes and conversations believable. He provided in spades. Thank you

Sarah Hendrix for always being my cheerleader when I was down. Also, my woman on the scene and primary researcher for Richland, Missouri and for Fort Leonard-Wood. Thank you for all your help. Any poetic license or mistakes made are my fault—and I took a LOT of poetic license when I described much of Richland, Missouri. Sarah is awesome and doesn't make those kinds of mistakes.

Timothy W. Long and *Katie Cord* for making sure Permuted Press and I met.

Michael L. Wilson for always emailing me with good news and *Hannah Yancey* for being my go-to person at Permuted.

Thank you to all of my editors for making me look like I know how to write.

Last but never least, thank you to the keystone of my heart, Jeff. Thank you for being a wonderful sounding board, proofer, and for supporting my publishing habit. I love you.

A note about the hospital at Fort Leonard-Wood in *Never Let Me Die:* It is nothing like I described on the inside. I made it all up. I have no idea what kind of locks are on the server room door. I don't even know what floor the server room is on. Please don't try to break into any hospital server rooms, especially not the hospital of Fort Leonard-Wood.

ABOUT THE AUTHOR

Jennifer Brozek is a Hugo Award-nominated editor and an award-winning author. Winner of the Australian Shadows Award for best edited publication, Jennifer has edited fifteen anthologies with more on the way, including the acclaimed *Chicks Dig Gaming* and *Shattered Shields* anthologies. Author of *Apocalypse Girl Dreaming, Industry Talk, the Karen Wilson Chronicles,* and the *Melissa Allen* series, she has more than sixty-five published short stories, and is the Creative Director of Apocalypse Ink Productions.

Jennifer is a freelance author for numerous RPG companies. Winner of the Scribe, Origins, and ENnie awards, her contributions to RPG sourcebooks include *Dragonlance, Colonial Gothic, Shadowrun, Serenity, Savage Worlds,* and *White Wolf SAS*. Jennifer is the author of the award winning YA *Battletech* novel, *The Nellus Academy Incident,* and *Shadowrun* novella, *Doc Wagon 19*. She has also written for the AAA MMO *Aion* and the award winning videogame, *Shadowrun Returns.*

When she is not writing her heart out, she is gallivanting around the Pacific Northwest in its wonderfully mercurial weather. Jennifer is a Director-at-Large of SFWA, and an active member of HWA and IAMTW. Read more about her at www.jenniferbrozek.com or follow her on Twitter at @JenniferBrozek.